BLOOD
OF AN
EXILE

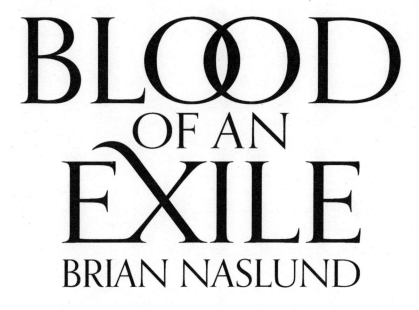

BLOOD
OF AN
EXILE
BRIAN NASLUND

TOR

First published 2019 by Tom Doherty Associates, LLC

First published in the UK 2019 by Tor
an imprint of Pan Macmillan
20 New Wharf Road, London N1 9RR
Associated companies throughout the world
www.panmacmillan.com

ISBN 978-1-5290-1612-3

1 3 5 7 9 8 6 4 2

A CIP catalogue record for this book is available from the British Library.

Map by Jennifer Hanover

Typeset in Bembo by Jouve (UK), Milton Keynes
Printed and bound by CPI Group (UK) Ltd, Croydon, CR0 4YY

Visit **www.panmacmillan.com** to read more about all our books
and to buy them. You will also find features, author interviews and
news of any author events, and you can sign up for e-newsletters
so that you're always first to hear about our new releases.

For my mother and father,
who taught me how to write.

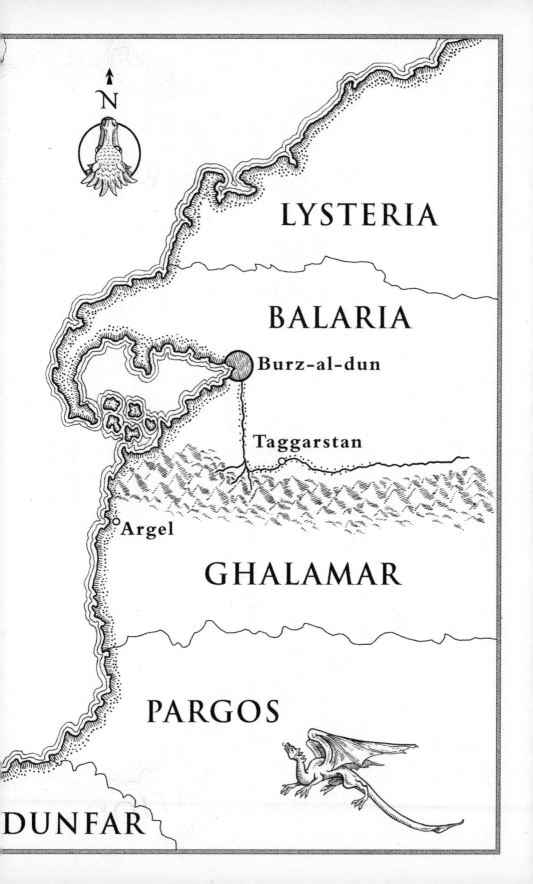

PART I

◆

They'll tell lies about me.
Enjoy them. Don't ask for the real story.
You won't like it.

—Silas Bershad

1

JOLAN

Almira, Otter Rock Village

On the day of the dragon slaying, Jolan woke an hour before dawn to prepare the supplies. Two spools of catgut stitches, all three healing mosses, one jug of boiled water, two skins of purified potato liquor, six tree-bark bandages, scissors, opium, all the knives, and, in case it was finally Bershad's day to die, a white seashell to leave in his mouth, so that his soul would find the sea.

Jolan worked methodically, taking each item from the shelves and placing it in the correct pouch of the leather traveling pack they used to transport supplies. There were two floor-to-ceiling shelves in the workshop, each one taking up an entire wall. One shelf held dozens of glass bottles filled with different salves, reagents, fermented animal organs, and moss poultices. Jolan and his master—Morgan Mollevan—had painstakingly gathered them from the countryside or grown them in the humid greenhouse out back. The second shelf was also full of glass jars, but each vessel contained the same thing: a toxic red-shelled snail. They were becoming overpopulated along the nearby riverbanks, and Morgan had been contracted by the local small lord—Crellin Nimbu—to find an antidote to the snail's poison. He and Jolan had been studying the snails for years, but the path to an antivenom had proved elusive.

Once the sun rose, the workshop would fill with a multicolored glow as daylight refracted through the bottles of their failed experiments.

Jolan used a stepladder to reach the Gods Moss, which Morgan kept in a small, locked wooden box on the top shelf so it was out of sight. The locals were too afraid of Morgan to rob the apothecary, but wandering thieves weren't uncommon, and the Gods Moss was the most valuable ingredient in the apothecary.

Jolan saved the bone saw for last, since it required the most careful attention. He laid the long blade across the big wooden table in the center of the room, tested each tooth, and sharpened those that needed it. The last dragonslayer to come through Otter Rock had every muscle in his leg torn to ribbons by the great lizard he'd tried to kill. As Morgan was sawing the man's leg off, the only thing louder than the dragonslayer's screams were his master's curses that the blade was too dull. Jolan wouldn't let that happen again.

He was finishing the last tooth on the bone saw, internally congratulating himself on his foresight, when Morgan came down from his bedchamber above the apothecary. He wore a simple gray robe. A pair of sealskin gloves were carefully tucked into his belt. The gloves were designed for the radical repair of arteries and organs deep inside a dying man's body. Morgan only took them out of the apothecary when there was going to be a dragon slaying.

Battlefield surgeons used them as well, but there hadn't been a battle in Almira for thirty years. Not since the Balarian Invasion.

"Coffee?" Morgan asked, frowning. He had jet-black, unkempt hair that shot out from his head in every direction. Jolan often wondered how a man could spend five hours straight measuring herb packets by candlelight, but forget that his hair required combing in the morning.

Jolan looked to the idle stove across the room, as if a pair of sad eyes could materialize a pot of freshly brewed coffee. His first responsibility, from his first day as an apprentice, was to have coffee ready when his master awoke. He had lingered too long on the saw.

"I'm . . . the bone saw needed sharpening, and—"

"Forget it, there's no time. Bershad will want to make his pass within the hour. Get the kit." Morgan disappeared out the front door, leaving it open behind him.

Jolan packed the bone saw in a side holster of the pack, slung the thick leather straps around both shoulders, and followed. A dozen yards down the road, he matched pace with Morgan, leaning forward to account for the added weight.

"Why is a dragon best slain in the early morning?" Morgan asked. He was fond of quizzes when he was annoyed.

"It'll be sluggish then, before it's had a chance to sun itself."

"And why does it need to sun itself?"

"They're reptiles. The largest known classification. Like all reptiles, their blood requires outside warmth to supply their energy. He won't reach full strength until nine, even ten in the morning. Before that, most dragons are either unable or unwilling to fly."

"Are there any exceptions to this rule?"

"Just one," Jolan said. "Ghost Moths are able to warm their own blood. But the source of the heat is unknown."

Morgan nodded once, the only sign of approval he ever gave.

"And why do I require coffee in the morning?"

Jolan paused before answering, realizing where this line of questioning was headed.

"Coffee beans stimulate the human mind, allowing clearer thought at a faster pace. They also stimulate the colon, creating the urge to—"

"Wardens and brutish men with swords can afford to live out their lives half drunk," Morgan interrupted. "They can always just bash a man's skull in if they don't have any better ideas. Our only weapons are our minds." He looked down at Jolan. "We are defenseless without them. Never forget that."

"Yes, Master Mollevan."

They walked in silence down the forest path that snaked toward town, but Jolan could tell Morgan wasn't finished talking. He had a way of tightening his hands into fists and releasing them again when he had more to say but didn't particularly want to say it.

"It was good that you sharpened the bone saw," he said at last. That was the closest Master Morgan ever came to apologizing for something. "We might need it today, even if it is the Flawless Bershad waiting for us."

"Is he really as good as they say?" Jolan asked.

"In my experience, legends never live up to their reputations." Morgan paused. "But Silas Bershad has killed more dragons than anyone else in Terra. The stories can't be entirely comprised of vapor."

Morgan's tone was academic and dry, but Jolan got the sense he was excited to see the Flawless Bershad in action. Jolan certainly was.

The apothecary was two leagues outside of Otter Rock. The people of Otter Rock did not trust the alchemists, with their glass bottles and carefully measured ingredients. They preferred to sacrifice goats to nameless mud gods by the light of the moon and hope for the best. But when their wounds grew painful enough, they all came trekking up the forest path for treatment.

Jolan was always amazed by how effectively a nasty rash or toothache could strip a man of conviction.

There was already a crowd when they reached the center of the village. It looked like every peasant, farmer, and craftsman had taken the morning off from his or her work to see the Flawless Bershad try to kill the dragon. At least thirty people milled around the square—their breath puffing in the cold of early morning as they made small talk with one another. The Flawless Bershad wasn't there.

"It seems we are not the only late arrivals," Morgan said. "He's probably drunk, same as every dragonslayer before a pass. Go check."

Jolan nodded and headed toward the inn.

He crossed a shallow river on his way, careful not to step on any of the mud statues the villagers had molded along the bank. Almirans were notorious in the realm of Terra for their habit of crafting these totems on the ground. Jolan stepped around one that was about a stride tall and shaped like a man, but covered in green fish scales. There was a crow's beak pressed into the face and black feathers radiating out from the head. Another totem was cloaked in willow bark and animal bones—it had river pebbles for eyes and an otter tail attached to its back.

Most Almirans kept a small pouch on their hip to collect items they felt had magical properties—sticks, leaves, animal parts, rocks. That way, they'd be ready to make a totem at a moment's notice if they wanted to conjure healthy crops from a freshly planted field, grant themselves safe passage while fording a dangerous river, or protect a newborn child from wet lungs.

On the eve of a battle, every soldier's yurt was guarded by a battle totem holding a scrap of steel.

Morgan had dispelled Jolan's belief in the totems' power a week after his apprenticeship began. Once he saw how Morgan conjured healing properties from roots, herbs, and mosses with carefully mixed concoctions and alchemical reactions, it seemed silly to rely on a statue to do the work for you.

Still, Jolan sometimes made totems when Morgan wasn't watching, just for luck. There was no recipe for that.

The riverbank of Otter Rock had been lined with an unusually high number of totems for months. Farther upriver, the villages were plagued by a strange disease that brought skin boils, seizures, and violent nightmares. The pestilence was traveling downriver—every few months they heard of another village becoming afflicted. The citizens of Otter Rock were convinced that forest demons were responsible, so they built more totems every day, hoping the gods would stop the malign spirits at the waterline.

Jolan knew better. The plague was caused by the inexplicable abundance of toxic red-shelled snails farther upriver. That's why Morgan had been hired to find the antivenom. But it was hard to convince a man who fell to shaking fits twice a day and dreamed of monsters every night that he was being poisoned by distant river snails, not possessed by a demon.

Better to suffer them their mud totems and try to work faster on the antidote. They were running out of time—by Jolan's calculations, the sickness would reach Otter Rock before the end of summer.

Jolan entered the inn's hall and found it empty except for a man behind the bar, struggling to lift a cask of wine. He was a sour and skinny man who had spent his entire life in Otter Rock. Three weeks ago, Jolan had prepared a special kind of soap for him to remove the worst case of pubic lice the young alchemist had ever seen. Demon-induced rashes and seizures weren't the only afflictions of backwater Almirans.

"Is the dragonslayer in here?" Jolan asked. The bartender jerked his head to the left as a response, but did not turn around or cease his struggle with the cask. Jolan looked toward the back of the room. There was a man there, passed out cold with his head and hands flat on the table.

"Him?" Jolan asked.

"Him," the bartender responded. "Was at it most of the night. Passed out an hour ago."

Jolan moved toward the man. He could tell that he was tall, even slumped over the table like he was, but he looked more like a beggar than a legendary dragonslayer. His face was obscured by a mess of long dark hair, full of tangles and silver rings tied into greasy braids. He wore a black woolen tunic and breeches, both covered in stitched repairs and patches. Jolan reached out to shake the man awake, but the dragonslayer spoke before Jolan's hand reached his shoulder.

"What time is it?" he asked, not moving anything except his lips.

"Half an hour past dawn," said Jolan, bending down to try and get a look at his face. He didn't quite believe that this was the Flawless Bershad—the most famous dragonslayer in the realm of Terra. Slowly, the man bent an arm and pushed himself up from the table.

His green eyes were bloodshot and glassy. His face was covered with small indentations where the rings in his hair had pressed against his skin as he slept. In no way did his dark, rough features bring to mind the handsome, perfect dragonslayer of the poems and songs and stories. He looked like he was somewhere between thirty and forty, but it was hard to tell exactly where. The world had gone hard on this man.

Still, the blue tattoos on his cheeks were unmistakable.

Every dragonslayer was given the same tattoo when their sentence was passed so that all men would know them on sight: a rectangular blue bar running down the length of each cheek. In Almira, any dragonslayer who abandoned his duty, spent the night in a real bed, or was caught within a day's ride of the capital—Floodhaven—was put to death. Other countries in Terra had slightly different customs, but dragonslayers were always outcasts—forbidden from enjoying the full comforts of civilization until their task was complete.

"Are you the Flawless Bershad?" Jolan asked.

"I am the Late and Hungover Bershad," he growled. "Where is Rowan?"

"I don't know who that is."

"Generally, it's him that wakes me up. Not strange children." Bershad pushed himself to his feet. He burped, tottered, and for a moment looked like he would collapse back into his chair, but instead headed for the door.

People began to cheer as soon as Bershad was out of the inn. He surveyed them placidly for a moment, then caught sight of a man standing next to a gray, leafless tree. He was tightening two long spears to the side of a donkey.

"Rowan!" Bershad barked, starting toward him. "Were you planning on waking me, or did you intend to kill the fucking lizard yourself?"

Rowan was unfazed. He finished his work on the spears and rubbed the donkey gently on the muzzle. He was a hard-looking man, with graying hair and a rough beard. Jolan noticed that even though he was short, his arms were long and sinewy. He had thick wrists, huge hands, and his knuckles were covered in dark hair. Men built like that made for good farmers or good fighters, depending.

Since he was preparing the Flawless Bershad's equipment, Jolan realized this must be his forsaken shield. Each dragonslayer was granted one—a man of low birth to assist in the hunting and killing of dragons. If a dragonslayer was killed by a dragon, his forsaken shield was executed afterward. So most of the time they were unlucky men or criminals who had been coerced into the duty one way or another. Jolan wondered how Rowan had been stuck with the job.

"Figured you'd want as much rest as possible after a night of such aggressive revelry," Rowan said, turning to face Bershad. "If you're ready, everything is set." He motioned to the hills in the east, where the dragon had made its lair the past three weeks.

Bershad sniffed, spat, and headed down the eastern path. Rowan followed with the donkey. Master Morgan was close behind, so Jolan hustled after them. The villagers did nothing for a moment, but Jolan soon heard them following in a noisy pack. They didn't want to miss the excitement.

And, of course, if Bershad did manage to slay the dragon, they wanted their share of the carcass.

As they moved down the path, Jolan noticed a long dagger strapped to the small of Bershad's back. It was strange-looking—the blade was thickest at the tip and it curved inward, the opposite of most weapons. The handle looked like a gnarled root cluster, and the grip was made from a complicated braid of sharkskin leather that somehow created a place for fingers overtop the irregular shape of the handle.

"That's a dragontooth dagger, isn't it?" Jolan asked Morgan.

"Yes."

"Do you think he made it himself?" Jolan continued. "I read they're near impossible to properly forge. Something with the calcium going soft unless you heat it just right. Plus—"

"I think you should focus on the living dragon down the road, not the teeth of dead ones," Morgan answered.

Jolan didn't respond. Morgan was clearly done with the conversation.

"What's your name, alchemist?" Bershad asked after they had been walking for a while.

"Morgan Mollevan. Of Pargos."

"You're a long way from home," Bershad said.

"All of us are a long way from home, my lord." Morgan didn't need to use Bershad's old title, shouldn't have, even—it had been stripped from Bershad the day he became a dragonslayer. But Morgan often did things that were not necessary and that Jolan did not understand.

"Let me ask you something, Morgan Mollevan of Pargos," Bershad said. "What's the strangest thing you've ever seen a wounded man do?"

"Strangest?" Morgan repeated, running a hand through his wild hair as he considered the question. "I once amputated a leper's legs to save his life. An hour after I was done, he was running around on his hands as if he'd been born that way. Never seen someone adapt to two lost limbs that quickly. Probably had something to do with the nerves in his legs already being—"

"No," Bershad interrupted. "I mean, have you ever seen something you can't explain? Someone who survived a wound when they shouldn't have?"

"My work is a game of odds," Morgan said. "People beat them occasionally, but no, I wouldn't say I've witnessed any miracles. Everything has an explanation, in my experience."

"I see."

"Why do you ask?"

Bershad spat into a cluster of ferns to the right of the forest path. "What can you tell me about the dragon?" Bershad asked. His steps were changing—becoming more fluid and energetic. His eyes were no longer bloodshot, but alert and clear. It was hard to believe this same man had been passed out with his face on the table fifteen minutes earlier.

A night of drinking did not flee so quickly from most men.

"It's a Needle-Throated Verdun. Male. Young, but fully matured physically. Migrated down almost a moon's turn ago to warm himself on the rock slabs in these foothills. We usually get one or two stopping off in spring before finishing the journey east for the Great Migration. Vicious monsters."

"He's just trying to survive, same as us. Keep his belly full and his body warm. To him, we're the vicious monsters showing up with spears and pitchforks."

Morgan glanced at Bershad and raised his eyebrow. "I would not have figured you for a philosopher."

"I'm full of surprises." Bershad scratched at his messy beard. "The Verdun'll be gone in another month."

"That's true," Morgan said. "But he's cutting further into the herds of our shepherds each day. And it's only a matter of time before he gets curious about the village. Otter Rock suffers enough as it is without an encroaching lizard, and with a dragonslayer such as yourself so close by—"

"I'm not blaming you for putting out the writ," Bershad interrupted. "And I'm not trying to avoid the thing. Just saying he'll be moving on soon. You don't need to issue another writ if it kills me. What else do you know about the dragon?"

"A beet farmer who saw him up close says he only has one eye. The other is sealed up by scar tissue."

"Someone else took a pass already?"

"Took it and missed, I'd say. But he'll be blind on that side."

"He'll also have an idea about what I'm up to," Bershad said.

"Needle-Throated Verduns are not known for their intelligence. Perhaps he has forgotten the previous incident."

Bershad grunted and seemed to mull that idea over, but said nothing.

They walked for the better part of an hour. It was a clumsy procession—Bershad, Rowan, donkey, Master Morgan, Jolan, and a noisy crowd of farmers and peasants. Hardly a discreet hunting force.

Jolan could hear some of Otter Rock's citizens complaining about the pace, and others complaining about the danger of getting so close to the dragon. But none of them turned away.

When they cleared the forest, Bershad stopped. Surveyed the long field of dead wheat that ended at the rock slabs of the Green Tooth foothills. There were oak and pine trees on either side of the field with trunks covered in moss. Thick shrubs blanketed the ground.

"This it?" Bershad asked.

"He's made his lair just beyond this field," Master Morgan said. "There's a tunnel dug out between the place those two rock slabs come to a point. He sleeps there, and roams along this line during the day. There used to be a hundred sheep grazing this field."

"Fucking death trap," Rowan said, mostly to himself.

"Yeah," Bershad agreed. "Let's get ready."

Rowan unbuckled an oak trunk from the donkey's flank and thumped it to the ground. He opened it and began removing pieces of armor, then passing them to Bershad, who cinched all the belts and straps himself. Jolan noticed the precision with which they performed the task—no words or wasted action—and figured they had done it hundreds of times. Bershad donned a hauberk made of black chain mail, a light lamellar breastplate the color of forest moss, matching greaves, gauntlets, bracers with thin bands of steel sewn into their sides, and a small steel gorget around his throat.

In the poems and stories, a warden donning his armor was a ritual full of honor, pride, and yellow light glinting off polished steel. The wardens were the protectors of Almira—well-trained and tasked by a lord or even a king to protect the realm with sword and horse. Commoners looked up to wardens as heroes and beacons of valor, and the nobility of Almira relied on their personal armies of wardens to control their domains.

But the Flawless Bershad was no warden, and he was no lord. Not anymore. He armed himself with the weary precision of an old farmer milking a cow.

Rowan moved behind Bershad and pulled a few final straps tight.

"What good is such light armor against a dragon?" Jolan whispered to Morgan, eyeing the thin breastplate and chain mail.

"Not much," he admitted. "But neither is a full set of steel plate when it comes to a dragon's claws or teeth. And it's far heavier."

Jolan nodded along, but if he had to fight a dragon, he'd want steel-plate armor.

The last piece was the mask. In battle, Almiran warriors always wore wood-and-leather masks that were cut into the shape of a god. Dragonslayers surrendered all lands and possessions when they were banished, but Bershad had been allowed to keep his mask. It was carved into the coal-black likeness of a snarling jaguar with crimson blood dripping from its mouth.

Most wardens preferred an animal's face, especially in a battle when it was hard to separate enemies from allies. But Jolan had seen all kinds—wild visages made from twisted bones and gnarled wood. The gods of Almira had no names, and they followed no rules.

The mask was attached to a black half-helm that protected his skull. Bershad pulled it over his face and adjusted everything. The two eye slits were large like a cat's, and Bershad's pale green eyes glowed within the darkness. Looking at the mask gave Jolan an uneasy feeling in his stomach. The same feeling he got when he was walking back to the apothecary late at night, heard a strange noise in the forest, and had to convince himself it was a prowling fox, not an imaginary forest demon.

Rowan pulled the two ash spears free from their place on the other side of the donkey and handed them to Bershad. He tested the weight of both and seemed satisfied. Then Rowan produced an ivory war horn from a saddlebag. It was the size of a boy's chest and had a hemp cord looped around two hooks. He checked the mouthpiece once for cracks in the wax lip and then tossed it to Bershad, who slung it over one shoulder.

Jolan had seen three dragon slayings in his life—none of them successful. Each man had approached the task a little differently, but all of them had used a horn. The report of an ivory horn created a low vibration in the inner ear of almost all dragon species, which flushed them out of their lairs. It also pissed them off. Jolan had been ten when he saw his first slaying attempt. The dragonslayer had been exiled because he was caught raiding a village that belonged to a small lord who was favored by the king. That was always a fast way to earn a pair of blue bars. He had dressed in full plate armor, mounted his donkey, and trotted around blowing a war horn as if it would call his old comrades into battle behind him.

But he had waited too late in the day. The dragon snatched the lord off his donkey, flew a thousand paces straight up into the air, and then dropped him on some rocks, splattering the dragonslayer open like a seagull cracking an oyster.

"Why don't they just sneak into the dragon's lair at night?" Jolan had asked Morgan while they carried the dragonslayer's smashed body back to the apothecary to weigh the organs, which Morgan did obsessively. His liver notebook alone was nearly two hundred pages long.

"Many have tried," Morgan had said. "But dragons are cunning with their lairs. Lots of dead-end passages and switchbacks. It takes half the night just to find out where the beast is sleeping, and by then they usually aren't sleeping anymore—they're very sensitive to uninvited guests. Sneaking into a dragon's lair at night is about as suicidal as trying to sneak into its belly. At least outside you can die with the sun on your face."

Bershad took a few steps into the field, eyes focused on the ground. He stabbed the dirt with the tip of his boot a few times, kicking up clumps of soft black earth.

"Need the rock?" Rowan asked.

"Definitely."

Rowan nodded, and went back into the saddlebag. He pulled out a white rock that wasn't much larger than a fist. Despite the size, the sinews of Rowan's forearm strained as he picked it up. There was a cylindrical depression bored through the middle of the odd stone. Rowan passed it to Bershad, who held it with a similar kind of effort.

"Try not to get killed," Rowan said lightly. Bershad grunted and turned to Morgan.

"Do not chop off pieces of my body trying to save my life. If it's that bad, give me some opium and let me die smiling. Preferably with some tits in my face."

Bershad pulled a blue-and-yellow seashell from behind his breastplate, rubbed it once, then tucked it back against his heart. Then he was off, taking long confident strides toward the dragon's lair.

Bershad moved fast for a man who was wearing a full set of armor, carrying two spears in one hand and a heavy rock in the other, and who had spent the night drunk. When he was thirty or forty paces from the lair, he stopped. Slammed his spears into the ground. Then he wandered around a bit, eyes fixed on the earth at his feet. After almost two minutes of searching, he dropped the strange rock in what seemed like a very specific place. Adjusted it once with his boot.

He went back and pulled one of the spears out of the ground, lifted the mask off his face, and put the horn around to his lips.

Bershad only blew once, but he made it last. A long call that was soft at first and grew louder. He held the note for what seemed like several minutes, until a shrill cry echoed from beneath the mountains. Bershad stopped the call, threw the horn far to the side, lowered his mask, and raised his spear. The dragon was awake.

A geyser of pebbles sprayed into the clear morning sky. The villagers gasped behind Jolan. Some of the rocks landed five paces from Bershad's feet, but he didn't even flinch. Just stood there like an armored scarecrow erected by a farmer. For a moment there was nothing, and then another, larger blast of rocky shrapnel burst into the air.

Before the pebbles landed, the dragon shot out—green hide darting toward the field, his tail kicking up more stones.

Even with his wings folded back, the dragon was the size of a large wagon. He coiled up behind a boulder at the edge of the field and eyed Bershad. Despite the distance, Jolan could make out the single, glowing orange orb of the dragon's remaining eye. He had red spikes jutting from his throat that twitched and vibrated with aggression.

Bershad wedged the butt of his spear into the rock and angled the point toward the sky.

Jolan had heard the same stories about the Flawless Bershad as everyone else: that when he fought, it was he who moved like a demon, and the lizard who slouched along like a man. That he killed dragons with a single, flawless spear throw. That he pissed on their carcasses and laughed at them when it was done.

The reality was different.

Jolan blinked, and the dragon was in the air, somehow summoning the energy for a pounce despite the early hour. Bershad crouched, hands clamped around the spear. The dragon rushed toward him— claws outstretched and gaping mouth filled with razor-sharp black teeth.

Bershad dove away at the last second as the dragon's snout slammed into the earth, throwing up a shower of dirt and wheat. The spear was nowhere in sight, but the dragon began twitching and thrashing. His tail beat against the ground in a random, angry rhythm.

Bershad was slow getting up, but once he was on his feet he moved fast—sprinting back across the field, arms pumping hard. He ripped the mask off as he ran.

Jolan expected to see terror on his face, something like the expression men got before Master Morgan amputated a limb. Instead, Bershad's face was painted with a wild kind of joy. Jolan had never seen it before.

It didn't last very long.

The dragon spun in a circle, his tail curling into a whip that lashed Bershad in the back of his left leg and sent him spinning through the air like a tossed coin. He landed fifteen paces away, bounced, then didn't move. The dragon didn't go after Bershad, just stood there licking at the dirt and sniffing.

Jolan squinted at the dragon. He could just barely make out the white rock, still with the butt of the spear wedged in it, lodged almost entirely inside the dragon's remaining eye.

"That's . . ." Jolan whispered. "Not possible."

"Lots of things seem impossible until someone does it in front of you," Morgan said.

Thick orange liquid poured down the side of the dragon's face and neck. The beast took a few steps back toward his lair, looking feeble, almost pathetic. He slipped a few times and then crashed to the ground. Didn't move. For a few eerie seconds, the field was quiet and still. Then birds began chirping their merry songs from the dense trees to the north.

"Jolan!" Morgan barked. "With me."

Jolan awoke from his daze and followed his master across the field. Morgan wasn't running—he'd want to keep his pulse steady for any surgery—but Jolan sprinted the last stretch and spread out the knives over a clear spot of grass so they'd be ready. Bershad was unconscious, but Jolan could see his chest rising and falling beneath his breastplate.

Still alive.

"It's his upper left leg and ribs," Jolan said as Morgan crouched beside him. Morgan snatched up a scalpel and made four fast cuts across the straps of Bershad's armor. He pulled the lamellar rib-guard away, then rolled up the chain mail that was underneath.

"What do you see?" he asked Jolan.

Jolan examined the wound—his leg and ribs were swelling, and there were a few cuts along his stomach where the lamellar had pushed the chain mail into his skin, but they weren't very deep. There was a circular wound on his thigh where a barb from the dragon's tail had punched through the hauberk, but the barb was thin and it had missed the arteries and the bone.

"He'll live. A few cracked ribs maybe, but otherwise his chest is fine. That cut on his leg is deep, but he should make out with nothing except a bad limp."

Morgan nodded once. "Disinfection, stitches, bandages. I'm going to have a look at this dragon before the peasants destroy it."

Jolan prepared a poultice for the wound on Bershad's leg. He mixed several different herbs into the bottom of a glass flask, including one pinch of Gods Moss, which Morgan had personally harvested from an old dragon warren in the Daintree jungle. It was extremely valuable because of its healing properties and Morgan would have whipped Jolan bloody if he saw him use it, since there were three cheaper disinfectants in the pack that would do the same job. But

Jolan figured the most famous dragonslayer in the world deserved the best ingredients. He added a bit of distilled water to the flask and stirred until the mixture turned into a paste. Then he picked up a skin of potato liquor and poured it into Bershad's wound.

The dragonslayer winced, but didn't wake up.

Jolan set the skin aside and dabbed the paste into the wound. He turned away to prepare a catgut stitch but his needle froze when he returned to the wound. It was already knitting itself back together, as if there was a second, invisible apprentice sitting across from Jolan and binding the flesh.

"Not possible," he muttered for the second time in ten minutes.

He'd seen Morgan use Gods Moss seven times before, but it had never done that.

"Careful, boy," Bershad said. He'd woken up. His eyes seemed more alive. Burning, almost. "Witnessing some things can be bad for your health." Bershad scooped the paste out of his open wound and flicked it away. Then he reached past Jolan, grabbed a bark-skin bandage, and wrapped it over his thigh.

Jolan was about to ask Bershad for an explanation, but a jerk of movement caught his attention. It was the dragon's left claw twitching. Morgan had been examining the folded flaps of skin that formed the Needle-Throated Verdun's wings when it happened. He cursed when the dragon started moving, then stumbled backward a few steps, looking surprised and furious at the same time, as if his favorite horse had bucked for no good reason.

The dragon decapitated Morgan with a single swipe of his claw.

There was a jet of blood and then just a twitching body. No head. The dragon lifted himself onto his back legs and released a terrible cry. Jolan heard much smaller, softer screams behind him. The last and bravest villagers were fleeing from the field. Frozen, Jolan couldn't think of anything to do besides move himself between Bershad and the dragon.

He fumbled around in his pockets for a seashell to put in his own mouth, but couldn't find the one he'd set aside that morning.

The dragon dropped its front claws back to the ground with a thundering pound. It took a few slow, unsure steps toward Jolan. Orange blood was still flowing out around the spear jammed in its ruined eye. The dragon sniffed the air once. Twice. Nostrils wet and dilated.

Jolan was an educated person. He did not believe in gods or demons, nor did he believe there was anything special about the enormous lizards that plagued the realm of Terra. They were just beasts. Wild and dangerous and more powerful than other creatures, but beasts all the same. Still, it seemed to him that in that strange moment, the dragon was trying to say something—to share some secret.

A spear hissed past Jolan's left ear and hit the dragon with so much speed that a jet of blood and bone spewed out the back side of its head. The dragon's neck kicked up from the strength of the impact, then the beast crumpled and died at Jolan's feet. He turned around to see Bershad was standing, but swaying a little.

"Not possible," Jolan muttered. No man should have the strength to pierce a dragon's skull like that.

"Remember what I said about witnessing shit, boy," Bershad growled. Then he vomited and collapsed.

———————

Jolan spent a long time looking for Morgan's head. He wandered along the ruts of the wheat field and checked the copses of trees. Mostly he just tried not to cry in front of Rowan and the Flawless Bershad. Even if the dragonslayer was unconscious, sobbing in front of a living legend seemed wrong.

The villagers returned from their hiding places in small groups, too. Nobody had seen the way Bershad had killed the Needle-Throated Verdun, so instead of gossiping about his inhuman strength, they just squabbled over who got what.

Most parts of a dragon's carcass—teeth, hide, organs, and bones—were notoriously difficult to use. For some reason, they almost always turned to rot within a few days. Sometimes hours. That was why Bershad's dragontooth dagger was so rare—most attempts at such a weapon ended with a soft, fungus-covered rod. But any fool could remove the lump of dragon fat at the root of each scale and boil it down to an oil that lasted ten times longer than any other animal fat.

In Almira, the local lord had claim to three-quarters of any dragon carcass. The rest went to whoever was brave enough to be there with a knife. Jolan noticed that the villagers were carefully setting Lord Nimbu's share aside. He'd recently built a new manor that was a ten-days' ride downstream from Otter Rock, but he would most certainly send riders to claim his dragon fat. Given the size of the

Needle-Throated Verdun, Nimbu's take would be worth two or even three years of taxes from Otter Rock.

Jolan left them to fight over the carcass. He didn't understand how Morgan's head could have gotten lost. But after twenty minutes of searching—which was the time it took Rowan to make a stretcher for Bershad from saplings and strips of leather and cloth—Jolan still hadn't found it. If he couldn't find Morgan's head, Jolan couldn't put a seashell in his mouth. Without a shell, his spirit would be forced to wander the countryside, looking for the Soul Sea. They were a long way from the coast, though. It would be easy for Morgan to get lost.

"Best leave it, boy," Rowan said after he'd gotten Bershad onto the stretcher and tied it to the donkey's harness.

"Might be he can find the sea on his own," Rowan added when Jolan didn't stop looking.

"And if he can't?" Jolan asked, voice trembling. Vision blurred by tears.

Rowan blinked, then put a hand on Jolan's shoulder. "Life's full of burdens, boy. Picking up a heavy one like this so early on isn't a good idea. You've got to pace yourself."

Rowan pulled gently on the donkey's lead, and they started back to town.

Jolan mulled over his situation while trudging back to Otter Rock behind Rowan, the donkey, his master's corpse, and the unconscious Bershad. The last piece in a dismal train.

In another few months, Morgan would have made Jolan a journeyman alchemist, which would have allowed him to take over the contract from Lord Nimbu. But as an apprentice, Jolan had the same rights as the knives he carried in his pack and the bottles of medicine on the apothecary shelves.

None.

The Guild of Alchemists would send a replacement for Morgan if Lord Nimbu paid them, but that wasn't likely. Morgan had made little progress with the red-shelled snails in five years of work, and Lord Nimbu had always been suspicious of his presence. He trusted mud totems more than glass vials of strange ingredients. Morgan had often wondered why the small lord had hired him at all.

No, Lord Nimbu would probably void his contract with the alchemists, sell the contents of the apothecary for a hefty profit, then
throw Jolan off the land. And there was nothing Jolan could do to
stop it.

Despite his knowledge, training, and years of experience, Jolan
was completely helpless. To make matters worse, he'd lost track of
the Gods Moss vial when the dragon woke up.

A rider blocking the path ahead interrupted Jolan's thoughts. The
man had a dark beard, sat atop a courser, and wore the purple cloak
and light silver armor of an Almiran sentinel. The sentinels were brave
men—part of the Malgrave army but not under the command of a
specific high-warden. They could be used as scouts, messengers, and
mounted archers, but they were mostly responsible for hunting down
dragonslayers that had strayed from their duty in Almira. Sentinels
were famous for their ruthlessness in bringing truant exiles to justice.

"Is that the Flawless Bershad?" the sentinel asked.

"Dunno," Rowan said. "Who the fuck are you?"

"Zim," the sentinel said, as if that was enough. He let his sword
arm hang low and relaxed by his side. "Answer my question."

"It's Bershad," Rowan said, letting go of the donkey's lead and
taking a step forward.

"Is he dead?"

"Napping. Tough work, killing dragons," Rowan said, with no
friendliness in his voice.

Zim squinted down at Bershad. "He doesn't seem to be living up
to his immaculate reputation."

"What would you know about it?" Rowan spat, and stared the
sentinel down. Jolan noticed Rowan's hand had drifted over the hilt
of his sword, too. It was an old, beaten thing with a jaguar on the
pommel and a leather grip worn down with dirt and sweat. Zim
eyed Rowan, then seemed to change his mind about something and
relaxed.

"I've been looking for that asshole for a fucking fortnight." Zim
produced a small roll of paper and tossed it to the ground at Rowan's feet. "When the Flawless Bershad wakes up, there's a message
for him."

"What's it say?" Rowan asked, frowning.

"I am the messenger. Not the mouth."

"You are a pimple on my donkey's ass."

"Watch your tongue, trash, or you will find it removed from your mouth. Along with the rest of your head."

"Idle talk," Rowan said. "Get gone back down the bloody road. If we meet in the wilds, we'll pick up from here."

Zim hissed, spurred his horse, turned, and galloped down the road. Jolan watched until he disappeared. When he turned back, Rowan was reading the message.

"What's it say?" Jolan asked.

"See for yourself. Not every day you read a letter written by a king."

Jolan took the paper.

Exile,

There is need of you in the capital. Whatever shithole barn you are sleeping in, wake up. Whatever lizard you are hunting, let it escape. Your banishment is lifted. Temporarily. Return to Floodhaven.

Hertzog Malgrave I, King of Almira

The king's royal mark was pressed below the signature—an eagle perched atop a great pine with his wings outstretched.

"What do you think the king wants?" Jolan asked.

"Whatever it is, can't be worse than this," Rowan said, picking up the stretcher again and heading into town.

2

GARRET

Almira, North of Swordfish Point

Garret leapt overboard from the whaler a league off the Almiran coast, under cover of mist and night. He swam with the tide, swirling toward land. It was almost dawn when he washed ashore, filled his wet fists with the sand of Almira, and walked off the beach. The taste of salt pervaded his mouth.

His equipment was wrapped in a waterproofed satchel made from a goat's bladder that he had tied to his hip. Inside: a plain but well-made hunting knife, one set of good boots, a compass, a leather traveler's cloak, six yards of hemp rope, a tobacco pipe, an empty canteen, putty and glue to disguise his face, and two pieces of flint. Garret unpacked everything amidst the short seaside grass that sprouted a hundred strides back from the surf, making sure nothing had been lost or damaged during his arrival.

In the distance, Garret could see the vague silhouette of a village—one or two watchtowers for seafaring dragons and a crude wall of driftwood. Had to be Swordfish Point, which meant he was exactly where he wanted to be, and right on schedule. For now, anyway. Garret's business was unpredictable. Always, there were complications.

The sky was pale gray, signaling the approach of dawn. Garret decided to enjoy a small moment of stillness before his long journey and watch the sunrise from the beach. He'd never been to this part of Almira—just the capital, Floodhaven—but he'd studied dozens of maps to prepare for his mission. He was currently in the northeast corner of the Atlas Coast, which was mostly farmland and rolling hills. People lived in small villages, worshipped spurious packs of nameless gods, and feared the movement of demons in the night. Floodhaven was due south along the coast, located where Almira's two great rivers—the Atlas and Gorgon—emptied into the Soul Sea to create the largest port in the country. South of Floodhaven was the Dainwood rain forest—a wild jungle teeming with dragons and jaguars. The only major city in the rain forest, Deepdale, had been ruled by the Bershad lords for generations until their house was set to ruin by the Almiran king. Now a high lord named Grealor ruled there.

For his part, Garret was heading west across the Atlas Coast until he crossed the Atlas River and entered the Gorgon Valley. He took one last look at the sea, then tucked his supplies into his goatskin and strode off with his back to the rising sun.

———

Two days later, Garret reached the bridge over the Atlas. The river was narrow—no more than a hundred strides across at her widest—but fording her was only possible in a handful of places because what the Atlas lacked in width she made up for in current and depth. Her waters blasted down from the mountains in a fury that did not abate until they reached the sea. Even wading ankle-deep into the current could take a man off his feet and drown him. A team of oxen could be swept away in seconds.

The river's violent and continuous current turned any bridge across the Atlas into a crowded funnel for merchant caravans and traders. That was good for Garret. Nobody would remember one man amongst the hundreds of people who would cross that day. He blended into a group of fur trappers who were crossing the bridge at the same time. As they walked, they compared prices and asked about road conditions to different trapping grounds.

"Got a silver a head for beaver at Cold Falls," one trapper said, grinning and waiting on the others to be impressed.

"Cold Falls folk always overpay, you'd think beaver hats were crowns the way they go after them," said another man, who was clearly drunk and swaying on the mule he rode.

"How was the road?"

"Not bad on the way up, but the bitch was totally washed out on the return. Going around took forever."

Almiran roads were notoriously rough and inconsistent. Garret had built delays into his timeline specifically for that reason.

He followed the rise and fall of their voices, memorizing the taste and shape of their accents. It had been five years since he'd impersonated an Almiran. He needed the practice.

A trading outpost began as soon as the bridge ended. Supply stores lined the main, muddy road and men poured out of them with sacks of salted meat and vegetables. Garret walked into the first cheap tavern he found. There were only two other customers. One was passed out in his chair, the other was molding a mud figurine directly onto the bar—sticking his tongue out as he carefully placed a crown of pine needles into its head.

Behind their horrific roads, Almirans' compulsive need to make decorative mud statues to their innumerable gods was the most well-known thing about them.

Garret sat down and motioned to the barkeep.

"What'll it be?" the barkeep said when he came over. The man's thick, country accent made him sound like he had a mouthful of mud that he was forced to talk around.

"Mead. Sweet as you got," Garret said in Almiran. His accent wasn't a perfect match of the trappers, but it was good enough to fool a distracted barkeep.

The barkeep filled a dirty mug with golden mead and passed it to Garret. There were a few shreds of blueberry skins and a piece of honeycomb the size of an acorn floating in the top of the drink. Garret took a sip. It was certainly sweet, but he wouldn't have called it good. He preferred the bitter ales of Balaria, but nodded approval all the same. Almirans liked mead.

"I been out east for a month," Garret said. "Thinkin' 'bout heading for Mudwall. How do things stand there?"

"Been trapping, eh?"

Garret nodded. "Beavers at Cold Falls. You'd think they were made o' gold, the prices I got. Was thinking I'd resupply and then head farther west."

"Mudwall's in bad shape." The bartender leaned in over the counter. "Tybolt still rules the city, but he's holding on by his ass hairs. Some small lord named Hrilian made a pass at him."

"That right?" Garret asked.

The Almiran lords all swore allegiance to the Malgrave king, but there was near-constant infighting amongst them for control of different cities and lands. From what Garret could tell, the king encouraged these miniature rebellions in an attempt to prevent a larger one aimed at his throne.

"I heard Hrilian even brought a catapult," the barkeep continued. "Fuck knows where a small lord got one, but it's caused a real ruckus. Tybby managed to fend him off, but had to call all his wardens to the city to break the little siege. The fighting's still going on in the woods, and Tybby's host is still camped outside Mudwall. They got the whole city locked up pretty tight. You might wanna resupply somewhere else."

Garret drained the rest of his mead. "Is the road to Mudwall clear?" he asked.

The barkeep frowned at the blatant disregard of his advice. Drummed a thick finger on the bar, then shrugged.

"Main highway's waterlogged to shit from the last storm. You wanna reach Mudwall before midsummer, you need to take the long way 'round. Head southwest along the Demon Hump Hills for a week, till you hit Carthorn pass. You'll know it by a stream where the north bank is covered with yellow wildflowers. Pray that path's clear, then follow it north all the way to Mudwall."

Garret slid two copper coins across the table and left. Now he was behind schedule.

3

BERSHAD

Almira, Floodhaven

It was an hour after dawn and the road to Floodhaven was already clogged for a league with farmers and peasants making their way to market. Everyone was trying to get a prime spot to sell their wares. Animals squawked and brayed while their owners cursed at their animals and at each other. Rowan surveyed the situation from the ridge where they'd made camp. Bershad stood up from his bedroll with a small groan.

"How's the leg?" Rowan asked.

"Almost there," Bershad said. The two-week walk along the Atlas River into the capital had slowed the recovery of his leg, but it hadn't undone the apprentice's work.

"Healed fast this time, even for you," Rowan said, dusting a few bits of sleep from his left eye. "Wish I knew what that kid put in your leg."

By the time Bershad had woken up and told Rowan what the apprentice had done, they were a day's ride from Otter Rock. Too late to turn around. Bershad had described the moss to Rowan when he woke up—deep green, like wet seaweed, and speckled with blue flowers—but neither of them had ever seen it before.

"Yeah," Bershad said, pushing a finger against his leg and feeling the dull pain.

"That second spear throw was a bit unusual as well, I'd say."

"Unusual is one word for it," Bershad said.

Whatever type of moss the kid put in Bershad's leg, it had given him a surge of strength he'd never felt before. His heavy spear had felt as light as a river stone in his hand.

"Well, for once the stories they tell about you will line up pretty close with what actually happened."

"Only if the kid talks. Everyone else was hiding in the woods, as I recall."

"What do you think it means?"

Bershad scanned the road. "No way to know. And if none of the two dozen alchemists I've asked have an answer, I'm not sure there is one."

"That crazy shaman out in the western hinterlands had a theory. Remember him? With all the bird shit in his hair? Horax or Horlin or something."

"That nut said I was the god of demons hiding beneath a man's skin. Bunch of crap."

"Yeah," Rowan agreed. "Demons don't have a god. That's nonsense."

Bershad grunted. He didn't believe in gods or demons any more than he believed in talking swords or honest kings, but something was happening to him. There was a heat inside of his bones that felt foreign and wrong, like a molten splinter running through his marrow. It scared him.

"Whatever it is, doesn't change the fact we need to get through there today," Bershad said, motioning to the crowd in front of the main gate.

"We'll cause a scene if you go down there," Rowan said.

"Walking around to one of the postern gates will take half the day," Bershad said. "Plus, I'd rather cause a scene than get stopped alone by an ambitious warden who'd rather cut off my head than read a letter. They'll be less inclined to fight if there's a crowd prone to rioting."

"Fair enough. You nervous?" Rowan asked. "About seeing King Hertzog and all?"

"Nervous isn't the word I'd use."

Angry. Violent. Those were closer.

Rowan gave him a concerned look.

"You're not planning on doing something stupid, are you, Silas?"

"Course not," Bershad said. "I generally like doing stupid things spur of the moment."

They broke camp and made their way down a narrow goat path until it intersected with the main road, which sloped gently uphill on its way to the city walls. Floodhaven had gotten its name because despite being situated between two powerful rivers, the stretch of land had enough elevation that it never flooded during the spring rains or the autumn storms. It was a rare advantage—most Almiran cities were plagued by deluges.

The first few farmers in the market line grumbled but moved aside as Rowan led their donkey into the crowd. Bershad followed behind, a full head taller than almost everyone he passed. They made it several hundred yards down the road before a peasant girl took the time to notice the man pushing past her.

She began to quiver when she saw the heavy blue strip of tattoo on either side of Bershad's face. The girl tugged at her father's sleeve and whispered, "Dragonslayer."

When her father didn't do anything, she screamed it.

Some people panicked, but most of them just backed up and eyed the doomed pair of men from a safe distance. There hadn't been an exile's head on the walls of Floodhaven for many years, not since Gralor the Stone Ear fell asleep on a river ferry and woke up at the docks to a headsman sharpening his scythe.

Bershad figured it was best to wait. Word would be passed down from wagon to wagon until it reached a sentry, and then a few of them would come riding up to kill him. Unless, of course, the king had been gracious enough to let his wardens know he was coming. Bershad doubted that. King Hertzog was an old, stubborn man who did not forget grudges. And he held a large grudge against Bershad.

While they waited, a few of the nearby peasants built mud statues and muttered prayers, but mostly they just stared at him. As expected, a group of Malgrave wardens rode from the main gate a few minutes later. Bershad counted twenty of them, which was a bit of overkill to deal with one wayward dragonslayer. Rowan dropped the salted pork he'd been eating and moved to Bershad's left. The bystanders backed away, allowing the wardens to surround and level spears at Bershad's and Rowan's throats. All of them wore eagle masks to show that they were sworn to the Malgraves.

A high-warden cleared a path for himself through the circle of mounted soldiers. His eagle mask had a bright orange slash of color running down the middle of the beak that made him stand out from the group. He wore a dark green cloak and his mask had a mane of blue horsehair attached to the back—as befitted his rank.

"Did you get lost, dragonslayer?" he said, as if this happened to him every morning and he had grown accustomed to the occurrence.

"I'm here on orders from the king," Bershad said.

"Funny, so am I. Except he says I'm to kill any dragonslayers I see. What am I to make of this discrepancy?"

Bershad knew his type—educated and highborn, but not very important. He was probably the third or fourth son of a small lord and was being groomed for a high-ranking station in the king's army so he'd be useful to the family when his older brother came into his inheritance.

"We have a letter, signed and everything," Bershad said. "If your men promise not to kill me when I move, I'll retrieve it from my pocket."

The high-warden nodded. "They promise."

Bershad pulled the king's letter from his inner breast pocket and tossed it up to the high-warden, who caught it deftly with one hand, keeping his other on the hilt of his sword. A good soldier, Bershad thought. Never letting his guard down. The high-warden read the note, checked the seal in the light of the sun, and then nodded at his men, who lifted their spears toward the sky in unison.

"Eaolin, Shermon. Get off your horses." The high-warden removed his mask and hooked it to his hip. He was young for an officer—bright blue eyes and an aquiline nose. "It's good to see you again, Lord Bershad." He smiled. "We best head inside the city. Bad policy to keep the king waiting."

———

As they rode toward Floodhaven, the high-warden kept pace next to Bershad.

"I apologize for not recognizing you," he said.

"We know each other?"

"My name is Carlyle Llayawin."

Bershad had been right—Llayawin was an old but minor house of the Dainwood rain forest.

"My father served your father for many years," Carlyle continued. "And I was in the crowd when you rode for Glenlock Canyon with your army. I am sorry for the way things ended for your family."

A lord from the Atlas Coast would never talk to Bershad with such empathy—the king's ire toward Bershad was their ire. But men of the Dainwood were more independent. Bershad appreciated that.

"How has house Llayawin found the new leadership?" Bershad asked. "I understand Elden Grealor has a different way of running things."

"Different is the word," Carlyle agreed. "Lord Grealor has no respect for the forest. He's built lumber mills all over the Dainwood and gotten rich off the industry. Dainwood lumber is worth a fortune, seeing as nobody had a chance to buy it until recently." Carlyle paused. "Apologies. It must hurt to be reminded of your homeland."

"The Dainwood isn't my home anymore," Bershad said. "I don't give a shit what Grealor does with it."

Sometimes Bershad almost believed that lie himself.

"All the same, it's not right." Carlyle grimaced. "That's why I took my men and came up here. Swore my sword to Princess Ashlyn Malgrave."

The mention of Ashlyn's name turned Bershad's mouth dry. On their trip south, he'd tried to avoid getting mired in daydreams about seeing her again. He hadn't been successful.

"You didn't swear to the king?"

"Technically, I'm the king's man, of course. But Hertzog Malgrave didn't have much love for five hundred Deepdale wardens looking for a new master. He kicked us over to Ashlyn to work the city's defenses. There isn't much glory in the life of a watchman, but being honest, I'm glad for it."

"Why's that?"

"I've had my fill of raids and skirmishes, and the king still runs plenty of those. Need to keep the high lords in line, and all that. No, guarding a wall and sleeping in a real bed each night suits me just fine. And I know that Ashlyn Malgrave won't go ordering me to chop down a forest anytime soon."

"No," Bershad said, swallowing. "She won't."

They rode down a large avenue toward the castle. Smaller roads and alleyways darted in and out of sight to their left and right—packed with carts, people, and doorways into different shops.

Castle Malgrave rose in the distance. It was an ancient fortress—the foundations built upon the highest point in the area centuries ago. The granite walls stood eighty strides tall. Beyond them, four tall spires poked into the sky. The two shorter towers stretched to an even height, four times as high as the city walls. The tops of those towers used to be archers' nests, but had long since been converted to plush chambers for visiting lords and royalty. The upper rooms of one tower were blackened and damaged on the western side. Bershad squinted, trying to make out the details. The masonry was saggy and deformed. It looked more like melted wax than solid rock.

"What happened up there?" Bershad asked, pointing.

"Fire," Carlyle said.

"Never seen a castle fire melt the castle."

"Neither have I. But fire is the story we high-wardens of the lower levels were told." Carlyle shrugged. "Happened two moons ago while the Balarian envoy was here."

"Did you see it?" Bershad asked.

"Sure." Carlyle nodded. "There was a pop in the middle of the night—like a lightning strike, although I remember the sky being clear. When I came out into the courtyard to get a look, the whole side of that tower was engulfed in flames. They looked queer, though."

"How's that?"

"Wrong color." He glanced up at the burned tower then back at Bershad. "I've seen plenty of holdfasts burn in my time. Gods, I've done the burning myself on occasion. The flames flicker out the windows, orange and yellow, same as a bonfire. But these were blue. *All* blue. And they weren't flickering out the windows. The stones themselves were doing the burning—turned white with heat in seconds. But it didn't last very long. Five, ten minutes at most. I was heading up to make sure everything was contained, but Princess Ashlyn turned me away."

"Ashlyn was in the tower when the fire happened?"

"Of course," Carlyle said, pointing to the third tower, which was half again as tall as the two smaller spires. "She's been using the Queen's Tower as her offices and personal chambers for years now, but she was working on something in that smaller tower the last few months. Before the fire." Carlyle paused. "Nobody knew what she was doing, exactly. Just rumors. Like I said, Ashlyn's a different breed of highborn."

Bershad had heard those rumors. Stories of Ashlyn Malgrave staying awake late into the night, using dragon organs to brew Papyrian potions in a massive cauldron that could change the weather and curse men's manhood. He also knew that was all dragonshit.

"The Floodhaven court always loved its gossip," Bershad said.

Carlyle smiled. "That is a fact."

Most Almirans never traveled more than a day's walk from the hut or shack in which they were born. They spent their days working a field and their nights worshipping gods that ruled the forest beyond their back fence. The isolation made them superstitious. Anything they didn't understand was demoncraft. And so much about Ashlyn was inscrutable to castle stewards, turnip farmers, and everyone in between. If she didn't have veins full of royal blood, the people would have named her a demon-worshipping witch, formed a mob, and burned her alive years ago.

"Anyway," Carlyle continued, turning them onto a wide avenue. "Not much sense worrying about burned-out towers when we're heading for this other one, up here."

He pointed to the fourth tower, which stood in the center and rose well beyond the other three. The tallest structure in Almira. Inside the tower, there were chambers, dining halls, granaries, kitchens, baths, armories. And Hertzog Malgrave, king of Almira.

"Yeah," Bershad said, pushing down his thoughts of Ashlyn. He needed to focus.

Carlyle led them through the main gate of Castle Malgrave, beneath yet another portcullis that was kept open for daily traffic into the fortress. On the other side there was a large courtyard, which was full of high-end merchant stalls set up for the courtesans. The carts sold rich spices from distant lands, casks of wine, and expensive gemstones destined for highborn mud totems.

Carlyle dismounted gracefully, with Bershad and Rowan following suit. Stable boys dressed in silk tunics appeared and led their horses away. The double door to the castle was ten feet tall, made from ancient Almiran oak and covered with sprawled carvings of gods' faces.

Three masked Malgrave wardens stood on either side of the door— their blue-and-black enameled armor reflected the sun. A steward sat at an ornate desk to the side of the door, scratching furious notes into a ledger. He was a gangly man, with gray thinning hair and deep, ravine-like frown lines cut into his cheeks and forehead.

"Your business in Castle Malgrave?" he asked as they approached, not looking up from his work.

"I present Silas Bershad, exiled dragonslayer, and his forsaken shield, Rowan. They are answering a summons from the king," Carlyle said, his voice stiff and formal.

The steward's quill froze. His eyes shot up to Bershad.

"Do you possess this summons?" he asked.

Carlyle produced the note from a pouch on his sword belt and handed it to the steward, who dotted the seal of the king in three places as he read.

"May I see your mark, dragonslayer?" the steward asked, still looking at the summons.

Bershad removed the glove on his right hand and rolled up his sleeve, revealing a blue sprawl of intricate tattoos that extended along the entire length of his forearm. The base of the tattoo—closest to his wrist—had been given to him at the same time they put the blue bars on his face. The symbols were ancient Almiran glyphs. They denoted his former rank along with his crimes and the reasons for his exile. The steward began to read them aloud.

"Son of the traitor, Leon Bershad. Former heir to Deepdale and the Dainwood province. Once betrothed to Princess Ashlyn Malgrave. Former commander of the Jaguar Army. Vicious temperament. Given to passion and bloodlust. Exiled for ordering and leading the massacre of Glenlock Canyon."

Those marks only covered the first few inches of Bershad's arm. Above that, the slayings began. Sixty-five dragons in the midst of their death throes twisted along Bershad's flesh—each one drawn by a different artist. A patchwork chronicle of impossible feats.

Almost all of the dragons had been killed with an ash spear through their mouth or eye. Flawless and clean. The only outlier was a Yellow-Spined Greezel etched on the middle of his bicep that Bershad had decapitated with his dragontooth dagger. The dragon had been a runt, but it was still a terrible fight—like wrestling a rabid boar armored with porcupine spikes. The poison from those barbs had given Bershad hallucinations for an entire week after it was done. When he came to his senses, they'd moved on to another province and he was famous for being the only man to behead a dragon, even if it was a runt.

Carlyle whistled at the sight of the tattoos. No other dragonslayer in the world had an arm like that. Most wound up with a seashell in their mouth on their first pass and never earned a single tattoo. The lucky ones managed two or three on their forearm.

But Bershad's tattoos snaked up to his shoulder, then poured across his chest and back.

If the steward was impressed, he hid it well—pulling Bershad's arm closer to his face and examining a few of the dragons. He moved to dot Bershad's skin with his quill several times, but stopped himself.

Satisfied, the steward released his arm and jotted down several notes in his ledger.

"I need another one added while I'm here," Bershad said.

"Your tattoo can wait. King Hertzog will not." The steward looked up from his ledger and frowned at Bershad. "You are filthy. I will send for wash-girls to clean you before you are presented to the king. Your forsaken shield will be given quarters in the servants' basement. High-Warden Carlyle"—he gave Carlyle the perfunctory glance that only stewards seem capable of, regardless of whom they are talking to—"that will be all."

If Carlyle was offended by the steward's curt dismissal, he didn't show it. He turned to Bershad. "It was an honor to see you again, my lord." The steward grunted at Carlyle's taboo use of Bershad's old title, but said nothing. "I hope our paths will one day cross again. Until then, I'll be on the walls."

Carlyle smiled, then strode off toward the stable, cinching his eagle mask back into place. The steward had already turned to the next person waiting to gain entrance to Castle Malgrave.

Bershad stopped Rowan before they parted ways.

"Keep your boots on while you're in the castle, Rowan. You catch even a whisper of drawn steel, take Alfonso and get him out of Flood-haven. Don't wait for me."

Rowan frowned. "Don't do anything stupid, Silas. He's the king."

"He's also the bastard that murdered my father and put these bars on my face. I'm not just gonna give a bow and kiss his hand." Bershad leaned closer. Tightened his grip on Rowan's shoulder. "We've made it a long way together, but there's no reason for you to follow me down the river if it comes to that. Promise me you'll run."

Rowan swallowed. Gave Bershad a long look.

"I promise."

Bershad clapped Rowan on the shoulder.

"Good. And don't worry so much. I'll try my best not to die."

————

Two female servants took Bershad to a chamber in the second tower. Judging from their hay-colored hair and pale skin, they were Lysterian—a frigid country on the far side of the Soul Sea. Bershad's longevity as a dragonslayer had made him famous across the realm of Terra, but in Hertzog Malgrave's castle, treating him with even a shred of respect was bound to earn a servant a score of lashes. Bershad figured the Almiran servants had pawned his clean up duty off on the foreigners in an effort to keep their backs unmarred.

The Lysterians put him into a steaming tub of hot water sprinkled with salts and lavender. Bershad submerged himself once and turned the water black. Dismayed, the girls drained the water and poured a fresh bath, sprinkling a larger portion of salts and herbs this time.

One girl toiled with the knots and rings in Bershad's hair while the other scrubbed his arms, chest, and back with a brush—removing dried scabs, mud, and dirt. She took special care around his leg wound. The scab had fallen off, leaving a light pink circle that would turn into a raised and gnarled mark. One more scar added to the mess.

When they were done scrubbing, one girl trimmed Bershad's beard while the other rubbed scented oil into his skin, moving her hands over the deep scars and marred flesh that covered his body. The girls whispered to each other in Lysterian while they worked.

"What's the big secret?" he asked.

The girl who'd been trimming his beard cleared her throat and spoke in a thick accent.

"Faye is confused by your name. You are called flawless, but carry so many marks upon your skin. These are the most she has seen on a man."

"Yeah, the stories tend to skip that part."

"Pardon?"

Bershad sighed. He didn't feel like explaining his name.

"I'm as clean as I'm going to get. Can you bring me a set of clothes?"

"Right away," said the serving girl.

They brought him clean clothes: pants, tunic, and jacket. All of it black with green trim. The jacket had a set of ivory buttons that Bershad couldn't figure out how to work.

"The fuck are these for?" he muttered to himself.

One of the serving girls smiled and helped him. She crossed the double-breasted jacket and hooked the buttons so they ran up the left side of his chest and closed his collar. It was the finest set of clothes

Bershad had worn in fourteen years. He hated them. But when he moved to unbutton the collar the girl slapped his hand away.

"If you're seeing the king, the collar stays buttoned," she said firmly.

"You're the boss."

While the Lysterians packed up their supplies, Bershad scanned the room for a weapon of some kind. An errant razor or scissor. Even a comb could kill a king. But there was nothing within reach. Not a real setback. Hertzog Malgrave had thrust a miserable life of wandering and killing around his neck. Bershad didn't have a problem murdering him with his bare hands. Just thinking about watching the life drain out of Hertzog's eyes filled Bershad's mouth with the bitter taste of adrenaline and rage. His fingers twitched from the tension flooding his bloodstream.

A nervous and talkative serving boy came to fetch him.

"King Hertzog was just starting to eat his supper in Alior Hall when I brought news of your arrival. He said to get you right away," the boy said. "I asked if the king would like to see you when he had finished his dinner, and he threw a dish of gravy at me. You can see the stain." The boy pointed. "In any case, we'd best hurry."

He led Bershad through the castle until they reached a set of double-oak doors. This one had an eagle-faced god with enormous wings carved into the wood.

"Ready?" the boy asked.

"Yeah," Bershad said. He tugged on his collar, which pulled one of the buttons free.

"Here, let me fix that."

The boy stood on his toes and adjusted the collar.

"I should warn you, there are a lot of wardens in there with their swords drawn," he whispered. "And the king seems very angry. I thought, if you wanted, you could have my seashell. Just in case . . . you know." The squire removed a bone-white clamshell from his pocket and offered it to Bershad. "It would be the greatest honor of my life to help the Flawless Bershad's soul find the sea."

Bershad couldn't help but smile. The boy would be whipped senseless if anyone found out he'd made that offer.

"What's your name, boy?"

"Dennys, my lord."

"Best keep the shell for yourself, Dennys. The sea isn't that far from here. I'll find it."

Dennys gave a serious nod, then opened the door.

Alior Hall was one of the smallest audience chambers in the King's Tower, named after an unpopular monarch who nearly bankrupted the nation and lost a war to the jungle nations south of the Dainwood. The king was eating dinner alone at the far end of the hall. Malgrave wardens ringed the walls, each of them wearing full armor and standing at attention with their swords drawn.

As soon as Bershad stepped into the room, a warden appeared from the left, shoved him back a pace, and carried out a violent body search. It was lucky Bershad hadn't been able to sneak a weapon up his sleeve after all.

"He's unarmed, my king," the warden said. Then he looked at Bershad. "But if he gets too close, he's a dead man."

With that, the warden nodded to Dennys, who scrambled in front of Bershad and led the way across the room.

"My king," he said, bowing low. "May I present to you the Flaw— I mean, that is to say, the dragonslayer is here."

King Hertzog stopped eating and steepled his hands together in front of his face, obscuring most of his features. There was a bearskin cloak slung over his shoulders, but the king still looked cold.

"Took your time getting here, exile."

Bershad counted the wardens—twenty-five. Checked the room for other exits, but didn't see any.

He shrugged. "My donkey's getting a little old to walk a full day. We took breaks."

The king glared at Bershad for a moment, then went back to eating his food. He pulled the wing off a crispy game hen and took a greasy bite. Bershad remembered Hertzog as a warrior king—more comfortable sitting atop a horse in a set of armor than warming a throne in an expensive robe. But the years had brought decay. He was old and bent where he used to be straight and strong. His once black hair had turned silver and thin. Still, his body had always been built for violence. Even now his broad shoulders took up the space of two normal men.

The king went for another bite of chicken, stalling to show he was in charge.

"What do you want, Hertzog?" Bershad asked.

Dennys gasped at the disrespect. Bershad didn't care. He'd had no patience for castle etiquette when he was eighteen, and the years of exile hadn't improved his tolerance for royal cock-jerking.

King Hertzog tried to ignore the insolence, but his face twitched. He sucked a piece of chicken from between his teeth and dropped the wing.

"There's work for you on the far side of Terra," the king said, his voice full of phlegm.

So, it was just another dragon. Some foreign lord had probably begged Hertzog to send his famous dragonslayer in exchange for a favorable tax break on imported goods. It had happened before, although Hertzog hadn't made the request personally. That was new.

"Where?" Bershad asked. "What breed?"

The king sipped from a ceramic goblet.

"Get out of here, boy," he said quietly, then shot Dennys a look.

The squire ran out of the room as if Hertzog had threatened him with a crossbow. The door slammed behind him.

Hertzog coughed from deep within his lungs, then washed it away with a longer gulp of wine. He wiped his mouth with a cloth-of-gold napkin and tossed it on top of his half-eaten meal.

"How are you still alive?" he asked.

Bershad shrugged. "Turns out killing lizards isn't as hard as people make it out to be."

"Sarcasm won't serve you well in this conversation," Hertzog said.

"I'm not sure what this conversation is about, yet. It seems a little more complicated than some foreign dragonslaying writ."

Hertzog stared at Bershad for several moments, then motioned to the warden standing behind him.

"I have a gift for you, exile."

The warden picked up a rectangular box made from lacquered oak that was propped against the wall. Placed it by Bershad's feet, then backed away.

Bershad stared at it. "That full of vipers or something?"

"Open the fucking box."

Bershad hesitated a moment, then bent down and unlatched the clasps. His old sword, which had been taken from him the day he was exiled, was inside. It was neither an Almiran nor Papyrian design, but lost somewhere in the middle. Ashlyn used to tease him for having the same taste in swords and women.

Unlike the double-edged and straight swords favored by wardens, this blade was single-edged and slightly curved. Thinner than
an Almiran broadsword—three fingers wide at the collar instead of
the usual six—but far longer than a typical Papyrian blade. The grip
added another foot to the sword's length, so it could be wielded with
one or two hands. It was wrapped in sharkskin leather for a better
grip and capped at the butt with a plain steel bobble that could crack
a skull. The black scabbard was made from leather and Papyrian
cedar.

"You check me for hidden weapons, then give me a sword?" Bershad asked.

Hertzog shrugged. "Go ahead."

Bershad picked it up and drew the sword a few inches. Tested the
edge. Slipping his fingers around the familiar grip felt like putting
on an old, favorite pair of boots he'd thought were lost forever. Except instead of comfort, touching the sword filled Bershad's body
with wrath.

"The cellar I threw it in flooded a few years back," Hertzog said.
"There'll be some rust."

Bile rose in Bershad's throat. His vision went blurry at the edges.
He couldn't think straight, all he could do was imagine sprinting for-
ward and ramming the length of rusty steel through Hertzog's heart.
He was about to do exactly that, but the king's face stopped him.

Hertzog was smiling. Face glowing with an expression of extreme
satisfaction.

The king was baiting him. Had to be. Bershad scanned the wardens again and noticed that five of them had crossbows tucked behind
their backs, loaded and ready to fire. Bershad hadn't survived this
long just to get himself killed over a lost temper. He forced down
the fury that threatened to burst out of him. Squeezed the sword's
grip until one of his knuckles cracked, then shoved the blade back
into its sheath.

"Why are you giving me this?" Bershad hissed through clenched
teeth.

Hertzog's smile faded. He leaned back in his chair.

"Because I want you to kill the emperor of Balaria with it."

Bershad frowned. After Balaria tried and failed to invade Almira,
they closed their borders. In the last thirty years, no Almiran had

cleared their legendary customs, let alone entered their capital—
Burz-al-dun.

"You're joking."

"Do I look like I'm joking? Do this for me, and the Crown will
lift your exile," Hertzog said.

That was an unprecedented proposition. An exile was permanent,
just like the tattoos.

"Why are you so desperate to see the emperor dead?"

"Do you care?"

"Yes."

Bershad had learned from experience that every offer from King
Hertzog came with strings, some of which could be tied around your
throat and pulled.

Hertzog coughed, then swallowed with effort. "Do you know
what occupies the minds of dying old men?"

"Not personally, no. As you can see I'm still full of youthful joy
and vigor."

"Family," Hertzog said. "And the emperor of Balaria stole half of
mine."

"How's that?"

"Their period of isolation has ended. The emperor himself came
to Floodhaven to negotiate a trade agreement two months ago. But
when he left, he took my daughter with him."

Bershad's stomach tensed. "Ashlyn?"

Hertzog's face twitched. "No. It was Princess Kira."

Kira was Ashlyn's younger sister.

"Kidnapped?"

"She's a fifteen-year-old girl, what else would have happened?
Those clock-worshipping bastards failed to conquer my country, so
now they've stolen my daughter instead. I won't allow it!" Hertzog
slammed his fist onto the table, then looked down at his scarred hand.
His voice softened. "A man protects his family, or he is not a man at
all."

Bershad glanced at the wardens in the room, curious how they'd
react to such a vulnerable display from their king. Their faces remained stoic. The king had probably chosen the men in the room
carefully—your average soldier couldn't carry a secret like this down
a short hallway.

"Guess you fucked up pretty bad, then."

Hertzog straightened up. His face darkened.

"You *will* get Kira back," he growled, all the vulnerability drained from his voice. "Then you *will* kill Emperor Mercer Domitian."

Bershad shifted the sword in his hands a little, trying to remind himself of the balance. Once he drew the blade, he'd have to move fast. But the offer to end his exile wasn't something he could completely ignore. He decided to play the charade out a little, just to see where it led.

"In case you've forgotten, you sent me to kill a man once before," Bershad said. "And all that came of that was a bloody massacre and a pair of blue bars on my cheeks. Why should I trust you this time?"

"Trust me. Don't trust me. I couldn't care less. My offer is made. Take it or leave it."

"What are you going to do if I refuse, exile me more?"

Hertzog's jaw tightened. "It would be a mistake for you to believe you have nothing left to lose. You have your forsaken shield, Rowan. And that donkey you're so famously fond of. I could snap my fingers right now and one of my wardens would be more than happy to drag Rowan into the donkey's stable, lock it, and incinerate them both. Perhaps I'll drag you down there, too, so you can watch."

That did it.

"I'll be honest, Hertzog, you had me fooled for a minute with the gift and the grieving father act, but there's the conniving king I remember. Rotting body packed with shit and lies."

Hertzog's face colored with fury. Bershad judged the distance between himself and the king. He could cover it in six, maybe seven long strides. That was a little too far. He might not finish the job before the wardens got to him.

"You want to know why I'm still alive, Hertzog?" Bershad stepped forward. The warden behind him followed, staying just close enough so that Bershad could slash his throat open in the same motion he used to draw his sword. "It's because I knew that for all these years, you were sitting on your ass in this castle, getting old. Waiting to hear I'd finally bitten down on a seashell. I knew that every time you heard a servant whisper about the latest dragon I'd killed, you doubted whether you'd outlive me at all. And that's what I wanted. For you to go down to the river knowing that I was still alive. That you'd failed."

Bershad looked down at the sword.

"But you've given me an easier way." He turned back to the king. "I don't give a shit if the emperor of Balaria kidnapped your daughter, but I've wanted to kill you for fourteen years. Think I'll pass on your shit-filled offer. I'd rather wrap things up right now. In this fucking room."

Bershad gripped the sword. Got ready to draw the blade. Hertzog licked his lips. There was sweat on his forehead.

"Princess Ashlyn predicted that response."

The mention of Ashlyn's name froze Bershad.

"But I wonder what you'll say to her when she asks you to do the exact same thing I have," Hertzog continued. "Somehow I don't think you'll angle up to stab her in the heart."

Bershad frowned. Before he could respond, he heard a woman's voice from behind him.

"Hello, Silas."

Ashlyn Malgrave was leaning against a stone pillar with her arms crossed. She was holding a leather scroll in one hand.

"Ashlyn," Bershad said, relaxing his grip on the sword. The rage that had crept up to the edges of Bershad's eyes retreated to his stomach.

He stared at his old lover.

Fourteen years had carved thin lines around the edges of her mouth, but the rest of her looked the same. Her black hair streamed down past her hips. Her large eyes and long nose made a sharp contrast to her soft chin. Ashlyn Malgrave's severe disposition had always leaked into her features too much for most people to call her beautiful. A poet once said that her face was like a storm you watched crawl across the horizon of the sea—it was stunning to behold, but the sight left you uneasy. Bershad never understood that. Seeing her face again was the closest he'd felt to being home since he was exiled.

"Fourteen years is a long time." It was all Bershad could think to say.

Ashlyn smiled, then motioned to the sword in Bershad's hand. "I see that my father has begun to fill you in on our proposition."

Bershad clenched his jaw. He was willing to do a lot of things to end Hertzog's life. And he was more than ready to follow him down the river. But he couldn't do it in front of Ashlyn.

"You want me to kill the emperor, too?" he asked her. "Why?"

"You're the perfect person for the job," she said, then crossed the room. She dropped the leather scroll on the table and took a seat. Folded her black silk gown in her lap.

Ashlyn's bodyguard, Hayden, had also entered the room while Bershad was preparing to kill the king. Ashlyn's mother, Shiru, had been a princess of Papyria—an island nation north of Almira that controlled the largest navy in Terra. King Hertzog had married Shiru for the beneficial alliance, but plenty of foreign customs came along with the princess and access to her homeland's fleet. In Papyria, every woman of royal blood was assigned a highly trained female bodyguard called a widow. Hayden followed Ashlyn like a shadow, and wore the black sharkskin armor of her order.

"Perfect person for the job," Bershad repeated. "How do you figure that?"

"Before I explain, there's an awful lot of drawn steel in this room." Ashlyn looked around. "Can everyone relax a little bit? Silas, come sit. Have a drink."

"I'm fine right here," Bershad said.

"As are my wardens," Hertzog added, still glaring at Bershad.

"Suit yourselves." Ashlyn poured herself a glass of wine and took a long drink. Even though nobody had moved or sheathed a weapon, the mood in the room shifted. Everyone lowered their hackles a little.

"Access to Balaria has proved impossible so far," Ashlyn said, putting the goblet on the table. "But you've traveled behind their borders before, correct?"

"Years ago," Bershad said, frowning. "Ten summers."

"That's why you're perfect for this. How did you get across?"

"A Ghalamarian Thundertail with my spear jammed in his throat carried me over the mountains and died a hundred leagues inside their border."

"Carried you how?" Hertzog cut in.

"My armor tangled on the barbs of his tail before he took flight. We were three leagues up in the sky before I knew what happened. It was either go along for the ride, or fall to my death."

Hertzog grunted. "There is not a single person in this court—from lord to whore—who believed that story when a Ghalamarian bard came around singing it."

"And yet every peasant in the Gorgon Valley believes I'm the god of demons," Bershad said, turning back to the king. "They throw salt at my feet to prevent my evil spirit from devouring their souls. One village offered me the life of a firstborn son, so I might spare the rest of them."

Hertzog let out a phlegmy sigh. "The Gorgon peasants are the reason every other country in Terra thinks we're a bunch of mud-worshipping savages."

"Last I checked, that was a fair description of most Almirans."

"We're getting distracted," Ashlyn said. "You were carried into Balaria by a Thundertail. What next?"

"A merchant caravan found me next to the carcass of the dragon three days later. I couldn't walk. Was drinking dragon's blood to stay alive. They took me to the nearest outpost—some fortress in the desert—where I was arrested as an illegal outlander and put into a dungeon below the fort. A week or so after that, some commander showed up and released me. He knew who I was, and wasn't in a rush to execute the Flawless Bershad for trespassing."

"What did he do instead?"

"The commander dispatched three score of soldiers to lead me through a pass in the Razorback Mountains and into Ghalamar. They marched me to some harbor city and told me if a dragon carried me into their country again, they'd cut off my head and send it back to Almira in a pinewood box."

"What's in those mountains?"

"Rocks. Trees. Stone Scale dragons ready to ambush anything worth eating. Hordes of bloodthirsty savages that'll cause problems if you don't take sixty soldiers with you. It's dangerous."

"How long did it take to clear the pass?"

"About a month."

Ashlyn took one last sip of wine, then pushed the cup away. "Would you be able to lead a group of people back to the Balarian border without getting them lost or killed in those mountains?"

Bershad weighed that. "You said getting across has proved impossible so far. How many times have you tried?"

Ashlyn paused. Rubbed the back of her neck for a moment. She always did that when she had to relinquish a secret.

"We tried ships first. Three of our fastest vessels set sail the morning after Kira was kidnapped." Ashlyn picked up the leather scroll she'd brought with her when she entered the room. "This is from

Lord Arnish, the commander of those ships. When he reached the Balarian coast, he was surrounded by frigates and imprisoned on a barrier island outside Burz-al-dun. He writes that he is no closer to gaining access to Balaria than he was three weeks ago, and warns that additional ships will likely meet the same fate as his."

"What about the mountains?"

"Three parties," Ashlyn admitted. "They were all murdered by Skojit marauders, we think. But you've made it through the Razors safely once before." Ashlyn paused. "I want you to do it again, this time with a group of people who can bring Kira home."

"Dragonslayers aren't exactly free to travel the world at their leisure, Ashe."

"You'll enter Ghalamar on the pretense of slaying a dragon far to the east. The squire who brought you in here heard my father order it, and that boy has the biggest mouth in Floodhaven, so the story's legitimacy is already spreading."

Bershad took a moment to think. He was more than happy to murder the king instead of running an errand for him, but he'd loved Ashlyn. Maybe he still did. That was worth something.

"So, I sneak a rescue party across the border, then I break off and kill the emperor for good measure?" he asked.

"Yes."

"Why not just bring Kira back without the royal assassination?" Bershad asked. "It would attract less attention."

"Because we need to send a message," Ashlyn said. "The lords of Almira will never stay in line if they see the Malgraves are too weak to impose consequences when their own flesh and blood is kidnapped and taken across the Soul Sea. And even if the High Lords don't rebel, do you really think the Balarians will scuttle back behind their border again for another thirty years after this? Once again, they think Almira's ripe for conquering—that they can turn us into a colony just like they did Ghalamar and Lysteria. The only way to keep Almira free is to bring Kira home and put a seashell in the emperor's mouth."

Bershad let out a long breath. Felt a wave of sorrow wash over him as he realized that Ashlyn had changed.

"Funny," he said quietly. "That's the same argument your father made when he told me to ride down to Glenlock Canyon and kill that mercenary general for him. And if I'm not mistaken, that bastard is still alive and Almira is doing just fine. You might not have become your asshole father, Ashlyn, but you have become a Malgrave. It's your dynasty that you want to protect, not Almira. And I'm not sworn to serve you anymore." He turned to Hertzog. "You saw to that."

"Silas," Ashlyn pressed. "I know that you don't want to keep killing dragons. I know that it's torture every time you use that spear and—"

"You don't know me at all anymore," Bershad snapped, even though everything Ashlyn said was true. "I won't trade black work like this on the promise that a Malgrave will keep their word." His voice choked. Turned into a whisper. "I've made that mistake before."

Ashlyn hesitated. "There is a greater good for the people to consider. Emperor Mercer has—"

"Don't dragonslayers already serve the people? Ridding the countryside of the great scaled menace so farmers can work their fields in peace?"

The rage surged back into Bershad's throat. Filled his mouth. The memories of all the dragons that he'd killed swarmed in his head. He threw his sword on the floor, then spat on it.

"I don't give a shit about the greater good."

Ashlyn glanced at the guards standing on the edges of the room before speaking again. "I understand. You have every right to doubt us. Doubt me. Sleep on it, at least. In a real bed, for a change."

She raised her eyebrows and inclined her head. Ashlyn had more to say, she just didn't want to say it here.

"An expensive bed isn't likely to change my mind. You two best start making other plans."

4

BERSHAD

Almira, Castle Malgrave

Dennys led Bershad through the castle, winding through passages and halls, down a twisting flight of stairs, and then up even more as they ascended one of the spires. The castle had once been a familiar combination of wonders—full of gardens, courtyards, and secret rooms that smelled of sea salt. Now the walls and rooms were strangers to Bershad. He felt lost inside of them.

As the rage from seeing Hertzog and shock from seeing Ashlyn wore off, Bershad felt lost in a much larger way, too. He'd refused their offer because he hated Hertzog, but he wondered if that was a mistake. It had been so long since he'd encountered a path that didn't involve trying to kill a massive lizard; it seemed foolish to throw this one away out of sheer spite.

Rowan was waiting in Bershad's room. Sitting cross-legged on the floor by the hearth with a cloth spread out in front of him and six spear points set up in a neat row. He had a seventh in his hand and was making careful strokes along its edge with a sharpening stone.

"So, you didn't get yourself killed after all. Good." He glanced at Bershad then returned to work. "Your armor is with the blacksmith, but I didn't trust him with your spear points. Man had farmer's hands."

"The blacksmith of Castle Malgrave?"

"Farmer's hands," Rowan repeated.

"How'd you get in here, anyway?" Bershad asked.

"Charm," Rowan said, but didn't elaborate.

The room had a massive bed and half a dozen cushioned chairs and recliners scattered around. This would be the first night Bershad had slept on something besides a tavern chair or a dirt floor in a very long time.

"So, what happened?" Rowan asked.

Bershad ignored the cushioned chairs and took a seat on the floor next to Rowan. "We've been offered a new job."

"Is the king dissatisfied with your dragonslaying performance?" Rowan set down the spear point and picked up another.

"I'd say he's a bit frustrated, seeing as he expected me to be turned to dragonshit more than a decade ago." Bershad pulled his boots off and angled his legs toward the hearth. "But Kira has been kidnapped by the Balarians, which appears to vex him far more than the Flawless Bershad."

"What does a kidnapped princess have to do with you and me?"

"He wants us to lead a rescue party into Balaria by way of the Razorback Mountains." Bershad paused. "Then he wants me to assassinate the emperor."

Rowan's hand stopped working the spear point for a moment—frozen halfway through a lick with the sharpening stone—and then continued. "That's a tall order. What's the emperor done to earn that kind of treatment?"

"Besides abduct a princess?"

"Yeah, besides that."

"Threatened the shiny, powerful future of the Malgraves," Bershad said.

"That'll do it."

"But if I kill him, Hertzog says he'll lift my exile and return my lands. Probably make you a high-warden or something."

"He's made promises to you before, Silas."

"Yeah."

"Plus, it sounds like a pretty elaborate plan for a man like Hertzog. He always liked to keep things simple."

"It was Ashlyn's idea."

"Ashlyn's in the castle?"

"I just saw her."

Rowan laughed to himself. "This is getting good. How's she looking these days?"

"Beautiful," he said. "Same as before."

"And would I be correct to assume she's the reason you didn't send Hertzog on the long swim today?"

"You would."

"Glad she was there, then." He tossed another log onto the fire and worked on the spear points for a while.

"So, are you gonna do it?"

"I told Hertzog to fuck off, but Ashlyn asked me to sleep on it."

Bershad winced at the things he'd said to her in the dining hall. "I owe her that much."

Rowan put down the spear point and the sharpening stone. "Seems to me we'll probably die trying to cross the mountains, given what you told me about that pass. Even if we do make it over the Razors and into Balaria, do you think the clock-toting bastards will just let you sail home after you open their emperor's throat? It's a suicide mission, Silas."

"Maybe. I've survived lots of those, though." Bershad shrugged. "Would you rather go find another dragon?"

"I'd rather retire to the mulberry orchard my sons work together. Meet my grandchildren. Spend my last days getting drunk on a porch and smoking a pipe."

Bershad smiled absently. "That will never happen if we stay on the same road we've been walking. It's only a matter of time before one of them gets me. Then some asshole sentinel will kill you and Alfonso, and our heads will guard the castle walls together until they rot to nothing."

"That's what you said sixty-six dragons ago."

Bershad stared at the fire.

"There's always the other way," Rowan continued. "From Ghalamar we could ditch this rescue party. Hide out in the wilds."

Rowan brought the idea up every few months. Bershad's answer was always the same.

"And if we get caught, they'll skin Alfonso alive, wrap you up in his hide, and light you on fire while I watch." Bershad left the last part unsaid—they'd gouge his eyes out after he watched Rowan cook, then they'd force him to go fight another dragon. "I won't risk that. Ever."

"People make it."

"Most don't."

Rowan grunted disagreement, but didn't push the issue further.

"So, if it's between killing another dragon or killing the emperor, what would you do?" Bershad asked. "At least we'll get something for killing the Balarian."

"We *might* get something," Rowan corrected, then let out a long breath. "But my opinion doesn't factor in here. The rest of this muddy country may treat oaths like unwanted bastard children, but I do not.

I swore to your father I'd look after you, and that's what I intend to do. I'm with you either way, same as always."

Bershad nodded. Rowan was the only friend he had, but Bershad had never gotten comfortable with the man's unwavering loyalty. His father had earned that from Rowan during the Balarian Invasion. Bershad had not, no matter what the old man said.

"In the morning I'll decide," Bershad said. "For now, clear out, will you? Don't want Ashlyn to sneak in for some nostalgia and find you here."

"Right, right." Rowan packed up the spear points and moved for the door, but stopped short. He glared at the bed. "All's I got was a pile of straw," he said. "Lucky bastard."

Bershad found a full pitcher of wine and drank from a silver cup while he stared at the fire. He listened to the servants moving down the halls. He'd never liked crowds. Even backwater villages like Otter Rock drove Bershad toward the drink, but Floodhaven was the largest city he'd spent a night in fourteen years. The movement of so many people in the castle felt like rats scurrying against his skin.

After emptying the pitcher, he stripped naked and got into the bed. The softness felt foreign and wrong after so many years of sleeping on the hard earth. Bershad didn't even try to sleep. He knew it wouldn't come. Not in such a soft bed. Not with this decision weighing on him.

Later, someone knocked on his door.

Bershad got out of bed, pulled his pants back on, but couldn't figure out the buttons on the shirt. "Screw it," he muttered, and went to the door half dressed.

Ashlyn Malgrave was waiting in the hall. This time, she was carrying his sword along with a thick roll of scrolls.

"Did I interrupt your dreams, Silas?"

Bershad's chest tightened. He resisted the urge to pull her into his arms.

"No, Princess." He let her into his bedroom. Closed the door behind her.

She stood in the middle of the room, staring at the dying fire for a moment. The embers ignited the outline of her body through her loosely tied silk dress. The shape of her arm, the curve of her hips.

"It's a crime to give me that," Bershad said, pointing at the sword.

Exiles weren't allowed to carry swords—anyone in Terra had the right to behead a blue-barred man on the spot if he saw a steel blade in his hand or on his hip.

"It's a crime to reject a gift from a king, too," she said, tossing the sword onto the bed. "You looked about ready to kill my father with that when I walked in."

"I was."

Ashlyn narrowed her eyes. Nodded.

"I didn't talk to him for ten years," she said. "After what he did to you, I could barely stand being in the same city."

"You two seem pretty close now."

"My older brothers died," Ashlyn said, her body tensing. "And someone has to take care of Almira after he's gone. I didn't want the job, but it's mine now and—"

"Ashe," Bershad said, stopping her. "It's all right. I've spent time blaming just about everyone else in Almira for what happened to me. Hertzog. My father. Myself, most of all. But I never blamed you." He smiled. Motioned to the room's window. "Remember when I used to climb up the side of the tower to get to your bedroom?"

Ashlyn's shoulders relaxed.

"I remember being worried sick you'd kill yourself trying to get laid." She laughed, then gestured toward the ceiling. "I'd have waited for you higher up tonight, but I think you're a little old to make the climb these days. And I needed to talk to you alone. Really alone."

"You gave Hayden the slip, then?" Bershad asked. He hadn't seen her in the hallway.

"She's just back a ways. Hayden's learned to grant me a false sense of privacy. And to let me have the things I want, in the rare event that having them is possible."

"So, this isn't your first midnight journey down the tower?"

She flashed the crooked and mischievous smile he remembered. "Like you said, Silas, fourteen years is a long time."

"Yes."

"The tattoos suit you," she said, touching the place on her cheek where the blue bar would go. "Lucky. Few wear the marks so well."

Bershad realized that she'd never seen the tattoos on him until today. After returning from Glenlock Canyon, he had been stopped at the gates of Floodhaven, stripped of his sword, then marked and cast off into the wild. No good-byes. No last words between lovers.

"I asked them for green to go with my eyes," he said. "Didn't happen."

"The blue works."

Ashlyn dropped her eyes to the carpet.

"I was sorry to hear about your husband's death," Bershad continued when Ashlyn didn't say anything.

"No, you weren't," Ashlyn said, smirking. "Havanath was a drunken fool. It's no sorry thing that Almira will not have him as their king."

"A lot of the commoners say you killed him. Cast a Papyrian curse or something."

Ashlyn scoffed. "They say your cock is a foot long, too. But we both know that's not true."

Bershad couldn't help but smile. He'd missed hearing filthy words come out of Ashlyn's beautiful mouth.

"Anyway, Havanath drank himself stupid on that pleasure barge twice a week—it was amazing he didn't drown sooner."

They stared at each other. Bershad knew she'd come to convince him that Emperor Mercer deserved to die, but he wanted to talk with her the way they used to first. Even if it was playacting. Even if it only lasted for a few minutes.

"Judging from the stories about you, you're still keeping up with the great lizards, right?" Bershad asked.

As teenagers, they'd ridden all over Almira together, searching for dragons that Ashlyn could study and sketch in her folios. They'd sleep together in the woods and talk to nobody except each other for days on end. It was the happiest he'd ever been.

"Hayden and I spent an entire afternoon following a Horned Black last week," Ashlyn said, another smile creeping across her lips. "We saw him fight with a rival male. They hook their horns together and tug until one of them submits, just like I always suspected."

"I'm surprised the king allows his heir to spend her leisure time riding beyond the castle and chasing dragons."

Ashlyn shrugged. "The king has to pick his battles. I will inherit the Malgrave crown, I will wear down my eyes on scrolls and maps and bureaucratic appointments, and I will protect the Malgrave dynasty as it passes through the ages. But I will not stop riding out to see a dragon when one comes near Floodhaven. That Horned Black was amazing—a perfect example of their functional bone structure."

Bershad smiled. "You are different," he said. "But only some of you."

"You, too." She paused. Looked around the room. "Speaking of bones, can I see it?"

Clearly, Ashlyn wasn't in a rush to get to business, either.

"See what?"

"I know you have it with you. Don't play coy."

Bershad let her stew a moment longer, then went to the saddle-bag Rowan had laid across the back of a chair and removed the dragontooth dagger. Handed it to Ashlyn grip-first. She tested the balance. Ran a fingertip across the sharpened edge.

"What breed did you take it from?" she asked, keeping her eyes on the weapon.

"A female Gray-Winged Nomad. Near Greenspur."

"Oh. I'm sorry, Silas. I know you always liked the Nomads best."

Before Bershad became famous in the realm of Terra for killing dragons, he'd loved them almost as much as Ashlyn. But he'd buried all of that a long time ago. It was the only way to survive.

"She was beautiful," he whispered.

Ashlyn gave him a sad look.

"How did you prevent the tooth from rotting?"

Bershad hesitated. The truth was, the Nomad had bitten through his stomach and broken the tooth off in his guts. Rowan pulled the tooth out and threw it in a saddlebag, then forgot about it while he packed the wound with Spartania moss and saved Bershad's life. They didn't realize the tooth hadn't gone to rot until almost a week later.

But if Bershad told her that, he'd have to tell her everything else, too. He wasn't ready to do that.

"It wasn't easy," Bershad said. "But now that it's preserved, the edge has never taken a scratch."

Ashlyn nodded. She knew him well enough to know she shouldn't push.

"The rest of you has taken some damage, though." Ashlyn motioned to his body, scars visible through his half-closed shirt.

"Yeah."

When Bershad was sixteen years old, he'd spent a week's worth of sleepless nights sitting on his own castle windowsill, wondering whether climbing higher toward Ashlyn's bedroom was the right thing to do.

Uncertainty wasn't a problem for him this time.

He crossed the room and kissed her. Put both hands on her cheeks, ran them down her black hair to the small of her back. He had kissed her hundreds of times. Thousands. But the familiar taste of her mouth after fourteen summers and fourteen winters was enough to make his hands tremble.

They broke apart and Ashlyn slipped both palms under his shirt, pressed her fingertips into his scarred skin. "I can't believe you're still alive," she whispered. "I can't believe a world made of such cruelty would do me the kindness of letting me hold you again. I missed you." She kissed his neck. His jaw. His tattoos and his lips. "I missed you and missed you and missed you."

"I missed you, too."

Bershad ran a hand down her forearm and stopped at her wrist. There was a Papyrian knife the size of a thumb strapped to the inside of her wrist with a sharkskin leather thong. She'd had it since she was ten.

"You still carry that?" he asked. There was a clear, fibrous strand wrapped around the thong that Bershad didn't recognize, but everything else was the same.

"You know Hayden," Ashlyn said. "She always said it's easier to protect me if I can protect myself."

Bershad touched her cheek. "I've carried the memory of your face to every corner of Almira. It was the only good thing I had. But now the memory feels so small, like I've been holding on to a pebble and pretending it was a boulder."

She kissed him again. Bershad could feel warm tears on her cheeks, and then the pinch of her teeth as she bit down on his bottom lip and released. She did that when she didn't have words for whatever she was feeling.

"Ashlyn," he said, breaking the embrace after a long time. They couldn't pretend forever. "I understand why Hertzog wants a seashell jammed into the emperor's mouth—he never could abide someone fucking with his family. But this isn't like you. When you were twelve, you rode a stallion into a High Council meeting with your face covered in mud, shouting at your father to stop issuing writs of slaying along the Gorgon because too many River Lurkers had been killed that year. Now you want to assassinate an emperor. Why?"

"Because if Mercer is still alive this summer, he'll kill every dragon in the realm of Terra."

That got Bershad's attention.

"How?"

"I'll explain." Ashlyn motioned to the carpet in front of the fire. They both sat down near the warmth. "When the Balarians agreed to visit Floodhaven, I told the High Council that they were coming to broker a trade deal with Almira that would make them rich and finally end Balaria's thirty-year isolation. That was partly true. The emperor and I did discuss the trade of lumber and salt, spices and opium, dragon oil and steel. But that's not all we discussed."

Bershad considered that. "Marriage," he said.

"That's right. My husband drowned in the sea four years ago like an idiot. Mercer's wife died before providing any heirs. It was only logical that we consider a match. For Mercer, it was the chance to succeed where his father had failed. To conquer Almira without so much as a drawn sword."

"And for you?"

"Mercer Domitian rules the eastern side of the Soul Sea with impunity, yet his true personality and goals have remained a mystery to me, despite my best efforts to plant a spy in the Imperial Palace. I needed to know my adversary. This was the perfect excuse. We used the trade negotiation as a chance to court each other, and I used the courtship as a chance to discover who Mercer Domitian really was. I didn't like what I found."

"What do you mean?"

"Mercer knew I was interested in the lives of dragons, so he exposed his own personal . . . enthusiasm, I guess you could call it. He thought it would provide us with a common ground, but he and I do not share any common ground as far as I can tell, particularly when it comes to dragons. Here, look at this."

Ashlyn unrolled one of the maps she'd brought with her. It was an atlas of every warren on the eastern shore of Terra.

"For decades, there have been rumors that Balaria has aggressively hunted their dragon populations to slake Burz-al-dun's deep thirst for dragon oil. But I never knew how far they'd truly taken things until two months ago. According to Mercer, there hasn't been a dragon sighted within a week's ride of Burz-al-dun since the last Great Migration, five years ago. There is only one warren left inside their borders where dragons still come to breed, but it's the largest in the realm."

She pointed to a triangle-shaped mass in the east that was outlined in green ink.

"They call it Tanglemire. The area has always been inaccessible to men because of a massive mangrove field that surrounds it on all sides. Every five years, thousands of dragons come to that patch of land to hatch their broods at midsummer, when the waters reach their warmest. But Emperor Mercer has spent the last three years cutting a road through the mangroves, while also mass-producing a new type of ballista that can shoot a dragon out of the sky from a thousand strides away. He showed me the plans—there are more gears and locking pins in the winch lever alone than I'd have thought possible, and he uses a mechanism powered by dragon oil to reload them incredibly fast. I suppose innovation is the inevitable result of a country that's worshipped a machine god for the last five hundred years instead of mud statues." Ashlyn shook her head in frustration. "When the summer solstice arrives and the dragons of Terra return to Tanglemire, Mercer is going to drag hundreds of those machines to the edge of the wetland and eradicate them."

"Why would he want to kill so many dragons all at once?"

"Simple economics. Burz-al-dun burns more dragon oil in a moon's turn than Almira uses in a year—they rely on it to power their entire city. Mercer's found a way to refine dragon oil so that it provides a far stronger and longer-lasting source of energy, but he still needs more oil with each passing year. Accessing the Tanglemire warren and harvesting dragons slowly would guarantee enough oil for generations. But culling them all at once will give Mercer a near monopoly on the most valuable commodity in the world. He'll set the price and dole out the supply to his empire, and every other nation in Terra, as he wishes."

"Why did he tell you all of this?"

"He thought I might be interested in doing the same thing to the Dainwood warrens after we were married. Then, instead of a near monopoly, he'd have a real one."

"That was pretty terrible judgment on his part."

"Yes."

"Why didn't you get into this back in the dining hall?"

"You didn't exactly give me a chance, Silas. And I never told my father about Mercer's offer. To be honest, I was afraid he'd have accepted it. I'm the one who brought up the idea of killing Mercer, but Hertzog thinks I want him dead because I've turned into the ruthless and cold monarch he wants to see inherit the throne. And he's proud of me for it. Thinks I'll guard the Malgrave line with a wet blade when he's gone."

Ashlyn paused. Stared at the map for a moment.

"The dragons of Terra are more important than nations and wars and dynasties. They keep our entire world in balance. Most of Balaria is already a wasteland because of overhunting. There are famines in Ghalamar and food shortages in Lysteria, too."

"It's not your responsibility to help countries on the far side of Terra."

"Maybe not, but half the breeds in Almira fly to that Balarian warren during the Great Migration. Gray-Winged Nomads. Snub-Nosed Blackjacks. Needle-Throated Verduns. Ghost Moths. I don't know why they travel halfway across the realm instead of breeding in the Dainwood, but it's always been that way. Same as the salmon who abandon the depths of the Western Sea and swim a hundred leagues up freshwater rivers to spawn each summer, I suppose."

"Ashlyn, look." Bershad swallowed. "I know how much you care about dragons, but you're the heir to Almira's throne. You're supposed to protect her people. Not her lizards."

"I am protecting Almirans."

Ashlyn unrolled another one of the maps she'd brought. This one focused on eastern Almira. She'd probably drawn it herself.

"You just came from Otter Rock, right?"

"Yeah."

She pointed to the village on the map.

"Did you notice a rather absurd number of mud statues on their riverbanks?"

"Must have missed them. I was a little preoccupied with the Needle-Throated Verdun your father sent me to kill."

"Well, they're there. The people of Otter Rock make them obsessively because these villages have been plagued by disease and famine for the last five years." Ashlyn tapped her finger against four villages that were all upriver from Otter Rock. "The sickness is spreading farther downriver each day. At this rate, the plague will reach Otter Rock in a few months."

"What does this have to do with dragons?"

She put her whole hand over the map.

"The Blakmar province used to be a rich hunting ground for Gray-Winged Nomads, but my father liked Crellin Nimbu's father—they fought together in the Balarian Invasion. So Hertzog sent dozens of dragonslayers there over the years. By my count, thirty Nomads alone have been killed in that region in the last twenty years."

Bershad nodded. He'd killed eleven of them himself in the early part of his exile. Although before that Verdun, it had been a long time since a writ had brought him that far north. "But they're gone now."

"Nomads are clever," Ashlyn said. "Eventually they abandoned the Blakmar province entirely, much to the surprise of the Nimbus. They should be one of the richest families in Almira given all the dragon oil they've taken over the years, but they spent most of it on priceless gems for their mud statues. Foolish."

Ashlyn shook her head.

"Anyway, the Gray-Winged Nomads were the only predators in that region that threatened the Almiran black bears," Ashlyn said. "When the bears no longer had to watch the skies and scurry off the riverbank every time a dragon's shadow swooped through the valley, they started gorging themselves on otter meat before each winter. It only took two seasons before they'd nearly eradicated the whole population. You can ride that river for weeks without spotting a single otter."

"We're still talking about animals, not people."

"I'm getting there. The otters ate fish. Insects. Worms. Whatever they could find, really." She licked her lips. "But they also ate a rare type of red-shelled snail that only lives in that province. The snails are poisonous to most creatures, but the otters were immune. Without a natural predator, the snails' rate of reproduction went out of control. There are stretches of river north of Otter Rock that are so choked with snails you can use their shells as a bridge to cross the current. The toxin is harmless to humans in small doses, but it causes rashes, boils, seizures, and hallucinations when consumed in large quantities." Ashlyn pointed at the villages north of Otter Rock again. "Those are the exact afflictions that have plagued these areas for half a decade. I strong-armed Nimbu into hiring an alchemist to try and find a cure, but the alchemist might as well be one man trying to beat back the evening tide with a paddle. The villagers farther north refuse his help—they'd rather hunker down in their sickness and build mud statues, hoping their gods will save them from the forest demons. And even if they wanted his help, he doesn't have much to give. Master Mollevan has made no real progress toward an antivenom in five years of research."

Bershad decided not to tell Ashlyn that her alchemist got killed by a dragon. Didn't seem like a good time.

"If Almira's dragons leave for Balaria this summer but don't return, every city and village and holdfast in this country will have a problem like this. And the Dainwood will be one of the worst."

"Why?" Bershad said.

"The jungles of your homeland are unique. The root systems of Dainwood trees are all intertwined below the ground—they stretch on for leagues and leagues. And they've been infected with a toxic flakey-white fungus for thousands of years. The trees remain healthy despite the fungus because Snub-Nosed Blackjacks burrow beneath the trees and spend half their waking hours gnawing the fungus away without damaging the roots. The fungus is toxic to trees, but it relieves the sinus problems that plague Blackjacks, so they love it."

Bershad scratched his chin. "And if the Blackjacks don't return . . ."

"All those leagues of lush forest will turn to rotten wood. Without the trees to hold the soil in place, the rainy season will bring floods. Mudslides. Thousands will die. Within a year or two, the Dainwood rain forest will be gone, along with every man and animal that lives in that jungle."

Bershad looked down at the map she'd sprawled across the floor. There was a single red circle and dozens of notes scrawled in the margin about one specific Ghost Moth. Ashlyn thumbed the edge of the map, but didn't explain it.

"How can you be sure killing Mercer will make a difference?" he asked. "If there's money to be made from killing dragons, the next Balarian emperor will try it, too."

"Maybe," Ashlyn admitted. "But when Mercer dies, the Balarian government will be thrown into turmoil. His brother Ganon—the heir apparent—is young and foolish and, from what I can gather, primarily concerned with elaborate parties to worship Aeternita, their goddess of time. Transporting the ballistas to the warren will require a massive logistical operation and cooperation from hundreds of bureaucrats. Ganon couldn't execute the cull this summer even if he wanted to. That buys us time. The dragons will migrate back around the realm of Terra before Balaria recovers from Mercer's death and the next chance to kill all of them won't come for another five years, when the next Great Migration occurs."

Bershad remembered Ashlyn as a bookish and shy girl—someone who didn't like ordering stable boys around, let alone ordering an emperor killed. The years between them had hardened her. "Seems like you've thought of everything."

"Nobody can think of everything, but I see the whole world now." She stepped toward him. "Dragons are dangerous predators. But they do more than kill livestock. Their impact cascades down to every plant and animal in their environment, including the people of Almira. Without dragons, the natural order of this world will fall apart. Everything from otters to algae to entire forests hinges on the presence of dragons. If Mercer succeeds, there will be more sicknesses. More famine. The Gorgon Valley will become a toxic swamp. The Dainwood jungle will be turned to a lifeless, muddy wasteland. But you can help me stop it."

Bershad tightened one fist into a ball. Relaxed it. A few hours ago, he'd planned on dying in a food hall with the king's blood on his face and twenty-five swords jammed through his chest. Everything had changed so quickly.

"I believe you, Ashlyn. And I'm sorry about earlier. I thought you'd become someone different. I was wrong." He paused. Tried to find a way to explain the feeling in his guts. "But I am different." Bershad pulled up his sleeve. "Sixty-six dragons are dead at my hand. Fourteen years of wandering and killing and nothing else. The connection I felt to the great lizards when we were younger is broken. The conviction I had is lost. And whatever you loved in me went to rot a long time ago. I can't help anyone."

Ashlyn studied his tattoos before speaking again. Eyes moving over the atlas of scars across his arms and chest and stomach.

"Silas, I know you've had to do terrible things to survive. I don't blame you. But those things don't have to define you. My father is old and sick. Soon enough, he'll be dead. What will you do when he's gone? Who will you be?"

He'd survived on his hatred for Hertzog for so long, he wasn't sure there was anything left underneath. Part of him was afraid to look.

"I don't know."

Ashlyn let her map roll closed. Set it aside.

"Your father threatened to kill Rowan and Alfonso if I refused to go. What will you do?"

"I have two ships in Floodhaven harbor right now. One can take you to Ghalamar tomorrow. The other will take you, Rowan, and your donkey out of Terra and across the Great Western Ocean. Right now."

Bershad was stunned.

"The journey across that ocean is almost as dangerous as the Razors," Ashlyn continued. "But if you make it, you'll be free. Your blue bars don't mean anything on the far side of the ocean. Nothing from this realm does."

Ashlyn left the last part unsaid. He would never see her again.

"I need help, Silas. But I won't force another burden upon you. You've carried enough of them for ten lifetimes. Whatever debt you owed for Glenlock Canyon, you paid it a long time ago. If you leave this realm, a part of me will never be whole again. But I'll understand why you had to go."

Bershad swallowed. His mouth was dry.

"I want the life that was taken from us. But all these years. All the things I've done, and had done to me. I don't know if I can go back. I just . . ."

He trailed off. Couldn't find the words.

"You don't have to know," Ashlyn said. "And you don't have to decide right now. There's time." She reached for his tattooed hand and intertwined her fingers with his. "But whatever you choose, there's one thing we definitely need to do before the sun rises."

She wrapped her arms around him. Pulled him close. She kissed his mouth and bit his bottom lip again. They stood like that for a few moments, feeling the warmth of each other's bodies. Bershad could feel Ashlyn's pulse against his chest. Her hands drifted along his stomach and ribs, then lower to the waist of his pants where they lingered for a moment before she started untying them. He managed to halfway unwrap her silk dress, tangled it at her waist, then got on his knees and yanked it the rest of the way down. He ran his hand up her thigh and kept going, feeling the warmth between her legs. They didn't make it to the bed, just dropped naked on the soft carpet in front of the fire. Falling into their old ways. Falling into each other.

Afterward, Ashlyn lay on top of him, resting her head against his chest. Eyes closed. She had a small, oval-shaped freckle on her left eyelid that Bershad had noticed after they spent their first night together. It hurt him to see it again. He could conjure the life they'd shared in his memory—full of laughter and carefree pleasure—but feared it was impossible to bridge the gap and return.

Bershad touched the queer translucent string that was tied around Ashlyn's wrist. Now that she was naked, it seemed even more out of place.

"What is this?" he asked.

She sat up. Rubbed her left wrist with her right hand for a moment. "That burden is mine to carry, not yours."

"Ashe."

"Trust me, Silas. Tugging on this thread will just make things harder."

Bershad hesitated. "Rowan and Alfonso are the only ones I've trusted for a long time."

"This'll be good practice, then."

She shifted so that she was straddling him again. Bershad could feel the wetness between her thighs pressing against him. She frowned down at the scar the Nomad had left on his stomach. "This wound should have killed you."

That one, and two dozen others.

"You're just trying to change the subject."

"And it's going to work."

Bershad grunted. "You're a little sharper than most of the people who see me like this."

"You mean the lady of Umbrik wasn't a student of human anatomy?"

"How do you know about that?"

"The usual way. Spies. Informants," Ashlyn said.

"Really?"

"My father has his armies, I have my informants. And I wanted to know about your life, even if I couldn't be a part of it. I've heard hundreds of stories about you. Most are about the dragons you've killed or highborn ladies' honor you've stolen, but others are about the damage your body takes without going down the river. My informants think they're backwater exaggerations because they only hear one or two of them. But I've heard them all. What's happened to you, Silas?"

"That's my burden to carry, not yours," he said.

If Ashlyn wanted to keep her secrets, he'd keep his, too.

"That's fair, I suppose." She traced a few more of his scars. "If we see each other again, maybe we'll be able to set our burdens down with each other then."

"Maybe," Bershad said.

She ran a finger down the bar on his cheek. "Whatever the truth is, nothing will change how I feel about you. I love you, Silas. Always have."

Bershad ran his hands up her thighs and rested them on her hips.

"I love you, too, Ashe. Always have."

Ashlyn leaned down and kissed him, long and deep. Her nipples touched his chest as she snaked herself up and down against him. She smiled as she felt his body react again. Reached down and guided him back inside of her.

"If we can't drop our burdens quite yet, we can do this again, instead."

————

Later, they lay in the bed, listening to the embers of the fire crackle. Bershad looked at the tattoos on his arm.

He could smell Ashlyn all over his skin. Taste her on his lips. It wasn't until that moment that he realized how tightly he'd guarded his memories of her. He'd locked them away inside a hidden cellar and stayed outside for fourteen years.

Now that the door was open, he didn't want to close it.

A few hours ago, he'd have gladly died so long as he did it looking down on Hertzog's corpse. And a boat that would get him out of Terra—out of this mess—was a better offer than he could have imagined. But Ashlyn was worth more to him than revenge or escape or a few more years of warm blood in his veins. If he ran from the chance to help her—to salvage the life that had been taken— what was the point of being alive at all?

"I'll do it, Ashlyn. I'll go to Balaria."

She turned to him. "You're sure?"

"Yeah."

Bershad ran his hand through her hair again. Pulled her on top of him and kissed her long and deep. Tried to memorize the feeling of her weight against his body.

They stayed in the bed together until the orange dawn streamed through the window, igniting the sea below the castle.

"I want to stay longer," she said.

"But you can't," Bershad finished. "It's all right."

He sat up in the bed.

"Tell me how all of this is going to work."

Ashlyn got out of bed and picked up her dress. Started organizing it in her hands.

"There's a ship called the *Luminata* waiting for you in the harbor. The captain is a Papyrian that you can trust. Your three traveling companions will be on the ship. One of them is a Papyrian widow named Vera Jinsung Ka."

"A widow?" Bershad asked. "They tend to attract attention, black armor and all."

"So do you, blue tattoos and all," Ashlyn said. "Vera was my sister's widow. It's her job to bring Kira back safely. You can trust her. The other is Elden Grealor's youngest son, Yonmar. He has a writ of slaying from the baron of Cornish that will give you legitimate entry to Ghalamar. He's also arranged a way to get across the Balarian border."

"You needed a Grealor for that?"

"I might have been able to find a way, but the Grealors are well-connected in Taggarstan from their lumber trade, and my father refused to send you into a foreign wilderness without at least one of his lackeys to watch over you."

"If I was going to run, I'd have done it a long time ago."

"All the same, that's the deal I had to make for my father to agree. Yonmar's a necessary evil, and Hertzog wrote the writ and documents of safe passage in his name. So keep him alive. You need him to get into Ghalamar, and to cross the border into Balaria."

"Who's the third person?"

"A Burz-al-dun local. I found him, but you definitely shouldn't trust him."

"Why not?"

"You'll understand about three seconds after meeting him." She paused. "Silas, none of the others know what you're going to Balaria to do. You should keep it that way unless absolutely necessary—that way nobody can betray you, even unintentionally."

Bershad nodded. It made sense.

Ashlyn pulled the dress over her head and started tying the ribbons that kept it cinched to her body. Bershad watched Ashlyn dress, enjoying the chance to see her go through at least one familiar routine from the past. He liked the way her fingers looked while she threaded the buttons that ran up the side of her rib cage.

"What are you going to do if I don't make it?" Bershad asked her.

Her fingers stopped moving, but she didn't respond.

"If stopping the emperor is this important, you wouldn't put all your hopes on five people and a donkey," Bershad continued. "So, what happens if we get killed?"

"After you leave, I'm going to begin raising an army," Ashlyn said without turning around. "If you fail, I'll start a war with Balaria."

Bershad was surprised, but realized he shouldn't be. Ashlyn had made it clear she was willing to do whatever was required to protect the dragons of Terra.

"Well," Bershad said. "Don't go launching any armies until you're sure I'm dead."

"I wouldn't have asked you to do this if I didn't think you could survive it," she said. "After so many dragons, one emperor shouldn't be a problem." She finished buttoning her dress and straightened the collar. "And when you come back, I will make you the lord of the Dainwood again. I promise."

"What about the Grealors?"

"I'll deal with them." She paused. "There are still some jaguars left, Silas. Deep in the jungle. The life that was taken from you still exists."

Bershad ran a hand over a scar on his forearm. "I'm not meant for a life at court, Ashe. All the broken oaths. All the lies and betrayals. Might be you found a way to live in that world without losing yourself, but I couldn't. That's why Glenlock Canyon happened. Truth is, I can barely stand spending a night behind these stone walls."

Ashlyn turned around to look at him.

"When you had the Wormwrot mercenaries surrounded in Glenlock Canyon, I remember a sentinel riding into Floodhaven with a message from you. My father sent one back, and you went to battle a day later. I've always wondered what was in his letter."

"It doesn't matter. I still did what I did." Bershad let out a heavy breath. "I'll help you, Ashe, but I can't go back to that kind of life."

"You won't have to. I'm not my father, Silas. And as far as I'm concerned, you can rule from Deepdale as you see fit. No need to lay eyes on this castle again." She took his hand. "However, I could make a regular habit of coming to see you."

Bershad squeezed her hand, then let it go. He'd longed to return to the Dainwood jungle—where the jaguars slept in the trees—in the same way he'd longed to be with Ashlyn again. For years, both were impossible. Now, suddenly, the path was clear.

"You're wrong," he said. "I need to come back to this castle one last time to drop off your sister."

Ashlyn smiled. Her eyes turned glassy with tears.

"I'll be waiting."

When he was alone again, Bershad sat with his sword across his knees, listening to the sea below and watching the sun rise. He thought about all the crimes he'd committed with a blade or a spear in his hand. Wondered if killing an emperor would make up for them.

Either way, Bershad had thrown himself back into the roiling currents of the world.

Now he had to swim.

5

GARRET

Almira, City of Mudwall

Garret reached Mudwall after dark. It was a moderately sized city named after the ancient dirt barrier that still protected its citizens. Almirans were not creative with their names. It was one of the last Almiran mud walls that hadn't been modernized by stone and masonry. The packed mash of earth and sticks and leaves rose thirty strides into the air.

The barkeep's assessment of the city seemed true enough. Garret could make out dozens of recently created indentations on the wall. Catapult damage.

Just outside the walls, the domed outlines of countless wardens' yurts were unmistakable, even in darkness. Garret made out four rows, with brazier stands set up every fifty strides and two sentries posted at each one. In the distance—past a rolling field—Garret could see the fires and yurts of another army about the same size. It wasn't a siege exactly. More of a prolonged standoff—each side daring the other to charge.

Almirans were strange.

Behind the mud wall, shingled roofs spread out in a loose system of concentric circles. In the center of the city, a holdfast rose half again as tall as the walls. That's where Lord Tybolt would be.

Garret squatted in a dark clearing a hundred strides off the main road and got ready. He took out his pouch of face putty and wetted the clay with water from a puddle. Once it was soft enough, he began putting it on his face.

Even in this backward country, it was amazing how well a man's description traveled. Height, hair color, and a defining chin or mole could get you arrested and lynched fifty leagues from the place you'd committed your crime. So Garret pinched out a new chin shaped like a man's ass, and gave himself a bulbous nose that looked like it had been broken five times over. He widened his brow and then rubbed enough of the makeshift putty on the rest of his face for the color to seem consistent. Anyone who saw him would remember an ugly, sunbaked Almiran. Not an outlander with delicate features and gray, unsettling eyes.

Now he just needed a uniform. There were two reliable opportunities to steal a man's clothes: while he was fucking someone, or while he was taking a shit. And Garret didn't see any whorehouses.

He was saved from having to guess which direction the latrine had been dug—the horrendous smell wafting from the west gave it away. Two braziers were posted on each end of the crap pit to mark the spot, but no sentries manned them. Garret had learned long ago that most armies were lenient when it came to protecting their latrines.

There was a ridge on the far side of the crap pit that gave Garret the perfect height advantage. He wedged himself between a shrub and a rock. Then he pulled his hemp rope free from his satchel, tied a quick noose at one end, and waited. Four soldiers who all seemed sober enough came to relieve themselves, so Garret stayed hidden. But half an hour later, a lone warden came stumbling down the gentle incline, lurching toward the crap tunnel with drunken sloppiness. Garret readied the noose.

The warden pulled down his britches and squatted.

Garret waited until the man was finished—he didn't want to get shit all over himself. But before the man could pull up his britches, Garret threw the noose around his neck in a smooth, practiced motion. One quick yank tightened the knot. Then Garret braced himself and pulled backward as hard as possible. Because he was standing on the ridge, five strides above the squatting warden, the man was pulled into the air and across the latrine. He landed in the shrubs, pants around his ankles.

Garret had pulled so hard that the man's boots remained on the far side.

The warden made a soft sucking sound as he tried unsuccessfully to squeeze air past the noose. Garret scanned the camp lines to see if anyone had noticed the airborne man. Nobody had.

He waited until the warden's face was purple and his chest still. Then he stripped the dead man's clothes, armor, and sword. They turned out to be a pretty good fit, although the sword had a slippery grip and terrible balance. He pushed his own jacket and clothes into the goat bladder and slung it over his shoulder. The bladder was a risk—most Almirans didn't use them—but there was no guarantee he'd be able to return to this spot. Garret covered the soldier's naked body with a thick layer of leaves and shit from the latrine. Then he hopped over the crap pit and began stumbling up the small hill, looking—from a distance—just like the drunken warden who'd gone down for a shit a few minutes earlier. At the top of the hill, Garret passed a group of men standing next to a brazier—two of whom were probably supposed to be down by the latrine.

"Took your bloody time with it, didn't you?" one of the sentries asked.

"Aye, what happened, you have a hard time saying good-bye?" said another. Garret pretended to stumble onto his hands and knees so they couldn't see his face.

"Damn stew gave me the shits," he said, mimicking the sentry's accent, which was a little softer than the fur trappers from the bridge.

"Ha, always the stew. Nobody ever admits the ten horns of ale is what got them squatting over the shit tunnel," a third sentry said. "You best make yourself scarce. A high-warden sees you this drunk and he'll have you flogged. Raimier would probably take a finger. You know how he is."

Garret did. Every outfit has at least one asshole officer.

"Raimier around camp?" Garret asked, glancing around and pretending to be afraid.

"Nah. He's behind the walls. Went to Tybolt's holdfast to deliver supplies for a totem."

"He's making another one tonight?" a sentry asked.

"Oh yeah. I heard he sent Raimier around collecting buttons from every warden who killed one of Hrilian's men today. And I'd bet my firstborn he's plugging his totem with enough gems to sink a Papyrian frigate."

"Fucking nobles, always making things as difficult as possible."

"Why so much fuss, anyway? We burned down the catapult yesterday morning."

"And then lost two score of wardens chasing Hrilian's bastards around in the woods last night. Being honest, I wouldn't have expected Hrilian's men to have that kinda salt. Must have hired a new lot. Some of Wallace's men, maybe. His wolves never make it easy."

"They're vicious bastards, all right. And they're still out there." The sentry gazed over at the tents. "I wish we were back behind the walls."

"Can't go back until we're sure Hrilian ain't just gonna roll another catapult up on us." He slapped his friend on the back. "Don't worry, though. Tybby's statue will sort the whole thing out. Fuck, if he's collecting buttons, I don't think I'll even bother to wear armor tomorrow."

They all laughed at that.

Garret took the opportunity to stumble down the line of yurts. As soon as he turned the corner out of sight, he became a sober sentry walking briskly as though he had an important task to accomplish. Almost every yurt he passed had a small mud statue with a scrap of steel in its hand. Some kind of ritual for luck in combat, Garret figured.

Most of the yurt flaps were closed, but inside the open ones Garret caught quick glimpses of men playing cards or dice, drinking horns of ale. One larger yurt had a warden and three camp-whores inside. The women were naked and lying on a woven mat, but the warden was on his knees, facing away from them and building a mud statue with enormous breasts and apples in her hair.

"Hurry up, will you, Gunther?" one of the women called to him. "You ain't the only horny sergeant in camp tonight."

"Not yet," the warden said, placing another apple. "It has to be perfect."

Garret moved toward the city, passing more rows of yurts and sentries posted around braziers. As he walked, he removed a coin purse that was attached to the dead warden's belt and emptied it in the mud. Then he pulled a few buttons off the inside of his tunic and put them in the pouch.

None of the soldiers in the camp paid much attention to Garret. It wasn't until he reached a small postern gate of the mud wall—which was an oak door on a massive iron hinge—that he was stopped. One sentry moved in front of the door and the other took two steps toward Garret.

"What's your business here?" the first asked.

"Got something for Raimier," Garret said, holding up the pouch.

The guard narrowed his eyes. "What's Raimier need with your fucking purse?"

"Ain't coins. It's buttons. My sergeant came up all in a huff 'cause Raimier's collecting buttons from the men who drew blood today, and he missed a few. Gave me the pouch and told me to give it to High-Warden Raimier himself, and nobody else."

"We got orders to keep the gate sealed till morning." The sentry kept frowning. "Who is this sergeant of yours?"

"Gunther," Garret said. "We're camped down by the latrines."

The first sentry rubbed his nose and sighed. "I can smell the fucking latrines on you, but I don't know a Gunther." He turned to his partner. "You?"

"I know him," the second sentry said. "He didn't go out raiding today, though. Why's he collecting buttons for Raimier?"

"Fuck if I know," Garret said. "I just do what I'm told. If Tybby wants buttons, buttons is what I deliver. He wants me plucking cock hairs next, that's what I'll do."

The first sentry grunted out a laugh. It didn't matter which country you were in, griping about the chain of command was always a reliable way into a guard's good graces.

"All right, all right. You can go in. Raimier was headed to the holdfast last I saw him. You best hurry, though. They're starting soon." He stepped aside and motioned to the second sentry, who seemed less sure about letting Garret inside, but opened the door with a heavy copper key and pulled it open all the same.

Garret saluted the two sentries and passed beneath the wall. The fifteen yards of darkness were cool and damp, and then he was inside Mudwall proper and walking up an avenue toward the tower. Garret smiled to himself. Infiltrating an occupied Almiran city was easier than he'd expected. Once, he'd spent almost a month working out a way into a Papyrian outpost, and they weren't even under attack.

The only people on the streets were other wardens. All the houses Garret passed had their windows shuttered. No candles in the sills. The doors were probably barred twice. Made sense. You only had to be a peasant in a city full of soldiers for a few hours to know it was best to stay out of sight.

That was true in every country, too.

As Garret walked, he studied the holdfast. It wasn't particularly well built—plenty of loose stones and sagging windowsills to make for an easy climb. The top three floors of the building glowed orange in the night. Garret could make out shadows moving along the ceiling and in front of the windows. They must have gathered for the totem ritual. Garret didn't know what that entailed, but lots of noise and people could always be turned into an advantage.

There was a tavern across the street from the tower that was full of drunken men singing and yelling and dicing. Garret made like he was heading to the tavern, but ducked into the side alley at the last second. There was a drainpipe running down the side of the tavern wall. It was a thick, circular ceramic thing. Garret grabbed the pipe with both hands and shimmied up the roof.

He surveyed the situation from the top. It was a long jump to the tower, but the tavern roof was thirty strides off the ground, maybe more. Doable. Garret traced a path back from the edge of the roof to make sure it was clear and could support his weight. He did a few quick squats to loosen his legs. He waited until the soldiers below started another loud song, then he sprinted off the roof, shooting himself up in the air as high as possible.

He caught the edge of a windowsill on the second floor. Steadied himself and froze, waiting for the cry of someone who'd seen him. When he heard nothing, he began to climb. It was easy work, but time-consuming because very few footholds and windowsills lay one on top of the other. He had to bank constantly to his left, wrapping around the tower in a lazy spiral as he moved upward.

At least they did something right when they built the tower.

The closer he moved to the top floors, the louder the sounds of drinking and revelry became. A drum boomed and laughter poured out of the window. When he reached the fourth level, he decided to venture a look. Garret inched his face past the sill and scanned the room quickly with one eye before moving away again.

Ten men, ten women. All of them wearing silk robes and ornately carved fox masks. Probably small lords under Tybolt and their wives. Two wardens guarded the door, and two more wandered around the room that he could see, meaning there were probably two or three more that he couldn't see. A long table was covered in food and cups of wine and ale.

Quite the celebration, but no sign of Lord Tybolt.

It would have been an easy thing to poison Tybolt. Cleaner, too. Garret could have brewed a coated dose of nightshade that wouldn't have taken effect for another two days. The lord would have gone to bed with a headache and died during the night. Cleaner than clean. Invisible.

But Garret had his instructions. He kept climbing.

The fifth floor was quieter, and stank of opium. Probably Tybolt's private quarters. Garret reached a window and risked a peek. Two people in the room.

One was a warden in full armor, no mask. The other was sitting in a chair in the center of the room. He wore a black robe, and a black fox mask with gleaming yellow eyes and tall, pointed ears. He was holding a sculpting tool that looked similar to a trowel. Had to be Tybolt.

Both men were staring at the statue.

Garret had expected to see a figure similar to the mud totem in the sergeant's tent, but this was something else entirely. The statue stood

as tall as a man, but was shaped like a woman. It was completely covered in bluebird feathers—arms outstretched and carved into massive
wings. Gemstones that had been planted amid the feathers twinkled
in the candlelight.

"My lord," said the high-warden, "I have the buttons."

Raimier.

"Yes, yes." Tybolt held out his hand without looking away from
the statue. "Give them to me."

After Raimier handed over the buttons, Tybolt placed them as the
totem's eyes, nipples, and navel. The rest went between her thighs.

"This will do it," Tybolt said, placing the trowel on the floor. "It
has to."

"My lord," Raimier said. "I must see to the men. We're to clear
out the woods at first light."

"Of course. Go. Tell the others to begin on your way out."

Raimier left, and Tybolt knelt in front of the totem so that he
couldn't see the window from which Garret was watching. Below, the
sounds of chanting lords drifted upward. They wouldn't be able to
hear a thing going on in the upper level. Garret couldn't help but
smile. This was perfect.

He moved like a cat, slinking through the window and into a
shadow. He snuck up behind Tybolt, who'd begun to chant a low
prayer spoken too fast for Garret to understand it. From the back, he
could see the lord's sweaty neck and thinning gray hair.

Garret picked up the trowel as he crept behind Tybolt, who'd
spread his arms as he prayed.

"Goddess of the woods and the sky, I ask your support. Show me
my enemies clearly in the light of day. Guide my wardens' blades so
they might—"

Garret clamped one hand over Tybolt's mouth and stabbed him
in the throat with the trowel. He held him still until he bled out,
then dropped him.

Garret left the trowel in Tybolt's throat. Wiped his hands on the
Almiran lord's robe. Then he left the same way he'd come in.

———

Garret escaped the city before the sun rose—walking confidently
through the front gate and waving at the four sentries posted there.

But he wasn't entirely safe yet. Once Tybolt's body was discovered, there would be chaos. Then there would be questions. If one

of the gate sentries happened to mention an unfamiliar warden with a butt-chin to the wrong person, they'd set hounds on him within a few hours. He had to assume that was the reality, and outrun them.

As soon as the road curved out of sight from the city, Garret darted into the woods and found a small, muddy lake. He removed the warden's uniform, buried it beneath a layer of thick mud, then took his traveler's clothes out of the goatskin bladder and dressed.

The face putty had hardened in the night, so Garret spent ten minutes throwing water on his face and scrubbing at the disguise. When he'd removed everything except the last bit of chin, he heard a splash on the far side of the lake. He opened his eyes, but all he saw was a series of ripples on the water. The size of the disturbance was concerning. Too big to be a turtle.

On instinct, Garret's hand moved to his hunting knife. Something was wrong—all the birds and insects had gone quiet.

A black, reptilian snout full of razor-sharp teeth blasted out of the water. Garret put his arm up defensively and felt teeth sink deep into his forearm. He hissed, cursed, then jammed his dagger into the dragon's jaw. Once. Twice. Three times.

The blade didn't do much damage, but the last strike got the beast to loosen its jaws just a little. Garret twisted away, felt a moment of resistance before one of the dragon's teeth broke and he was set free.

Garret grabbed his goatskin bladder and ran.

When he was thirty strides away from the lake, he risked a quick look over his shoulder. The dragon wasn't much larger than a canoe. It was bleeding from the eye and mouth, but it wasn't chasing—just glaring at him from the shallows.

He turned and ran flat out for twenty minutes before letting up his pace. Stopped in an open meadow to catch his breath, heaving air in and out of his lungs and cursing himself for being so careless. He was used to working in countries like Balaria and Ghalamar, where dragons were rare within a day's ride of a city. But Almira was different—the great lizards were as common as salamanders out here.

If he wanted to survive in the backcountry, he needed to be far more careful.

Garret headed west, where he'd slip the line of wardens that Tybolt's men planned to fight that day. It wouldn't be difficult—they were looking for an army of wardens, not a single man traveling alone.

6

BERSHAD

Almira, Floodhaven Docks

When he left the castle, Bershad kept his face hidden beneath a cloak to avoid causing a riot. He and Rowan jostled through the crowd at Floodhaven harbor until they found the *Luminata,* which was a single-masted fishing dogger tied to a slip between a lumber barge and a Ghalamarian carrack that was resupplying.

The carrack was an explorer's ship, destined for the Great Western Ocean beyond the Soul Sea. Her belly could carry six months of supplies and one hundred men to the far side of the world, where an unexplored continent had been discovered.

The nations of Terra had been sending out carracks for almost a decade, looking for fresh resources on the new world. Ghalamar and Lysteria—two countries that had been plagued by famine and drought for years—were searching the hardest. The few ships that successfully crossed the open ocean and returned again brought tales of a strange, bountiful land. The water of the harbors and rivers was so clear you could see all the way to the bottom, where the seabed was carpeted with delicious oysters and clams and crabs. The land was blanketed by an endless forest full of ripe fruit and herds of vibrant game. And, if all the stories were to be believed, fire-breathing dragons filled the skies and clans of unfriendly native warriors lived beneath the ground. Despite the dangers, more ships set sail every month. Ghalamar and Lysteria were desperate.

Briefly, Bershad wondered if that carrack was the ship Ashlyn had offered him passage upon, but he didn't linger on the question. He'd made his decision.

As Bershad and Rowan approached the small dogger, a short Papyrian man with sun-soaked skin came up the dock to meet them. His head and face were clean-shaven, and he wore a cloth headband to keep the sweat out of his eyes. His tunic was as red as the fish on his sail. He grinned at them, his face bursting into a patchwork of smile lines and wrinkles.

"You are Ashlyn Malgrave's cargo?" he asked, voice thick with a Papyrian accent.

Bershad nodded.

"That makes me Torian. And this is the *Luminata*, your transportation across the Soul Sea."

"I'm—"

Torian stopped the introduction by wagging a finger at Bershad.

"Ah, don't need the name. Don't want the name. I get asked later, you were just two strangers with a bit of coin and the desire to see Ghalamar. Didn't see no tattoos or famous faces." He smiled easily. "Now if you don't mind, we're ready to go and your friends are already belowdecks waiting for you. You can leave the donkey with me; I'll take care of the animal and your supplies."

"Friends?" Rowan asked. Bershad hadn't told him about their companions yet.

Torian smiled again and motioned toward the ship. "Belowdecks."

Torian shouted a few orders at the crew, which comprised three other men. They were younger than Torian, but dressed in the same tunic and wearing the same headband. Bershad had a feeling they were his sons.

Bershad clambered belowdecks and found three people waiting for him: a lord, a widow, and a man chained to a support beam. All of them watched Bershad and Rowan as they climbed down.

The lord was sitting on a bench with a map stretched over a barrel. He had short flaxen hair and wore a set of fine riding clothes: supple deerskin boots, a blue silk tunic, and a cloak made from a jaguar's hide. He narrowed his eyes.

"You are the Flawless Bershad?"

Bershad removed the hood of his cloak as an answer.

"And you're the Grealor."

"Lord Yonmar Grealor." He said it slowly, as if it was a magical incantation instead of a name.

Bershad eyed the cloak strewn across Yonmar's shoulders. Almirans were constantly using animal hides and bones for their totems, but Bershad's family had honored the jaguars of their homeland by leaving them alone. When they ruled the Dainwood, it had been a crime to kill one—punishable by death.

Bershad didn't put stock in rituals and prayers—in his experience, the gods never helped anyway—but he'd always loved the jaguars of Dainwood. Seeing Yonmar's cloak made his pulse quicken with rage.

Yonmar followed Bershad's gaze, then lifted the edge of the pelt.

"Oh, so sorry. I'd forgotten your ancestors used to worship the vile tree cats. My men have killed so many of them over the years that I had to start throwing some of my pelts away." He shrugged. "No room in the wardrobe, you know?"

"Take that off," Bershad hissed. "Or I will tear it from your body."

Yonmar smiled. "You'll do no such thing. You're here because of Princess Ashlyn. I'm here because of the king." He patted his chest. "Our papers of safe passage into Ghalamar are in my name, and I'm the only person who can get us across the Balarian border. That means that I am the one in charge of this journey. If you do one thing I do not like, exile, I will make sure the last thing you see is your forsaken shield cooking inside your donkey's hide. Clear?"

Bershad glared at Yonmar. Thought about killing him on the spot. Ashlyn's warning was the only thing that stopped him.

"What makes you so confident you can get us across the border?"

"Oh, it's been arranged. I have a man in Taggarstan, but he'll only deal with me." Yonmar drummed his fingers against a leather satchel on his hip, which had the Grealor family crest branded upon it, but didn't elaborate further.

Bershad was having trouble resisting the urge to knock all of Yonmar's teeth out, so he turned to the widow, instead. She had black hair pulled into a tight bun behind her head, and a straight dagger on each hip. Widows were notoriously vicious with their blades, known for slipping them into the seams and gaps of a fully armored man, slicing a few arteries, then ducking and dodging until the man bled to death on his feet.

"Vera, right?"

"Yes."

Her cheeks were peppered with small, circular scars left over from an adolescent pox, and she was wearing black sharkskin armor. Same as Hayden. The armor was covered with small nooks and crannies, as if a thousand tiny rivers had dug their way into the surface and then gone dry. Wealthy merchants and lords all over Terra wore expensive sharkskin gloves and boots, and the best sword makers used it as leather grips for their weapons. But Papyrian widows were the only ones who used sharkskin for armor. They'd worked out a method to treat it that didn't involve boiling—just tanning and salting for months—so that it became strong and flexible. Each piece was molded perfectly to the wearer's body, cut and shaped so that it fit like a silk garment. Sharkskin armor was far lighter than plate, far stronger than other leathers, and twice as expensive as both of them combined.

There were three separate cords of hemp rope wrapped around Vera's left thigh, and a leather satchel tied to the curve of her right hip. Papyrian slings—each with a different range—and a bag of lead shot. Bershad had never seen a Papyrian widow fire a sling, but he'd heard plenty of stories.

A shepherd with a wool sling and a stone shot could kill a wolf from a few hundred paces away if he was skilled or lucky. But the widow's version of the weapon was something else entirely.

Hundreds of years ago—before the widows guarded Papyrian royalty—they were a secretive clan of female warriors who'd spent generations perfecting their warcraft while living on a remote island in the Papyrian archipelago. Papyrian slings were made from hemp and specifically designed to maximize range and velocity—the only weapon with a longer range was a Balarian longbow. Papyrian shots were made from perfectly rounded lead molds, and could punch through steel helms and chain mail as if they were paper. Their longest slings could rain havoc onto an entire cavalry division before a single horseman lowered his lance.

"Glad to have you with us," Bershad said, nodding. They'd need as much help as they could get if they wanted to survive the Razorback Mountains.

The man chained to the beam stirred. He was dirty and skinny and looked like he'd just been pulled out of a gutter.

"So, uh, does everyone know each other besides me?" he said in a Balarian accent. "Introductions, then. I'm Felgor. No title or fancy nickname or anything. Just Felgor for me." He peered past Bershad, looking at Rowan. "Who're you?"

"Rowan."

"Huh. What do you do?"

Rowan shrugged. "Cook. Fight."

"Gonna be a lot of that?" Felgor asked, turning to Bershad. "Fighting, I mean."

"My life'd be turning over a pretty big new leaf if we did this peacefully," Bershad said.

"Too bad," Felgor said. "I'm not much good in a fight."

Bershad studied the man and his chains. Ashlyn said not to trust him, but hadn't said why. Bershad was curious.

"What are you good at?"

"Oh, quite a few things. But if I had to summarize, my skills are mostly centered around sneaking into places I'm not supposed to be, and taking things that don't belong to me."

"You're a thief."

"Guilty as charged. Literally. I was in the Floodhaven dungeon up until a few hours ago."

"That's obvious," Rowan muttered.

"We need him," Vera said, reading Rowan's disdain.

"Why?" Rowan asked.

"Because in Burz-al-dun, trying to walk just four city blocks in the same direction comes with complications," Felgor said. "Stealing a princess out from under the palace is quite a bit more involved. I have some experience, though."

Bershad turned to Vera. "What stops him from betraying us once we reach Balaria?"

"It's been considered," Vera said, "but he's got a strong incentive to behave."

"What incentive?" Bershad asked.

"The home front and I aren't on the best terms," Felgor said, managing a smile through lips that were crusty with thirst. He had the smallest teeth Bershad had ever seen. "Turns out I have a death sentence in Balaria, Ghalamar, and Lysteria. And as of a few days ago, Almira, too. But I'm supposed to get a big fat pardon when this is all squared away—same as you. Pretty good deal, I think. Death sentences are inconvenient."

"He also knows I'll cut his feet off if he tries anything," Vera added.

"Yeah," Felgor said, wincing. "That, too."

Bershad glanced around the room. It wasn't the last group of people he'd pick to cross a dangerous mountain range with, but it was fairly close.

"My donkey gets seasick," he said. "Got to tend to him."

Bershad headed back up the steps, but turned around on the third rung. He might not have chosen the crew, but he had to live with them.

"We're all in this mess together now. Give Felgor some food and water. He'll die in the mountains like that."

7

ASHLYN

Almira, Castle Malgrave

Ashlyn ate her breakfast alone on a porch that overlooked the Soul Sea. A dragon skirted the horizon while she ate—flying low over the waves and skimming its hooked tail across the surface. It was a Naga Soul Strider—female, judging from the size. Very rare to see this close to the Atlas Coast. Ashlyn watched carefully, barely touching her food, as the dragon trawled the sea. Eventually, her tail jolted from an impact, and the dragon flicked a wriggling marlin into her mouth without missing a wingbeat. Ashlyn had been eight years old when she first saw a Naga pull that trick. She'd demanded that Hayden take her down to the fish markets so she could measure and weigh a marlin and use it to calculate the size and weight of the dragon.

She thumbed the translucent strand that was wrapped around her wrist. Last night, Silas had suspected there was more she wasn't telling him about it. She'd wanted to tell him the full truth, but her plan was stronger if the pieces remained divided from one another. Ashlyn had dedicated her life to uncovering the hidden mysteries of the world, drawing the connections between dragons and nature and men. She didn't like keeping her discoveries a secret—especially from Silas—but she'd do what was necessary to protect Almira's future.

Her father had asked to see her and Elden Grealor that morning. When Ashlyn was done eating, Hayden escorted her to the main hall of the King's Tower, where her father was already seated on the

Almiran throne, draped in a massive bear cloak despite the sunny, warm morning. The room was ringed with Malgrave wardens.

Once Ashlyn had taken a seat next to her father, the king nodded toward the door and two wardens brought Elden Grealor into the room.

"My king," Elden said, approaching the throne and bowing low on one knee. He had a massive forehead and a receding hairline. The hair that remained was gray and long and full of bear claws woven into intricate braids. The totem bag on his hip was full to the point of bursting. "And Princess Ashlyn, what a pleasure to see you this morning. It's as if the sun has risen again, twice as bright."

Ashlyn smiled and thanked him. But she also remembered when she was third in line for succession and the lords of Almira were more than happy to ignore her. That was a weakness in men—most lacked the foresight to imagine a future vastly different from the present.

After Leon Bershad was executed and Silas exiled, Hertzog had wanted to insult the Bershad legacy as much as possible, so he offered Deepdale and the Dainwood province to whoever won a tournament of single combat. Elden Grealor—a small lord with little power or wealth—was the champion. He and the king had been close friends and allies since then.

And Elden Grealor had become rich.

The Dainwood rain forest was home to fertile farmland, fortified holdfasts, and endless leagues of wet jungle. For generations, the Bershads had revered the forest and refused to fell trees for profit, making it the last untouched source of lumber in the realm of Terra. But the first thing Elden did after taking power was build scores of mills on the edges of the jungle and begin cutting them down. He wasn't as wealthy as the other members of the High Council—who'd been taxing their vassals for hundreds of years—but he was getting closer every year. And his army of wardens, who all wore bear masks to show their allegiance to Grealor, got larger every day.

"The exile has accepted the offer?" Grealor asked, rising from his bow.

"Yes," Ashlyn answered. "Bershad and Rowan are probably boarding the ship as we speak."

"It seems he took some convincing," Elden said, squirming a little. "Were any terms added?"

It had been hard for Ashlyn to lie to Silas, but she'd done it. Lying to both Elden Grealor and her father was easy.

"Relax, Elden. Dainwood's vassals and incomes will still be yours if Bershad returns. He did not want them back."

"Good," Elden said, blowing out a sigh. "I just hope Bershad truly knows the way. I'll take it personally if Yonmar winds up dead in the Razorbacks."

Ashlyn shrugged. "There's a very good chance that he will wind up dead."

"Ashlyn," her father warned.

"I accepted the consequences of sending those five into the mountains when I gave the order," Ashlyn said. "You should, too. In fact, we must all assume that Silas and your son will not reach Balaria alive, let alone infiltrate Burz-al-dun." Ashlyn squeezed her fingers into her palm as she said the dreadful words. "Resolving this peacefully was always a long shot. We must prepare for the more likely outcome."

Ashlyn paused. Took a breath. She'd lied to Elden about Dainwood because she needed his help now.

"We need to raise a host of wardens in Floodhaven that is fit for war with Balaria. If Bershad fails, we must attack them."

"Attack Balaria?" Grealor asked. "What do you mean?"

"Which part is unclear?"

"No. You didn't fight the clock-worshipping bastards the first time, Princess. I did." Grealor's face tightened. "You don't know what you're asking."

Ashlyn knew exactly what she was asking. It was a terrible thing. And she knew there was a chance she'd go down in history as a warmonger and a tyrant. But she was willing to face that consequence if it kept the world in balance.

"Enough, both of you," Hertzog said before Ashlyn could respond. "Ashlyn, raising an army to get Kira back is the next logical step, but it needs to wait."

"It can't wait," Ashlyn said. "The summer solstice is only four months away. Even if we start raising an army today, we'll be hardpressed to have it ready for war in time."

"What does midsummer matter?" Grealor asked.

"If we don't have an army gathered by the solstice," Ashlyn said carefully, "every warden in Almira will scatter back to their homelands to build their totems for the High Summer Sacrifice."

Generations earlier, in the dark recesses of Almira's history, the High Summer Sacrifice was a bloody ceremony that culminated with the ritualized murder of virgins in villages across Almira. All of it was done to ward off the forest demons. Thankfully, her people had left that practice behind hundreds of years ago. Now, they settled for moon orgies and murdered goats at the feet of enormous mud totems that took days to build.

"We cannot raise an army twice, nor can we wait until after the High Summer Sacrifice," she continued. "If a war is coming, it must arrive before the summer solstice."

"This isn't why I summoned the two of you," Hertzog said, eyeing Ashlyn suspiciously. "We have a more urgent issue. High Lord Tybolt is dead."

Hertzog paused to rattle off a series of coughs from deep in his lungs. When it was over, he took another sip of wine and collected himself.

Tybolt was an eccentric but loyal high lord who'd controlled Mudwall for thirty years. His presence had stabilized the surrounding area and kept Cedar Wallace—a far less trustworthy high lord who ruled the westernmost provinces of Almira—from organizing an open rebellion.

"Dead," Ashlyn repeated. "How?"

"Murdered in his chamber two nights ago. A sentinel arrived this morning with the news."

They were all silent for a moment.

"One of Wallace's small lords was making a pass at Mudwall, wasn't he?" Grealor asked.

"Lord Hrilian," Ashlyn said. She'd been monitoring the situation carefully. "But it was my understanding that Tybolt had scattered the attempt."

Almira was a country defined by land squabbles and unrest amongst the nobility. Attacks on Mudwall—or any fortification along the border of two high lords' lands—weren't uncommon. A high lord dying during one of them was.

"Perhaps Hrilian sent an assassin when his attack failed?" Grealor asked.

"It's possible," Hertzog said. "But Tybolt died at the top of his tower, with his entire retinue of small lords feasting and drinking below him. It's far more likely that one of them killed Tybolt."

"Whatever the circumstances, Mudwall is now a problem," Ashlyn said, putting the pieces together. "Tybolt had no heir. No family at all. There will be a fight amongst his small lords for control of Mudwall, all while Hrilian's men are still lingering beyond the walls."

"The fight has already begun," Hertzog said. "A high-warden named Raimier has claimed the city for himself under the pretense of securing Mudwall before I choose a proper successor. However, Raimier was the last person to see Tybolt alive, and there's a good chance he's the bastard who killed him."

"What about Tybolt's wardens?"

"Some stand with Raimier," Hertzog said. "But most have aligned with whatever small lord was first to pay them. It's a goatfuck, and if we don't fix it, we could lose Mudwall entirely." The king swallowed, throat strained. "We cannot raise a Malgrave host in Floodhaven because I have already sent five thousand of our wardens to deal with that mess."

"That's half our army," Ashlyn said. "Was that necessary?"

"It's the only way to guarantee that we regain control. Hrilian's men came pouring out of the woods the morning after Tybolt was killed and began a full-scale siege. This could be Cedar Wallace's attempt to get the entire region under his thumb. Wallace already has too much influence over the Gorgon Valley. I'm not going to hand him a stepping-stone to the Atlas Coast, too."

When Ashlyn became heir—and was pulled into Hertzog's inner circle—the aspect of ruling that surprised her the most was how little control her father truly had over the high lords of Almira, especially Cedar Wallace. He was a beloved war hero who won fame during the Balarian Invasion by breaking the siege of Gilroy and leading the vanguard during the final battle in Black Pine Valley. But Wallace was also notoriously ambitious when it came to expanding his lands. To limit his power, Hertzog had been fighting a quiet war of proxy skirmishes and minor land disputes. For decades, it had worked. But Hertzog was right—it was very possible that Cedar Wallace was finally ready to fight in the open.

The timing couldn't have been worse. If Bershad failed, Ashlyn needed the lords of Almira to stand together against Balaria. Instead, they teetered toward the precipice of civil war.

"There must be a way to avoid violence," Ashlyn said.

"There is. Hrilian will concede Mudwall without a fight if he has no chance to win. That's why I sent so many of our wardens."

Avoiding violence with the threat of more violence wasn't exactly what Ashlyn had in mind, but it wasn't her choice. Not yet, anyway.

"Assuming that works, who will take over control of Mudwall?" Ashlyn asked.

"Mudwall will go to Elden," Hertzog said, turning to his vassal.

"I'm honored, my king," Elden said.

"I'm sure that you are. So honored, in fact, that you *will* do as Ashlyn says. Go to Deepdale, raise a host of wardens fit for war with Balaria, and bring them back to Floodhaven. When this mess with Kira is over, you'll get Mudwall."

Elden Grealor's face hardened once again, but he was trapped. "Yes, my king."

"Good," Hertzog said. "Leave today."

"Of course," Elden said, rising. "I will send word once I reach Deepdale and begin preparations."

When Elden was gone, Ashlyn and her father sat in silence for a few moments. After Hertzog exiled Bershad, her plan had been to never speak with him again. But when her two brothers died and she became heir, they'd been forced to build an uneasy truce. Even now, neither of them were comfortable sharing a room alone with the other.

"The exile truly refused Deepdale?" Hertzog said eventually.

"Yes."

"You're lying." Hertzog grunted. "You've been doing that a lot lately. The fire in the eastern tower. This whole business with sending the exile after Kira."

"I've lied to you my entire life," Ashlyn said. "And you've done the same to me."

Her father had vehemently opposed sending Bershad after Kira when she first proposed the idea. But for some reason, once Ashlyn agreed to send Yonmar Grealor along, Hertzog and Elden both supported the plan. That didn't make sense—even if Elden thought Bershad didn't want the Daintree back, he was a threat once his exile was lifted. The two of them had something planned, Ashlyn just couldn't figure out what it was. And for the time being, she couldn't afford to make enemies out of them while trying to uncover the truth.

Hertzog grumbled. "Well, I've also ensured that Elden Grealor will be a loyal asset to the Malgrave dynasty."

"I appreciate that," Ashlyn said. "But I do not like placating men like him."

"Men like him," Hertzog repeated. "What does that mean, exactly?"

"He's shortsighted. All he cares about is gold."

The king narrowed his eyes. "Maybe that's true, but it's not the real reason you despise him. You make an enemy out of anyone who tries to hurt the forests and wildlife of Almira. You always have. A ruler cannot afford to draw such hard lines in the ground."

"Isn't that exactly what a ruler is meant to do? Make clear the lines of order and morality?"

"You will soon become an unmarried, half-Papyrian queen to a country of glorified warlords. Just look at the chaos in Mudwall. Every lord in Almira will be against you in some way—either in secret or out in the open. Order and morality are luxuries you won't be able to afford."

Ashlyn shifted her position in the chair. Their conversation had traveled into unfamiliar territory. She and Hertzog both preferred to focus on the concrete aspects of ruling—border decrees and troop movements, treaties and alliances. The philosophical implications hadn't come up before. Ashlyn wanted to be a better ruler than her father, but she hadn't even taken the throne yet, and she'd already started down a path of deception.

"There must be a way to stop all of this infighting," Ashlyn said. "A way to trust the high lords, instead of bribing or strong-arming them into obedience."

"The last high lord I trusted was Leon Bershad," Hertzog said. "I treated him like a brother. And look what became of that. Keeping power comes before using it." Hertzog grunted. "When I'm dead, you'll understand. Your authority will stand on the edge of a precipice, always. I have spent most of my reign bickering with the high lords so that I could maintain control of Almira, and even now, one dead man in Mudwall throws things into chaos." He broke into another series of coughs. "Steel and gold are the only two ways to move the lords of Almira. Remember that. They will not see an intelligent, thoughtful queen who wishes to serve the greater good. They'll see a half-breed woman come to take their money and power."

When Ashlyn was a teenager, she'd have argued with her father about that. She used to believe that anyone could be moved by the greater good once they saw it. Getting people to look was the problem. Now, though, she wasn't so sure. Otherwise, she'd have tried to change Emperor Mercer's mind instead of ending his life.

"Perhaps that's the burden a ruler must carry," she said. "To see the larger picture—and serve the greater good—even when the people do not."

"Speaking of the larger picture, Elden Grealor isn't sharp enough to puzzle out what you meant by the summer solstice, but I know you a little better. You wouldn't send the exile to kill Emperor Mercer just because of Kira, and you certainly wouldn't start a war over her."

"Would you rather I had done nothing?" Ashlyn asked.

"Of course not. That clock-worshipping bastard kidnapped my youngest daughter," Hertzog said. "I'd jam a seashell into Mercer's mouth myself if I could. And I was glad to see that you're willing to get your hands dirty. But I want to know the real reason."

Ashlyn had found a way to live with her father, but she'd never forgiven him for the things he'd done to Silas. Hertzog didn't deserve to know the inner workings of his daughter's mind.

"If we both want the same thing, what does it matter?"

"Ashlyn."

"Father."

"I know what you think of me," Hertzog said. "That I'm a short-sighted and brutal man, stuck in a warlike and tribal rut, along with the rest of Almira. And the world might be more complicated than I admit, but it's simpler than you'd like. When there are men with swords drawn standing outside your walls, you must defend yourself, or you will not be queen of this muddy country for very long. Remember what I said—steel and gold are the only two ways to rule Almira."

"I understand, Father," Ashlyn said.

"No, you don't." He stifled a cough. "But you will."

———

That night, Ashlyn was working late at the top of the Queen's Tower, which had a ceiling made from domed windowpanes that looked up into the star-filled sky. The room used to be a lavish bed-chamber, but Ashlyn's mother, Shiru, had it converted to an obser-vatory. Ashlyn used to stay up late with her mother learning the Papyrian names for the constellations. There were three telescopes, each facing a different section of the sky. Ashlyn kept them cleaned and calibrated so she could look at the stars when she needed to forget the world below.

She conducted the vast majority of her business from this room. Her contracts, provincial maps, and intelligence reports were stacked in neat piles on the large desk. The eastern wall was covered with a dozen of her most recent dragon sketches. There were more than fifty folios of dragon drawings in the basement archives—everything she'd done since she was a ten-year-old girl with no sense of scale or per-spective.

When her mother was alive, she had indulged Ashlyn's love of dragons. Shiru had hired a Papyrian alchemist—Gayella Stern—to tutor her on the natural world and teach her to draw. For nearly ten happy years, Ashlyn had absorbed everything Gayella could teach her about plants, rivers, animals, and—most of all—dragons. How to track a dying one without getting yourself killed. Once you found it, how to dissect its body and learn as much as possible from its or-gans before they went to rot. Ashlyn had surpassed Gayella when it came to drawings, but she'd always felt as if she'd barely managed to scratch the surface of the alchemist's knowledge before Gayella was taken from her.

When Shiru died, Hertzog banished Gayella because he'd sus-pected the alchemist knew about Shiru's affair with Leon Bershad but had kept it a secret. Hertzog gave her one day to leave the Almira, and threatened her with a pair of blue bars if she ever returned. Ashlyn had no idea where the alchemist was now, but hoped she had found her way back home.

Ashlyn spent the evening reading reports from her informants on the far side of the Soul Sea. Balaria was still a bottomless pit from which no information ever escaped, but their surrounding colonies were not as mysterious. Agricultural calamities continued in Ghala-mar. Crop shortages so bad that entire villages had been abandoned as people moved on, looking for food. It had taken Ashlyn months of research to figure out exactly what caused the famine. The wheat farmers had eradicated the low-valley Green Horn dragons, which frequented their fields to hunt a specific breed of red-tailed fox. Without a natural predator, the foxes decimated the pond-frog population. This, in turn, allowed the frog's main source of food—the meadow wasp—to see an exponential increase in numbers. The wasps alone wouldn't have caused the famine, but Ghalamarian wheat was prone to an ergot fungus that was spread through the tiny hairs on wasps' legs with unstoppable industry. The fungus turned good wheat into a mash that, when eaten, would make adults shit themselves to death within three days.

It was similar to her problem with the red-shelled snails in the Blakmar province, just far larger in scope.

Finding all these connections had taken months of work. Ashlyn imported fox scat, frog specimens, wheat, and living wasps from Ghalamar. Then she'd started her own miniature wheat field in a greenhouse and spent weeks watching the wasps. Examining their tiny legs for fungus. Tracing the small, hidden connections that ran between all living things.

Once Ashlyn mapped the source of the famine back to the over-hunting of Green Horns, she'd dispatched carrier pigeons to Ghalamar, explaining the problem and urging them to allow the dragons to return. The stewards had written back with idiotic and insulting questions. How could the elimination of Green Horns—which had been celebrated as a great victory—possibly cause a wheat fungus? Why was a princess of Almira sticking her nose into their problems? She'd heard rumors that the Ghalamarians called her the Mad Wasp Princess because of those messages. The people of Floodhaven court—who'd seen her laboring inside her tiny wheat domain and obsessing over wasps—probably had their own names for her.

Ashlyn didn't care. The nobles could call her whatever they wanted. The wheat famine was in danger of destroying Ghalamar, and the exact same thing could happen to Almira if Emperor Mercer succeeded. Whispered rumors were a small price to pay if it gave her a chance to stop that ruination.

She unrolled a map that showed every country with a shoreline on the Soul Sea, then began plotting the Great Migration. Charting the movement of dragons made her feel closer to them. The younger Needle-Throated Verduns were already starting their journey. In addition to the one Silas had killed, there had been sightings all along the eastern coast of Almira. Looking at the map and seeing how much was at stake, part of Ashlyn felt naïve for relying on five people and a donkey to stop a war.

Tomorrow, she would try to convince her father to recall the Malgrave wardens from Mudwall. The sooner she had a reliable army, the better.

Later, when everyone was asleep in the castle except for Hayden, who stood watch outside her door, Ashlyn moved to the far side of the room. There was a table of alchemical supplies. Glass jars. A copper alembic. Steel clasps. Bamboo needles. A flame that used dragon oil and could be adjusted with a small crank beneath the desk. She'd been studying dragons all her life. She measured their carcasses whenever possible. Weighed organs. Explored the anatomy of the different species. That was the habit that had bred the rumors of her demoncraft. She'd had a much larger research station in the eastern tower, but it was destroyed in the explosion, so she had to make do with this meager setup. Despite that setback, her work was more important now than ever. She wouldn't let limited tools stop her progress.

She unwound the translucent cord from her wrist and laid it flat on the table. Ashlyn still couldn't believe that such a small object had caused such damage in the eastern tower. She'd found it last year—a long strand of barbed nerve tissue that ran down the spine of a one-hundred-year-old female Ghost Moth.

Ashlyn moved her hand across it. Felt the interwoven texture, which reminded her of a spider's thread, but far thicker. That texture had led Ashlyn to start calling the strange organ a dragon thread.

This was the only thread she'd found, despite having dissected two hundred and eleven dragon corpses in her life—fifteen of them Ghost Moths. It was clearly part of a rare and hidden system—some unusual combination of biology and elemental power—but its true purpose and full potential eluded her. For now. Ashlyn thought about what her father had said—that gold and steel were the only ways to rule Almira. For him, that might be true. But Hertzog Malgrave was confined by the limitation of armor-clad soldiers and the obedience of the liege lords who commanded them.

If Ashlyn could unlock the mechanism beneath the dragon thread, those constraints would no longer apply to her.

She took a deep breath. Felt her pulse quicken. Activating the thread always made her nervous, especially after the fire in the eastern tower. Her palms dampened. Mouth went dry. She squeezed on the thread and was about to rip her hand down the length when two firm knocks came from the door.

"Princess Ashlyn," came Hayden's voice. "A steward to speak with you."

"One moment," Ashlyn called, annoyed. She tied the thread back on her wrist and adjusted the sleeve so it wasn't visible. Even Hayden didn't know about it.

When she opened the door and saw the steward's face, her stomach dropped. The man's eyes were glassy, skin puffy from tears.

"Princess," he said. "Your father is dead."

8

GARRET

Almira, South of Mudwall

Garret was bleeding in the woods. He'd managed to escape the dragon, but a splinter from the lizard's tooth was lodged deep in the muscle of his forearm. That was a problem, but he'd been unable to pry it out after an hour of painful attempts, and he needed to keep moving. If anyone from Mudwall was smart enough to look for him, a bloodhound would be able to track him from leagues away now that he was bleeding.

Garret found a shallow creek with a gentle current and splashed down the middle of it for an entire afternoon, staying in knee-deep water as much as possible to hide his tracks and his scent. He paused every fifteen minutes to listen for signs of pursuit or more dragons, but heard none.

This mess would cause more delays. Getting himself bitten by a dragon had been stupid and sloppy. Little mistakes would kill a man in this business, which was why Garret always stressed the details. Careful planning and precise action—that was the key to good work.

Once Garret was sure that he wasn't being followed, he cut through a valley that was dominated by oak trees until reaching the main road heading south. Rather than walk the highway, he skirted the edge, being sure to stay under tree cover and hiding from sight anytime he spotted another traveler. By dusk, he reached a large fork in the road—one branch heading southwest to Deepdale, the other east toward Floodhaven. This was the spot. Garret waited until dark, then ventured out of cover and located a stump seven paces directly south of the fork. There was a red pin in the bark, and behind that pin a hollowed notch containing a rolled scrap of paper. There was only one word scrawled in ornate cursive.

Deepdale.

Garret traveled south for four days—using the road at night and moving into the trees during the day. Sleeping for only a few hours at midday. The landscape turned mossy and wet and full of insects. Turtles with flashes of orange and red on their heads sunned themselves on river rocks. Every pond and lake he passed was full of colorful fish. And every passing bird or shadow from a cloud put Garret on alert, thinking another dragon might be descending.

He worried about his left arm. Despite being unable to remove the tooth, he cleaned the wound and changed his bandage once a day, but the pain was getting worse by the hour. This was not a friendly country to open wounds—things got infected easily in warm, damp climates, and it would only get warmer and damper after he crossed the Gorgon and headed into the Dainwood rain forest.

By the fifth day, the edge of tooth that he could see protruding from the wound had turned green. Garret's arm smelled like sour milk. If he didn't get the tooth out of his arm soon, he was going to have a serious problem. Garret turned into the woods and found a thin creek that provided decent cover. He sat down on a sunbaked rock, dropped his goatskin bladder, and started removing his shirt— quickly on the right side and gingerly on the left, as if his arm was a newborn he didn't want to awake from a nap. He found that it was too painful to pass the sleeve over the wound, so he used his hunting knife to cut away the fabric and bloody bandage.

Garret found a few thick patches of moss growing along the river-bank and dug them free with his knife. He stacked them on the rock, planning to plug the wound with the moss after he removed the tooth. He moved over to a deep pool, pushed his arm under the water, and held it there hoping the cold would dull the upcoming pain a little.

"You'll die if you plug your arm with that moss," someone said from behind him.

Garret froze. His knife was five strides away on the rock. He turned around. There was a boy perched on the riverbank. He was thin, no older than fifteen, and wearing a dirty gray robe. He was carrying an overloaded backpack, but no weapons. Garret decided that he didn't need to stab the boy to death just yet.

"The moss cleans it," Garret said.

"Some moss does. Not that kind."

"What do you know about it?"

"More than you, apparently." The boy splashed out to the rock. He moved with a spindly sort of awkwardness that made Garret think these woods weren't his home. He'd grown up with a roof over his head. "That's turtle dung moss. Pack it into your wound and it'll turn black in two days—there are too many little creatures that use it as a home. They'll use *you* as a home, too, and in five days you'll either be dead or, if you're very lucky, grabbing for your ale glass with a stump."

Garret did not like that image. He returned to the rock, glared at the moss for a moment, searching for tiny creatures, and then pushed it into the river.

"Do you have a better idea?" he asked.

The boy heaved the backpack off his shoulders and opened it up. He searched around for a few moments, then produced two glass jars, both filled with moss.

"These are what you need. Crimson Tower and Spartania moss." The boy placed the jars on the rock. Garret peered at them.

"Those don't look that different from what I had," he said.

"Maybe not," the boy said, "but it's like comparing a garden snake to a Red Skull in terms of potency. Turtle dung is a common moss, it grows everywhere." He pointed at the jars. "Those only grow in dragon warrens."

"So?"

"So, the three warren mosses all have powerful healing properties. Spartania is a natural disinfectant—it'll stop your wound from festering. Crimson Tower reduces swelling and pain."

Garret did not care about the difference between common moss and warren moss, but he very much did not want to deal with an infected, hurt arm in the jungles of Almira.

"Fine, I'll use them."

The boy nodded, then unscrewed the jars and took out a few pinches of each moss.

"So what happened?" the boy asked.

"What does it look like?" Garret said. "I got bit by a dragon."

"Happens. From the tooth, I'd say it was a juvenile Lake Screecher. You're lucky, they're a pretty small breed. A Blackjack would have taken the entire limb." He paused, frowning at the wound. "How long has that been in your arm?"

"What do you care?" Garret muttered, turning back to the tooth. He took a deep breath and pinched it between two fingers. Pulled, then gasped in pain and stopped. Moving the tooth even the length of a thumbnail clipping sent shocks of pain up his arm.

"Gods, let me help you," the boy said, rooting around in his pack again. He came up with a vial of blue liquid this time.

"What is that?" Garret asked.

"A numbing tonic. Derived from the poison dart frogs in the Dainwood."

"Poison frog? Is it safe?"

"Of course. It's been diluted. The numbness will only last a minute or two."

The boy pressed around the wound with his fingers a few times, then pulled the stopper on the vial and poured the blue liquid all over it. Within moments, the heat and pain from the tooth disappeared and his entire forearm went numb.

The boy corked the vial and put it back in the pack. He rummaged around some more and came out with a set of long metal tongs, then moved his attention back to Garret's arm. He took a few moments to get the edge of the tooth clamped down by the tongs, then drew the tooth free in one smooth motion, setting it down on the rock. Before a single drop of blood escaped from the wound the boy had stuffed wads of each warren moss into it. Then he produced a thin bark-skin bandage from his pack and wove it around Garret's arm.

"The tooth started going to rot," the boy said while he wrapped. "That's why I asked how long it had been in your arm. The putrification spreads quickly, but I think we'll be okay. I just wish I still had some Gods Moss."

"Why?"

"It's the strongest of the three warren mosses. Gods Moss carries the same properties as Spartania and Crimson Tower, it's just more powerful. It also stimulates organ functions. You can erase a decade of drinking damage to a man's liver with the right Gods Moss tonic. But it's so rare, most people don't even know it exists. For the few people who understand what it can do, a single vial sells for a thousand gold pieces."

The boy swallowed. He looked ashamed all of a sudden.

Garret's fingertips started to tingle, and then all the warmth returned to his arm. There was still a bad pain, but it was noticeably better than before.

"Well, these two seem to be working, at least."

"Good." The boy's face brightened. "The infection should clear up in a day or two."

The boy admired his work for a moment, then glanced at Garret's hunting knife and took a few steps back, his confidence melting away again.

"What's your name, boy?"

"Jolan."

"What are you doing in this forest, Jolan?"

"There are no laws preventing people from wandering the woods." Jolan's lips tightened.

"Are you a healer?"

"I am not anyone."

"Just a runaway who's lugging around a backpack full of rare ingredients and a head full of moss facts? I know the alchemist's trade when I see it."

Jolan fixed his eyes on the ground. "I was an apprentice. But my master died before I could make journeyman. Nimbu, the local lord, sold our apothecary and cast me out." He looked Garret in the eye. "Like I said, I'm nobody."

Garret knew he should kill the boy. Witnesses only caused trouble. But now that he was hurt, there was value in having a healer around, especially one who knew the land and could probably spot dragons far better than Garret. Plus, it was always easier to get into a city if you had a kid with you. For reasons Garret never understood, people trusted children.

"Well, Jolan the Nobody, I am in your debt," Garret said, standing up and sheathing his knife. "I'm headed to Deepdale. Do you know it?"

"Everybody knows Deepdale," Jolan said, frowning. "Where are you from, exactly?"

Garret had been too preoccupied with the dragontooth in his arm to fake an Almiran accent, and he'd learned from failure that pretending to be a local only worked for short interactions.

"Far away."

"I know all the countries in the realm. Is that a Ghalamarian accent? It sounds a little odd, but—"

"Do you know if the road to Deepdale is clear?"

Jolan shook his head. "Doubt it, this time of year. But I'm heading south as well. I know a route through the hills that won't be washed out—the key is to avoid the floodplain."

"Why didn't the people who built the road avoid the floodplain?"

Jolan shrugged. "There are a lot of dragons in the hills."

"Of course there are."

"They usually don't attack people in the forest. That's a misconception."

Garret held up his bandaged arm.

"Usually."

Garret weighed his options. He couldn't risk falling further behind schedule because of a flooded road. "If you guide me to Deepdale, I'll rent you a room with a featherbed and buy you as much food as you can eat when we arrive."

Jolan frowned at him, head tilting on his skinny neck. "Are you an outlaw?"

"Do you care?" Garret said. "Food and a bed. Yes or no?"

———

Jolan was quiet for a few miles, but once he began talking the boy did not shut up.

As they cut and picked their way through dense forest, steep hills, and heavy undergrowth, he prattled on about the types of trees and flowers and insects they could find in the different places they passed: cypress groves, reed-lined ponds, winding riverbanks. He talked about his old master and the poisonous snail they studied on some river in the north. About the proper way to brew coffee in the morning and set a broken bone. About the town he grew up in, and the sicknesses that had plagued the area since he was a small boy.

"Everyone thinks it's forest demons, but there's no such thing.

That's the first thing Morgan taught me. Then he showed me how the venom from the red-shelled snails was poisoning the water table. He got some of the villagers in the north to stop drinking from the river, but the whole area was corrupted—even freshly dug wells. And the villagers thought the purification process was demoncraft, so . . ."

"They just made mud statues instead?"

"Yeah."

Garret stopped to take a sip of water and check the sky for dragons.

"What gods do they worship where you're from?" Jolan asked after taking a sip from his own canteen.

"Never had much use for gods," Garret said, avoiding the real question.

"Seems lonely. I know the gods aren't real, but there's a value to them, I think."

Garret grunted. "What value?"

Jolan thought for a few moments.

"Here, look at that." He pointed to a yellow butterfly that had landed on a turtle's head. "The butterfly drinks the turtle's tears for their salt because he can't produce any on his own. And the butterfly is so light, he doesn't hurt the turtle. There are a thousand relationships like that on this hill alone—different creatures working together."

"Your point?"

"Almirans use their totems to worship the nameless gods of the forest. The gods may not be real, but the connections between all living things are. Honoring them is worth something."

Garret put his canteen away.

"I've known a few alchemists," Garret said. "They didn't talk like you. Always seemed more interested in where to find rare ingredients than anything else."

"That's because the money's all in the health tonics and pain tinctures, not long-term study. But Morgan always said that it was lazy to take from a world you didn't understand. And it left the alchemist's job half finished. He taught me to look for connections instead of just knowledge. He used to say that being able to name every mushroom in a forest isn't nearly as valuable as understanding everything the mushroom touches."

They started walking again. Both of them struggled to climb over a mossy outcropping that was crawling with orange spiders and yellow, finger-sized lizards.

"I thought I was starting to really understand the way the world works. But I was wrong. Back in Otter Rock, I saw something that I can't even begin to explain. The people of this country would call it demoncraft, just like the water purification. But this was very, very different."

"How?"

"I know how water purification really works. But this . . . shouldn't have been possible. I have to figure it out."

"Why's it so important?" Garret asked, not caring enough to ask what the boy had actually seen.

Jolan chewed on that. "All my life, I've healed the sick. But for each fever and infection and plague I can cure, there are ten that elude treatment. And it's not just because I'm young. Morgan spent five years trying to stop the red-shelled snail pestilence, but got nowhere. What I saw could change all of that. It could save thousands of lives. Ten of thousands, even."

"Sounds a little far-fetched."

"You wouldn't understand. You didn't see it."

"Fair enough. But if you saw this thing I wouldn't understand in Otter Rock, what are you doing down here?"

"The Daintree warrens are the only place in Almira where Gods Moss grows. And that's the key."

"Gods Moss again? Sounds like you're just trying to get paid."

"No." Jolan frowned. "That's not the point at all. Gods Moss is so naturally valuable that nobody's ever tried to explore the limits of its capability. But I will."

Garret gave Jolan a look. To his surprise, the boy seemed to be telling the truth.

They kept walking. As a rule, Garret didn't like people. That's why he was so good at his job. But he didn't mind the boy so much. It was rare to meet someone with an honest heart who wasn't also a moron.

After three days, they reached the Gorgon River, which was a wide, inexorable beast—more than a league across in most places. Her current wasn't as strong as the Atlas, but she was dangerous in more insidious ways. Insects hovered over her waters in an incessant and vast horde, cramming themselves into the mouth and eyes of anyone that was available. There were larger animals, too. Lithe and cunning jaguars, vicious crocodiles, and the enormous river dragons that some locals believed guarded the spirit of the river. On the other side of the Gorgon lay the Dainwood, which was all canopied darkness and jungle savagery.

"What are those called?" Garret asked, pointing across the river at the colossal, twisted trunks on the far side of the bank. He'd never seen such massive trees.

"Dainwood trees," Jolan said. "They don't grow anywhere else."

The boy paused for a moment, but then continued talking. Like he always did.

"Dainwood trees are actually very interesting. Their root systems are all—"

"Jolan, please. I don't think I can handle any more facts today."

The boy gave an embarrassed nod. Then looked out over the water.

"I've never seen the Gorgon before," Jolan said. "Gods, she's beautiful."

"You say that now," Garret responded. "Wait until we're halfway across."

Jolan frowned. "This doesn't look like a crossing."

"It isn't."

"Then why would we cross here?"

Garret didn't respond. Just started wading into the water.

"Do you have any idea how dangerous that is?" Jolan called from behind him.

Garret stopped. Turned around. "You said that Deepdale was due south from here, but the nearest crossings are fifty leagues to the east and west. I am not wasting three days just to cross a river without getting my boots wet."

"You've already been bit by one dragon," Jolan reminded him. "Are you that eager to repeat the experience? I can't help you if you get eaten."

That was a fair point.

"Do you have a suggestion?"

"I can build a raft," Jolan said. "Give me an hour."

Garret glanced back at the water. About fifteen strides out, the scaled back of some unknown creature humped out of the surface. It was three times longer than the dragon that had bitten his arm.

"One hour. That's it."

Jolan made Garret gather straight logs while he worked on the lashings. The boy was gangly and uncoordinated when it came to walking through the woods, but his fingers worked with rapid, practiced alacrity. As promised, the makeshift raft was ready within the hour, including two oars made from hard, straight branches.

Garret began pushing the raft into the water, but Jolan bent down at the waterline and started molding a little statue with his hands.

"Seriously?" Garret asked. "After that whole speech about the gods not being real?"

"The gods aren't real," Jolan said, pulling two blueberries from his pack and using them as eyes. "But a little luck can't hurt."

Garret shrugged. He'd known a sergeant in the Balarian army who refused to wipe his ass the night before a battle—said the stink kept the arrows away. In the end, building a mud statue for luck wasn't much different. And it was more sanitary.

"Give it some of those fish scales, at least," Garret said, pointing to a few that were floating in an eddy.

Jolan smiled. "Good idea."

———

When they were halfway across the river, the birds and insects went quiet. Jolan's body turned rigid, his eyes went wide. They both looked down into the swirling green depths as a massive shadow snaked against the current. The aquatic dragon was ten times wider than their silly raft.

When it was gone, they paddled the rest of the way as fast as they could. Neither of them spoke until their boots were sucking mud on the far side of the shore.

"What breed was that?" Garret asked. "It was huge."

"Glad we took the raft and made the totem now, aren't you?" Jolan said, smiling. "That was an Almiran River Lurker. I wish he'd surfaced so we could have gotten a look."

"You didn't look much like you wanted him to surface while we were out there."

"Well, you were scared, too!" Jolan said. "Now, do you want me to change that bandage, or should we wait and see if it gets infected from all the animal shit in the water?"

Garret frowned, then started rolling up his sleeve.

"What's the rush to get to Deepdale, anyway?" Jolan asked, opening his bag of medicines.

Garret didn't respond.

"You're worse than Morgan was."

"What do you mean?"

"Secrets. All the alchemists have a lot of secrets. About history and poisons. About dragons, especially. Master couldn't tell them to me until I became a journeyman . . ." Jolan trailed off and focused on the bandage. "Dragon warrens, they were the key to everything. But he never talked about them."

"Some secrets will get you killed, boy."

"Yeah, I've been told that before."

"Master Morgan again?"

"No," Jolan said, a serious look creeping across his face. "Someone else."

Jolan finished his work. Stood up and oriented himself against the sun. "Let's keep moving. If we keep a good pace, we can reach Deepdale in a week."

9

ASHLYN

Almira, Atlas Coast

Ashlyn looked down at her father's face. Someone had combed black dye into his beard to hide the silver and gray. He would have hated that. Hertzog Malgrave was a lot of things, but vain wasn't one of them. He would have wanted to go down the river without hiding who he really was, both inside and out.

As news of the king's death spread, peasants and wardens and lords across Almira would cease work and spend a week in mourning, drinking to his memory and retelling stories of his heroism in the

Balarian Invasion. There would be other things, too. Darker things. Spells and sacrifices performed in basements and cellars and moonlit fields. Ashlyn wondered how many goats and chickens would be bled out beneath the stars. Hundreds. Maybe thousands. If Hertzog had died five hundred years ago, the lords would be sacrificing children in his honor instead of animals.

Almira was considered a backward country in the realm of Terra, but Ashlyn was thankful that her people had at least evolved beyond that dark and terrible custom.

Traditionally, the deceased royalty of Almira were sent back to the Soul Sea from a castle courtyard that opened into the harbor, so there was no chance their souls would get lost. The lords and ladies of the court were all invited to watch their fallen liege return to the place where all souls were born. Afterward, most of them got blind drunk and cried to the waves. It wasn't uncommon for the ceremony to degenerate into a sorrowful orgy.

Despite being Papyrian, Ashlyn's mother had wanted to follow the Almiran custom for her burial. But when she died, Hertzog didn't send her back to the Soul Sea from Floodhaven. Instead, he took her to a small, hidden river a day's ride north of the city. People whispered that he'd gone alone because he was still so furious with her infidelity that he'd actually buried her corpse without a shell and covered it with rocks, but Ashlyn had never believed that.

Before he died, her father had asked to be taken to that same hidden river. No ceremony, no nobles screwing each other, just Ashlyn saying good-bye next to a hidden river. The nobility of Floodhaven was shocked by the decision—and clearly disappointed they didn't have the opportunity to show their loyalty through a display of grief—but Ashlyn honored her father's decision. She was the queen now. They needed to see that she was in charge, not Almiran traditions.

Ashlyn was escorted to the river by Hayden and a score of her personal wardens for protection. They helped Ashlyn lay Hertzog Malgrave in his boat, then melted into the forest and formed a perimeter, giving her space to say good-bye.

When Ashlyn was alone, she waited for a wave of grief to wash over her, but it didn't arrive. No tears. No trembling fingers. Ashlyn had never forgiven Hertzog for what he'd done to Silas, she'd just found a way to live with it. And her father had been dying for years—they'd both planned for it. Both known that one day soon, she'd be in this exact spot.

Ashlyn thumbed the seashell that she'd brought with her. Light cream, with twists of orange and green. Hertzog had chosen it himself a year ago, when his cough started producing blood.

A squirrel ventured down from a nearby tree and skittered along the banks of the river. Trout darted in and out of the clear water beneath the funeral boat, which was painted dark blue.

She needed to say some words. That was one tradition she would keep.

"Hertzog Malgrave was a good king of Almira," Ashlyn began. "He raised two strong sons and two beautiful daughters. Halted the Balarian Invasion at the battle of Black Pine. Forged thirty years of peace and prosperity."

Ashlyn paused. There was nobody else here, why was she talking as if there was? She started over.

"My father was quick to lose his temper and slow to forgive his enemies. He ruled the lords of Almira through violence, intimidation, and the threat of two blue bars on their cheeks." She swallowed. "But he was loyal and generous to his friends. Fiercely protective of his family. We saw Almira through different eyes, but we both loved our country in our own way."

Ashlyn opened her father's mouth and slipped the seashell inside. Closed it again. "Good-bye, Father. May your soul find a calm course back to the sea. I will keep Almira safe. I promise."

She pushed his boat into the current, causing the trout to scatter. Watched until it disappeared around a bend in the river. For the first time in her life, Ashlyn was the only Malgrave in Almira.

She had never felt so alone.

———

When Ashlyn returned to the castle, she headed straight to the dovecote, which was guarded by three Malgrave wardens and managed by an ancient steward named Godfrey. He had a thin layer of pigeon shit permanently coating his shoulders.

Almira had the most unreliable roads in the realm. They were muddy and poorly maintained—every spring half of them got washed out by floods. Hertzog had struggled for years to build a reliable highway system that would allow him to better move and communicate with his armies, but her father couldn't prevent the spring monsoons or conjure enough viable quarries in his country to build paved roads in the Balarian style. This poor infrastructure, combined with a fragmented and chaotic religion, was one of the main reasons that Almira had remained a backward and divided country—ruled by superstition and feudal warlords instead of centralizing and innovating like Balaria.

Expanding the Almiran network of carrier pigeons to avoid the roads entirely had been Ashlyn's idea, which made Godfrey one of the busiest men in Castle Malgrave.

She'd spent the last seven years working with Godfrey to breed and train their pigeons to make longer journeys at a faster pace. She'd started with a dozen birds, but now had hundreds spread across the realm of Terra. Some birds were trained to go to the castles and holdfasts of Almiran lords. Some to the barns, mills, and forest huts of commoners Ashlyn paid to spy on their own lords. Some went to the remote outposts of alchemists she'd hired to study different aspects of the natural world. Others went to foreign nations like Papyria. And others still went to the secret informants that Ashlyn had planted on the far side of the Soul Sea.

"Hello, Godfrey," Ashlyn said, lowering her head to slip past the low ceiling of the dovecote. The steward was in the process of sending out Ashlyn's messages to the small lords of Almira, requesting they bring as many wardens as possible to her coronation.

Now that her father was dead, Ashlyn knew that calling so many wardens to Floodhaven was a risk. And if the only thing she wanted to accomplish as queen was to remain in power, she would never do such a thing. But Ashlyn refused to be that kind of ruler.

She'd burn the Malgrave throne to ash if it meant saving the dragons of Terra.

"Good morning, my princess," he said, lowering his head. A moment later his bushy eyebrows twitched as he realized his mistake. "Ah, forgive me. Good morning, *my queen*."

"It's all right," Ashlyn said. "I'm not used to it yet, either."

Godfrey nodded. "We become accustomed to all things with time, my queen. Just think how far our pigeons have come." He motioned to a white-winged female. "Layla was born in this very dovecote. It was her entire world for a time. But just this morning she returned from Papyria—flying over mountains and across long leagues of the Soul Sea. You taught her that."

Everyone had thought Ashlyn was insane when she started training birds to cross the Soul Sea—most homing pigeons couldn't reliably travel more than a few dozen leagues over familiar land. But Ashlyn had trained hers to travel up to five hundred leagues over open water without getting lost.

"Ruling a country is not so different from what you've done with these birds," Godfrey continued. "It seems impossible until you settle down and begin doing it."

"I hope you're right," Ashlyn said.

She'd always liked Godfrey—he took excellent care of the birds and seemed impervious to the troubles of the world beyond the dovecote.

"Speaking of Layla, let me get the message that she carried back."

Godfrey opened a locked chest in the corner of the room with a key that only he and Ashlyn carried. He removed a small, rolled parchment and handed it to her. The wax seal was pressed into the shape of an orca's fin rising up from the ocean. Empress Okinu's personal symbol. It had required very careful work to get a letter like this into her private dovecote. After Ashlyn's mother had died, there were rumors that Hertzog Malgrave had killed Shiru with his own hands, instead of her dying during childbirth. It wasn't true, but it wasn't easy to convince a distant island nation of that through letters alone.

The empress of Papyria had never forgiven Hertzog for the death of her sister, and Hertzog was stubborn enough to let relations with the island empire turn icy and distant. Ashlyn could not abide the loss of such a valuable ally. She had spent years secretly rebuilding the Malgraves' relationship with Papyria.

The official channels of royal communication were shared by a hundred eyes in both countries, and neither Hertzog nor Okinu were willing to extend anything beyond the most basic level of correspondence, so that avenue was closed off. Instead, she'd cultivated an academic relationship with one of Empress Okinu's high councilors—a woman named Noko. Ashlyn was initially wary of putting even the smallest ounce of confidence into a stranger, but over the years she'd begun to trust Noko. They shared the same interest in the mechanisms that powered the natural world. Noko was more focused on flowers and plants than dragons, but they both trusted logic and observation above all else. So, she took a risk.

A year ago, when Hertzog's cough began to worsen, Ashlyn asked Noko to deliver a private letter to the empress on her behalf. The message had been simple. After her father died, Ashlyn knew that she would be the female ruler of a country that, above all else, respected the strength of men. The odds would be stacked against her at every turn, which meant she needed allies who saw her gender as an advantage, not a weakness. Ashlyn suggested that she and the empress open a private line of communication with each other, so they might prepare for the day that she ruled as queen of Almira.

Ashlyn knew it was morbid to plan for the death of her father behind his back, but the world was a morbid and unforgiving place. No sense denying that reality.

Empress Okinu accepted. They had exchanged dozens of letters in the following months—each message Ashlyn sent was meant to build favor with Papyria. When the empress complained of ongoing illnesses on her outer islands, Ashlyn recognized the problem, then sent a new method for digging cisterns that kept the water clean and ended the outbreaks. When a score of adolescent Milk Wings harried a remote township, Ashlyn suggested the local soldiers lure the dragons into the wilderness using rags soaked in milkweed, which mimicked the smell of a potential mate. No piece of advice was too small.

All that effort had been geared toward influencing the contents of the letter Ashlyn now held in her hands. Okinu's reaction to Hertzog's death would either give Ashlyn a wealth of options, or none at all.

Ashlyn took a deep breath and broke the wax seal with her thumb.

For the eyes of Queen Ashlyn Malgrave,
Losing a parent is never easy, but it happens. I would imagine that you feel a bit like one of your baby pigeons who has hatched from her egg only to find the nest devoid of support and nourishment. But you are not a lonesome bird, my dear niece. You have proven yourself to be a valuable and loyal ally, and you have powerful friends in Papyria.
Simply ask for the support you require, and it shall be yours.
With love,
Empress Okinu, Eternal Majesty of the Papyrian Empire

Ashlyn allowed the message to roll closed against her thumb, then tucked it into her dress. She let out a long, slow breath of relief as she considered her response. More than anything, she needed a way to get Almiran wardens across the Soul Sea if Bershad failed.

"There was a second arrival today as well, my queen," Godfrey said.

"Who?"

"Asper, my queen."

"Finally," Ashlyn said. Asper was her Mudwall pigeon—she'd been waiting to hear from the steward there for two days, hoping to receive good news so that she could order the five thousand Malgrave wardens riding west to turn around. With her father dead, she needed to consolidate power.

She opened the paper.

For the eyes of Queen Ashlyn Malgrave,

I regret to inform you that the violence in Mudwall has escalated in recent days. Lord Hrilian's men have been marauding the countryside beyond our walls. His men capture the local peasants, then bring them within sight of the wall and lynch them, one by one. He is hoping to lure High-Warden Raimier out of the city to engage in open combat, where he will most surely be defeated, now that Hrilian has the numbers. And, I must admit, Raimier's control of the city is dubious at best. The small lords suspect him of treachery.

In your previous message, you mentioned that Malgrave wardens were on their way. I beg you to spur them forward with all haste. I fear that Mudwall will become a nest of demons and violence if help does not arrive soon.

Uylnar Went, High Steward of Mudwall

Ashlyn stared at the wretched words after she had read them twice. Felt hot anger rise in the back of her throat.

"When would you like to draft your responses, my queen?"

"Right now," Ashlyn said.

She wrote back to Uylnar Went first, assuring him that her Malgrave wardens were riding to his aid as quickly as possible. Ashlyn needed more soldiers in Floodhaven, but she would not ignore peasants who were being hung from the trees. There was always a different path forward. Lord Hrilian and his marauders had closed off one road, which meant Ashlyn needed to open another.

Ashlyn would ask the empress for ships from Papyria, but that wasn't all. It was time to find out exactly how much goodwill Ashlyn had built with her aunt.

PART II

10

BERSHAD

Realm of Terra, the Soul Sea

Rowan and Alfonso got seasick as soon as the *Luminata* left Flood-haven harbor. When possible, Rowan vomited over the side of the ship. When it wasn't, he did his best to hit a bucket. Most of the time he missed.

Alfonso was worse. The poor creature didn't understand what was happening. He whinnied and brayed and then made a mess of his stall. Bershad stayed with him, rubbing his muzzle and trying to calm the donkey down. Told him it would be over soon. During the rare occasions the beast was actually calm, Bershad used the time to scrape the rust off his sword. Beneath the decay, the blade was still keen.

Two days into their journey, Bershad came out of Alfonso's little stall with a full bucket of donkey vomit. Felgor was perched on the rail, looking out over the sea. Vera had unchained the Balarian as soon as they were out of the harbor and the ruse of a prisoner transportation wasn't necessary, but she'd made it very clear that she would cut off his feet if he made trouble. Even now, she watched Felgor from across the ship as if he might jump into the Soul Sea and swim for his freedom.

Rowan was sitting against the ship's mast and staring at his feet. There was a bucket between his legs.

"Ah, but I've missed the sea!" Felgor said, beaming with happiness. "Spent the first half of my life on a ship about this size, although not nearly as nice. My parents were part of a traveling band of trou-badours, so they could barely afford a seaworthy vessel. Makes you good at improvising, but it takes a toll on—"

"Felgor," Rowan said, without looking up from his feet. "Shut up."

Felgor looked down at him. "A natural sea dog, this one."

Bershad emptied the bucket into the sea and looked out. In the distance, he could see the hazy outline of islands that marked the center of the Soul Sea. Every ship that crossed the sea gave those islands a wide berth—the currents and channels between them were famous for bashing errant ships to splinters. There were other alleged dangers, too. Strange animals and enormous dragons.

And for Almirans, the place was sacred.

"The islands seem smaller than I remember," Felgor said, following Bershad's gaze. "Maybe I've just gotten bigger." Felgor glanced at Yonmar, who was molding a totem onto the gunwale. "What's all that, anyway?"

"The heart of the sea is the birthplace of the gods," Yonmar said without stopping his work. "It would be foolish to pass by and not honor them."

"Fucking Almirans and your mud gods, I love these things. Let's see it."

Yonmar glared at Felgor for a moment, but moved his hands away so everyone could see his work. It was an arm-sized totem, body formed from mud, sprouting bear claws and willow twigs. Yonmar had used two rubies for the eyes. It wasn't bad work.

Felgor studied the little totem. "What'll you do with it when you're done?"

"Send it back to the sea," Yonmar said. "Nothing's permanent."

"You're gonna part with two rubies so some gods don't get homesick? What's so special about this place?"

"Before the gods were born, the realm was ruled by dragons and demons," Yonmar said. "Everything was hard rock and hot ash. Then the forest gods emerged from the heart of the sea and climbed onto the shores. They brought lush trees and warm-blooded animals with them. And once they'd filled the land with plants and life, the gods pulled men from the heart, too, so that we can live with honor and courage amidst their creation. When we die, if we can get back to the sea and the gods deem us worthy, we join our ancestors and live in the heart for eternity."

"What if you're not found worthy?"

"Your soul is cursed," Yonmar said. "And you're turned into a wandering demon. Tortured by sunlight. Haunted by nightmares."

"Shouldn't you two be making totems, then?" Felgor said, glancing at Bershad and Rowan.

"My soul is pretty well fucked at this point," Bershad said. "Even if it wasn't, they snatched my totem bag at the same time they took my title and gave me the bars. Exiles aren't allowed to ask the gods for help."

"You, too?" Felgor asked Rowan.

"I still got mine. But I'm not worried." He glanced at Yonmar. "The gods can smell desperation."

Several tense moments passed.

"The whole thing seems silly to me, but I love you Almirans for it," Felgor said, breaking the silence. "All of you tote around these bags of sticks and bones and precious gems. A pickpocket can die rich and happy just prowling the Foggy Side of Floodhaven, snatching purses."

"At least I don't worship a fucking clock," Yonmar muttered.

"Common misconception, there," Felgor responded. "Balarians don't worship Aeternita. We made her."

"Men can't make a god."

"Sure you can. All you need is some metal, wire, gears, and a bunch of people to agree with you. And it's not just clocks—it's all the machines of Balaria. Whole thing works out better than your Almiran setup, too. Aeternita serves us, not the other way around. Life's more comfortable and we don't have to stop what we're doing all the time to make little statues."

"If it works out so well, why'd Balaria try to invade Almira thirty years ago?" Rowan asked, still staring at his bucket.

"Dunno," Felgor said. "I was two years old."

Bershad did. Balaria had touted all sorts of reasons for the war— honor, conquest, civilizing the mud worshippers. But it all came down to food. Balaria had expanded their empire so quickly, they couldn't sustain their population even before the famines in Ghalamar and Lysteria. After the invasion of Almira failed, Balaria was forced to seal their borders just to keep the refugees out of the empire's heartland.

"Because just like rocks and burned trees, you can't eat metal, either," Bershad said. "And Aeternita doesn't make food."

Felgor shrugged. "Hey, I'm just a simple thief trying to keep my blood warm. I don't fuss with the whys of life and all that philosophical shit. It's exhausting." He turned to Vera. "What about you Papyrians?"

"What about us?" Vera said.

"You worship some sky god or something, right? I was always hazy on that."

"Papyrians don't worship gods at all. We simply respect the moon and the stars."

"Why's that?"

"The moon brings the tides that take us to the sea. And the stars guide us upon her waters."

"That's all?" Yonmar asked, frowning.

Vera looked at him. "You ever find yourself in the middle of a storm at night, and nothing to guide you besides a black sky, and it'll make more sense."

———

After passing the Soul's heart, the *Luminata* hit a storm. The ship was tossed from wave to wave, tipping and rising at steep angles as the rain battered the deck. Torian and his crew worked tirelessly for a week—shouting at each other, adjusting the sails, tightening ropes only to loosen them again when the wind changed.

On the morning that the storm broke, they spotted the bone-white coast of Ghalamar. The shore was colored by thousands of tiny shells washed ashore and bleached by the sun. From a distance, the wavering cream line of the coastal cliffs beyond looked like a great snake stretching out endlessly on either side. There was a small harbor and city on the coast, and beyond that, the dark gray Razorback Mountains, which separated Ghalamar from Balaria.

"Argel." Torian pointed as everyone clambered above deck for a look. "Northernmost city in Ghalamar."

"Argellian whores have really nice breath," Felgor said. "Top five in the realm, I'd say."

Vera glared at him, tightened her grip on one of her sheathed daggers.

"Is there no other place for us to get ashore?" Bershad asked Torian. "A harbor with fewer eyes?"

"Plenty, but not around here. North is all rocks and mountains and then Balaria—no paths inland. South is that cliff. One man in ten can scale those heights. The other nine end up dead and pulled out by the tide. We can go around it if you're willing to tack on an extra month of travel."

"I'm not." If Bershad didn't reach the emperor before the summer solstice, there was no point in going at all.

"Then we've got to make port in Argel."

"You've been here before?" Vera asked.

Bershad nodded. "This is where they took me down from the mountains. The pass is a day's ride northeast of here, give or take. Hidden by a grove of pine trees and razor bush."

"Were you well received?" Yonmar asked.

Bershad had spent two weeks drinking with different Argellian lords and merchants—who all wanted to hear the story of his airborne entrance into Balaria—before Rowan finally tracked him down and they'd been compelled to move elsewhere. Ghalamarians did not hold the same disdain for dragonslayers as Almiran nobility, but they still executed exiles who lingered too long in one place.

"Depends on who we run into," Bershad said.

The quay of Argel was almost empty. Ships rocked lazily on the water, but there were no sailors or workers in sight. Just customs agents. Torian and his crew docked the *Luminata* in silence, and six armed and armored agents came over.

Balaria had subsumed Ghalamar and Lysteria into their empire almost a hundred years ago after a series of successful military campaigns. The two countries kept their names and small scraps of their autonomy so long as they supported Balaria with taxes, food, and soldiers. The Ghalamarian borders weren't sealed like Balaria, but clearing customs wasn't a simple thing, especially when it was a dragonslayer, a Papyrian widow, and a Balarian thief with a death sentence asking to be let in.

Yonmar hopped off the boat to meet the agents. A tall man stepped forward from the group. He had a steel cap on his head, stringy blond hair flowing out beneath it, and a patch of beard on his chin that dangled down to his Adam's apple in a braid.

"Papers," he said, thrusting out a hand.

"What's your name?" Yonmar asked, frowning.

"Adelon. *Sergeant* Adelon."

"Well, Sergeant, I am *Lord* Yonmar Grealor. So watch your tongue."

"Don't matter to me if you're Aeternita the fucking goddess of time, everyone needs papers to get into the city." The man sneered. "Where are yours?"

Yonmar's face was a mess of anger and embarrassment, but he produced King Hertzog's documents of safe passage and handed them over. Adelon read them quickly.

"You'll need to see the baron," he said, then he pointed at Bershad without looking up from the papers. "You and the exile both."

"We need to do no such thing," Yonmar said.

By way of response, Adelon motioned to the men behind him. Four moved to board the ship, and the fifth ran for reinforcements, who soon poured out of a customs house farther down the dock.

"My men will search and document your ship's contents while the baron decides what to do with you. If everything's in order, shouldn't take more than a few hours."

"King Hertzog's decree supersedes some saltwater baron's port regulations," Yonmar said. "Now let us disembark and be on our way."

"Don't know what *supersede* means, and I honestly don't give a shit." Adelon folded Yonmar's papers behind his breastplate. "You and the exile come with me, or you sail back into the Soul Sea. Your choice."

————

Bershad gave his sword to Rowan—it was too suspicious to be seen with the blade. Then he and Yonmar headed into Argel, escorted by Adelon and twenty soldiers. Everyone else stayed on the *Luminata*.

They passed over a flood wall and moved down a deserted street.

"Where is everyone?" Yonmar asked as the soldiers led them down the avenue.

Nobody answered him, but after a few more blocks a noise rose in the distance. It was soft at first, but growing. People were chanting.

"Axe! Axe! Axe!" the voices sang.

Then they hushed for a second before erupting again into a howl of cheers and whoops.

"Gods," Yonmar said. "I know what they're doing."

"A wood-chopping contest?" Bershad asked.

Yonmar glared at him. "They're executing Skojit."

The chanting grew louder as they turned a corner onto the main square, which was packed to bursting—hundreds of people filled the open area. Small children were propped on the shoulders of parents. Every roof on the square was covered with people. Men sitting on the eaves, trading skins of ale and wine back and forth. Others milling behind them, jostling for a better view. Everybody loved a good execution.

A makeshift raised platform had been built out of pine and erected in the center of the square. There was a pile of headless bodies behind the platform. Across from the corpses, a man was being led up a set of stairs by a soldier. The prisoner's hands were bound and a burlap sack was wrapped over his head—a long trail of black matted hair protruded from below the sack at all angles and stopped near the middle of his back.

The soldier yanked the man to the center of the platform and kicked him to his knees. To the left, a lord in an expensive ermine cloak sat on a bench. He was leaning forward, with one elbow resting on a knee, the other lazily balancing a naked sword pointed into the platform. He was middle-aged, clean-shaven, with thinning brown hair cropped closely to his face.

"That's Garwin," Bershad said to Yonmar. "The baron of Argel."

Bershad had feasted with Garwin for several nights during his previous stint in Argel. The baron was stern and serious when sober, but he was fun to drink with.

Garwin motioned with one hand and the soldier removed the sack from the prisoner's head. His face was beast-like, covered in a wild beard that stretched down to his navel. Bushy eyebrows obscured his eyes and a thick scar ran down one side of his face, disrupting the hair in a rough ridge of hewn flesh. The crowd fell silent.

"Name?" the baron asked.

"Logon of the Hidden Lakes," the prisoner said, his voice full of defiance.

"Charge?"

When the prisoner did not respond, Garwin looked to the soldier, who took half a step forward.

"Murder. Rape. Cannibalism." The soldier paused, and Garwin motioned that he should go into further detail. "This bastard invaded a small Ghalamarian mining plot—just a man and his family set up well below the Line of Lornar. The miner's head was caved in by an axe and his body left for crows. The woman was chained inside the cabin. She had been violated until she died. The children were . . ." The soldier trailed off.

"Finish the tale, Sergeant," Garwin urged.

"They were eaten. Not by animals, mind you. Their bones were stacked in piles, their little skulls at the top. Three of them, no older than ten."

The crowd rumbled in horror. Men called out for his blood.

Garwin waited for them to quiet and turned back to the savage. "Do you have anything to say?"

The Skojit raised his head and spoke in a low growl. "Might be the man was murdered. Kids eaten. There are tribes in the Razors who do such things. But I had no part in the flatlander's story. The men of the Hidden Lakes do not eat people."

"Where did you capture this Logon of Hidden Lakes?" Garwin asked.

"A league or so north of the ravaged camp, but still below the Line," the soldier said. "Stone drunk and passed out beneath a tree. Blood on his hands and an axe next to him. No animal carcass nearby to justify the blood."

Garwin took a moment to absorb these facts and then spoke to the prisoner.

"If you confess, I'll grant you a clean death." Garwin gestured toward the pile of headless men. "Either way, you will not see the sun set tonight. Decide."

Logon of the Hidden Lakes scanned the crowd, his face unreadable.

"Your offer does not move me, flatland lord," he said at last. "Your people sneak onto our lands and dig into our earth. Like rodents, you are. Taking what is not yours and expecting to have it for free. Trying to heal your poisoned and hungry country." He glared at Garwin. "Do with me what you will, but I did not eat that man's children."

The people roared again, calling for punishment. Garwin stood up from his bench.

"Feed him his manhood," he said loudly. "See that he chokes on it."

The crowd went wild. Two men held Logon's arms while a third cut off his balls and jammed them into his mouth. They wrapped a length of rope around his face several times so he couldn't spit them back out. One soldier clamped a hand over his nose. The savage's face turned red and then purple. Then he swallowed with a great deal of effort and the guard let him drop against the wood planks of the platform, legs thrashing. He bled to death a minute or two later, and they dumped his body off the platform and went to retrieve the next man.

"As you can see, the baron is occupied at present," Adelon said, smiling and revealing a set of yellow, broken teeth. "You'll wait for him in the keep."

They led Bershad and Yonmar to Argel's main keep, which had a dragon's corpse hanging from the uppermost crenellations. The carcass had been stripped of its fat—only torn scales and rotten bones remained. Probably been hung there for two or three days.

"That a Red Skull?" Bershad asked, squinting at the flash of crimson on the head.

"What do you care?"

"Not a good idea to keep the carcass around for decoration like that," Bershad said. "Red Skulls mate for life. And they're known for developing a mind for revenge when some assholes kill their partner." Bershad squinted at the dragon, judged it to be a male by its size. "And the females are quite a bit larger than the one you have there."

"You worry about living dragons, we'll worry about the dead ones. How'd that be, exile?"

"Suit yourself."

The baron's office was tucked away in a room at the back of Argel's main keep. The chamber was small, but well adorned—tapestries on the walls, soft rich carpets on the floor. Bershad yanked off his boots, rubbed them on the carpet a few times, and then flopped onto a cushioned chair.

"You were a lord once," Yonmar said. "How can you behave like that?"

"I was a lord," Bershad said, closing his eyes. "But I wasn't much good at it."

Garwin executed Skojit all morning. Every few minutes the cries rose up again as he allowed the crowd to choose the punishment for a particular man. They seemed to favor the axe.

While Bershad and Yonmar waited for the killings to end, servants brought ale, wine, cheese, and cuts of pork and bread. Yonmar ignored the refreshments, but Bershad drank and ate a heavy portion of everything available.

"You don't feel like this is a good time to be sober?" Yonmar asked Bershad as he downed his third horn of ale.

"Not really, no." The city was making Bershad's skin itch.

Yonmar shrugged and returned his attention to the window. They knew when the executions were over because a sad murmur rumbled through the crowd, followed by the sounds of men and women leaving the square. A few minutes later, Garwin burst through the door to his office, followed by Adelon, who stayed by the door.

"Wretched business," Garwin said, more to himself than his two guests. He kicked off his own boots, crossed the room barefoot, and collapsed into his chair behind the main table. He squeezed his nose between two thick fingers and then looked up at Bershad.

"So it's true," Garwin said. "You're still alive."

Up close, the baron of Argel's face was a battered thing. He had been hit in the face with a mace or a maul or some kind of blunt object. There were deep pits of scar tissue on his cheek and chin and forehead. His nose had been broken and not repaired, and the top half of his ear had been pinched off. The life of a Ghalamarian baron wasn't defined by border skirmishes and battles like an Almiran's was, but it wasn't peaceful, either.

"Do you know why I do that?" Garwin continued leaning back in his chair.

"You got tired of boar hunting?"

"I do it for the people," Garwin said. "You have to show them the blackness that waits beyond these city walls. Helps them appreciate their lives of comfort and safety."

"Nothing like a pile of headless savages to boost morale," Bershad said. "I'm surprised, Garwin. I'd have thought a soldier like you would find a more honest method of ruling. Intimidation and spectacle is a rich man's game."

"Everyone's a critic of the nobles until they become one and have to actually make decisions," Garwin said.

"You forget, I used to be a noble," Bershad said.

"How'd that work out for you?"

"Not well," Bershad admitted. "Doesn't make me wrong."

"You know what my subjects are doing right now?" He looked out his window. "Every lowborn man, woman, and child is walking down to a river outside of town to wash themselves clean of that business this afternoon. The whole ritual makes them feel like they've accomplished something meaningful. For today at least, they forgot about the grain famine Ghalamar has endured for years. They forgot that their lives, and their children's lives, will be marked by labor and toil and little else, with most of the profit going to the heart of an empire they'll never see. How else do you rule a people whose lives are made of such mundane drudgery besides through distraction? Your country does the same thing with their mud gods and human sacrifices."

"Almirans haven't sacrificed humans for five hundred—"

"Quiet, boy," Garwin said, cutting Yonmar off. "The adults are talking."

Garwin looked at Bershad, waiting for an answer.

"If your people are plagued by famine, maybe you should provide better seeds instead of bloody distractions," Bershad said. Ashlyn had mentioned there were famines in Ghalamar because they'd killed too many dragons. Bershad didn't know how a lack of dragons led to a blight on wheat, but he was sure that Ashlyn could tell him.

"I seem to be fresh out of high-quality seeds. Did you bring me some?"

"No."

"Didn't think so." Garwin crossed his arms. "So, what are you doing here?"

"The same thing I'm always doing."

"There are no dragons near Argel right now. We had a male Red Skull a while ago, but a lucky dragonslayer managed to kill it. Poor bastard got so drunk that night that he tumbled off the ramparts while taking a piss and killed himself, but that doesn't detract from the achievement. I'm sure you noticed the carcass on your way in."

"I did. You really shouldn't keep it hanging like that, though. If he was m—"

"Spare me the fucking lecture, Silas, and tell me why you're here."

"Come now," Bershad said. "Is that any way to treat an old friend? I'm sorry for criticizing your leadership style, okay? I'm an asshole, you know that. But I seem to remember your parting words on my last visit being far more hospitable. Something about women and wine? I don't remember exactly."

"May you live long enough to return, so I can put wine in your hand and a woman at your side."

"That's the one," Bershad said, leaning forward and smiling. "A Ghalamarian saying? I just love these little foreign adages. Well, I have returned very much alive. I see the wine, but not the woman."

"My men have seen a woman," Garwin said. "A Papyrian widow, sworn to protect the royal family of that *great* island nation. And I see this Almiran lord." Garwin looked at Yonmar for the first time. "Who has the snide look of a fourth or fifth son that nobody gives a shit about."

Yonmar's jaw tensed and the flesh around his collar reddened, but he said nothing.

"I'll tell you what I do not see," Garwin continued. "I do not see any good reason why I should be finding you in my city today, drinking my wine and getting my carpet dirty."

Bershad drummed his fingers on the table a few times. Then he gave Yonmar a look. This was supposed to be his job, might as well let the bastard do it.

"If you had let me finish a sentence," Yonmar said, "I would have told you that we travel with documents of safe passage from King Hertzog Malgrave. The exile is traveling to Cornish to execute a writ there, and I am escorting him."

"Cornish?"

"The baron requested Bershad personally," Yonmar said. "King Hertzog obliged—he is in a relationship-building mood these days."

"Why are you with him?"

Yonmar leaned back, relaxing into his story. "Almira is happy to share our famous lizard killer, but King Hertzog wants to make sure he doesn't go wandering off."

"We keep dragonslayers in line on this side of the Soul Sea, too, lordling."

"All the same."

Garwin rubbed his scarred face. "I suppose you have these documents?"

"Your sergeant took them from us."

"Adelon," Garwin said. The soldier crossed the room and produced the papers. Garwin read them carefully, his lips moving as his eyes scanned the words.

"I was planning to strike east," Bershad continued while the baron read. "Heard there's good foraging along the pine forest foothills all the way to Cornish."

"What's your excuse for the widow?" Garwin asked, raising the paper with King Hertzog's seal and examining it in the light.

Judging from the way that Yonmar's shoulders tightened, he hadn't bothered to create a good answer to that question, so Bershad did it for him.

"I've been trying to fuck the widow for a fortnight now—you know I have a thing for Papyrians," Bershad said. "But it's proved a slow process. Papyrians are like wild jaguars in bed, but they take the most convincing."

Bershad pulled a fake smile across his face.

"Pretty thin, exile," Garwin said, tossing the papers onto the desk.

"Thin? We travel under the king's name," Yonmar protested.

"Look, lordling. The king of Almira might get his ass licked by every mud lord on the other side of the Soul Sea, but things are done differently here. The emperor of Balaria holds sway, not your king."

Adelon stirred behind them, shifting his spear from his right hand to his left. "We should put them in a dungeon."

"Did I ask for your opinion, Adelon?" Garwin asked. "No? So keep your fucking mouth shut." Garwin sighed and squeezed his nose between his fingers again. "Do you take me for a fool, Bershad? Some thick-headed baron you can trick into letting you into the mountains, as I did the other three groups of adventuring Almirans?"

"Who said anything about mountains?"

"Your presence in this office says much and more about a great many different things." Garwin looked up. "I'm told there was an incident with an Almiran princess and a Balarian envoy several moons ago. Any chance your trip across my country is related to that?"

"What do you care about an Almiran princess, Garwin?"

"I swear allegiance to a count, who in turn swears allegiance to a duke, and it runs all the way up the chain until it reaches the king of Ghalamar, who himself is buried so deep in the pocket of Emperor Mercer Domitian of Balaria that he shits lint." Garwin smiled. "The emperor cares about the Almiran princess, which means that—by a long chain of command—I care."

Bershad took one final sip of wine. "So, the nobles finally dug their claws into your back and turned you into another fucking puppet with a title. I'm disappointed."

Garwin bristled. "Let me explain something to both of you. There are no Lysterian barons or counts left in this world. There is no Lysterian king. They are ruled by Balarian viceroys, who have sucked their decaying countryside dry. The only reason Ghalamar gets to keep a scrap of autonomy—and a fraction of our own meager harvests— is because we follow Balarian directives when we receive them.

It's the only way to survive. And I have been directed to close my port against any suspicious foreigners, particularly Almirans."

So, the emperor of Balaria was a few steps ahead of Ashlyn. That was unfortunate.

"You'd ignore a writ of slaying?" Yonmar asked, still struggling to grasp the notion that he hadn't gotten exactly what he wanted. "That's . . . that's simply not done."

Garwin pushed the writ of slaying back across the desk, but he kept Yonmar's document of safe passage. Then he spoke in a flat voice, eyes fixed on Bershad's face.

"In accordance with the laws of Terra, you, Rowan, and your donkey are free to execute this writ of slaying in the eastern province of Cornish. I have no authority to tell you otherwise, and wish you the best of luck on your quest. Anyone else I see traveling with you will be arrested and executed for illegal entrance to Ghalamar. And rest assured, my eyes see a great deal." He glanced at Yonmar. "I suggest you get rid of this idiot, take one last pass at that widow, and then send her back to Papyria or Almira or wherever the fuck she came from."

11

ASHLYN

Almira, Floodhaven

Ashlyn stood over her desk, frowning down at the ledger of numbers while she performed a few more calculations in her head. The ledger contained the latest head counts of wardens sworn to each lord in Almira. It was strange to reduce so many men to simple slashes of ink, but it gave Ashlyn comfort. She knew practically nothing of battle tactics. Would have no idea how to lead men into war. But numbers made sense to her. They could be organized and ordered. Shifted to suit her needs.

Ashlyn had been sending dozens of pigeons every day, asking every lord on the Atlas Coast with whom she had regular contact to provide their latest numbers of available wardens. She trusted them to be accurate. The lords of the Gorgon Valley were a different story—most of them hadn't responded to her inquiries at all, and the ones who did had given vague answers of dubious veracity. Ashlyn had been forced to estimate. She'd given some of the smaller western lords no more than a dozen slashes in their columns. But for Cedar Wallace, she'd assigned eight thousand, which was disturbingly close to the ten thousand wardens Ashlyn had sitting in her own column.

And Ashlyn had a feeling Cedar's number was soft.

Her coronation wouldn't be held for almost two months—the lords of Almira needed time to travel to the capital. But Ashlyn couldn't wait that long to begin raising an army. She had sent word to Elden Grealor telling him about her father's death and urging him to raise as large a host of Deepdale wardens as possible—ideally ten thousand—and return to Floodhaven as soon as possible. She'd also called an emergency meeting of the high lords. They were waiting for her now.

"My queen," Hayden said, stepping into the dressing chamber. "The High Council is waiting in the garden room, as you requested."

Ashlyn had been the power behind the bureaucracy of Almira for almost five years. She wrote decrees and land deeds. Settled property disputes and tax complaints. Set salt and wheat prices. But she had never called a High Council meeting before. Never ordered them to do something for her. It felt like the difference between studying a pile of old dragon bones in the safety of her observatory and chasing a fully grown Needle-Throated Verdun that could turn around at any time and eat her.

Ashlyn knew the high lords would be against her—they resented being ruled by a woman, and her Papyrian blood only made things worse. Given the situation in Mudwall, calling the high lords to Floodhaven was particularly risky. Wallace was already on the cusp of rebellion, and he could unite the others against her if they saw her as weak. But if she established her authority now and made them believe she would be sympathetic to their personal interests, Ashlyn was confident the odds of the lords mounting a rebellion, at least in the short term, would be relatively low.

"I'm ready."

Ashlyn came down from the Queen's Tower and crossed an open bridge that was connected to the upper levels of the King's Tower. She looked to the west while she walked—where the forests of Almira stretched out in all directions—and noticed a Ghost Moth dragon winging a graceful path through the clear blue sky. It was close enough for Ashlyn to make out the twin, almost leaflike tendrils that hung down from either side of its snout and looked similar to a moth's antennae. The tendrils were as long as a grown man's arm and covered in snow-white powder. Ashlyn had a theory that Ghost Moths used their tendrils to track foxes and badgers and other den creatures, but she hadn't been able to prove it yet.

She stopped walking. If her father was still alive, she would have told him to start the High Council meeting without her so she could spend more time watching the Ghost Moth. That wasn't possible anymore. Most likely, it never would be again.

"My queen?" Hayden asked from behind her. "Is something wrong?"

"No." Ashlyn took one last look at the dragon. "Let's go."

Besides the observatory, the garden room was Ashlyn's favorite place in the castle. The floors of three rooms had been gutted so the peach and orange trees could grow freely in the sunlight that poured in from all sides through large rectangular windows. The stone floor of the room was covered with thick loamy soil and planted with grasses and flowers.

The four lords of the High Council were chatting around a large table: Cedar Wallace, Yulnar Brock, Doro Korbon, and Linkon Pommol. They went quiet when she entered.

Cedar Wallace sat upright and alert. Hero of the Balarian Invasion, and bitter rival of the Malgraves ever since. He had a large mole on one cheek, and while age had turned his black hair into a snow-white field, he had maintained the strength of a warrior, unlike the other members of the council. He was also the only member who was armed—a broadsword with an emerald in the pommel was slung over his chair. It wasn't unusual—Cedar and Elden had both brought their weapons to the High Council meetings when her father was alive, too. Ashlyn knew it would make her look weak if she prohibited the blade now that she was in charge.

She wasn't worried. Hayden was armed, too.

Yulnar Brock was next to him. He'd fought bravely in the Balarian Invasion, but in the last thirty years he'd rarely gone more than an hour or two without a meal that could feed a family of peasants for a day, making him grotesquely fat.

Doro Korbon had never been a warrior. He solved his conflicts with taxes, bribes, and well-paid wardens. Ashlyn thought he had an unfortunate number of physical similarities to a beaver.

Linkon was the only high lord who hadn't fought in the Balarian Invasion. He was half the age of every other man in the room, and possessed less than half the money and power. His father, Ronuld, had died two years ago after falling off his horse while drunk. Before getting himself killed, Linkon's father had gambled away the vast majority of his Gorgon Valley lands. Linkon had inherited his father's seat on the High Council, but the debts had come along, too. He had very little actual influence over Almira's fate. There were only two thousand slashes in Linkon's column.

"My queen," Linkon said, rising from his chair and bowing at the hip. "May I offer my deepest and most heartfelt condolences for the loss of your father."

The others grumbled even more hollow platitudes.

"Thank you, high lords. Sit."

They reshuffled themselves and looked at her. Waiting.

"I have called this council meeting because Almira faces difficult times ahead. My father has died. My sister has been kidnapped."

"I hear Mudwall's quite the mess as well," Cedar Wallace said. He thumbed the large mole on his cheek with a dirty, cracked fingernail, and added, "My queen."

"That's true, Lord Wallace," Ashlyn said. "I'm glad you bring that up. It is my understanding that Lord Hrilian, your vassal, is the main instigator of that particular conflict."

"He has a good claim to Mudwall. His great-grandfather ruled it for almost forty years."

"Good claim or bad claim, he is not pursuing it legally. Skirmishing lords are part of life in Almira, but lynching peasants in front of the city walls is unacceptable. If those reports have any truth to them, your vassal has a pair of blue bars in his very near future."

Cedar Wallace cocked his head, but said nothing.

"I want the fighting in the west stopped. I will choose who inherits the incomes of Mudwall."

"Then choose, my queen," Cedar Wallace said.

Ashlyn had been considering that for days. There were no good options. Going back on her father's agreement with Elden Grealor would jeopardize their relationship—and she needed his wardens now more than ever. But publicly choosing him would turn the other high lords against her during the infancy of her reign. Better to lure them into her favor with possibility.

"I will choose the next lord of Mudwall after my coronation," Ashlyn said. "However, there is an army of Malgrave wardens riding to Mudwall as we speak. If they arrive and see crimes being committed, they will bring justice to those who are responsible."

"Is that a threat, my queen?" Cedar asked.

"A promise."

Cedar Wallace stared at her. Ran his tongue over his teeth.

"I'll send a rider, my queen."

"Send a fast one. Next issue, my sister," Ashlyn said before Cedar Wallace could speak again.

Doro Korbon straightened in his chair. "My queen, it was my understanding that Lord Arnish had already been dispatched to bring her back."

Korbon was part of an ancient family that had lorded over a large portion of western Almira for three hundred years. He wasn't as powerful or as aggressive as Cedar Wallace, but the Korbons and Wallaces had been tight-knit allies for generations.

"You understand correctly, Lord Korbon," Ashlyn said. "But Lord Arnish has made no progress in his efforts to retrieve my sister. Diplomacy is not working. And I will not let Balaria's aggression go unchecked. I will have my sister back in Floodhaven before midsummer, even if I have to invade Balaria to do it."

"Invade?" Cedar Wallace asked. "With what army?"

"My army," Ashlyn said. "Every small lord in Almira is coming to Floodhaven for my coronation next month. They have already been instructed to hire as many local wardens as possible and bring them here. In addition, each of you will call half of your forces to the capital."

Originally, Ashlyn had planned to order all their wardens into the city, but then realized that was far too risky. By only summoning half of their armies, Ashlyn's most loyal allies—the Atlas Coast wardens and Grealor's men—would outnumber the Gorgon lords.

"That would be . . . nearly twenty thousand wardens," Doro Korbon said.

"Closer to thirty." Ashlyn had counted the ledger columns very carefully. It wasn't enough soldiers to conquer Balaria, but certainly enough to distract Emperor Mercer until the dragon migration was over. Once it ended, Ashlyn would call the army home. It was a messy solution, but she didn't see any other option if Bershad failed.

"Raising so many of our wardens so quickly will be difficult," said Yulnar Brock. "And expensive."

"I will, of course, show my gratitude for your service," Ashlyn said. "Once your wardens are inside Floodhaven, I will decrease the Crown's taxes and levies on your lands and holdings by ten percent. For five years."

Yulnar Brock licked his lips. "Would a ten-year decrease be possible?" he asked.

"No," Ashlyn said. "But if all of your wardens arrive early, seven years is something I will consider."

"A very generous offer," Brock said. "Very generous indeed. I can live with those terms, my queen."

"As can I!" Doro Korbon piped.

Linkon bowed his head, a smile on his lips.

The lords could choose to spread this extra wealth back into their lands—provide more food, lower taxes, or build better roads for their people. Ashlyn knew they would most likely use it to fill their own private treasuries instead, but the greed of the high lords was a problem for a different day.

Cedar Wallace scoffed. "I don't need your petty tax break, Queen." He leaned forward. "Last I checked, I already won a war with Balaria for the Malgraves. Why should I ship my wardens across Terra just because you can't keep your sister in her bedroom?"

Ashlyn had expected this from him.

"If a more agreeable tax rate does not move you, Lord Wallace, perhaps the spoils of war will. Should you distinguish yourself as you did during the Balarian Invasion, you could wind up controlling a large portion of Balaria in addition to the western reaches of Almira."

Ashlyn would never actually allow that to happen, but she could see the possibility of it snatch Wallace's interest. He kept his dark eyes fixed on her for a few long, tense moments. Ashlyn could feel Hayden shift behind her.

Linkon cleared his throat. "Raising an army is one thing," he said in a soft voice. "But soldiers cannot walk on water. We don't have nearly enough ships to transport that many wardens across Terra."

"True," Ashlyn said. "But Papyria does. I have already called their fleet of warships down from Half-Moon Bay."

"The empress agreed to send her fleet?" Linkon asked, surprised. "I'd thought the Papyrian alliance chilled to the point of breaking."

"You thought wrong. Seventy-five Papyrian warships will depart for Almira within the next moon's turn."

Ashlyn let that sink in. She could tell that an invasion of Balaria was the last thing the high lords expected her to do as a newly made queen in the dawn of her reign.

"War, then," Linkon Pommol said, shrugging and reaching across the table toward a bowl of fruit. "Something to look forward to, at least. These council meetings were getting dull."

"Oh, are you planning to get up on a horse and do some actual fighting?" Cedar Wallace asked, crossing his arms. "Not like you have many wardens to hide behind."

"What my wardens lack in numbers, they make up for in constitution," Linkon said.

"Constitution for sucking cock, maybe." Cedar Wallace cracked a grim smile.

"You make jokes," Ashlyn said. "But Linkon has pledged his soldiers to the war effort. You hesitate and make up excuses. To me, he's the braver man in this room."

It was a cheap shot—and not a long-term strategy for controlling Wallace—but Ashlyn needed to solve her problems one moment at a time. If tax breaks and war spoils didn't move Wallace, pride might.

Cedar Wallace tightened his jaw and glanced between Ashlyn and Linkon a few times. Eventually, he nodded.

"I was just having some fun. Don't worry, Queen, I'll help raise your little army."

"Good," Ashlyn said. She rose from her chair. "I suggest that all of you begin sending messages back home. My coronation is not far away."

————

Linkon Pommol was waiting in the hallway when Ashlyn left the garden. He held his arm out to escort her. Hayden trailed them—five steps behind, as always.

"You've started your reign quite aggressively, my queen," Linkon said in his light voice.

"You disagree with my orders?" Ashlyn asked.

"I wouldn't dare. But for me, calling such a large portion of my wardens to Floodhaven is no small task. As you know, I can only afford to keep two thousand wardens under my employ at any given time."

"I do know that."

"So my little sliver of the Gorgon Valley will be left quite vulnerable."

"Perhaps you should have tried to curb your father's gambling habits," Ashlyn said.

"Perhaps," Linkon said. "Anyway, as a method of control, forcing every member of the High Council to divide their army in half is brilliant. Wallace and Korbon can't cause nearly as much trouble this way."

That was only true if Ashlyn was able to fill Floodhaven with enough loyal wardens from the Atlas Coast before the Gorgon wardens arrived, of course. Otherwise, Ashlyn could wind up creating a rebellion within her own city. She had to take that risk. And geography was on her side, at least—her most loyal wardens were far closer to the capital than Wallace's men.

"And rescuing Kira from the clutches of Balaria must obviously be a priority," Linkon continued. "Lest it be known across the realm of Terra that Ashlyn Malgrave can't protect her own kin."

They walked a few dozen paces in silence.

"Do you have business with me of which I'm unaware, Linkon?" Ashlyn asked when the young lord made no move to alter his course away from her offices. "I have work to do."

"I was hoping we might discuss a certain opportunity in private. Your observatory, perhaps? It's such a unique room, I'd love to see it again."

"Very well," Ashlyn said. They passed the long walk through chambers and up winding stairwells in awkward silence. Servants had cleaned the observatory while she was away—stacking everything in neat piles and throwing a sheet over her alchemy station in the corner. Her dragon sketches, however, remained pinned on the wall.

"What do you want, Linkon?" Ashlyn said, sitting back into her familiar chair and motioning for Linkon to sit as well.

Linkon studied the drawings that were tacked to the eastern wall. "These are quite beautiful, my queen. I've never seen their equal."

Ashlyn winced. She'd have to ask her servants to get rid of those. The queen of Almira couldn't flaunt dragon illustrations in front of visitors.

"These are interesting as well," Linkon said, pointing to three smaller maps of Almira. There were pins scattered across the geography, each marking the current location of a pigeon. Some were in cities, others in remote villages or isolated mills. Colored strings connected them all back to Floodhaven. "What are these used for?"

"Those are my pigeon routes," Ashlyn said, eager to move the conversation away from her dragon sketches. "So I can tell which lines of communication are currently open."

"You have birds who can reach all of these areas?" Linkon said, eyes fixed on the maps as if he was trying to memorize them.

"Falcons are always a problem," Ashlyn said. "But yes."

"I had no idea you'd expanded your reach so dramatically. Very impressive."

That map only tracked her Almiran communication lines. She had another that was entirely dedicated to her Papyrian birds. She kept most of those birds in the castle dovecote, but there was currently a score of Papyria-trained birds scattered along the northern rim of the Dainwood. Ashlyn had moved them south several months ago so she could quickly communicate with Noko while traveling the Gorgon and surveying River Lurker populations. She kept meaning to send a few sentinels to collect them, but it had been a long time since she had riders to spare.

But Linkon did not need to know any of this.

"Lord Linkon, I don't believe that you walked all this way to compliment my drawings or my pigeon routes."

Linkon continued looking at the maps for another moment, then took a seat across from her.

"You are correct, my queen. I am here to acknowledge a struggle we both share. The other high lords think of me as a weakling child," Linkon explained. "A green boy who has never fought in a war or cut a man's head off in a duel over grazing rights. A silly way to measure a lord's value in my opinion, but alas, this is the world we live in. It is not unlike the way they think of you." He put his palms up in the air. "No offense intended, my queen."

"I'm aware of the High Council's perspective. What's your point?"

"Their scorn toward me is an advantage. They drop their guard around me—speak more freely of their personal interests. Please, allow me to be your eyes and ears in the High Council when you are not present. Perhaps I can dig up some useful information that can be used to bring Cedar Wallace and his western lackeys under tighter control."

Ashlyn leaned back in her chair. "And what would you expect in return, Lord Linkon?"

"A gift to the queen doesn't require reciprocation, of course," he said. "But if you were in a generous mood, awarding me Mudwall would be . . . very much appreciated. I promise that you'll approve of the way I treat the land."

Ashlyn raised an eyebrow. "Don't make me play a guessing game with you, Linkon."

Linkon smiled. "My lack of military experience is not the only way that I am different from the other lords of the High Council. Unlike them, I take great interest in your studies of nature. And more specifically, of dragons. If I were awarded Mudwall, I would be willing to sign a contract promising to only harvest sick or aging dragons from the countryside, just as you do for your private research. If my information is correct, the surrounding area is populated by a large number of River Lurkers—a very important aspect of the region. Almira must have healthy rivers, after all."

"How did you come by that information?"

"Like I said, Queen, I take great interest in your studies. Most of your sketches and folios aren't seen by anyone except your personal stewards and the eccentric court alchemists, but I have been making quite frequent visits to the archives. I think you'll find that I am by far the most open-minded member of the High Council." He leaned closer and lowered his voice. "I could be a great ally to you, if you allow me to help."

"And here I assumed that you already were a great ally to me."

"Of course, my queen. And once again, I am not like the other high lords."

"I won't argue with you there," Ashlyn said.

Linkon stood up. "I meant to ask, has there been new information discovered about that fire in the eastern tower?"

"It was a fire. What more were you hoping to learn?"

"A very strange fire. I've never seen stones melt like that. There must have been something quite flammable in there." Linkon looked around the room, eyes rolling over the thin sheet that covered her alchemy station. "There have been a lot of strange events these past few months, in fact."

Ashlyn didn't say anything.

"The Balarians pop free of their shroud and visit with Almiran royalty," Linkon continued. "A strange fire in the eastern tower melts stone like candle wax. A princess disappears. And then a famous dragonslayer is brought to the capital for the first time in fourteen years. The giddy scholar in me can't help but feel like we are on the precipice of some great event."

Her father had never paid Linkon much attention—he had never trusted the younger generation of Almiran lords, who hadn't fought in the Balarian Invasion—but very little slipped past the young lord.

"As I'm sure you've heard, Bershad took a ship to Ghalamar under a request from the baron of Cornish. There's nothing strange about a dragonslayer going to kill a dragon."

"Nothing strange about a dragonslayer being called to the capital?" Linkon raised an eyebrow. "By that logic, there's nothing strange about that tower fire, either."

"There you have it, nothing strange at all. No precipice in sight." She turned to her papers. "I'm very busy, Linkon. I will see you at the next High Council meeting."

Linkon gave a little nod. "Until next time, Queen Ashlyn." He threw one final smile at her. "That has a nice ring, don't you think?"

"I don't spend much time thinking about how my name sounds. Good-bye, Linkon."

––––––––

Ashlyn released a long breath when Linkon was gone. Rolled her shoulders in a few circles. Linkon was more subtle than the other high lords, but he wanted the same things. Power and money. Silas would have hated him.

"You did well, my queen," Hayden said.

"Well enough for now," Ashlyn said.

"They agreed to bring their wardens to Floodhaven. That is what you wanted, yes?"

"Agreeing to me in a room is one thing, delivering thousands of wardens to Floodhaven is quite another. I think Cedar Wallace is going to be a problem."

"That man is a snake," Hayden agreed.

"Everyone on the High Council is a snake. Wallace just doesn't bother disguising it."

"I could kill them for you," Hayden said, keeping her face unreadable. "Just blink your eyes twice, and I'll slit their throats tonight. We could replace them all with women."

Ashlyn couldn't help but smile, but she made sure not to blink, just in case Hayden was being serious.

"Very well," Hayden said after a moment. "But my offer still stands." Hayden's face broke into a rare smile of her own.

Ashlyn reached for the pitcher of wine on her desk and poured. If she drank too much, her mind would turn foggy and she wouldn't get a bit of work done tonight. But a single glass helped loosen her thoughts after a long day.

"I didn't think being a queen would feel like this," she said.

"What did you expect?"

"I'm not sure, exactly. More freedom. More choices. But the past has decided so much for me."

"A dependency on the past is something that queens, peasants, and everyone in between all share. The only thing you can do is work to create more options in the future."

"That's true. More widows in Floodhaven should help."

"My queen?"

Ashlyn couldn't help but smile.

"Empress Okinu has agreed to send three hundred of your sisters to Almira, along with the ships."

"Getting that many widows from the empress couldn't have been easy."

"It wasn't."

Widows were far more precious than ships. There were only a few thousand of them in Papyria at any given time, and it took eighteen years to train one, whereas a ship was built in a few months. The larger obstacle, however, was the breaking of tradition. Ashlyn's royal Papyrian blood earned her protection by Hayden, but that was it. The only Papyrian in the world who was protected by more than a single widow was the empress herself, who famously filled every shadow in her palace with a black-armored guardian.

Offering so many widows to Ashlyn—and sending them out of Papyria—was an unprecedented gesture.

"When my father was alive, it would have been impossible," Ashlyn continued. "But I am the queen of Almira now. This is what the empress wanted when she shipped her sister across the sea to marry Hertzog Malgrave—for a half-breed to sit on the throne of Almira.

My work to repair Almira and Papyria's relationship is finally paying dividends."

"Agreed," Hayden said. She lingered in the room, resting her hand on the hilt of the short sword on her hip and looking uncomfortable.

"Is there something else?" Ashlyn asked.

"There is, my queen." Hayden hesitated. "I'm hoping you'll stop lying to me about what happened in the eastern tower. If there's a danger, I need to know about it."

"Hayden, as I told Linkon—"

"Please, Ashlyn. Do not insult me with the same lie you gave that soft-palmed lord. I know there is more." She stepped farther into the room. "Your mother was a woman of secrets, too. Even before she fell in love with Leon Bershad, I watched her being eaten away by the feelings she locked inside of herself. I never asked her to share them with me, though I often wanted to. I will not make the same mistake with you, Ashlyn. I can do more than protect you from knives and swords."

"You don't talk about my mother very often," Ashlyn said.

"Neither do you."

Ashlyn paused. She couldn't carry her secret alone forever, and Hayden was the only person in Floodhaven she truly trusted.

"I'll try to explain." She began unwinding the dragon thread from her wrist. "Do you remember the last Ghost Moth that we rode out to see? The female."

"Yes, the one that fell from the sky. That was over a year ago."

"One year and three months. When I dissected her body, I found this barbed nerve string running down her spine. I'd never seen something like it before. I weighed and measured it, along with all her other organs. But unlike her heart and lungs and stomach, this string didn't necrify. So I kept it. Tried to figure out what it was. First, I went to the archives to search for more information. I'd already read everything down there about dragons, most of which is focused on ways to kill them. But there have been a few stewards and alchemists over the generations who took an interest in the great lizards' anatomy. Dissections. Drawings. That kind of thing. It was possible I'd missed something hidden within their research."

"And?"

"Nothing," Ashlyn said. "No mention of an errant nerve string or any kind of irregularity along the spine. So I expanded my search."

She took a breath.

"While there isn't very much useful information about dragons in the archives, there are hundreds of records of men and women accused of witchcraft, or consorting with demons. Their crimes and victims. The alleged spells." She paused. "The methods and tools of their demoncraft."

"Ashlyn . . ." Hayden said.

"I wasn't looking for an actual spell," Ashlyn said. "I was just looking for some mention of the nerve string. There was nothing recent, but two hundred years ago a goat herder on the northern edge of the Atlas Coast was executed for performing blood magic with a translucent thread she claimed originated in the body of a Ghost Moth. One hundred years before that, a shaman from the west was caught stealing children from nearby villages and sacrificing them beneath a tree-sized totem in the woods. After the wardens killed him, they noted in a brief report to their small lord that there was an odd, clear rope affixed to the altar where he'd been murdering the children.

"And lastly, deep in the annals of an obscure Gorgon Valley clan, a warlord's wife was put to death for accusations of demoncraft. It was five hundred years ago, so that wasn't an uncommon occurrence, but the details stood out. She was accused of calling down storms on passing riverboats with a blood-soaked rope made of dragon-skin that never went to rot."

Hayden absorbed all of this. "The stories do share a certain similarity."

"Yes." Ashlyn nodded. "And in all cases, blood was mentioned. But when I drew blood from myself and put it on the thread, nothing happened. So I spent weeks treating the dragon thread with different combinations. I started with animal blood—one species at a time, then mixed together. When that didn't work, I tried different amounts mixed at different temperatures. I pulled the blood from different veins in my body. Mixed it with other animals. Other people, too, which wasn't easy to do in secret. I even tried my moon's blood when the time came. Eventually, I realized there must be a missing element. Something to start the reaction.

"I began with alchemy ingredients, both healing and venomous. When those didn't work, I tried adding rare herbs that were once thought to contain magical properties, thinking there might be a correlation. Alder. Foxglove. I went through weeks of trial and error, watching for changes in the thread. Nothing worked, so I tried another approach. Diet."

"My queen?"

"Ghost Moths mostly eat medium-sized mammals," Ashlyn explained. "Fox. Badger. The occasional bear if the dragon is large enough. If an external element triggered a reaction, it made sense for the source to originate from their food. So, I started reducing animal organs and testing them as reagents. Don't ask me how long it took to arrive here, but I eventually tried the liver of a fox who'd prowled the wilds of the Dainwood for his entire life. After that, things happened very quickly." She tightened her fist around the base of the thread. "You should step back, Hayden."

Ashlyn snapped her hand down the length of the thread fast enough so the small barbs broke skin. A blue crackle of light sprang from the thread and transferred to Ashlyn's fist. She held her arm up, palm facing Hayden, so the widow could see the charged tendrils snapping between her fingers as if a miniature storm raged in her hand.

"Black skies." Hayden whispered the Papyrian curse with her eyes fixed on Ashlyn's hand.

Ashlyn smiled. "All my life—even as a girl—I've mocked the rituals and totems to which Almirans cling. I've discounted their bone charms and muttered incantations as superstition and foolishness. But I realize now they were scratching at the surface of a much larger system—one that I hadn't noticed, despite how carefully I'd been watching. There is a kind of magic in this world. I believe that now. It runs down the spines of dragons and connects to the animals and rivers and earth." She paused, rolling the lightning across her fingers. "And, now, to me. The only way to activate the thread is with my blood. Believe me, I checked."

Hayden frowned. "But that isn't strong enough to melt a tower."

"No," Ashlyn said, shaking her hand so the lightning dissipated to nothing. "Adding more fox tissue has no effect. And more of my blood creates more tendrils, but they become no stronger. This is where the witches and shamans of the past stopped—with a spark and an incomplete understanding of what they'd discovered. But once I learned how to activate the string, I knew there was more. That's when I moved to the eastern tower. I'd started the reaction, but I hadn't completed it. So I spent months trying every permutation of animal organ and blood mixture I could conceive of in an attempt to create a stronger reaction. I must have fifty notebooks filled from the work. Nothing. And then . . ." Ashlyn trailed off. Cracked two knuckles on her left hand and stared at them afterward.

"Ashlyn?" Hayden asked when she stayed quiet.

"Emperor Mercer, of all people, is the one who made me consider warren moss again," Ashlyn continued. "I'd obviously tried the warren mosses to activate the cord, but when they didn't work, I wrote them off. That was a mistake, since I was now working on a different aspect of the reaction. During his visit, when Mercer proposed culling the dragons of the Dainwood, I pretended to be interested in the idea to keep him talking. I knew he had the means to extend the longevity of the dragon oil that he burned, but I didn't know the method. When Mercer saw an opening to Almiran warrens, he became far more forthcoming with me. Showed me the formula for refined dragon oil." Ashlyn smiled. "I doubt he expected me to understand it at a quick glance, but I did. He's using warren moss. Mostly Spartania and Crimson Tower, since they're the most common. He combines the moss with several other reagents prepared in a specific order and temperature. Once I saw the formula, the principles of the reaction were obvious. And it was only logical that warren moss would react with the only other part of a dragon's body that doesn't necrify besides their oil."

"The dragon thread."

"Yes. It just needed to be activated first. I knew I should wait until the Balarians left before trying it." She met Hayden's eyes. "But I'd been working on the thread for more than a year and didn't have anything to show for it besides a spark in my palm, and I felt foolish for missing something so obvious. So when we finished our negotiations for the day, I went to my personal alchemy stores. I didn't have any Spartania or Crimson Tower on hand. But I always keep a vial of Gods Moss. So I used it."

"That was the night the tower exploded?"

Ashlyn nodded. "Mercer had been mixing a quart of Spartania moss per barrel of dragon oil. I knew Gods Moss was more potent, so I only used a pinch. Just one pinch of Gods Moss added to a shallow tray. I mixed in the other reagents according to his formula, put it over a low heat, and watched. Nothing. So I drew a vial of my blood and began titrating it onto the tray, one drop at a time. I was waiting for a reaction when a steward showed up in the eastern tower, saying that Emperor Mercer was in a lower chamber and wanted to see me." Ashlyn sighed. "At the time, I'd thought it was an unlucky coincidence, but not anymore. Mercer was baiting me into revealing my hand in the same way that I was baiting him. I found out later that he'd sent one of his envoys snooping around the eastern tower on several occasions before that night. That's why he gave me the formula. He knew I'd try something, and he wanted to see what it was.

"Everything would have been fine if I'd stopped the titration. But he caught me by surprise. I left the thread in the basin and locked the laboratory. Told one of my wardens to guard the door and let nobody inside. Mercer was waiting in a chamber one floor below. A moment after I entered the room, we heard the explosion. It sounded like a bolt of lightning. When I got back to the tower, the door to the laboratory was gone. And inside, there was a power unlike anything I have ever seen. The stones were glowing blue—lightning sparked across the room in vaulting arcs. The rocks melted like candle wax. I was so excited, so amazed at my discovery, that I didn't realize the warden guarding the room had been destroyed along with the door. His body was reduced to black cinders and sprayed against the outer hallway."

Ashlyn looked down at her hands.

"Did the emperor see inside?" Hayden asked.

"Yes. I can still remember the hungry look in his eyes as he watched the reaction. I knew that I needed to get rid of him as quickly as possible, before he saw the source, so I went into screaming hysterics until he ran down the tower for help. When he was gone, I yanked the dragon thread out of the tray, which stopped the reaction. When Mercer returned with help, it just looked like a bad fire. I lost track of Emperor Mercer in the confusion, and by the time things calmed down, he'd left Floodhaven."

"And Kira with him."

Ashlyn nodded. She wrapped the thread tightly around her wrist and pulled her sleeve down. "Mercer might not understand exactly what I did, but he knows it's powerful."

"You should have told me earlier," Hayden said. "This gives the emperor enough cause to want you dead."

"I doubt that," Ashlyn said. "He wants the power for himself. If he kills me, the secret is lost. That's why he kidnapped Kira—to ransom her in exchange for the thread. Or the thread's secret, at least."

"But he hasn't asked for it yet."

"No. I'm not sure why. Perhaps he's waiting until rumors of Kira's kidnapping have spread and I've become desperate."

Hayden chewed on that. "Three hundred widows is enough to turn this tower into a fortress, at least." She touched the back of her bun. It was the only nervous tick Hayden possessed, and something as unsettling as the thread's power was the only kind of thing that could bring it out. "Do you have any more Gods Moss with you?"

"I keep a vial locked in that chest over there." Ashlyn pointed to her alchemy station in the corner of the room. "I've already treated it with the necessary reagents, but I can't control the thread's power yet. Even the small tendrils of lightning get away from me half the time. If I used it again, I could melt another tower. Turn my legs to cinders. Or kill everyone in the castle."

"Then I suggest you practice. You have discovered something extraordinary, my queen. A magic that will move the tides of the world. You cannot live in fear of it."

Ashlyn looked at the thread.

"I know."

––––––––––

Ashlyn stayed up late into the night, checking the math in her ledger and writing letters that would be lashed to pigeon legs the next day. It was a few hours before dawn when she sealed the last message and set it aside. She would bring them to Godfrey herself in the morning. That was the only way to be sure they weren't read by anyone else before taking flight.

Ashlyn tamped out the candles on her desk and moved to the small bedroom that was attached to the observatory. She preferred the chamber's simple solitude to the lavish apartments below.

She took a few deep breaths, enjoying the smell of the extinguished candles—piney and fresh like the depths of a forest. Ashlyn sat on the edge of the bed and unwound the dragon thread from her wrist. Hayden was right—she needed to be ready to use it if necessary. Behind a secretly dispatched dragonslayer, armies of wardens, and ships of Papyrian cedar, the thread was her last resort. She would sail to Balaria herself with a barrel of Gods Moss if that was what it took to stop Emperor Mercer's cull.

Ashlyn stretched her neck and dug her thumb-knife across her palm, pressing just deep enough to draw a teardrop of blood. She stroked the thread three times so the lightning crackled and wrapped around her fingers, then allowed the bolts to cascade up her arm and across her shoulders. She took another deep breath, which pulled the current beneath her skin, where she could feel it welling inside of her like a storm. It made her lungs hot and her pulse quicken. She released her breath—which allowed the lightning to seep from the surface of her skin—but kept the current close to her chest and head like a cowl. There was a balance to commanding the power—not unlike running across a fallen log that had bridged a river. If you kept an equilibrium, crossing was simple. If you teetered, you fell into the torrent below.

She continued breathing in and out, allowing the lightning to expand and contract around and inside of her body, careful to rein it back anytime it strayed from her command. If Ashlyn ever had to combine the thread with Gods Moss again, she knew that control would be extremely difficult. She remembered the way the lightning had arced across the walls, melted stone and metal as if they were wax. Those bolts would kill her if she didn't practice with the weaker current first.

She closed her eyes. Tried to steady her heart rate and calm her mind. Then she started to count her breaths. In and out. Anytime she lost control of the lightning's ebb and flow, she started her count at zero.

After dozens of tries, Ashlyn reached a count of one thousand breaths. She opened her eyes, then opened her palm to face the wall and began guiding the lightning back into her fingers. It was a difficult and strange process—almost as if she were goading the lightning to follow the currents of her bloodstream to a specific point on her body. Once it was all corralled in her fingers again, she took careful aim at the wall. One finger at a time, she fired a miniature bolt at the connecting mortar of the stones. Each snap of lightning left a scorch mark the size of a cat's eye. She hit her target three out of five attempts. Not good enough, but getting better.

She wondered what the high lords would do if they saw lightning cascading from her fist. Plenty of Almirans already believed she was a witch who made pacts with demons. They were closer to the truth than they realized.

She cracked her knuckles, then activated the thread again. It was too late to get much sleep. Might as well practice until dawn.

12

BERSHAD

Ghalamar, Town of Argel

Bershad and Yonmar were marched back to the docks by Adelon and another soldier. The town was empty except for a few patrolling soldiers—the citizens of Argel were still down by the river, washing their sins away.

Felgor was pissing off the dock when they returned to the *Luminata*. He gave them a smile and wave, but Adelon shoved him roughly back onto the ship.

"Hey, easy!" Felgor yelped, adjusting his pants as he stumbled onto the deck.

Adelon grunted, then motioned for Bershad and Yonmar to get aboard, too.

"Trouble in town?" Rowan asked from his spot on the ship.

"Trouble with the baron. You and I are free to move inland, but they are ordered to turn around and head home," Bershad said, motioning to Yonmar, Felgor, and Vera. "Grealor's papers were about as useful as a pile of the donkey's shit."

"Where does that leave us?" Vera asked.

"Fucked, I'd say," Rowan grunted.

Adelon leaned against a dock post and began eating an apple. When he saw the entire group glaring at him, he stopped chewing.

"I'm to wait until your mast is a toothpick on the sea," he said, sucking a piece of apple from between two of his teeth. "Baron's orders."

Bershad sighed. They could split up here and reconnect in secret along the foothills—he'd shown Vera where the entrance to the pass was on a map of Ghalamar. But the baron of Argel would probably have him followed all the way to Cornish and arrest him if he strayed from the main road. The plan had gone to shit in an impressively short period of time.

"Tide's waiting," the other soldier added.

Bershad was about to take everyone down into the hold of the ship—where they could figure out another plan—when an old and familiar sensation hummed along his bones like the pulse of a secret drum. He didn't get the feeling very often, but it always meant the same thing.

Bershad turned to Rowan. "Let's have the dagger."

Rowan pulled the knife belt from a canvas sack and tossed it to Bershad.

"Impressive-looking weapon," Adelon said through a mouthful of apple. "That a dragontooth?"

"That's right," Bershad said. "Made it from the seventh lizard I killed." Adelon nodded absently. Bershad took a step closer. "It'll cut through chain mail or steel as easy as a cleaver through tenderloin." Bershad glanced around the dock. Empty.

"Good for the dagger," Adelon said, straightening up a bit as Bershad got closer.

"Only problem is the length. Can't reforge a tooth, so you're stuck with this range." Bershad stepped closer, then spoke a little softer, as if he had a secret just for Adelon. "So you have to get real close before you can use it."

Adelon frowned and let his mouth hang open, revealing a bite of chewed apple rind. His eyes darted to the handle of Bershad's dagger. He tightened his grip on the ash spear.

"Hey now," Adelon started to say, "I said you're free to—"

Bershad drew the dagger and cleaved the top of Adelon's head off, slicing just above his eyebrows. Adelon's steel cap flew through the air—a billowing ribbon of blond hair still attached—and splashed into the water. Disappeared into the murky blue.

Adelon's eyes turned into two huge, white orbs of surprise. Apple chunks dropped out of his slackened mouth. Bershad slammed his open palm into Adelon's chest, sending the body into the water behind the skull. There were a few ripples, and then nothing. It was the first man Bershad had killed in fourteen years.

Vera drew both of her long daggers before anyone else reacted. She stabbed the other watchman in the neck with one dagger while slipping the other blade between his chest and back-plate, directly into his heart. He was dead before he hit the dock.

Bershad moved over to Alfonso and started checking his saddle-bags, looking for his horn and armor. "We need to get out of this city in the next five minutes."

"You've killed us all," Torian growled. "We'll all bite down on seashells for this." He spat. "Bastard!"

"Don't go grabbing a shell just yet," Bershad said. "You'll be fine if you set sail right now."

"You'll be dead before you reach the gates of the city," Torian said. "And I'll be sunk by a Ghalamarian warship before I'm half-way across the Soul Sea."

"There will be no warships summoned today," Bershad said.

"Why not?"

Bershad felt the tremor in his bones again—stronger this time—and looked toward the mountains in the east. Pointed. A massive dragon swooped down along a cliff and headed toward the city. Its head was colored deep red where the black scales receded and exposed a cap of crimson bone. "Because that Red Skull is about to attack Argel."

"Black skies," Torian muttered, backing up onto the *Luminata*.

"Here," Rowan said, yanking Bershad's breastplate out of a wooden crate and passing it to him.

"It'll head for the keep," Bershad said, pulling the breastplate on and cinching it tight. "If we're going to get out of Argel, it needs to be right now." Bershad took his jaguar mask from Rowan and slipped it over his face. Felt the familiar pressure against his cheeks.

Vera grabbed a pouch full of shot for her sling and tied a long rope around Felgor's wrists. She wrapped the other end around her wrist as if it was a leash for a dog.

"What are you doing?" Felgor asked.

"Keeping you within reach, Balarian."

Yonmar was frozen in place, watching everyone else prepare to run through the city.

"Grab that pack," Rowan growled at him. "Food's in there."

Yonmar picked it up, struggling with the uneven weight. Bershad found his horn buried in the bottom of the crate and slung it over his shoulder. Picked up a spear and checked the point. When he turned around, everyone was looking at him.

"Follow me," he said, his voice muffled by the mask.

———

The Red Skull attacked Argel as they were moving through the main square. The dragon was almost twice as large as the one strung to the keep. Definitely a female. She tore out a large chunk of city wall and sent it careening into the keep, demolishing the upper section of the tower. When the soldiers saw the breed, half of them dropped their weapons and ran.

"I warned those bastards not to hang a fucking Red Skull," Bershad muttered as the beast hammered its tail into the roof of a stable and sprayed shingles across the square in an explosion of sharpened chaff.

Bershad had slain two Red Skulls before, but even in the morning they were bastards. One had nearly torn his head off and the other had broken every bone in his foot. At full strength, they were flying atrocities. Not only did this lizard have a body full of hot blood, but she'd come down here with revenge on her mind. If the dragon spotted the townspeople down by the river, she'd kill every last one of them.

The soldiers in the town garrison who hadn't run away were preparing the defense—armored men poured out of the barracks on the far side of the square. They carried crossbows and halberds. Sergeants were shouting and waving men into positions with good cover. It was an organized effort, but that didn't improve their odds much.

"This way," Bershad grunted, skirting the far wall of the square so they were as far away from the fight as possible. The Red Skull was surrounded by soldiers who were winding crossbows as fast as they could.

"Loose!" one of them screamed. "Shoot the fucking thing!"

The clatter of crossbow bolts hitting the dragon's scales sounded like a hailstorm. The dragon screamed and broke the stone roof of a blacksmith's forge with a violent swipe of her claw. A ruined soldier's body landed a few strides from Bershad, his head twisted so violently that his spine had popped out the back of his mail shirt.

"Make sure Alfonso doesn't step on that," Bershad said over his shoulder. He didn't want the donkey hurting his ankle.

After they cleared the square, they rushed down an empty avenue toward the eastern gate of the city. The sounds of violence grew faint behind them. The gate was about twenty strides high—a massive door painted white and set in a stone arch made from red brick. Yonmar saw the path to freedom was clear, dropped the bag of food, and broke into a flat-out run.

"Idiot," Bershad muttered.

When Yonmar was ten strides from the gate, the Red Skull landed on top of it, cracking the brick arch. Her claws dug into the alabaster wood of the gate for support. Countless crossbow bolts stuck out of her armored hide like thorns.

"Fuck!" Yonmar cried, trying to turn around but falling on his ass instead. He started to scuttle backward, but froze when the dragon howled at him—spreading her wings and hunching forward in an attack posture.

Alfonso twitched with fear, then shat all over the road. Rowan cursed and strained to keep the donkey from bolting. Vera dropped the rope tied around Felgor's wrists and rushed forward in a low crouch. She reached Yonmar just as the dragon lurched forward, jaws open wide. At a full run, she grabbed Yonmar by the shoulders and yanked him to the left, barely getting them both clear of the Red Skull's teeth. After missing her prey, the dragon rose high over the walls, heading back toward the keep.

Felgor's eyes were darting between Vera and a narrow alley to his right. Bershad walked over and clamped a fist on the Balarian's shoulder.

"You're not skipping out on us that easily," Bershad growled.

Felgor glanced at the alley one last time, then nodded. "Can't blame a guy for giving it some thought though, can you?"

"Fucking hell," Yonmar gasped. "That was . . . that was . . ."

"There's no time," Vera said, grabbing Felgor's rope again. "We have to keep moving."

Outside the gate, there was a river to their right and steep mountains to the left. Straight ahead, a wide road made from crushed seashells cut through a long open meadow that turned to thick forest. "We need to reach those cottonwoods," Bershad said. "Then we'll use the forest's cover to reach the pass."

Nobody wasted any time getting down the road. When they were about halfway between the gate and the tree line, Alfonso and Rowan started lagging behind. Bershad stopped to wait for them, checking the sky for the dragon. She was still circling around the keep and shrieking every few minutes.

"He's about tapped," Rowan said, trying to pull the beast of burden along.

"Leave the animal and let's go!" Yonmar hissed.

Bershad grabbed Yonmar by the front of his shirt and yanked him close.

"Listen to me very carefully, Grealor. Hertzog and your father can't protect you out here. And I don't care if you've got a flying fucking carpet that'll spirit us across the Balarian border, I will cut your lungs out of your chest if you threaten my donkey again."

"He's slowing us down."

"So are you," Bershad said. Then he moved toward Alfonso and cut the heaviest pack of equipment off his back. "Now let's keep moving."

"Uh, guys?" Felgor said, pointing toward the river.

Hundreds of Argellians were huddled against the riverbank, trying and failing to stay out of sight.

"They need to run," Bershad said. "They should have been running this entire time."

"Well," Felgor said, "they're not."

Bershad looked back at the dragon. She was still circling the keep, but her arcs were getting wider and wider. It was only a matter of time before the Red Skull fanned out far enough to see hundreds of helpless humans trapped against a riverbank.

"Shit," he muttered.

"What do we do?" Vera asked Bershad.

Bershad rolled the spear across his fingers a few times. The dragon veered to the south and swooped down by the river, screaming overtop the heads of the townspeople. He could hear them shouting and pleading for mercy.

"You four head for the trees," Bershad said, lifting the horn off his shoulder. "I'll catch up."

"Silas," Rowan started to say. "It's the middle of the fucking day."

"Yeah. Vera, you know where the entrance to the pass is. I'll meet you there."

"What if you—"

"Then you'll just have to rescue Kira without me," Bershad said.

"Get her back to Almira and tell Ashlyn I tried to keep my promise as best I could. Now go!"

Bershad headed back toward the city before anyone could argue further. The dragon kept circling as he moved, but didn't attack. If Bershad was lucky, she'd taken a few bad wounds and exhausted herself. If not, he was a dead man.

When Bershad was in range, he stopped and slipped his hand behind his breastplate to make sure his seashell was there. Then he raised his mask and put the horn up to his lips. There was no risk of enraging the Red Skull any more than she already was, so Bershad blew as long and loud as he could. When his lungs were out of air, he heaved in a new breath and did it again. And again. And again. On the fifth call, the Red Skull snapped her head around to find the source of the horn.

"That's right," Bershad whispered, lowering the mask again. "I'm the one making all the noise in your head."

The dragon bolted upward like a loosed arrow, so high she turned into a black dot in the sky. Bershad found a good bit of ground and the right grip of his spear. The dragon dove.

"That's it," Bershad whispered. His heart pounded behind his eyes. His stomach churned with fear. "Come and get me."

The Red Skull careened toward the earth. Bershad could see every scale on her face. Hear the tendons of her jaws strain as her mouth stretched open. He could have named each one of her dagger-length teeth. He crouched and aimed his spear at the dragon's right eye, but it was too small of a target. Moving too fast. At the last moment, Bershad saw a long, bloody gash on the left side of her neck. The scales had been scraped off, exposing soft, vulnerable flesh below. He shifted his aim, crouched a little lower.

When the Red Skull's shadow turned his world black, Bershad dove left. Felt the earth jerk and rumble from the dragon's impact. Heard the snap of bone and sinew as she plowed into the ground. Then silence. Bershad couldn't see anything. His mask had gotten twisted when he fell. He pulled it off and wiped the sweat from his face. Tried to get his bearings.

The Red Skull was dead. Bershad's spear was buried in her neck, although he wasn't sure that was what had killed her. She hadn't slowed down at all—didn't try to snatch him up in her jaws. She'd either been too furious to think clearly, or too tired to care. Luck was the only reason Bershad was still breathing. He walked over to the dragon's head and touched her forehead.

"Sorry, girl."

Bershad knew he'd done the right thing. The dragon would have killed hundreds of people. Women. Children. Everyone. But having a good reason to do something terrible doesn't change the way it feels while you're doing it.

———————

Bershad picked up Alfonso's tracks in the forest and found the others waiting for him by a small creek. It looked like Felgor had just finished throwing up.

"Dragon's dead," Bershad said. He turned to Alfonso. "How is he?"

"Tired," Rowan said, rubbing the donkey's muzzle. "Scared."

"Makes two of us," Felgor said. "Never seen a dragon before. That was quite a first impression."

"You've never seen a dragon?" Yonmar asked. "How is that possible?"

"I grew up in Burz-al-dun." Felgor shrugged. "We don't have 'em there. I heard they were dangerous, but I was thinking more like the way a bear's dangerous. Although I've never seen one of them, either. I can't believe you actually killed that thing."

"I figured you for dragon shit," Vera admitted, then smiled at everyone's look of surprise. "What? So did all of you." She considered the trees. The forest grew thicker as it rose into the mountains, trunks tangled into each other and underbrush rooted itself between dead stumps and mossy loam. "I'm glad you survived, though. This place has turned to wilderness already. I can see how the others got lost out here."

Rowan cleared his throat. "I hate to interrupt this little orgy of gratitude, but we don't have any food," he said.

Bershad frowned. "None?"

"Lord Grealor over here dropped it all back in Argel."

"There was a dragon!" Yonmar said.

"You never drop the food," Felgor said. "Even I know that."

"What about that sack you cut off the donkey's back?" Yonmar asked. "What was in that?"

"Extra chain mail and steel slats for my armor," Bershad said. "Which we can't eat."

"Well, can't you hunt for more?" Yonmar was clearly unfamiliar with details of the hunting process.

"Of course I can," Rowan said. "But traipsing around this side of the Razors looking for a goat or a deer is a quick way to wind up killed by Skojit or eaten by a Stone Scale lying in wait to ambush me." He sniffed the air. "Plus, the higher we go the harder it'll be to find food." Rowan seemed to add this information up and find a rather unfortunate total sum. "I believe this will soon turn into a bit of an unpleasant trip."

"Yeah," Bershad said. "We might as well get started."

13

JOLAN

Almira, Deepdale

The walls and towers of Deepdale seemed like part of the forest—huge gray stones festooned with moss and thick vines, as if the city had been pushed up from the earth below, rather than built on top of it. The crenellations of the outside wall were decorated with dozens of large stone jaguars, some of them prowling, others carved in lazy postures that made them appear to be dozing atop the city, paws and tails dangling.

"An old Bershad lord had them carved," Jolan said when he saw Garret eyeing the great felines. "The jaguars."

"Huh." Garret grunted. Jolan couldn't tell if he liked them or not. Garret was a hard man to read.

Morgan had spoken of Deepdale often—he had completed his apprenticeship in this city, years before. The Bershad lords had always been accommodating to the alchemists, and Morgan often bragged about the research he'd conducted under the guise of a useful lesson for Jolan. But he also relayed the history of the jaguar lords, who had worshipped and protected the Dainwood jungle for generations. Master Morgan always sounded a little bitter when he talked about the destruction of their dynasty.

There was a crowd forming along the eastern wall, which didn't make a lot of sense to Jolan, seeing as the main gate was off to the west. He squinted and tried to see between the shoulders and bodies that blocked his view. When they got a little closer, his eyes widened—he could see a scaled tail now, barbed at one end and almost fifteen feet long.

"Dragon," he whispered. "They killed a dragon over there."

Garret glanced over. "Good for them."

"Let's go take a look," Jolan said.

"You're not worried it'll spring to life and cut your head off?"

Jolan winced, regretting that he'd told Garret that detail. "Not really," he muttered. Then he trotted off toward the crowd. If Garret didn't want to look at the dragon, that was fine by him.

Jolan wormed his way through the crowd until he could see the beast. The dragon had marbled scales of black and white, each one twice as thick as a piece of plate armor. Its back had three warped ridges running toward the tail, and its snout was turned upward like a bat's. There were dozens of spears poking out from between the scales—it must have taken fifty men to kill it that way.

"Ugly bastard," said a bearded man wearing a jacket of chain mail. "What kind is it?"

If the man didn't know, he definitely wasn't a local. This was the most common dragon in the Dainwood.

"*Draconis var coruptan,*" Jolan said, using the alchemical classification, all of which were written and spoken in Balarian.

"The fuck does that mean?" the bearded man asked, then spat.

"It's a Snub-Nosed Blackjack, moron," said a tall man with long black hair that was festooned with silver rings. Definitely a Deepdale man.

"Huh. Well it was a fucking asshole. Damn near bit my arm off."

"They'll do that," the tall man said. "Rynolf'll probably die, too. His liver's jelly."

Jolan noticed a pile of meat and blood near the Blackjack's snout. He craned his head to get a better look. He could make out the remains of an arm and the shiny, broken remnants of what looked like a gilded breastplate. Jolan thought he saw a piece of torn flesh with a little strip of blue as well.

"Was that the dragonslayer?" Jolan asked.

"Aye," the tall man said. "Starkland . . . Stuckland. Something like that."

"Stravalund," the bearded man corrected.

"Whatever. All the soft-palmed lords from Floodhaven are the same."

"I'm from Floodhaven," said the bearded man.

"Good for you."

"What did he do?" Jolan asked.

"The same thing every dragonslayer does," the bearded man said. "Pissed off Hertzog Malgrave." He let out a breath. Threw a worried glance around the group. "Don't suppose I get a pass here, seeing as the dragon's dead."

Jolan realized the bearded man must have been the dragonslayer's forsaken shield. That meant he was supposed to follow the exile down the river today.

"The law is the law," the tall man said. He gave the forsaken shield a look. "But in the Dainwood we go our own way. We'll get you a belly full of rain ale first, at least. Who knows, might be we lose track of you before you lose track of your own head."

"Careful with that," said another local. "Grealor's in the city. His wardens don't abide exceptions."

"Fuck Elden Grealor and his bear-masked assholes." The tall man spat. "They don't hold sway over me."

Someone put their hand on Jolan's shoulder. Clamped down.

"Seen enough?" Garret said.

Jolan wanted to watch them field dress the dragon. The people of the Dainwood had their own unique way of slaughtering the great lizards. They cut each scale free and set it aside so the fat at the root could be shucked off. Then they removed all the organs and meat instead of letting them go to rot inside the carcass. They'd eat everything that could be eaten except for the heart, which was left inside the rib cage to fertilize the site of the bones. No other people in Almira, or the entire realm of Terra, bothered with such effort. Jolan could already see a few men squatting near the dragon, sculpting figures from the mud and adding totems. It was bad luck to leave the gods out of a dragon kill.

But Garret's grip and eyes made it clear that he wasn't willing to wait around.

"Yes," Jolan said.

"Good. Let's go."

At the city gate—which was a massive portcullis so wide four car-riages could pass underneath at the same time—Jolan and Garret were stopped by a fat guard with a lazy eye.

"Business in Deepdale?" he asked without a hint of interest in the answer.

"Givin' the boy up fer apprenticeship," Garret said, slipping into a surprisingly good Almiran accent.

"Uh-huh." The guard spat to his right. "Which trade?"

"Whichever one'll take him."

"Ha!" The guard clapped Garret on the shoulder, brightening up a little. He gave Jolan an appraising glance with his one good eye. "Bad apple, eh? Give 'im to a chimney sweep, that'll show him."

The guard waved them through and turned to the next person in line.

"Why'd you tell him that?" Jolan asked as they headed into the heart of the city, walking on the edge of a wide avenue that was busy with carts and horses.

"Everybody needs a reason to enter the city."

"No," Jolan said. "Why did you tell him *that,* about the appren-ticeship? We could have told him anything to get through."

Garret glanced down at him. "The best lies are the ones you carve out from truth. You've been sold into an apprenticeship once before. I figured you'd know how to act if we got more questions."

"Oh."

Jolan knew that he probably shouldn't have gone to Deepdale with Garret. He should have kept moving through the hill coun-try on his own, like he'd planned. There was something very un-settling about the man he'd found in the woods with a dragontooth in his arm. It wasn't just the shifting accent and secrecy. Garret had a quiet, calculating look about him at all times, like a fox who could sense that he was in a dangerous spot, but continued hunting anyway.

Jolan was curious about him, though. He wanted to know where he was really from, and what he was doing in Almira. But in the back of his mind, he also wondered if it was the same kind of curi-osity that Morgan had had about that Needle-Throated Verdun.

They found an inn on the western side of town called the Jag-uar's Mask. A gentle, misty rain had begun to fall while they moved through the city, and the inn had several small streams of water flowing off its slate roof by the time they arrived. Someone had set up three large stoneware buckets to collect the water.

"They're for rain ale," Jolan explained happily, even though Garret hadn't asked. "It's a special drink in Deepdale, can't find it anywhere else. They use forest hops and rainwater to get the flavor."

Garret didn't respond. He just pushed the oak door open and went inside.

There was a large common room with half a dozen round tables set up by the hearth. Two staircases on either side led to the rooms above. Garret spoke to the innkeeper—an old man with a white beard that extended down to his belt buckle—and then pressed a small stack of coins into his hand. He motioned for Jolan to follow him into the common room. They took a seat close to the fire, and after a few minutes an old woman emerged from the kitchen.

"What'll it be?" she asked, then burped. Jolan was pretty sure she was drunk.

"As much food as the boy can eat," Garret said, true to his word. "And two rain ales."

Jolan smiled.

They sipped their beers while waiting for the food.

"What do you think?" Jolan asked. "It's kinda like those bitter ales you Balarians like, right?"

Garret licked his lips. "Fresher hops."

Jolan smiled again. Wider this time. Garret hadn't exactly admitted Jolan was right about his homeland, but he'd come close.

Half an hour later, Jolan had eaten an entire chicken, three pork sausages, several thick slices of ham, two warm rolls, and a bowl of root stew. Both he and Garret were on their third rain ale, and Jolan felt dizzy and carefree for the first time since Morgan had been killed by the dragon.

"It all seems like a long time ago, now," Jolan said after talking about his apprenticeship for a few minutes. "Used to be I'd spend weeks doing nothing besides grinding down herbs and boiling water for Master Morgan. But life outside the apothecary moves much faster."

Garret took a sip of beer, looking like he was giving the comment careful consideration. The drink hadn't changed his quiet demeanor, but his body was a little more relaxed.

"Traveling has a way of making the past seem further away," he said after a while. "Something about all the miles underneath your heels plays tricks on your mind, I think."

"You've traveled a lot?"

"Yes."

"What's the farthest place you've ever been to?" Jolan asked, taking a sip of his own beer. It was almost empty, and he wondered if Garret would buy him a fourth.

"I did some work beyond Taggarstan once. Out in the free nations of Juno."

Jolan fiddled with one of the chicken bones for a moment, debating whether he should ask his next question. The beer gave him courage. "What work do you do, exactly?"

Garret's eyes flicked from his beer to Jolan's face, but there was no malice in them. No anger. His gray eyes didn't seem to carry any kind of emotion—they took the world in, but gave nothing back.

"You should get some sleep, Jolan. The featherbed was expensive."

14

BERSHAD

Ghalamar, Razorback Mountains

Felgor and Yonmar struggled with the mountain.

The Balarian thief continued to vomit sporadically, but eventually he had nothing left and just heaved air onto the ground and followed it with globs of phlegm and spit.

"Fucking dungeon," he muttered while hunched over. "Turned me soft."

Yonmar may have dressed himself in prim travel clothes of supple leather, but he was sticky with sweat before midday and walking slower than Felgor by the afternoon, despite the thief's frequent breaks to empty his stomach.

"First adventure?" Bershad asked Yonmar when the group stopped to take water. Yonmar had removed both of his boots and was sitting on a rock, inspecting his feet for blisters. He glared at Bershad but said nothing.

"You'll get used to it," Bershad said. "Or you'll get eaten by a Stone Scale." He untied a goat's bladder from the side of Alfonso's pack. It had been filled with wine, but Bershad had emptied it and filled it with water from the first creek they passed. He took a long drink, holding the bag high above his head and letting the liquid pour down in a long stream.

"You drink like a Papyrian," Vera observed.

Bershad swished the water around in his mouth a few times before swallowing. Offered her the skin. She took it and drank in the same graceful way, then passed the skin to Yonmar, who sucked from the spigot like a pup nursing on his mother's tit. He passed it to Felgor when he was done, who ventured a small sip. When that didn't cause him to retch, he took several much larger ones.

"What happened to the drunken dragonslayer?" Yonmar asked, motioning to the water. "From your reputation, I expected you to stay soaked in wine this whole trip."

Bershad scratched at his beard. "Shouldn't believe everything you hear about me." He could barely pass an hour behind city walls without filling his belly with wine, but out in the wild, he felt different. The rhythm of the forest kept his body relaxed and calm. Always had.

"So, what do we do if the Skojit attack?" Felgor asked, looking around in the woods.

"We're miles south of the Line of Lornar," Bershad said. "Only danger down here is slipping on a loose rock."

"That family was killed south of the Line," Yonmar pointed out.

"I doubt that," Bershad said. "Those soldiers have to fill quotas for Garwin just like tax agents. We could scour these woods for a month, don't think we'd ever find those slaughtered miners."

Vera frowned. "Swine have stronger morals than you mainlanders."

"Last I checked the widows weren't known for their ironclad scruples," Yonmar said. "Spies and assassins masquerading as bodyguards."

"At least we don't murder people to fill . . . quotas," Vera said.

Bershad shrugged and took another long drink. "We'll sleep south of the Line tonight. Tomorrow, might be worth coming up with a plan for the Skojit."

———

Near dark, Vera scouted ahead and found a place to camp beside the bend of a small mountain river. When they caught up with her, she'd already managed to pull four trout from the water with a piece of cord and a steel hook. They were gutted and skewered and she was starting a fire beneath them.

"Handy little assassin," Felgor said, turning to Yonmar and smiling. "Saved your ass."

"We all have a part to play," Yonmar said.

"What's yours again?" Bershad asked. "Pissing off barons and losing our food?"

"That wasn't my fault," Yonmar said. "Ghalamar tightened their regulations."

"Is that what you're gonna say when you can't get us into Balaria, too?"

"That will be different. I've made a deal in Taggarstan that cannot be undone."

"Why?"

Yonmar glared at Bershad. "I don't need to explain myself to the demon of Glenlock Canyon."

Bershad felt his stomach sink. The mention of Glenlock Canyon did that to him. He let the conversation drop.

They shared the fish and warmed themselves by the fire. The pine needles of the tree above them were as long as fingers, and they cast spiked shadows over their campsite. Yonmar complained about his feet, then started making another mud figure. Felgor and Rowan traded drinking stories. Vera sat off to the edge of the firelight, saying nothing.

Bershad ate his fish. Didn't say much. Argel had put him in a low mood. Felgor prattled on for a while about nothing much and Bershad had him just about tuned out when there was a short silence and then a question that caught his attention.

"Why do they call him the demon of Glenlock Canyon, anyway?" Felgor asked Yonmar.

"That's how our friend here earned his blue bars," Yonmar said with an oily smile. "Nasty bit of business."

Things were quiet. Rowan looked like he was about to break Yonmar's face open.

"Well," Felgor said, "let's hear it, then! I shared plenty of stories with all of you so far."

When Bershad again refused to look up, Yonmar cleared his throat and leaned forward.

"Fourteen years ago, the young heir to the Dainwood was sent to quell an uprising in the eastern part of his province. You see, toward the end of the Balarian Invasion, Almira had a bit of trouble coming up with fresh soldiers. More than half of our wardens had been killed. Most peasants of fighting age, too." Yonmar paused to pull a bone from his totem bag and placed it carefully on his mud statue. "So King Malgrave used mercenaries. He hired a particularly vicious outfit called Wormwrot Company. They were led by a young but sadistic commander. What was his name again, exile?"

"Vergun," Bershad muttered. "Vallen Vergun."

"Exactly. Vergun." Yonmar smiled. "When people reminisce about the war, everyone talks about Cedar Wallace and the battle at Black Pine, or Hertzog's charge to the sea after the Balarians retreated. But the only reason Almira managed to even fight in those battles was because of Vergun's and Wormwrot's bloody work. After the war was won, Almira's treasury couldn't cover the bill. Not even close. So, for sixteen years the king was forced to pay off his debt to Vergun at a steep interest rate. Damn near doubled the original cost of the hired legions."

"That's the problem with large debts," Bershad said. "They tend to linger."

"Vergun kept his army in Almira to make sure he got paid," Yonmar continued. "They took over a town called Glenlock on the eastern coast of the Dainwood. Vergun and his men collected their gold in installments and . . . how shall I put it? They enjoyed the taste of the Dainwood's countryside. But the war had been over for a long time, and Almira's wardens had been replenished. The king figured it was time to strike a better deal. That's where he came in." Yonmar motioned to Bershad. "Hertzog sent the young jaguar lord to negotiate better terms for the rotten deal. As a show of strength, the king allowed Bershad to take three thousand wardens with him. His first military command.

"But this is where things get sticky," Yonmar continued. "See, instead of trying to negotiate with Vergun, Bershad rode down to Glenlock and started a fight. He managed to kick Wormwrot Company out of the city, and they fled into the nearby hills. Bershad gave chase, and a few days later he cornered Wormwrot Company in a box canyon. The mercenaries were trapped. Thing was, Vergun had snatched a few hundred Almiran prisoners during his retreat. Peasants, mostly, but he grabbed a few small lords, too. Lined them up at the mouth of the canyon, necks tied to cottonwood trees, and dared Bershad to charge. And a day later, the evil bastard did it."

"It wasn't that simple," Bershad growled.

Yonmar shrugged. "Simple or not, the exile got hundreds of innocent Almirans killed. Women. Children, even. And then there was the massacre afterward. The wardens who were there said Bershad howled like a demon as he cut down the soldiers. Ran murderous lines through their ranks, horse and blade dripping with blood and gore. Cutting at the hanging corpses as he rode. Of course, he didn't get all of them." Yonmar smiled. "Rumor has it that Vergun escaped and fled back east across the Soul Sea. The rest of his army became crow's food."

That was the story everyone in Almira had been told. And it was accurate except for one detail Bershad had kept to himself all this time. The only other person who knew the full truth was Hertzog Malgrave. But Bershad didn't bother correcting Yonmar for the same reason he hadn't told Ashlyn the full story at Castle Malgrave. It didn't change anything.

"This unfortunate incident happened to occur about the same time Shiru Malgrave went into labor with her fifth child," Yonmar continued. "The birth went hard on the queen, and the child was stillborn. Just before the queen followed her dead child down the river, she told King Hertzog that the baby hadn't been his child at all. Leon Bershad, high lord of the Dainwood and friend to the king, had been making rather frequent visits to the queen's bedchambers over the last few years of her life. In his grief for Shiru, so they say, Leon Bershad confessed his crimes when the king confronted him. Hertzog Malgrave executed Leon the day before Bershad rode back into Floodhaven with children's blood on his hands. So nobody argued much when Hertzog ordered a pair of blue bars put on the young heir to the Dainwood." Yonmar looked at Bershad and called out to him. "Tell me, exile, do you ever wonder how things would have played out if you hadn't gone all bloodthirsty in that canyon?"

Bershad glared at Yonmar, rage boiling up inside his throat. "Do you ever wonder what your lungs would look like if I cut them out of your chest?"

Nobody said anything for a while after that.

Felgor licked his lips. "Well, I'm no soldier and I'm definitely no lord, but it sounds like they backed you into a crap-covered wall, then got angry when you came back smelling like shit. The king brought those mercenaries into Almira, not you. And anytime soldiers draw swords, innocent people wind up dead. That, I've seen firsthand. One man's never responsible for all of it." Felgor looked at Bershad. "Being honest, I like your other name better."

Yonmar flinched. "Well, look at that. The thief sides with the murderer. Should have expected the criminals to stick together."

Bershad nodded at Felgor but didn't say anything. He'd stopped searching for a justification or forgiveness for Glenlock Canyon a long time ago.

Yonmar kept talking, and Bershad was having trouble fighting the urge to cut his tongue out, so he got up from the fire and dug a candle out of a saddlebag, lit it with a stick from the fire, and moved over to where Alfonso was grazing. First, he saw to his sword, wiping the blade with a goatskin oilcloth and then searching for any remaining rust spots he hadn't taken care of during their journey across the Soul Sea. He rubbed each of them away with a sharpening stone, glad to have the routine back again.

Bershad was worrying at a crescent-shaped rust mark the size of his fingernail when Vera abandoned the campfire and walked over to where he was sitting.

"If you came over to hear my side of Glenlock Canyon, don't bother," Bershad said.

"I don't care about your past unless it's going to affect my future," Vera said. "I came to get a better look at your sword."

Bershad looked up at her. He couldn't get a good read on the widow yet.

"It belonged to my uncle," he said. "Gregor."

"I've never heard of an Almiran carrying a Papyrian sword. You mainlanders are famous for those enormous blades. We make fun of you for them."

"Gregor used to travel to Papyria every spring during the early years of Hertzog's marriage to Shiru. He was a good ambassador. He liked places that were different from his home. Can't say the same for most Almirans." Bershad worked a piece of rust loose from the blade and flicked it aside. "Anyway, Gregor admired Papyrian craftsmanship so much that he asked a smith there to design this one for him."

"What's it called?" Vera asked.

"No name," Bershad said. "That part's all Almiran. No names for our gods or our blades."

"I see. It's a custom design, yes?"

"That's right."

He offered the sword to Vera hilt-first. She took it and nodded approval as she tested the balance.

"Is your uncle dead?" Vera asked, passing the sword back to him and sitting down. Alfonso came over to sniff her open palm, then wandered off to eat more grass.

Bershad shook his head. "Exiled, like me. Except his was voluntary. Gregor forswore his titles and property when I was a boy. All of his Dainwood lands and holdings went to my father, but the sword went to me. Then he took a catboat out of Floodhaven harbor and disappeared. Last anyone saw him, he was heading directly into the heart of the Soul Sea. Nobody's heard from him in twenty years."

"Why did he leave?" Vera asked.

Bershad shrugged. "Didn't say. Might have been he knew my father was fucking the queen and didn't want to be around when Hertzog found out. That's what most people think. But my father said Gregor was changed by the Balarian Invasion. He took a bad injury that nearly killed him, and after that his mind became a cage that rattled too easily in the wind. He needed a quiet place to find peace."

Bershad stopped talking and focused on a freckle-sized spot of rust near the guard of his blade. From the corner of his vision, he saw Vera move to stand up.

"What are the names of your daggers?" he asked. Vera had done well during the Argel attack. He wanted her on his side when the next fight arrived. And nothing bonds two killers like a conversation about their weapons.

"*Kaisha,*" she said, patting the right dagger. "And *Owaru.*"

"Beginning and end," Bershad said, translating the Papyrian words. "I guess that makes you the middle."

"You speak Papyrian?"

"You'd shudder at my accent."

Vera smiled at that and rubbed her thumb against *Owaru*'s handle, which was made from orca bone.

"I'm glad you're with us," Bershad said. "Not sure we'd have escaped Argel without you."

"Yonmar wouldn't have, anyway." Vera scowled at the lord.

"I wouldn't have been too upset."

"If we didn't need him alive, I wouldn't have saved him." She moved her right arm in a slow circle. "Strained my shoulder a bit hauling him out of the way."

Bershad finished with the sword and slid it back into the scabbard. Set it aside. Then he unstrapped his breastplate, shucked off his mail, and went to work on the links by the candlelight, looking for tangled or bent rings. He found six, and went over to a sack of replacements in one of Alfonso's saddlebags. He rubbed the beast's snout after he'd taken the rings, watched his ears twitch happily.

"Seems like that donkey receives the majority of your affection," Vera said when he sat back down to start replacing the rings.

"With donkeys, you know where you stand," Bershad said. "True of all animals. Dragons might be vicious killers, but I never saw a great lizard pretend to be anything besides exactly what it is."

"Is that why you hate Yonmar so much?"

Bershad glanced at the young lord, who was massaging his feet and staring at the mud figurine he'd made. "I've known worse."

"Like who?"

Bershad looked at Vera. She seemed genuinely curious.

"Before I got my blue bars, I was the heir to a powerful family. Our lands were fertile and wild. And our wardens were some of the most feared warriors in Almira. There was this small lord named Umbrik who had a few holdfasts and a coffee plantation along the northern border of our province. No wardens under his command. He wanted to win my favor so when I became a high lord, I gave him a few soldiers to start his little army. He'd bring me shipments of reserve wine and coffee and rain ale each moon turn. Tell me about the different jaguars he'd spotted in the forests because he knew I liked them. I thought we were friends."

Bershad paused for a moment to slip one of the missing rings into place.

"A year after I was exiled, I came through Umbrik's lands for a writ. Hertzog made sure that I was never sent too far into the Dainwood—too many deep-rooted loyalties that might sprout—but Umbrik was far enough north to be acceptable. I was excited to see a familiar face. Sleep under a roof. Maybe even in a bed, if Umbrik was feeling especially generous. But the small lord came down from his muddy little tower with his sword drawn. He was wearing a jaguar cloak, just like Yonmar is now. He yanked the cloak from his shoulders, threw it on the ground, and pissed on it while I watched. Said he'd go out and kill himself a fresh one in the morning. Then he told me exiles had no place on his property, and to get my donkey and my tattooed face out of sight."

"Charming man," Vera said.

"Back then, everybody assumed I'd be dead soon. And they didn't want to risk angering the king by showing me respect. Funny thing is, I came through Umbrik's lands again almost ten years later, after I was famous. He'd ingratiated himself with the Grealors by then—set up a dozen lumber mills on his land and turned those thousand-year woods into gold. He even managed to build a nice little town near his plantation that he named after himself. Umbrik's River or Glade or some shit. Pretentious bastard. Anyway, by the time I came through a second time, it was normal for the lords of Almira to invite me into their manors and castles if they were sure Hertzog Malgrave wouldn't find out. So Umbrik dispatched a warden to fetch me from the tavern I was drinking in and bring me to his freshly constructed villa. He insisted on throwing a feast in my honor so his wife and children could meet the Flawless Bershad."

"Did you go?"

"Sure," Bershad said. "Never turn down kitchen-cooked food and the chance to sleep in a bed—that's a rule of dragonslaying. Mostly me and Rowan have been doing this for fourteen years." He motioned to the fish and thin sleeping mats. "Anyway, Lord Umbrik fawned over me just like he did when I was the heir to the Dainwood. And when he passed out from drinking too much ale, I took his pretty wife upstairs to their marriage bed and fucked her senseless until dawn."

"So, some of the stories about you are true." Vera smiled.

Bershad shrugged. "Point is, an animal will never pull shit like that on you. If you know how to look, you'll always know where the wild things of this world stand."

Vera stared at Bershad for a few moments. "Speaking of wild things, how did you know that dragon was going to attack Argel?"

"Seeing it come down from the mountains was a clue."

"Maybe it was, but you cut the top of that man's head off before the Red Skull appeared. How did you know it was coming?"

Bershad hesitated. "You've got a pair of eyes on you."

"Answer my question," Vera said.

Bershad had started feeling the approach of dragons in his bones about five years into his exile, after he'd already taken three or four bad wounds and used the moss to heal his body. Bershad knew the two were connected, he just didn't know exactly how. But he couldn't tell Vera the full truth, so he told her something close.

"Even before I had these blue bars, I'd been around dragons my entire life," he said. "The Dainwood has more Blackjacks than Flood-haven has stray cats. And the world changes when the great lizards are nearby. Goes quiet and still." He shrugged. "Once you learn to recognize that, dragons have a hard time surprising you. That's all I did."

"I don't believe you."

"Suit yourself."

Vera squinted at him. "Most men would be proud of killing that Red Skull. You saved a lot of lives. Why aren't you?"

"The people of Argel strung that dragon's mate against a stone wall and left him there. If someone did a thing like that to your lover, what would you do?"

"I don't have a lover."

"Pretend you do."

Vera hesitated. "I would kill them."

"Me, too. Slaying that dragon was the only thing to do, but that doesn't make it right. Just necessary."

Vera studied his face. "You're not what I expected."

"What did you expect?"

"A drunken brute who didn't know how to do anything besides stab things with a spear. Or his cock."

"Well, give it time," Bershad said. "We don't know each other very well yet."

Vera snorted. Bershad caught a flicker of a smile on her face before she turned back toward the fire.

———

The Line of Lornar was a wall in celebration of death. Every fifteen yards there was a human skeleton propped up by pine branches and twisted into a position of cruelty. Their bones were bleached white and their skulls were painted red. Behind them, their rusted weapons hung in a tight bundle of rotting hemp rope.

Dozens of massive black birds with white-tipped wings and hooked beaks filled the pine branches. They called to each other in short, mournful cries.

"Whose bones are these?" Vera asked, approaching one.

"Soldiers of Ghalamar who got caught on the wrong side of the Line."

"I've always wanted to see it," Yonmar said, touching one of the bone clusters with shaking fingers. "My brothers used to tease me and try to give me nightmares with stories about the wall of bones. They said the demon spirits of the soldiers still haunt the mountainside."

"Demons aren't the problem up here," Bershad said.

"Still," Yonmar said. "I should make a totem for good fortune."

He started to open the bag on his hip.

"If you pull something out of that bag, I will shove it down your throat," Bershad said. "Now check your weapons and let's go."

The enormous birds followed them up the mountain like sentinels. The branches over Bershad's head creaked and shifted every time one of them landed. They moved through a forest of paper birch, Ghalamarian ash, and white oak trees. Every few minutes they passed a large boulder that was festooned with moss and lichen. Bershad gave all the boulders a wide berth.

"Why are we going so far around those?" Felgor asked between pants after they spent twenty minutes circumventing a particularly large boulder by way of a steep hill and a thicket of thorn bushes.

"No good way to tell the difference between a boulder and a Stone Scale waiting to devour anything that comes within snatching distance," Bershad said. In theory, he knew that he should feel a tremor if it really was a dragon, but Bershad didn't want to risk it. Stone Scales were tricky bastards.

"Oh."

After that, Felgor started hiding behind Rowan every time they passed near a boulder.

The signs of spring were everywhere—mountain flowers starting to rise, green leaves poking from the tips of low-hanging tree branches. The changing season made Bershad think about all the dragons that would begin their migration to Tanglemire in the next few weeks. They didn't have much time.

As they climbed higher, their path narrowed into a slim game trail that was littered with deer tracks and fox prints. The woods grew quiet. Bershad led them through the forest while Vera covered their back trail. She had a drawn dagger in her right hand and a loaded sling in the left, ready for anything that might creep up behind them. Rowan, Felgor, and Yonmar walked in the middle. Yonmar clutched his sword in a way that made it clear he had never swung the blade in defense of his life. Bershad didn't know whether to be angry or jealous. His own life had been colored with violence for so long, he could no longer imagine what a peaceful version of his soul would feel like.

Around evening a cold rain started misting down from higher elevations. They made camp for the night between two great pinyon trees whose branches twisted and mingled with each other overhead, forming a small respite from the damp. It was the best chance they had to stay slightly dry during the night. Bershad dug a deep pit and sparked a fire using dried pine needles as kindling that he'd saved in his pocket once he saw the rain coming.

"I'll get us something to eat," Rowan said, removing a bow from Alfonso's pack along with a few arrows.

"I can help," Felgor said.

"This is a little different from robbing food carts and windowsills for scraps," Rowan said.

"Doesn't mean I won't be good at it."

Rowan squinted at the Balarian. "Fine. Just stay quiet."

"Rowan," Vera called as they were heading away from the fire. "Keep him in your sights. Always."

Rowan smiled and smacked Felgor on the back. "Relax. Felgor here knows I'll shoot him directly in the asshole if he tries to run."

They disappeared into the fading light. Vera pulled some water from a nearby spring while Bershad fed the fire, making sure the light didn't reach beyond the rim of the pit. Yonmar donned his armor with the clumsiness of a man who had never done it by himself before. He wasn't strong enough to wear the armor during the day, but the young lord was eager to protect himself while standing still. Bershad had also noticed that while he was more than happy to let

Alfonso lug his armor around all day, Yonmar always kept that leather satchel on his hip.

The three of them sat by the fire in silence until Rowan and Felgor returned about half an hour later.

"Success!" Felgor announced. He was cradling something in the front of his shirt. "Got two rabbits and a bunch of wild onions."

"You did?" Vera asked.

"I got the rabbits," Rowan said, approaching the fire. The animals were tied to his belt. "And the onions. Felgor the forager here only managed to find a bunch of sour crab apples that taste like shit."

"They're not for us. They're for Alfonso." He walked over to the donkey and began feeding him the tiny apples. Alfonso chomped one after the other and twitched his ears at the taste. "See? He likes them."

Bershad shrugged. "It's not the worst thing. The grass'll thin out the higher we climb."

Rowan gutted the rabbits, chopped each onion in half, and dumped all of it into the pot. Everyone watched the water simmer up to a boil.

"I do not think a meal has ever smelled so good," said Yonmar, fiddling with his chain mail jacket.

"The taste'll disappoint," Rowan said, stirring the mixture. "Wish we had some salt."

"Did you say salt?" Felgor asked, turning away from Alfonso, who had eaten all the apples and was now sniffing Felgor's shirt, looking for more. The Balarian approached the fire and produced a surprisingly large black pouch tied by a leather thong. He opened it, licked a finger, and dipped it inside. Came out with a fingertip covered in small white granules. "What do you think, four pinches? Five?"

"Where the hell did you get that?" Vera asked.

"Nicked it from that blond-haired soldier back in Argel. Right before Bershad lopped the top of his head off."

Rowan smiled. "You can't hunt for shit, Felgor, but this makes up for it. Seven pinches, I think."

Felgor added the salt and Rowan tasted it. Nodded approval. Bershad found his pipe and packed it with Almiran tobacco and a bit of crushed opium to help relax his legs and feet after the long day of walking. He watched Felgor's eyes brighten as the poppy smell wafted around their fire, and passed him the pipe. Felgor had fed his donkey and improved the meal—that earned him a few drags, at least.

"What got you thrown in Floodhaven's dungeon?" Bershad asked him.

"Not good manners to ask a prisoner how he earned his chains," said Felgor between puffs from the pipe.

"But you're not a prisoner anymore."

"Invisible chains keep you bound the same as iron ones. I'm still a prisoner. Of you, and her." He motioned to Vera, who sat on a rock apart from them sharpening her blade. "And even if all of you go into the ground before me, I am still a prisoner of these mountains."

"Quit stalling and tell us," Rowan said without looking up from the pot he was stirring.

Felgor offered the pipe to Vera. When she waved it off, he passed it back to Bershad without offering it to Yonmar. Then he rubbed his chin a few times, hiding the smile spreading across his lips. "Some of them eagle-masked bastards caught me robbing a brothel in the Foggy Side of Floodhaven."

"Dungeon and the block is a pretty steep punishment for robbing a whorehouse," Bershad said.

"Depends on who you rob. Wasn't just any brothel. It was for . . . *special* tastes."

"Children?"

Felgor shook his head. "It was highborn only. And they were the types who still take their mud god worship a bit too seriously. You know, the ones who get a little extra horny on full moons? I swear to you, there were fifty lords and ladies in that room rutting like pigs."

Yonmar shifted uncomfortably, probably because his family was notorious for their full-moon orgies.

"Get caught trying to take a turn?" Bershad asked, offering the pipe to him again.

Felgor took a deep pull. "Highborn tail isn't really for me," he said, smoke drifting out of his mouth as he spoke. "I was there for the silver and the gold and the priceless gems that were packed into the human-sized mud sculptures they had watching the whole thing. You Almirans bring a lot of money to your orgies."

Bershad leaned back against the trunk of the pine. "So how'd you get caught?"

"Same way every thief gets caught. I got greedy. Used to be I'd only rob a room if it was empty. Safer that way. But I saw a chance for a better payout and I took it. There was a ruby the size of my fist in one of those statues. I figured they'd take it with them when they left, so I went for it, right there in the middle of the orgy. Some lord saw me and yelled out. I figured having his cock all the way up a courtesan's ass would distract him, but alas . . ." Felgor spread his arms out in feigned desperation. "Then it was the usual drill: irons, dungeon, rats nibbling at my ankles. I was only a day or two away from the block, but some blue-eyed widow sprung me from the line."

"Hayden," Bershad said. "That widow's name is Hayden."

"If you say so," Felgor continued. "Anyway, this Hayden said she had alternative thoughts about my future."

"What did she say, exactly?" Bershad asked, still curious as to why Ashlyn had added Felgor to their crew.

"Apparently Princess Ashlyn had gotten ahold of my Balarian records. Not sure how. Justice in the homeland isn't doled out the same way as in Almira, where a lord hears your story and just does whatever the fuck he pleases. Everybody gets a trial in Balaria, and every trial gets written down. Word for word. They got a whole building full of the records in Burz-al-dun. Pretty place, I robbed it a few times."

"What made your record so interesting?"

Felgor shrugged. "When I was fourteen, I was arrested in the Imperial Palace of Burz-al-dun, posing as a chef's assistant. I hadn't stolen anything, and they never figured out how I got mixed into the servant crowd, so they gave me three lashes and let me go. But the charge was in the record, even after all these years. 'Gaining Illegal and Clandestine Entrance to the Imperial Palace,' I believe it was. The blue-eyed Papyrian read it back to me."

Felgor took another pull on the pipe.

"Anyway, this Hayden character asked me if I could sneak into the palace again. I told her there was no way to be sure, but I doubt if the powdery bastards closed up my entrance. Would have caused a real shitty situation, if you know what I mean."

"I don't."

"Anyway," Felgor said, ignoring him, "then she asked if I could lead other people into the palace the same way I came in all those years ago. I said sure, as long as they aren't too fat. Then I got turned over to Vera and that bastard." He pointed his pipe at Yonmar.

"And neither of you thought this was worth mentioning?" Bershad glared at Vera and Yonmar.

Yonmar dug into the ground a bit with a stick he'd picked up, keeping his eyes on the dirt. "You talk too much, Balarian."

Felgor leaned back and pulled his boots up next to the fire. Smiled. "You know, I've heard that. There was a whore in Naropa who said I talked more during sex than any other man she'd fucked. A whore said that! And who knows how many men actually put their prick in her, I mean Naropa is known for its whores."

Bershad turned to Vera, who just shrugged. "I assumed Princess Ashlyn told you."

"She didn't."

Same as she hadn't told the others what Bershad was planning to do when they reached the Imperial Palace of Burz-al-dun. Bershad didn't like it, but he couldn't deny the shrewdness.

"Because you could be captured," Vera said, coming to the same conclusion. "Tortured." She flicked her eyes between Bershad and Rowan. "The less a man knows, the less he can say when he's getting his fingernails torn off, or his balls stuffed up his own ass."

"People do that?" Felgor asked.

"People do whatever it takes to get answers," Vera said.

For a while, the only sound was Rowan's ladle moving around the rim of the pot and the steady scrape of Vera sharpening her dagger.

"Stew's ready," Rowan said. "Prepare for disappointment."

They ate in silence, all of them crowded around the pot and passing around two large spoons. The food tasted like grass and dirt, but Bershad was so hungry he didn't care. When the pot was empty, Rowan let Alfonso lick the rim.

"The salt helped," Rowan said to Felgor as he added a small log to the fire. "Thanks."

"Just wish you'd stolen some garlic, too," Bershad said.

"Or some lavender," Vera said, staring at the fire. "Lavender and wild rice and that would have been a proper meal."

"Papyrians use lavender to flavor their stews?" Felgor asked. "I always thought it was just something whores put in their soap."

"How much of your knowledge is informed by brothels?" Vera asked.

"'Bout half I'd say."

"Animal," Yonmar muttered, shifting in his armor.

"Oh, like you never spent a minute of your life in a brothel, Lord Gelden?"

"It's Grealor."

"Whatever."

Felgor continued talking about things he'd learned in brothels while everyone else talked about their favorite spices. After a while, Bershad felt his bowels tighten in an uncomfortable way and took his leave to deal with it.

He found a large boulder about fifty yards away. They were too high up for Stone Scales to be a problem anymore, so he dropped his pants and squatted. It was the first time he'd been alone since Flood-haven Castle. His thoughts drifted. The consequences of his decisions over the last few weeks began to sink in. Two days into the Razor-back Mountains. Dead men and another dead dragon behind him. A country ahead where he'd be executed on sight if he was caught. The odds of him ever seeing Ashlyn again got smaller with each passing footfall. Thinking of her hurt his chest.

Bershad started finishing things up. He didn't like how much his emotions had traveled during a simple task like shitting.

There was a soft twang from the trees, and then there was an arrow stuck in Bershad's thigh.

"Fuck!"

He fell from his squat, barely missing the pile of his own shit, and scrambled to the other side of the boulder with his pants around his ankles. There was a soft curse a couple dozen feet off in the trees from the archer who'd just bungled the job of waylaying him mid-shit. Then the soft whisper of a blade being drawn from a leather scabbard.

Bershad was unarmed. Stupid to have taken a shit without a weapon. The arrow in his thigh was burning, and crouching was pure agony, but it had taken him in the meat of his leg. Not serious. He tore his pants the rest of the way off, wiped his ass with them, and chucked them toward camp in a tight ball. They caught the branches of a pine and snapped a few twigs on their way down.

The archer headed in the direction of Bershad's soiled pants. It was amazing how blind people were to cheap tricks in the middle of a fight. Most men were rubbed down to terrified fools as soon as swords were drawn. As the footsteps approached, Bershad circled around the other side of the boulder so he stayed out of sight.

The archer paused as he came around the boulder, searching. Ber-shad slipped behind him. All he saw was a short figure in a bear cloak. He leapt forward, clamped both hands onto the short man's head, and slammed it into the side of the boulder as hard as he could. The sound of a skull hitting rock made a wet crunching noise.

The body went limp, but just to be sure, Bershad flipped him over, grabbed the blade from his hand, and ran it across his throat. It wasn't until the blood was spurting from the wound that Bershad realized he had just killed a girl. No older than twenty. She had curly red hair and the most crooked teeth Bershad had ever seen. The final bits of life were draining out of her, but she was foggy from getting her skull caved in and didn't seem afraid. Just confused and lost.

"Sorry, girl." He realized it was the same thing he'd said to the dragon he'd killed in Argel.

Bershad heard metal on metal clanging together from the direction of their camp. The Skojit must have been waiting for one of them to separate before attacking. Smart. Bershad moved slowly, favoring the leg without an arrow in it and trying to warm his freezing balls a little with his left hand. The girl's comrades would assume she put an arrow through his neck, so he'd have surprise on his side if he was careful.

Bershad came up to the two pines. Everything was chaos and violence. Four Skojit had attacked. The stew pot had been turned over and rolled down the hill. The fire spilled from the confines of the pit he'd dug. Vera was darting around the strewn fire, pursued by the largest Skojit, who wore a suit of mismatched iron armor wreathed in animal furs. He was swinging at Vera with a two-handed sword. He took two big swipes, and each time Vera ducked, bolted forward, and stabbed him with one of her daggers—first in the thigh, then high up on the right side of his rib cage. On the second strike, her dagger got stuck in his body and she abandoned it, slipping away before the Skojit could swing at her again.

Papyrian widows were trained to kill heavily armored men with a frightening kind of efficiency—they dodged and they weaved and they stabbed at your vital organs until you collapsed, not even realizing that the woman in front of you had poked your liver and lungs and heart with holes. The Skojit that Vera was fighting had probably planned on cutting her in half and then helping his friends kill Rowan. Instead his boots were filling with blood and he was dead on his feet. Just didn't know it yet.

Rowan was not as graceful as Vera, but he fought like a cornered wolf. Two Skojit had come for him, and one of them was already on the ground—his skull cleaved in two and his legs twitching. Rowan's short sword whipped around to meet the other Skojit, parrying his attacks while he wrestled himself up close and began beating at the Skojit with his elbows and knees and steel-tipped boots.

The last Skojit was working on Felgor—yelling hard curses in an angry tongue and swinging a stone club from left to right. Felgor was unarmed and panicked, ducking away from each blow as best he could, moving away from the fire.

If anyone needed help surviving the next few seconds, it was Felgor.

Bershad panned to his right, staying beyond the light of the spilled fire. Then he rushed forward, thigh screaming in pain. He reached the Skojit just as he was making another wide sweep with the club. It would have turned Felgor's head into a bowl.

Bershad did not entertain half measures when he was stabbing someone in the back. He crunched his stolen blade diagonally through neck and collarbone and breast, carving into the Skojit's chest until his blade became tangled in his spine several inches above the navel. The Skojit made a desperate gurgle in place of another battle cry, and fell over. Blood sprayed up from the gash in a torrent of red, drenching Bershad's bare thighs and arms and chest.

In seconds, the blood from the Skojit had made a small pond on the ground beneath Felgor's feet. The thief was sweating and panting, his fingers twitching.

Bershad left the sword in the dead man, and locked his eyes on Felgor.

"He's dead," Bershad rasped. "You're not."

After a close call like that, a reminder helped.

The other Skojit were dead, too. Rowan was wiping his sword off. Vera had one leg propped on the armored man's chest and was yanking on the dagger she'd stuck between his ribs. Bershad's leg was tightening up with a bad kind of pain. He yanked Felgor's cloak away from his shoulders—tied it around himself in a makeshift skirt—then limped back to the ruined camp and plopped down next to the fire.

"I see they sent an archer down after you," Rowan said, motioning toward the arrow stuck in Bershad's thigh. "I'll get some bandages."

Bershad nodded absently, scanning the camp of dead men. Alfonso was off to the side, munching grass and unmoved by the carnage. Rowan moved to his pack and started pulling out bandages and a jar of moss they kept for his dragonslaying injuries.

"Just the bandage, it's not bad," Bershad said. He didn't want the others to see what the moss would do. Rowan nodded and handed Bershad the bandage. Put the jar away.

"Where's the Grealor?" Bershad asked when he'd removed the arrow.

"Bad news, there." Rowan grimaced. "They went for him first. Must have thought with all that nice armor he was the biggest threat. Well, besides you." Rowan grabbed hold of a body. He pulled Yonmar closer to the fire where there was enough light to see. Felgor and Vera came over as well.

There was an arrow sprouting from the middle of Yonmar's forehead. He had an annoyed look on his face like he'd just been tapped on the shoulder during an important task.

"Must have just had two bows. One for you. One for him." Rowan grunted from the labor of moving the corpse. "Lucky."

Bershad sighed, leaned down, and pulled the jaguar cloak off the corpse. He folded it carefully, then placed it on the fire. Pictured the ashes floating down into the sea eventually. Then he took a white seashell from the leather pouch he kept around his neck and put it in Yonmar's mouth. Even the souls of assholes deserve a little help getting back to the sea.

When that was done, Bershad sat down on a boulder and rubbed his leg for a few moments, thinking. Ashlyn had told Bershad to keep Yonmar alive. That hadn't panned out so well. He turned to Vera. "Yonmar said he was going to sneak us across the Balarian border from Taggarstan. How was that going to work?"

Vera finished wiping the blood off her dagger and sheathed it. "I'm not sure. The Grealors made some kind of deal with a man there."

"Hand me his satchel," Bershad said.

Rowan pulled the leather satchel off Yonmar's corpse and threw it to Bershad. Inside, there was a poorly balanced knife, a purse with twenty silver pieces, one rolled-up parchment that had been flattened by travel, and an ornately carved rosewood box.

Bershad unrolled the parchment first. He read it twice, frowning.

"Well?" Felgor asked. "What's it say?"

"It says, 'Bring this letter to the Seven Anchors in Taggarstan and present it to the vampire, along with payment, and your passage to Balaria will be arranged.'"

"Vampire of Taggarstan," Felgor repeated. "You're sure?"

"I know how to read, Felgor. Why? Do you know him?"

Felgor licked his lips and glanced at Yonmar's dead body. "Not personally, no. But I've heard of him."

"Well, he's the man we need to see."

"What's the payment, though?" Vera asked.

All of them looked at the rosewood box. A bunch of Almiran gods with animal faces and wild hair were carved into the side. Bershad unclipped the silver clasp and opened it. Inside, there was an emerald egg the size of a fist. Bershad picked it up and held it next to the fire.

"Well, there's the answer to that question."

"Finger my ass while Aeternita watches," Felgor said. "That's a big egg."

"If you steal this egg," Bershad said, "I'll knock all those tiny teeth out of your mouth and sell you to a brothel so you can suck cocks for a copper a pop. Are we clear?"

Felgor scrunched up his nose. "You know, I'm getting a little tired of all these threats to my body. What'll it take for you to trust me?"

"I'll let you know when I see it," Bershad said, closing the rosewood box and giving it to Rowan. "Let's move the bodies away from here and try to get some sleep. There's plenty more walking to be done tomorrow."

15

JOLAN

Almira, City of Deepdale

Jolan woke up two hours after sunrise. It was the longest he'd slept in five years. Even after leaving Otter Rock, when he was wandering the wilds of Almira, he had been unable to stop himself from rising with the sun. A few times, he even moved to prepare a pot of coffee on a stove that no longer existed. The rain ale and featherbed had solved that problem.

Jolan's mouth was dry and his head felt as if his skull was suddenly too small for his brain. Finally, he understood the feeling the drunks of Otter Rock were trying to remove when they stumbled up to the apothecary after a long night at the tavern, asking for a tincture or a tonic to ease their pain.

Jolan actually did know how to brew a tonic that would erase a hangover entirely, but it required four ingredients from a warren: Gods Moss, eggs from a mirror frog, marrow from a purple strangle-vine, and Dainwood beets. No way he was drumming those up today.

"Too bad," he muttered to himself as he sat up, looked around, and then very nearly shat himself. Garret was in the room, sitting in a chair near the circular window that encompassed most of one wall. He was wearing his leather traveler's cloak, and there were new, dark streaks along the shoulders and sleeves. Soot or grime of some kind. Garret's hunting knife was in his lap and he was smoking a pipe.

"How was the bed?" Garret asked, blowing a two-pronged curl of smoke from his nostrils.

"I didn't know sleep could be like that," Jolan answered. "Thank you."

Garret looked out the window. "Something is wrong with my hand," he said.

"Even with the Crimson Tower moss, there will be pain for several weeks, most likely."

"Pain I can handle. There's a clumsiness in my fingers. Tingling and weakness. I can barely make a fist."

Jolan frowned. He had thought the tooth had only hit muscle, but it was possible a tendon or a nerve had been nicked as well. "Let me see your arm."

Garret extended his forearm. Jolan crossed the room and unrolled the bandage. The injury itself seemed like it was healing nicely—the wound had scabbed over and there was no sign of pus or rotting flesh. But Garret's fingertips were pale white, as if he'd been walking around in the cold for three hours without gloves.

"Damn."

"What is it?" Garret asked.

"Dragon rot."

"That is not an adequate answer."

"It's a rare complication with dragon wounds," Jolan explained. "A fragment of the Lake Screecher's tooth must have traveled up your arm through a blood vessel and gone to rot near the wrist."

"Can you get it out?"

"I never learned how to perform surgeries like that. I'd just make it worse. It can be treated with a tonic, instead. But it takes warren ingredients." Jolan thought of what he'd need. Ran through a mental inventory of his pack.

"Jolan," Garret said. "I need to leave Deepdale in the next hour. Can you fix this or not?"

Jolan licked his lips. "I already have fermented lemon lace and ginger. So, the only thing I'm missing to make a decent dragon rot tonic is norishroot. If you take regular doses for seven days, the nerve damage should go away."

"Should?"

"Will," Jolan corrected himself. "It will go away. An alchemist in the city should sell norishroot, and I think we passed one on the way in. But even a small amount is expensive."

Garret produced five gold coins from an inner pocket of his cloak and held them out to Jolan. "Wake the alchemist up if you have to. I cannot stay here much longer."

Jolan took to the streets, cursing himself for screwing up Garret's wound. Master Morgan would have never let something like that happen. Had he pulled the tooth out at an angle and caused the fragment to break off? Maybe that wasn't it at all, and he'd just numbed the arm improperly?

"No," Jolan whispered to himself, "then he'd never have regained feeling at all. Definitely dragon rot."

He was so caught up in his own thoughts, that Jolan didn't notice the tolling of the alarm bells or the steady growth of traffic as he moved east—everyone was heading in the same direction, and lots of people were pointing down one of the main thoroughfares.

"It's Lord Grealor," a tanned man near Jolan said. "I recognize the cloak."

"The fuck it is," said another.

A woman screamed from farther down the avenue and a group of wardens pushed their way through the crowd, hands on their swords and serious looks on their faces.

"Back to your business!" a warden called. "Stay away from the manor! Back to your business!"

Nobody listened. They just fell in behind the warden.

Jolan spotted the apothecary on the other side of the avenue. But the crowd—and his own curiosity—were pulling Jolan farther down the street. He gave in and started working his way through the mob. He'd see what the fuss was about, and then he'd go back to the apothecary. He turned the corner.

A man had been hanged from the mouth of a stone jaguar.

The statue was perched atop the roof of a great manor. A rope had been strung around the big cat's jaws and skull, the man lynched by a twenty-foot length of hemp cord. He was swaying back and forth in the wind about thirty strides above the street, the soles of his expensive leather boots visible to everyone below. The man's face was purple and twisted. There was a steady trickle of piss dripping off his boot.

"I'm *telling* you, that's Lord Grealor," the tanned man repeated. "I watched the bastard ride into the city a week ago and he was wearing that same jaguar cloak." The man spat. "Fucking asshole."

"Why was he back in the city?" Jolan asked.

"Came back to raise another host and take it to Floodhaven. Guess that won't be happening."

"If that's Elden Grealor," said the second man, "why the fuck was he in this manor, and not the castle?"

The tanned man smiled. "Everybody knows Elden had a honeypot he kept in there. Way I heard it, he kept a few of them in there. Real pretty ones."

"You're a liar. And that ain't Lord Grealor. If members of the High Council are spending their time swaying from jaguars these days, we're all liable to wind up in a fix."

"Funny thing, now that you mention it." The man scratched at his face. "Lord Tybolt wound up with a mouth full o' shells up in Mudwall not too long ago. That's what my nephew said, anyway. Although, he's been known to tell a tale."

"Is that what we're callin' lies these days?"

"Mudwall . . ." Jolan repeated.

He'd met Garret just a few days' walk from there.

Jolan squeezed between the two men and worked his way back to the apothecary. He passed three wardens who wore green tabards, black chain mail, and had jaguar masks hanging on their hips. The feline visages were similar to the one Bershad had worn at Otter Rock, but not quite as scary looking. Those masks meant they were part of the Jaguar Army, Bershad's old wardens. They served the Grealors now, but were famous for having kept their jaguar masks all these years, rather than carve new ones in the shape of a bear to signify their new allegiance. Morgan had talked about them sometimes. Said that any other wardens would be lynched for such a brazen display. But the Jaguar Army were some of the most fearsome warriors in the realm of Terra, so lords tended to look the other way so long as they fought when they were asked.

All of the wardens were staring at the hanging man.

"How the fuck are we gonna get him down?" one asked.

"We gotta get into the manor, first," said another. "Cumberland says Grealor's wardens have barricaded the door and drawn steel. They think we killed him."

"Gods, they want a fight?"

"All I know is that if I was a high-warden who lynched my own lord, I'd start pointing fingers pretty quick, too. The lackeys from the capital all think we're still Bershad men anyway."

The first warden shook his head, keeping his eyes high. "What a goatfuck. Let's see if we can rustle up some more men."

Back at the apothecary, the shopkeeper was just unlocking the door.

"They catch a pickpocket or something?" she asked Jolan, motioning to the crowd. He ignored the question, knowing that if he told the woman what had really happened, she'd close the shop and go have a look for herself.

"I need half an ounce of norishroot and a sterile glass flask." Jolan showed her the gold coins. "And I need them quick."

———

Half an hour later, Jolan was back at the inn. Garret was waiting for him, still smoking his pipe and staring out the window. The hunting knife was back in its sheath on his hip.

"Somebody murdered a lord," Jolan said as he unpacked the norishroot and glass flask. He dug up his mortar and pestle and started grinding the herb down.

"Did they."

"Strung him up above the street by a jaguar statue. He's just sway-ing out there for a big crowd to see."

"How do you know he didn't hang himself? Might be he got de-pressed or something."

Jolan stopped his work for a moment. Glanced at Garret. Now that he was back in the room with the quiet, mysterious man, he became painfully aware of how easy it would have been to disappear into the city instead. But now there was nothing left to do but finish the tonic.

He ground the norishroot into powder, put it in the glass flask, then added the fermented lemon lace he'd taken from Morgan's apothecary. He winced when he saw he'd have to use all of it. Lemon lace was far less common than norishroot—he could have sold that vial for a sack of gold instead of a few coins. But the tonic wouldn't work without it, and despite Jolan's growing fear of Garret, he couldn't bring himself to offer him a faulty product. He sliced four thick discs from a piece of ginger and added them to the flask, too. The lemon lace would react with the norishroot and create a power-ful tonic that would kill the dragon rot in Garret's body. The ginger was just for flavor.

"That about done?" Garret asked.

"Yes." Jolan plugged the flask with a cork. Wrapped the glass bottle in leather so it wouldn't crack on the road. He handed it to Garret. "Take a sip once a day until it's empty. Your hand will start feeling better after a few days, but keep drinking it until it's gone. That's important."

Garret stood up and took the flask. After taking a swallow, he stowed it in the goat bladder that sat on his hip. "I'm in your debt once again, Jolan," he said. Garret extended his left hand, struggling a little with the motion. There were five more gold coins in his palm. Jolan looked at the money, then looked at Garret's other hand, hang-ing loose at his right side, just below the hilt of that razor-sharp hunting dagger.

"It was nothing," he said. "I don't need that. Really. I just . . . I just want to see the Dainwood dragon warrens."

16

GARRET

Almira, City of Deepdale

Garret wasn't happy about having to murder the boy, but Jolan was too smart for his own good. He held out the money and waited for Jolan to take it so that he could slash his throat open. But the boy didn't move.

He just stared back at him. No begging. No pleading. It made Garret like him even more, but it didn't change the fact that Jolan needed to die.

The thundering of boots on loose wooden steps interrupted the moment. Three wardens wearing black chain mail burst into the room. They had bear masks on their hips. One was a sergeant, the other was extremely fat for a soldier, and the third was lean and careful, sticking to the far end of the room. All of them had hands on the grips of their sheathed swords. That was a mistake—it was a small room, and drawing long steel would be difficult. Should have done it before coming in.

The sergeant had thick jowls and droopy eyes. He stepped forward, looking at the boy. "Are you Jolan of Otter Rock?" he asked.

"I . . . no," Jolan said.

The sergeant looked around the room a moment, scanning the alchemy equipment and the backpack full of ingredients. He sniffed, then spat on the floor near Jolan's foot.

"That is interesting news," he said. "Because you match his description, and I don't know too many boys who tote all that alchemist shit around for fun. 'Cept apprentices. Ex-apprentices in your case."

"What's this about, Sergeant?" Garret asked. He didn't want to cause a scene. Scenes created attention. And attention would put him even further behind schedule than he already was.

"That kid burned down an apothecary that belonged to Lord

Nimbu up north, then took off. Apparently Nimbu holds a grudge for that kind of behavior. He's had sentinels posting ransoms all over Almira for the past month—puttin' 'em around inns and the like. Took a while, but word got down here in the south. Thought you could hide in Deepdale, eh, boy?"

"My name isn't Jolan," Jolan insisted. "I'm from a town called Briarwood in—"

"Save it." The sergeant stopped him with a mailed hand. "Elden Grealor is hanging from a manor and leaking piss into the street; I've got no time for lying children. Some lord will decide your fate." The man's droopy eyes slid over to Garret. "You were traveling with him?"

"You could say that," Garret admitted. There was no point trying to hide it—the innkeeper was probably the one who'd reported the boy. The sergeant seemed to think everything over. He ran his tongue over the front of his teeth while he stared at Garret.

"You best come with us, too, then, until we get this cleared . . ."

Garret rushed forward and jammed his hunting knife into the sergeant's right ear—the silver tip poked out of his left temple, a worm-sized piece of brain seeping from the wound. The sergeant's droopy eyes came to life briefly, then lolled back in his head. His knees went slack. Garret yanked his knife free from the man's skull and heaved his corpse into the fat warden, who tried to dodge his dead sergeant but failed. He lost his balance and fell down against the far wall.

Garret darted left—moving to slit the third soldier's throat—but somehow the quick bastard had gotten his weapon drawn and managed to parry the attack. A ripple of pain shot up Garret's arm as his knife clanged off the steel. On instinct, he chopped at the man's throat with his left hand, but with the dragon rot he couldn't tighten his fingers enough to make it a killing stroke.

The soldier gagged, but raised his sword for a counterriposte at the same time. It was bad luck to have been arrested by a capable warden—the steel hanging in most of those idiots' scabbards was just for show. Garret skipped backward, avoiding a strike that would have cut him from collarbone to lung. He flipped his knife into a reverse grip and prepared for the next attack, but he never had the chance. The fat warden crashed into him with a desperate tackle, knocking the air out of Garret's lungs and sending him to the ground with a thump, then landing on top of him.

Call it a killer's instinct or call it luck, but Garret's knife ended up in the fat man's eye when they fell. Blood spurted onto Garret's face. The warden's jaws clamped together so hard that three of his teeth cracked before he died.

The third warden walked toward him, rubbing his throat.

"Fucking asshole," he muttered, raising his blade.

Garret had always assumed he would meet a violent end, but lying on the floor of an inn, covered in blood and weighted down by a fat corpse wasn't quite the death he'd pictured.

Then a flying stone pestle crashed into the warden's temple. The man dropped to the ground like a piece of timber, either dead or unconscious. Garret yanked the hunting knife out of the fat man's eye, stood up, crossed the room, and slashed his throat.

Jolan was quivering in the corner. Staring at the carnage and taking fast, shallow breaths.

"You were about to kill me," Jolan said, not looking away from the bodies.

"Yes."

Jolan took a few more breaths, then looked at Garret.

"Go ahead, then."

17

BERSHAD

Skojit Territory, Razorback Mountains

With Yonmar dead, they moved much faster.

Felgor seemed to wake up stronger each morning, despite the long leagues of walking and meager rations. Rowan had used more of Felgor's stolen salt to turn a few rabbit chunks into jerky so they'd have something to eat throughout the day.

"It's the sunlight," he said when Vera questioned his sprightly step. "Balarians are like sunflowers—all we need is some golden rays and a bit of water."

"Guess you won't be needing any more rabbit then, eh?" Rowan had said.

"*Like* sunflowers, I said. It's a metaphor. That's when you talk about one thing, but really it's a symbol for—"

"I know what a metaphor is," Rowan said.

"Course you do, my dear Rowan," Felgor said. "Course you do."

Rowan mumbled something to himself about sunflowers and stew and idiot Balarians, but Bershad could tell the thief was growing on his forsaken shield. Rowan always had a soft spot for the outcasts and malcontents of the world.

They spent many days moving along a series of game trails, avoiding the larger paths that could be used by Skojit. The ground was full of sharp stones, prickly grass, and patches of snow in the shadows that hadn't yet been warmed enough to melt. The first time he'd come through the pass, the Balarians took him around a lake near the summit of the mountain. Bershad kept his eyes out for the two ridges that would lead back there, but everything looked different coming from this side. He hadn't bothered to check his back trail when he was being marched out of the country the first time.

At one point, Felgor huffed his way up next to Bershad while he was taking some water.

"I have to thank you," Felgor said.

"That right?" Bershad grunted, wiping some sweat from the edge of his beard.

"My head would be splinters if it wasn't for you." Felgor squinted off into the distance. "So yeah, I do."

Bershad lowered the water skin. Studied Felgor, but didn't say anything.

"You know, you're an awfully sullen person for a man who fills his day with so many good deeds," Felgor continued. "Saving that town. Saving me. Only one of us you didn't save was Yonmar, and being honest, that asshole bothered me. Won't miss his highborn ass none."

Bershad still didn't say anything. Felgor moved to leave.

"Time comes," Bershad said, stopping him. "Might be the situation is reversed. And I'm the one with a blade coming down toward my neck." He offered Felgor the water. "You want to thank me, return the fucking favor, yeah?"

After the Skojit ambush, they all agreed it was better to camp with-out a fire. Instead, Bershad, Rowan, and Felgor wrapped themselves in their cloaks and gnawed on salted rabbit meat. Vera was the only one who seemed untroubled by the cold. At night, she wrapped their extra cloak around Alfonso instead of using it for herself.

"Pretty sure you're the first woman I've known who can stand a chill better than a man," Rowan said. "My wife was always com-plaining about drafts."

"You had a wife?" Felgor asked.

"Why's that so hard to believe?"

Felgor didn't answer. Just wrapped himself tighter in his cloak.

"Cold is relative," Vera said. "I've had far worse."

"Gods, where?" Rowan asked.

"The islands of Papyria hook north. Very far north."

"You're from all the way up there?" Felgor asked.

"Nobody is from there anymore. But for hundreds of years that's where widows have been sent to train. One of the most distant is-lands on the Papyrian archipelago is called Roriku. There is a moun-tain there that is crusted with ice even in the height of summer. I spent eighteen years there."

"What was it like?" Rowan asked. "The training, I mean."

"It was cold, Rowan. Much colder than this. Many of my fellow widows did not survive."

"Why do it then?" Bershad asked.

"Every widow who completes the training earns her sharkskin armor. We spend a lifetime protecting Papyrian royalty. The empress herself is guarded by one hundred and eight of my sisters at all times." Vera shrugged. "I wanted to be one of them."

"If you signed up to protect the empress of Papyria, it must burn your piss to be up here on this mountain with a bunch of outlander men, chasing after an Almiran princess," Felgor said.

"That is one way to put it." She moved a stray hair behind her ear. "But at least I'm not cold."

Everyone laughed at that. Bershad kept looking at Vera, though. Saw a look he didn't recognize on her face. Sadness.

Rowan saw it, too.

"I just realized you were Kira's widow," he said. "You must have been."

Vera gave a slow nod. "That's right. I've been by her side for almost her entire life." Vera trailed off. Looked down at her fists. "And I will never forgive myself for allowing her to be taken."

"It wasn't your fault," Rowan said. "You couldn't watch her every second of the day. Nobody could have."

"That doesn't matter. Protecting her was my sworn duty, and I failed. There is no excuse."

Nobody said anything for a few moments. Bershad could imagine the sort of guilt and pain Vera was holding. He carried something similar.

"Kira is still alive," Bershad said eventually. "And so are you. Shame won't help you get her back. You've got to stay focused on the job ahead."

Vera didn't say anything, but her face started to look a little less grim.

"Kira was just a child when I got my bars," Bershad said, thinking it'd be good to lighten the mood a little. "What kind of person did she grow up to be?"

Vera considered that. "She's beautiful. Funny. Always able to make people laugh with an effortless kind of grace. Kira was the center of attention at every feast and festival. People fall in love with her within moments of meeting her."

"Sounds like my kind of princess," Felgor muttered.

Vera chewed her lip for a moment.

"But she's also reckless," she continued. "Slower to forgive than her father and more devious than her sister. Full of wild passion."

"Now I like her even more," Felgor said, closing his eyes.

"Careful, Balarian. I once broke every bone in a small lord's hand for a comment like that."

Felgor put his palms up in mock surrender, but didn't open his eyes. "No offense meant, little spider."

Days later, their path was interrupted by a river. It rushed from the mountains in a blue torrent—crashing across rocks and steep drops.

"We need to cross this," Bershad said, raising his voice to be heard over the river's roar.

"You're sure?" Vera asked. The current was moving with such ferocity that fording the river looked impossible no matter where they tried it.

Bershad nodded, looking up the river. "A good trail continues on the far side, but if we stay on this bank it's a wild mess. I definitely crossed somewhere around here with the Balarians."

"How?" Felgor asked, eyeing the water.

Bershad shrugged. "It was easy in autumn, the river was barely running. But with the spring snowmelt . . ."

"A different river," Rowan said. "So how are we getting across this thing today?"

Bershad looked at everyone's curious faces, and then pointed about a hundred yards up the river. There was a fallen tree stretching across the water.

"That wood's rotten," Rowan said when they got up to the trunk. "And the donkey is going to trip and die if we try to lead him across."

"It's just damp. We've taken Alfonso across worse than this."

"Ten years ago, maybe."

Bershad looked at the log. It probably was starting to rot, but the log was three feet wide at its thinnest spot near the other bank, and he didn't think they'd find a better crossing. The land on their side of the river was covered with thick forest and jagged slices of rock. If they had to stray too far from the river Bershad was afraid they'd get lost.

"The thief first. Then the donkey."

To Bershad's surprise, Felgor perked up at that.

"Time for a little hop?" he asked cheerfully.

"That's right," Bershad said.

"Not a problem."

Felgor heaved his small backpack across the river, and then tip-toed across the trunk—arms outstretched and feet close together. He leapt off onto the far side of the river and performed several quick bows. Then his eyes darted around, scanning the considerable gap he'd managed to put between himself and his captors. He had a look on his face like he'd been told a secret he didn't quite believe. Bershad moved to cross the trunk, but Vera was ahead of him.

She took two steps forward and unwound one of the slings from her thigh. Loaded it with a lead shot from the pouch on her hip.

"I see your head filling up with ideas, Felgor," Vera said. "Better you keep your skull empty. Show me your back, and I'll show you a shot through the knee. The donkey can take a cripple up the mountain just as easily."

Felgor pressed his lips into a thin line. "One of these days, little spider, you're going to start trusting me."

"But not today."

Bershad nodded at Vera. "Now Alfonso."

Rowan sighed and picked up the donkey's reins. He stepped onto the wooden trunk and began to lead him across. Alfonso sniffed when he reached the makeshift bridge, tested the trunk with one hoof, snorted, and then followed.

When they were halfway across, the wood started to sag.

"Best hurry, Rowan."

Rowan grunted and kept going, placing his feet carefully as he neared the far bank. He was two or three steps from the far bank when the trunk splintered.

Alfonso let out a panicked whinny, and then scrambled forward, hooves clopping at the rotten trunk and sending pieces of wood into the churning water below. His muzzle rammed into Rowan, who fell forward and managed to grasp a rocky ledge before Alfonso used the middle of his back as a bridge onto solid ground. A heartbeat later, the trunk snapped and went careening into the river.

"Just damp, you bastard?" Rowan yelled, getting up and rubbing his back. Alfonso was already cropping at the tall grass on that side of the river, the near-death experience forgotten. Bershad looked over at Vera.

"Guess we're stuck with each other," he said.

Vera removed the shot from her sling in a smooth, practiced motion and put it back in the satchel she kept on her hip. "The Balarian is responsible for getting me into the Imperial Palace. I do not want to be separated from him for long. Is there another crossing higher up?"

"No idea." Bershad scanned the thick forest ahead. It would be difficult to stay close to the river—the bank turned into a high shelf of rock on their side, and the twisted trees grew too close together to walk through.

"What's the plan now?" Felgor called from the other side.

"The trail's just up there on your side," Bershad called over the rush of water, pointing. "It follows the river until it reaches a dragon warren. We'll meet you there."

"How far?" Rowan called back.

"A day for you. Maybe a little less. But this side is for shit so we'll be behind you."

"Armor?" Rowan asked.

"Just the mask." If they were climbing up this side of the river, the rest was too heavy. "One of the spears, too."

Rowan nodded and moved over to Alfonso's pack. He unstrapped the jaguar helm from the saddle horn and grabbed one of the empty water skins, then wrapped them both up together and tossed them across the water. Bershad caught it, slung the skin over one shoulder, and fixed the mask onto a belt hook. The spear came next—Rowan tossed it a few feet to Bershad's right so that he could snatch it from the air.

"Stay with the river, you can't get lost," Bershad said, then turned back to Vera. "You ready?"

She nodded and motioned for Bershad to lead the way. On the other side, Rowan and Felgor disappeared, following the easy trail that wrapped its way up the mountain in lazy switchbacks.

Within a hundred yards, Bershad and Vera descended into a gloomy devastation of trees and boulders. They tried to pick their way through it at first, sticking close to the river and hoping for another crossing, but after three hours they were both sweaty and covered with scratches from the tree twigs and sharp rocks they had to clamber over on all fours.

Bershad stopped and leaned over the bank just enough to fill the water skin. He had to hold it with both hands to keep it from being torn free and lost.

"We can't keep going along the river," he said after taking a few gulps of water and passing it to Vera.

Vera nodded. "Agreed."

Bershad found a narrow ridge of rock that they could follow, but it was moving them in the wrong direction. They would lose a lot of time if they didn't find a drainage path or ravine they could use to climb higher, but there wasn't another option that he could see.

They followed the ridge for most of the morning. Around noon, Vera stopped. "You're not limping anymore."

"Huh?" Bershad turned around.

"Your leg. The arrow. Yesterday you were limping." Vera was frowning.

Bershad looked down and rubbed his leg. Even without moss, he healed faster than a normal man.

"I'm used to pain," he said.

"No," Vera said. "This is something else. An arrow through the meat of your leg from, what, fifty yards?"

Bershad shrugged. It had been more like thirty.

"You shouldn't even be walking."

"It's a good thing I can," Bershad said. "Otherwise you'd have to carry me."

This was the first time anyone besides Rowan had been around long enough to watch him recover from an injury. Bershad realized he should have been more careful about it.

Vera kept frowning at him. "What's the worst wound you ever took?"

"We don't have time for this." Bershad moved to continue across the shelf. But Vera stopped him with a hand on his shoulder.

"Tell me."

Bershad couldn't tell her about his worst injury, which was when that Gray-Winged Nomad had bitten into his stomach outside of Mudwall and made a mess of his guts. Along with the dragontooth dagger, he'd gotten two apple-sized scars on his belly from the lizard's fangs. Rowan had plugged the wounds with moss and lugged Bershad around in a litter for two weeks, figuring the Flawless Bershad was finally done for. But he was walking by the third week and killing dragons again by the fourth.

"I got my foot chewed to the bone by a Red Skull once," Bershad said instead.

"That should have crippled you," Vera said.

"Guess that makes me the luckiest bastard in the realm of fucking Terra," Bershad said in a voice that was closer to a snarl than he'd intended. "Are we going to stand here talking all day, or are we going to move on?"

Vera stepped back a few paces. She looked at him like he was a horse that wasn't entirely broken, but she still had to ride. "No," she said. "Let's go."

They hiked for hours, but never found a ravine or drainage back to the river. As evening approached, they passed through a field that was strewn with massive rocks from an ancient landslide. The trail of rocks ended at a steep but climbable cliff.

"We should wait up there," Vera said, pointing at the trail.

"Why?"

"If there are men following us, this is a good place to get acquainted with them."

She had a point. Bershad hooked his spear through a loop on the back of his sword belt.

"All right." He began to scale the first big boulder, struggling for good handholds.

Vera gave a short grunt that could have been her version of a laugh, then stepped forward and lifted herself up with practiced grace.

"Don't slip," she said as she passed him.

When Bershad reached the first ledge of the cliff, breathing hard from the climb, she hauled him over the lip. There was a flat area about forty paces across before the cliff rose again.

"Dark soon," she said, pointing at the western sky.

"This is as good a spot as any," Bershad said. "In the low light, it's too easy to fall trying to get higher."

"For you, maybe. You climb like a drunken child."

Bershad ignored her, scanning the mess of trees and rocks they'd crossed that afternoon. "You really think Skojit'll follow us?"

"What would you do if a group of outlanders hiked through your land and killed a bunch of your friends?" Vera asked.

"I don't have any friends," Bershad said. "But I get your point."

Bershad hunkered down beneath a rocky overhang with a long shadow. Vera tucked herself next to him, sitting so close to Bershad that he could smell the faint scent of Papyrian oil in her hair. They had a clear view of the field below, but were both hidden in the shadows.

They waited for hours. The moon cast a pale light over the rocks and trees below. A few mice picked their way around between Bershad's boots, hunting for scraps. All of them scattered when an owl swooped down from a nearby tree. Bershad watched the owl's wings beat until it disappeared into the gloom.

Bershad was about to ask Vera what Papyrian owls were like, but she tightened her shoulders, then went still. Bershad scanned the ledge without moving anything except his eyes, trying to figure out what had spooked her. He would have missed the two white eyes in the darkness if the Skojit hadn't blinked right as Bershad's gaze was passing over him.

The Skojit's face was gaunt, wreathed by wild, unkempt hair. He watched for a while longer, then he disappeared below without a sound.

Vera and Bershad didn't move or speak for half an hour. Then, it was only whispers.

"What do you think?" Vera asked.

"Hard to say. But he was awful subtle for a man who didn't think anyone was up here. Our tracks couldn't have been too difficult to follow."

"Agreed. What next?"

The Skojit answered the question for him. Off in the distance— maybe four hundred yards past the place they'd separated from the trail—the yellow-and-orange glow of a fire appeared. Soon it grew into a massive pillar of light in the dark trees.

"Shit," Bershad muttered.

Without a sound, Vera got on her belly and crawled to the edge of the cliff.

"To follow us so carefully and then light a fire like that," she whispered as Bershad came up behind her. "Doesn't make sense."

"Could be they figure the trail's gone cold."

"You don't believe that," Vera said.

"No," Bershad said. "And even if I did, I'm not going to cross these mountains looking over my shoulder every ten minutes. How far can you sling one of those rocks?"

"If I can see them, I can kill them. But I need room to swing it." She motioned to the fire. "At night, and tangled in those trees, I can probably only get one or two shots off. The sling is better suited for open spaces."

If there were more than three or four Skojit, this would be difficult.

"Let's go take a look," Bershad said. "Quietly."

"You're the loud one," Vera said. "Look at this."

Vera grabbed a handful of his hair. Scoffed. Then she unwound two lengths of leather cord from her hair and used it to tie Bershad's hair in a tight knot.

"I can stop the jingling," she whispered as she worked, "but these rings of yours reflect moonlight like fucking mirrors."

Bershad shrugged. "It'd be dawn by the time we got them cut out."

They crept down the cliff and crossed the field, heading toward the fire. When they got within a few hundred strides, they crawled the rest of the way, using a thicket of scrub pines for cover as they snuck up on the Skojit camp.

Six men. They were roasting a mountain goat and talking by the fire. They wore the same wild combination of thick furs and mismatched armor as the Skojit who'd ambushed them before. But this group seemed to have scavenged more expensive gear from the corpses of their enemies—steel mail, scale gloves. One had a gilded breastplate that looked freshly forged.

"Think they crossed the river after all?" one of them asked. His hair stretched down to his waist, but was cut into a Mohawk and dyed blue. The Skojit spoke a heavily accented version of Ghalamarian that was filled with slang and odd pronunciations, but Bershad could more or less understand it.

"Not all of them. Two came this way," another one said. He was short and wiry, but sat closest to the fire and seemed to be the only one eating food. He had the casual confidence of the man in charge.

"But you can't find them," Mohawk said.

"Footprints and broken twigs aren't the only way to find flatlanders." The leader took a bite of goat using a long, curved knife. Grease ran down the side of his face. He nodded his head. Seemed to like the taste. "Eat."

The others began slicing off pieces of meat. For a while there was just the sound of men chewing. Attacking the Skojit while they were eating wasn't a bad idea—nobody was holding a spear or axe. But they each had knives, and a man could do a lot of killing with a small blade if he had a mind to. Better to wait until some of them went to sleep.

"Crow, you ever seen a man killed like Splitnose?" Mohawk asked the man next to him. He seemed to be the talker in the group. "Cut damn near in half down the middle."

"Thunderclap killed a man like that once," Crow said, talking around a mouthful of food. "Axe."

"Dragonshit," Mohawk said. "Thunderclap did a boy like that and you know it. Ten years old at the most. And skinny."

Crow gave Mohawk an angry glance but said nothing. Just swallowed and took another bite. They had four or five big skins of wine in the camp, all of them full, but nobody was drinking.

"Yeah, it's a real piece of work we're chasing, I think," Mohawk continued. "Smashed in Red Legs's skull, too. We found her away from the others."

"I always liked Red Legs," one of the other men said.

"You only liked her 'cause she'd do that thing with her mouth on your cock."

The man shrugged. "I liked her jokes, too."

The men reduced the goat to a pile of red bones within twenty minutes. The skinny leader kept his eyes on the forest, scanning one way and then another with watchful eyes.

"Right, then," he said eventually. "Crow takes first watch."

The men grumbled but did as they were told. They arranged themselves in a circle so that each man could stand up fast and cover a different part of the woods. They also tucked their weapons inside their cloaks, being careful to cover the steel and prevent it from catching the moonlight. They pretended to snore while Crow perched on a rock, only watching one direction. After a while he pretended to doze off, too.

Bershad motioned for Vera to follow him, and crawled back beneath the scrub pines until they dipped down into a low spot. He leaned close so that his lips were right next to her ear.

"Ambush," he whispered. His nose filled with the scent of Papyrian oil again—all lavender and lilacs.

She nodded. Brought her face around to whisper in his ear. "Still want to kill them?"

"They'll just keep after us if we don't." He thought about how they could get this done just the two of them. It wouldn't be easy. "Circle around to the other side, I'll be waiting back where we were. Kill the sentry with your sling. Might be they hold fast. Might be they scatter. Either way, kill the next one that gets up, then I'll throw the spear and charge. Soon as I'm surrounded, you make your way in and get as many as you can from behind."

"Simple enough."

"You try to get too clever with your killing, you'll just get tangled up in your own genius."

Rowan had told him that.

Vera melted into the darkness. Bershad moved back to the edge of the camp and waited. The sentry, Crow, was still pretending to sleep. Bershad slid his mask over his head and cinched the straps tight.

The familiar pressure on his cheeks and forehead was comforting. His breath was hot on his skin. He waited. A few minutes later, Bershad heard a faint whooshing sound from the far side of the camp.

Crow's head exploded. Red mush and bits of skull blew through the air in all directions. A scrap of scalp landed in the fire. Skin and hair bubbled on the flames. At first none of the other men moved. But Bershad could see the milky white orbs of open eyes searching in the moonlight. A moment later the skinny leader sprang up with a howl, and the rest followed and scattered in different directions.

"Fuck," Bershad hissed.

Vera's next shot hit the Skojit that had charged in Bershad's direction. The rock took a massive chunk of flesh off his back, exposing a mangled mess of meat and shattered bone. The Skojit fell forward on his face. Tried to get up. Failed. Slumped over.

After the shot, the skinny leader switched directions almost immediately, heading toward Vera. He had a short sword in each hand and moved with the calm determination of a man who had been ambushed before. He'd be on her before she had time to reload the sling.

Mohawk and the other two Skojit were looking in different directions. Scanning the darkness for someone to kill. Bershad picked the one who was closest to discovering him and threw his spear. Impaled the Skojit just below the place his two collarbones met.

There was a wet sound. Blood flooded down his chest. The Skojit dropped to his knees and died. Bershad drew his sword.

When Mohawk and the other Skojit—a short and beefy man with a pot belly—saw Bershad was alone, they fanned out in opposite directions. Mohawk to the left and Pot Belly to the right. The firelight put an orange glow on their skin. Mohawk was carrying a double-headed axe made from two enormous slabs of sharpened stone. Pot Belly had a crude mace—one thick piece of oak with iron barbs hammered through the tip.

"You're the one," Mohawk said, continuing to move to the left. He was a big man but he had quick, agile feet.

"I'm the one," Bershad said, his voice muffled behind the black, feline visage.

"Some mask," Mohawk said. "A cat, is it?"

"Jaguar."

Mohawk nodded, as if it had been a crucial question. "I promise not to crush it with my axe, if you promise not to cut me in half," he said. Smiling now. Bershad smiled, too, but all Mohawk saw was the jaguar's snarl.

"Deal."

Bershad knew from experience that panic—not poor odds—is what generally kills outnumbered men. Most people get over-whelmed and start whipping their head one way and then the other, trying to keep all their enemies in sight. Bad for your balance. The Skojit knew that, too, because they fanned out so far to either side—working to divide Bershad's attention until one of them got a view of his back and put a hole in it. They were patient and careful, nei-ther one eager to get killed in a deal where they'd been given such a clear advantage.

But Bershad didn't panic. He waited until the two Skojit were as far away from each other as they were going to get, and Mohawk was in midstride and just a little off balance. Then he charged Pot Belly, who seemed like he would be easier to kill.

The beefy Skojit had just enough time to look surprised and then pull his mace back before Bershad was on him—rushing at full speed and thrusting his sword toward the Skojit's fat chest. Pot Belly swiped his mace across himself in a clumsy parry. Bershad's blade got tan-gled between two of the iron spikes, and he felt the grip being wrenched away as the Skojit pulled his mace down and to the left.

Instead of getting into a pushing and pulling match for it—which would have taken about as much time as Mohawk needed to decapi-tate him from behind—Bershad let go of his sword. The grip whipped out of his hands and slammed into the dirt with a heavy thud. Pot Belly smiled. Came around for a killing stroke. But Ber-shad grabbed the Skojit by his furry collar and started head-butting him in the face.

Three quick hits, as fast and hard as Bershad could make them. The forehead of Bershad's mask was reinforced with steel strips, so Pot Belly's face lost some of its shape with each crushing blow. After the third hit, his eyes rolled back in his head and he dropped his mace. Went limp.

Bershad dove to his left just in time to dodge Mohawk's axe. The Skojit sheared his friend's arm off at the shoulder, cleaving flesh and bone as if it was a dried-out log. Pot Belly fell to the ground and started the jolty twitches dying men get.

Mohawk bulled toward Bershad, his axe coming in sweeping arcs of violence. He whirled the weapon with frightening coordination—twisting and weaving it through the air with both hands. Bershad ducked and skipped from side to side, staying one very small step ahead of the crescent-shaped death the Skojit was bringing down on him.

Bershad shifted left, tripped, and slammed mask-first into the dirt. Rolled away just as the stone blade crunched into the area his head had occupied a moment earlier. Got to his feet just as Mohawk brought his axe around for a sweeping horizontal cut. He ducked the axe swing and crashed into Mohawk's legs.

The big bastard stumbled but didn't fall over. He cracked Bershad in the back with the butt of his axe. Once. Twice. There was a spike on the end that punched through Bershad's cloak and bit into flesh.

Bershad drew the dragontooth dagger from the small of his back, reached around Mohawk's leg, and hamstrung him. The Skojit groaned as the muscles in his leg ripped apart.

Then, finally, the big bastard fell over.

Even as his ass and ruined leg hit the ground, Mohawk brought the axe around for a final, murderous effort. But Bershad caught his arm and drove the dagger through all the meat and tendons in the Skojit's wrist. The axe fell from his maimed hand. Bershad slit his throat in one brutal motion. The blade nearly cut Mohawk's entire head off, sharp as it was.

Bershad felt the old bloodlust rising in his chest, hot and tight, but pushed it down. Vera was still fighting. He picked up his sword and rushed into the darkness, following the sound of grunts and scrapes of metal on metal. When he found Vera and the skinny leader, they were wrestling on the ground. Vera had managed to get herself behind the skinny Skojit, who looked like he was bleeding from four or five different stab wounds, but somehow wasn't dead. She was working hard to slit his throat with one of her daggers.

The leather armor on Vera's left shoulder had been sheared off, exposing links of chain mail beneath. The Skojit was holding the dagger off his neck with one mangled hand and twisting the fingers of Vera's free hand with the other. Every muscle in his wiry arm was bulging at the pressure he was grinding into her bones.

Bershad rushed forward and stomped his boot into the back of Vera's dagger—shoving the blade deep into the Skojit's throat.

Dark blood poured from the wound, then from the Skojit's mouth. Bershad stomped again. Killed him. Bershad stepped back and took a few deep breaths, trying to calm the mad tide rushing through his head. Vera untangled herself from his body with the stiff, timid movements of someone who knew there was about to be a lot of pain coming her way.

"You got the others?" she asked between heavy breaths.

Bershad nodded, pulled off his mask, and wiped the stinging sweat from his eyes.

"Bastard was quick," she muttered, pulling her blade out of his throat with a wet sound.

Bershad looked down at the corpse. Then at Vera's left hand. Every finger was twisted and bent—each one going in a different, unnatural direction.

"That's an issue," Bershad said.

She looked at it and grimaced, as if she was just now noticing the problem. "Black skies. Shouldn't have let him get ahold of me."

"Let's go back to the fire. I'll see what I can do."

18

ASHLYN

Almira, Castle Malgrave

Ashlyn sat on a canopied balcony built along the inner wall of Flood-haven. She had spent every morning there for the last two weeks, watching the arrival of the wardens of Almira who'd come for her coronation. Her father had told her once that it was good for a warden to see his liege as he entered the capital. It reminded him who he answered to if he misbehaved.

Ashlyn was doing it for a different reason. She sat with her leather-bound ledger in her lap taking an inventory of the traffic into the capital. Presently, Crellin Nimbu was riding at the head of fifty wardens. He was a relatively poor small lord who ruled Otter Rock and a few other villages in the Blakmar province. None of his wardens wore the same type of armor or rode the same breed of horse, but all of them wore yellow cloaks and masks carved into the faces of otters to show that they were sworn to Nimbu. Most of the masks looked freshly carved.

He'd most likely hired the new wardens in anticipation of the profits he'd receive from the dragon that Bershad killed for him at Otter Rock. If the money fell through, or the wardens found better pay elsewhere, they would drop their new otter masks in the mud and make different ones. Among the small lords, a warden's loyalty was almost as temporary as a mud totem set next to a river's edge on a rainy day.

Truth be told, loyalty wasn't much stronger for the high lords. They just paid better.

Kira would have liked watching the wardens arrive—she always adored the fanfare of Floodhaven court. During feasts, she would flit from table to table, chatting with different lords and laughing at their jokes. Everyone liked her immediately—it was one of her gifts. Ashlyn felt a pang of sadness when she realized that feasts and royal audiences were pretty much the only time she'd seen her younger sister in the last seven years. They'd never spent much time together as children, but once Ashlyn became the Malgrave heir, they'd become strangers. On the surface, Ashlyn appeared to be the loyal and protective older sister—the queen who was willing to launch a fleet and an army to help her family. But Ashlyn didn't feel like a good sister. If she had to choose between rescuing Kira and stopping Mercer, she knew what her choice would be. That knowledge made her feel ugly and cold, but it didn't change her mind.

Ashlyn faked a smile and waved at Lord Nimbu as he passed below the portcullis. He saluted her with a violent double tap on his chest. Ashlyn rolled her eyes—she'd never shared Kira's enthusiasm for elaborate displays.

She ticked off the new wardens in her ledger. One slash at a time, her army was being assembled.

Ashlyn leafed through the pages and worked out a quick sum of the wardens who had arrived so far. Small lords had been pouring into Floodhaven from the Atlas Coast for weeks. Nearly five thousand strong and more arriving every day. As for the high lords, Linkon Pommol had delivered one thousand wardens—the entirety of his obligation. Lords Brock and Korbon had both managed about half the requested amount, also with more arriving every day. That made a total of nearly thirteen thousand wardens in Floodhaven.

But the area for Cedar Wallace's tally sat empty. Not a single wolf-masked warden inside the city.

He claimed delays from heavy spring rains in the west. That made Ashlyn nervous, but not nearly as nervous as the fact that there had also been no news from Deepdale or Mudwall in weeks. She had no idea how soon Elden Grealor's host would be ready. She did not even know if Uylnar Went was alive in Mudwall. When messages stopped arriving in her dovecote, Ashlyn had dispatched half a dozen sentinels to both cities. Nothing. Without information, she was blind. More importantly, she couldn't control the army she'd summoned to the capital without the return of her Malgrave wardens and Elden Grealor's men from Deepdale. If the lords of the Gorgon didn't feel outnumbered in Floodhaven, they would get ambitious. Ashlyn couldn't afford that. Not now.

An hour later, one of Carlyle's wardens came onto the balcony, his forehead wet with sweat. He started to speak, but was breathing too hard to understand.

"It's all right," Ashlyn said. "Take a moment to collect yourself."

The warden nodded. Took several long, deep breaths.

"My queen," he said. "They're here."

———

Ashlyn stood on a high balcony of the King's Tower, looking through a telescope. Seventy-two Papyrian frigates dotted the horizon of Terra. Each mast was eighty strides tall, cut from ancient Papyrian cedars. It looked to Ashlyn as if a burned-out forest was lurching across the sea toward the castle. The hulls were all dyed deep black by the oil of a Milk Wing Dragon—a breed rarely seen beyond the islands of Papyria. Their sails were down, but their oars were digging hard toward shore. The leading ship of the fleet had strung a massive Papyrian banner to its mast—an orca leaping above a tree-covered island.

Ashlyn counted one last time to be sure, then closed the telescope and scratched a few quick notes in her journal. Seventy-two ships.

"Only three missing," she said to herself. "Three is not bad for a fleet that size moving along the Broken Peninsula. Not bad at all."

"How long until they make port?" Hayden asked.

"At that pace, eight . . . maybe nine hours," Ashlyn answered. "But there is a coastal wind moving along our shore they have almost reached. They should open their sails again soon."

As if the sailors had heard her, the ships raised their sails—dozens of colors popped across the horizon: reds, blues, striped oranges, and blacks. The burned-out forest transformed into a floating garden of fabric.

"Two hours," Ashlyn said. "Maybe less."

The arrival of the Papyrian fleet meant that one way or another, she could stop the emperor's dragon cull. She'd have much rather seen a single ship appear on the eastern horizon that carried Silas, her sister, and news of Mercer's death. But Ashlyn would have rather had a lot of things happen differently in her life. There was no point in wasting time wishing for an easier reality. This was what she had.

"Someone find Lord Pommol," Ashlyn said, rising. "I would like him to ride with me down to the dock. The other high lords can walk."

Ashlyn and Linkon made the journey to the harbor in a covered palanquin, surrounded by Carlyle and a score of his wardens. Traffic came to a halt along the main avenues as her retinue moved through the city. Men shouted for a clear route through the commotion.

The trip reminded her how vulnerable kings and queens were. They were like the tallest tree in a grove—easiest to spot, and the most valuable to cut down.

"If you don't mind me asking," Linkon said after they'd been traveling for a few minutes, "what did I do to deserve the honor of traveling in the queen's palanquin?"

"You're a clever man," Ashlyn said. "I'm sure you can guess."

Linkon tapped his lips a few times. "The others haven't delivered all of the wardens you requested?"

"Correct," Ashlyn said. "Korbon and Brock are coming along, though. Wallace is not."

"I see," Linkon said. "What will you do about it?"

"Become more persuasive."

Three hundred widows standing next to her would help.

Linkon nodded and leaned back on his cushion. "You're something of a mystery, my queen. I'm still trying to puzzle out why you're so keen on invading Balaria."

"I want my sister back."

"That's a good enough reason to convince the small lords to go to war. And the small-minded high lords. But not you—the diligent student of nature and history. There must be something more you expect to gain from the invasion."

"Of course there is," Ashlyn said, easing into the most convenient explanation. "I expect to gain control over my country. As you say, I am a student of history. And the archives are bursting with warlords and kings who shored up control over armies and countries and even entire continents by establishing an enemy, then starting a fight with them."

"I see," Linkon said. "That's certainly a tactic that has some merit, although it comes with some considerable collateral damage. Win or lose, many Almirans will be killed in a war with Balaria."

"I learned a long time ago that almost everything in this life comes with collateral damage, Lord Linkon."

Ashlyn thought of Silas, and the places she'd asked him to go. The things she had convinced him to do.

"Perhaps that's true," Linkon said, then glanced out the window before speaking again. "Still, I can't help but notice the timing of your plans. If I'm not mistaken, we'll be setting sail for Balaria just as the Great Dragon Migration is reaching its height."

"I didn't choose the time at which the Balarians kidnapped my sister."

"No, but seeing as you carry such a fervent interest in the great lizards, it seems like a happy coincidence that you're able to follow the beasts across Terra on their travels."

"There is nothing happy about invading a country," Ashlyn snapped, letting an extra barb creep into her voice. "And what exactly are you suggesting? I'm invading Balaria so I can get a better look at some dragons? Are you insane? I am the queen of Almira now. I have more important things to worry about."

Linkon's face turned pale. He realized he'd overstepped.

"Of course, my queen," he murmured, giving a little head bow and fidgeting in his seat. "I apologize."

Ashlyn watched him, but didn't say anything. Of all the lords on the High Council, Linkon had the sharpest eyes, which meant he was the most likely to uncover her true intentions. But for right now, she believed her lie had convinced him.

They arrived at the docks. Hayden pulled the black lacquered door to the palanquin open. Ashlyn squinted at the bright sun as she stepped down. Shielded her eyes with one hand.

The high lords of Almira had arrived as well, each one of them standing beneath a different colored silk canopy, some of which were still being tied down by scurrying servants. Cedar Wallace stood beneath a blue bolt of fabric with his hands clasped behind his back—the emerald on the pommel of his sword glinting in the sunlight. Doro Korbon's eyes shifted between the ships and Ashlyn. Yulnar Brock was lying sideways on a sofa working through a plate of sauce-drenched meatballs.

"Lords," Ashlyn said.

"My queen," they echoed in unison.

Ashlyn turned to the sea, and the ships that filled it.

The closest ship was less than a hundred strides out. The black hull was the length of three buildings strung together, the masts taller than any tree growing within a hundred miles of Floodhaven. A dozen or so bald Papyrian sailors scrambled around the deck and the rigging, calling back and forth to each other in their language as they prepared to dock.

A single widow emerged from the hold and walked down the gangplank. She had the dark eyes and black hair of a full-blooded Papyrian. There was a forked scar running down her left cheek and over her lips.

"Queen Ashlyn, my name is Shoshone Kalara Sun," she said in a thick Papyrian accent that reminded Ashlyn of her mother. The memory tightened the back of Ashlyn's throat, but she pushed the emotion down. "Empress Okinu asked me to express her condolences regarding your father once more."

"I appreciate that," Ashlyn said. She glanced back onto the ship. "How many are with you?"

"There are one hundred and seven of the empress's widows in the ship behind me. Another one hundred and ninety-two are spread between the four other ships at this dock. A precaution in case we were hit by a storm and separated. I'll admit that some of my sisters are fresh from their training on Roriku Island, but even an inexperienced widow is twice as useful as those metal-covered sweat-machines that you Almirans prefer."

Ashlyn smiled. "Good."

"I also have this." Shoshone removed a letter from behind her breastplate and handed it to Ashlyn. It bore the orca seal of Papyria, cast in ocean-blue wax. Ashlyn opened the letter and read:

Queen Ashlyn,

You have provided many gifts to Papyria over the years. Now I provide a gift to you. I look forward to the exchange of many more gifts in the future.

With love,
Empress Okinu, Eternal Majesty of the Papyrian Empire

Ashlyn folded the paper in half and tucked it into her gown. She glanced around the dock, seeing the uncertain eyes of the high lords. Ashlyn had never put much stock in the ceremony that seemed to surround soldiers—all the marching wardens with their clinking armor, battle totems, and chest-thumping salutes seemed like wasted effort. But now that she was a young queen surrounded by chauvinist warlords, she understood the value of spectacle.

"Bring them out," Ashlyn said.

"Widows!" Shoshone called.

They poured from the ships like a river of black silk. The whisper of their armor was a gentle wind cascading over everyone on the quay. The widows flowed around Ashlyn and formed a crescent wall of sharkskin leather. Some widows were barely older than Kira, but their faces were all defined by a hardened discipline.

Yulnar Brock dropped the rib he'd been chewing and watched with an open mouth as the widows moved into formation around Ashlyn. Doro Korbon looked like he might actually run away and hide. But they weren't the ones Ashlyn was concerned about.

Cedar Wallace remained still as the widows disembarked. His eyes were fixed on Ashlyn. Unlike every other man on the docks, he did not seem impressed. That, or he was just hiding it better.

When the widows had formed up behind her, Ashlyn stepped forward.

"High lords, our fleet has arrived."

Doro Korbon's mouth twitched a few times. "Most impressive, my queen."

"Yes, yes, a fine fleet, my queen!" Yulnar Brock said, necks jiggling.

"Thank you," Ashlyn said. "I have been keeping track of the wardens coming to Floodhaven. Lord Pommol has delivered in full, showing his wisdom. Lords Korbon and Brock, I'm not dissatisfied with your numbers, but I would imagine all of your wardens will arrive in the next eleven or twelve days, yes?"

Korbon was staring at Shoshone, who stared right back. "Yes, my queen. Eleven days sounds about right."

Ashlyn turned to Cedar Wallace. Back at the first High Council meeting, she'd shamed him into providing a hollow promise of support. If she had more time, Ashlyn would have found an elegant way to convince Wallace to fall in line—there had to be a way to defuse the rivalry her father had spent decades exacerbating. But Ashlyn was out of time.

She had no choice but to give him an ultimatum.

"Lord Wallace. Where are your wardens?"

Wallace stepped forward. Cleared his throat. "The roads have been very difficult, and—"

"The condition of Almira's roads is not an excuse for disobeying my orders," Ashlyn interrupted. "There are no excuses for disobeying your queen. If you fail to bring your wardens into my city by the eve of my coronation, you will no longer enjoy my protection in Floodhaven. Do I make myself clear?"

Wallace's jaw tightened. He looked like he wanted to draw his sword and rush her, but instead his eyes flashed across the armed widows standing behind Ashlyn. He knew that while they would certainly protect Ashlyn, they could also be sent out into the night with their blades drawn.

"Clear, my queen," he said. "My wardens will arrive on time. As promised."

Ashlyn hesitated. There was something in Wallace's tone that Ashlyn didn't like, and most certainly didn't trust. Still, she'd gotten the answer that she needed—there was nothing more to be gained by pushing him further right now. She gave him a slight nod of acknowledgment.

Shoshone took a step forward. "What are your orders, my queen?"

"Your widows will secure the castle. I'd like you to join me in the Queen's Tower so that we might become better acquainted."

"Very good, my queen."

———

An hour later, Ashlyn sat in her private chamber with Hayden, Shoshone, ten of the newly arrived widows, and Linkon Pommol. He had his hands pressed flat against his thighs and was sitting very still, like a rabbit who had spotted a predator.

"Shoshone," Ashlyn said. "Who were you responsible for protecting in Papyria?"

"I served the empress's youngest sister for many years, my queen."

"Kasumi?" Ashlyn asked. "Didn't she die of a fever a decade ago?"

"That's correct."

"What have you been doing since then?"

Shoshone bowed her head. "The empress has many enemies. Sometimes it is better to seek them out rather than wait for their arrival."

"You're an assassin," Linkon said.

"I am flexible with my duties." Shoshone smiled, the scar on her face turning an unsettling shade of white.

"I see." Ashlyn was willing to use the newly arrived widows as assassins, but didn't want to define her rule with murder. Perhaps the threat of a widow's blade in the night would be enough to keep Cedar Wallace in line. "Right now, getting the high lords to bring their armies to Floodhaven is the priority."

Hayden cleared her throat. "Due respect, my queen, but the priority is keeping you alive. Your coronation draws near."

"You suspect a threat?" Shoshone asked.

There was a knock on the door. Every widow in the room moved her hand to her blade. Hayden stepped outside for a moment and came back in.

"My queen, there is a sentinel outside who says he has ridden from Deepdale with a message for you. I've checked him for weapons; he is unarmed."

"Bring him in."

"My queen," the sentinel said, kneeling. He was a tall man with long brown hair and dozens of blackheads on his bulbous nose. He was wearing Grealor colors, but they were covered in mud and grime.

"Rise," Ashlyn said. "Is Elden on his way back to Floodhaven yet?"

"No, my queen." The sentinel swallowed once. "Lord Grealor is dead."

————

"How could this have happened?" Ashlyn said to nobody in particular.

After the sentinel had delivered his message, Ashlyn sent him away, then moved up to her observatory to figure out a response. Only Hayden and Shoshone came with her.

"There are still plenty of Bershad loyalists in Deepdale," Hayden said. "The Jaguar Army in particular. If Elden was trying to raise a host of wardens as you requested, he might have added enough pressure that they lynched him."

"No," Ashlyn said. "The Jaguars are soldiers. They don't murder lords from the shadows. This is different. And familiar."

"Familiar how, my queen?" Shoshone asked.

"A lord dies—there are no witnesses. And chaos follows. Same as Mudwall."

The sentinel had brought other news from Deepdale. Three of Elden's sons were in the city when he died, and all of them believed they should inherit Dainwood. The oldest had already been killed in a duel—the other two had entrenched themselves in different parts of the city and divided the southern wardens' allegiance. To make matters worse, both brothers had come to the same conclusion as Hayden and blamed the Jaguars for Grealor's death. Problem was, the Jaguars had responded to the accusation with drawn swords. They'd won several skirmishes despite being vastly outnumbered, then disappeared into the jungle.

"You think Mudwall and Deepdale are related?" Hayden asked.

"I think that Cedar Wallace has benefited from both events." Ashlyn stared at the map. Looked at her ledger. "I can't rely on another lord's wardens to resolve the situation in Deepdale. I have no choice but to send Malgrave wardens south."

Hayden frowned. "Half our wardens are already in Mudwall. With all the traffic into Floodhaven, our men are needed here to keep the peace. And protect you."

"We have Shoshone and her widows to protect me now," Ashlyn said. "This is what will happen—three thousand Malgrave wardens will go south tomorrow morning. That leaves enough men in Flood-haven to guard the walls. We will use the small lords of the Atlas Coast and Linkon Pommol's wardens to fill in the gaps within the city until our forces return from Mudwall and Deepdale."

"That leaves you far more vulnerable than I am comfortable with," Hayden said. "Especially if Cedar Wallace's wardens show up before ours return."

"If there was a better option, I'd take it," Ashlyn said. "But there isn't. I'll prepare the orders right away. Our wardens need to stabilize Deepdale, then bring as many wardens as possible back to Floodhaven. Hayden, organize the men and let them know that they ride south at dawn."

19

BERSHAD

Skojit Territory, Razorback Mountains

Three of Vera's fingers were dislocated. They twisted away from her hand in an unsettling way. Her smallest finger was destroyed—the bone poked through the flesh in two different places and her nail faced her wrist.

"Most of this can be salvaged," Bershad said, examining her hand in the firelight. "But that pinky needs to go."

Vera winced and nodded. "Fix the others first."

"It's going to hurt a lot," he warned.

She just motioned with her other hand for Bershad to get on with it.

Bershad gripped her first finger.

"On three. One—"

He snapped her first finger back into place. Vera sucked in and pounded her foot hard against the ground.

"Two."

He snapped the second back into place.

"Three."

The third was the farthest out, so Bershad had to yank hard before he felt the bone lift and slide back into place. When it was done, he handed her one of the Skojit's wineskins. Vera took four or five big gulps.

"Piss for wine," she muttered.

Bershad drew his dragontooth dagger, wiped it clean, and held it over the fire for a few moments. He untied a leather pouch filled with Spartania moss from his belt and opened it up. There was a bolt of silk bandages on top, which he set aside, and then he pulled several clumps of moss out and crushed them between thumb and forefinger. He placed the pellets on top of the silk, and then picked up the knife again.

"The moss will keep it clean when I'm done," he said.

He guided Vera's hand to a log that one of the Skojit had been using as a seat. He pressed her recently relocated fingers together—isolating the ruined pinky.

Surgeons and alchemists always made a big deal of tying people down and drowning them with opium before things like this, but Vera seemed calm enough. Besides, they didn't have any opium—he'd left his pouch with Rowan.

"Ready?"

"Yes."

Bershad slammed the knife down, severing Vera's pinky just below the knuckle.

Before her blood had time to spurt, he plugged the wound with Spartania moss and wrapped the silk bandage around her finger stump and hand. He cinched the silk tight using a small twig as a lever and then sat back on his haunches. Vera was breathing a little heavy, but overall hadn't taken the loss of her finger with much drama. She picked up the wineskin and drank some more. Bershad watched her white throat bob up and down.

"What now?" she asked, wiping off her mouth with the back of her undamaged hand.

Bershad squinted at the eastern sky through a copse of cedars. "Dawn soon. We best head back to where we spotted them and keep on climbing."

"You sure this is the last of them?" Vera asked.

"No. But a camp full of dead men has a good shot at convincing any other Skojit we're not worth keeping after." Bershad took the wine from her and drank. She was right, it tasted like piss.

They made it back to the rock shelf as the gray glow of dawn was burning off into daylight.

"The very last thing I want to do right now is climb this cliff," Vera said.

"Life's full of disappointments."

Vera was slowed by her wound. Every time she lost her grip on a rock or missed a handhold, she muttered a Papyrian curse under her breath. Eventually, they reached a drainage that finally allowed them to cut back toward the rushing river. Bershad had hoped to find an easy crossing, but instead they just found more rapids and currents that pounded down on the rocks in an endless roar.

Bershad dipped one foot into the current and was nearly swept away by the ankle. He had to grab onto a small bush to avoid being sucked into the torrent.

"Not crossing here," he called to Vera. It was hard to believe a broken trunk had caused such an inconvenience. Their only option was to keep climbing.

At midday Bershad called a stop.

"Need to change your bandage," he said, between breaths.

"So soon?"

"Sweating and battering it against the ground like this, it'll rot faster. Better a bandage change than a black hand that I have to cut off, right?"

Vera examined her hand, as if checking for signs of rot, and then sat down against a twisted tree and let him do his work. Bershad unwound the old bandage, packed it away to boil in water later, and removed the used clump of Spartania. He replaced it with a fresh piece.

"You're good at all of this," Vera said as he worked.

Bershad grunted as he plugged the finger stump with fresh moss. "I've had some practice."

"If that's true, how come you didn't put the moss in your arrow wound?"

Bershad looked up at Vera. Her dark eyes studied him.

"Don't say it wasn't bad enough," she continued. "I'm not an idiot."

Bershad hesitated, keeping both hands on her wrist. His instinct was to hold back the truth, like he'd done with Ashlyn. Like he'd been doing for years. He hadn't put moss on his wound because he didn't want Vera to see how quickly he'd heal when it touched his skin. Seeing that would only lead to questions he couldn't answer.

"It's a long, dangerous walk over these mountains," he said. "Figured we best conserve."

Vera squinted at him. "You're lying."

"Honesty was never part of our agreement." Bershad finished with her wrist and started packing up the moss and bandages. "Let's go," he said, motioning with one arm.

"No." Vera grabbed a chunk of moss from the pouch and wadded it up.

"What're you doing?" Bershad asked.

"If you won't tell me the truth with your mouth, I'll get your leg to do it," Vera said. She unlatched the sling from her thigh and, like a snake, wrapped the leather around Bershad's wrists and strapped them to a tree over his head.

"What the fuck?"

"Quiet."

He struggled but it didn't do any good. Vera grappled him into submission easily, yanked his pants down, and jammed the moss underneath the bandage on his leg. She pulled his pants back up roughly. Then she put her hand around Bershad's throat and looked him square in the eyes.

"If you take that out, I'll tie you up, cram it back in again, and we'll never get anywhere today. Clear?"

Bershad glared at her. He'd have to kill Vera to stop her, and he didn't want to do that.

"Have it your way, widow," Bershad said. "But you won't like the place this path takes you."

"I'm used to that problem," she said, releasing his hands and stalking off into the forest.

———

Normally, the plants and trees would have thinned out as they climbed higher, but since they were heading toward a dragon warren, the opposite happened. Tall, colorful flowers became more frequent. Moss carpeted the ground. Vines stretched up the trunks of every tree and snaked along the limbs, sprouting bright yellow parasol flowers that intermingled with the green pines. Their beauty was deceptive. Beneath the vibrant colors, the warren plants were strangling the natural forest to death. The slow, insidious struggle for power and resources was easy to mistake for peace.

Near dark, they came across a calm and lazy stream that fed into the impassable river. The water was warm and filled with fat, colorful fish darting around in the clear, moonlit water. Their heads popped up sporadically to feed on the evening wave of insects.

"How is the water so warm?" Vera asked, breaking a five-hour silence. She held her hand over the steam that was rising off the surface of the river.

Bershad didn't respond. He was still pissed at her for the moss.

It was too dark to keep moving. They found a spot to camp at a horseshoe-shaped bend in the stream that overlooked a deep pool from a mossy shelf. Near the bank, a great tree had been pulled down by vines—the roots yanked halfway out of the earth, creating a space with a decent overhang for shelter. Bershad worked on a fire while Vera prepared her fishing line and began making casts into the pool. After the lines were drawn, she picked at the spot on her shoulder pauldron that had been sheared off by the skinny Skojit, as if there was a way to regrow the ruined armor. Neither of them spoke. Bershad finished the fire, then checked and cleaned his weapons. The moss had been doing its work all day. He knew what Vera would see when she removed the bandage, and he wasn't looking forward to her reaction.

It didn't take long for Vera to pull two of the enormous yellow-and-blue fish from the river. She gutted and cleaned them and set them to cook on a flat stone she'd placed in the fire.

"Strangest river fish I ever saw," Vera said.

"All this comes from the dragon warren higher up," Bershad said, realizing that continuing the silent treatment was both useless and childish. "It changes the landscape. Makes it richer. The fish are like fat lords high in their keeps and castles. Gorging themselves on the world below. Well, above in the fish's case. Everything up here lives longer, too. You might have just killed a hundred-year-old fish."

She gave him a queer look. "How do you know so much about warrens?"

"The Dainwood is full of them," Bershad said. "I used to explore them as a kid. They aren't as dangerous as the stories make them out to be, just hard to understand. Nobody knows how the dragons create them or why the creatures inside grow like they do. And when men can't comprehend a thing, they get scared of it. Spin up lies about demons lurking amid all the fertile wealth, guarding dragon eggs."

Vera grunted. Checked the fish with her undamaged hand, then leaned back and gave Bershad a long look. "Are you going to make me tie you up again or are you going to show me that leg?"

"You're sure you want to see this?" Bershad asked. "I can get you over these mountains and into Balaria without complicating things for you."

"I'm sure."

Bershad stood up and unbuckled his pants. Pulled them down and flicked the moss away. The firelight made it easy for Vera to see that his arrow wound was healed—nothing but a pink, raised scar remained.

"Happy?" Bershad asked, pulling his pants back up and sitting down.

Vera fiddled with the bandage on her hand. "That is not what I expected," she said without looking up.

"What did you expect?"

"I'm not sure." Vera raised her eyes. "This is how you've survived all these years?"

Bershad nodded. "The third dragon that I killed gored me in the back. Pierced my liver and a kidney. Rowan plugged it with Spartania moss out of habit—every warden knows how to keep a wound clean—but we both figured that was the end. He stayed up with me in a barn, waiting with a seashell in his hand. But I never needed it." He shrugged. "We were back on the road a week later."

The fire crackled. Flames reflected in Vera's eyes. "What are you?"

"Most people would say I'm a demon. That's why I've hidden it for so long."

"I'm not most people," Vera said.

Bershad leaned forward and picked at the fish a little. He was tired of lying, but wasn't sure how to begin explaining it.

"Tell me what it feels like, at least," Vera said, seeing his struggle.

Bershad thought about that.

"It's as if there's something inside of me that doesn't belong. Just like the dragon warren doesn't belong at the top of this mountain. And it's getting worse. The last time someone put moss in my body, it gave me a wild strength that was so powerful I threw a spear through a dragon's forehead. Do you know how much force that takes?"

"More than a man should have," Vera said.

"Exactly." He paused. "What would you do if you were me?"

"I would search for the truth," Vera said. "No matter the cost. It is like you said, men are most afraid of things that they do not understand. You'll never be able to control something that scares you."

"I've been searching. I've asked every alchemist and shaman I've met for the last fourteen years if they've ever seen anything like this. None of them have."

"Search harder," Vera said. "Then use the strength to protect the people you care about. That's what I would do, anyway." She studied him. "But you aren't traveling to Burz-al-dun to protect someone, are you?"

Bershad hesitated. "I have a debt that I need to repay."

"A debt," Vera repeated. "You're talking about what you did in that canyon?"

"That, and every black thing I've done since." Bershad rubbed the tattoo on his forearm. Thought of all the dragons that were burned forever into his skin. And his soul.

"And rescuing a kidnapped princess you've never met, from a country that's exiled you, is going to pay that debt? I haven't known you for very long, but I don't believe that for a second."

Bershad grunted. "Anyone ever told you that you're irritatingly observant?"

"Silas, what are you planning to do when we get to Burz-al-dun?"

"It's better if you don't know."

"Why?"

"Same reason Ashlyn didn't tell me Felgor's part in all this. The less you know, the less you can tell a torturer." He paused. "I'll help you get to Kira. But then I have to go my own way. I made a promise to Ashlyn Malgrave that I intend to keep, no matter the cost. You understand that, don't you? You've come all this way because of a promise you made to a Malgrave, too."

"Yes," she said.

"I can still help you," Bershad said. "Having a demon on your side is a good thing."

Vera looked out at the river for a long time, then stood up. The leather of her armor sighed as she stretched both arms over her head, then dropped them down to her hips. "You don't look like a demon to me, Silas. You look like a man." She licked her lips. "What do I look like to you?"

Bershad frowned. "You're not afraid of me?"

"Do I look afraid?"

"No."

"Then answer my question."

"You look like a woman, Vera." He paused. "A beautiful woman."

Vera released the straps of her sharkskin breastplate and pulled it off. Then she unwound the sweat-stained linen shirt beneath and tossed it on the ground. Her nipples were small and dark, encircled by the smallest areolas Bershad had ever seen. She pulled the leather ties around her hips loose and shucked off her pants and boots in one smooth motion. Between her thighs there was only a small tuft of smooth black hair, glistening like silk in the orange firelight. Her body was nimble and lithe. Even while naked she carried herself with the balance of a killer. Vera turned around and took one step toward the steaming river—the muscles of her back and thighs defined by the flickering shadows cast from the fire.

"Come on," she said over her shoulder. "We're both filthy."

Vera crossed the mossy shelf and hopped into the water with a light splash—leaving Bershad alone to make a decision. Bershad assumed that if he somehow managed to reach Burz-al-dun, he'd die there. Passing up one last chance at pleasure seemed foolish.

Bershad pulled off his clothes. Walked over to the edge of the pool.

Vera was standing hip-deep in the water. She untied her hair and let it drop past her shoulders. It was so long the tips touched the water and writhed around her in a black swirl. Her nipples had hardened in the night air, and the silver reflection of the moon outlined the shape of her breasts and collarbone and neck. The small, dark oval of her navel was just above the waterline.

She gazed up at him, scooping water with her uninjured hand and pouring it across her chest. The moonlight illuminated the outline of Vera's lithe frame, but it also exposed Bershad's own jagged scars and battered flesh. Notches cut from his shoulders. Dents and rends along his chest and rib cage. Scores of teeth marks dug out from his forearms and legs.

"Get in," she said. "I'm not going to fuck you if you're covered in mud and shit."

He lowered himself into the water. Felt the warmth start relaxing his knotted muscles and stiff joints. The sandy river bottom was soft on his feet. He waded over to her. She kept a ghost of a smile on her lips as she raised her hands out of the water and rubbed her palms along his chest and arms. Massaging his muscles and then running her fingertips along his ruined skin.

He rubbed a hand along her arm and noticed a long, vertical scar running from hip bone to the base of her armpit.

"First big mistake I ever made," she said when she saw him looking. She held up her left hand, with its missing pinky. "And I'm adding to the list more and more. At this rate, I'll look like you before long." She dipped her wounded hand into the water. Wincing a little at first and then relaxing.

"The warmth will help it," Bershad said.

He ran his thumb over her scarred cheeks. Then Vera stood up on her toes and pressed Bershad's shoulders down with her palms.

"Turn around and sit," she said.

Vera guided him backward to dip his hair in the water, then she combed through the matted tangles and rings with her right hand. Explored his scalp with her fingers, massaging the base of his neck and just above his ears.

"Bad time to be short on soap," she said, continuing to rub. "But I suppose this is better than nothing."

Bershad turned around and pressed his face against her smooth belly. He kissed along her rib cage and moved one hand between her legs. She sighed, wrapping a hand into his long, wet hair. Bershad grabbed her ass with both hands and lifted her out of the water. Set her on the mossy shelf above the river. Her body was steaming from the heat of the river.

Bershad lay down on top of her. There was the slightest resistance and then he slipped inside. Vera gasped and then dug her nails into his back as he began to move in and out. She squeezed her legs around him and he took her by the wrists and pressed her arms over her head. Leaned in close to kiss her lips and neck.

Vera sat up just enough so that her full lips brushed across his ear. The mossy smell of the forest filled his head—traces of lavender wafting from Vera's hair. A thousand summer insects vibrated their song through the trees and across the water like a great, secret heartbeat. Every scar on his body began to burn, and he felt his pleasure building deep down. Vera closed her eyes. Mouth open and skin flushed.

When it was over, they lay together on the moss, intertwined and quiet. Vera ran her finger along Bershad's thigh, down to the place he'd been shot with the arrow.

She sat up. Face masked by shadow and hair. "How have you kept this a secret for all these years?" she asked. "Didn't people notice?"

"Exiles have to keep moving. I've spent more time with you than anyone else in fourteen years, apart from Rowan. Most people only get glimpses of me, and they see what they want to see. The world wants a hero, not a demon."

Vera ran a hand through his hair. Kissed him.

"I don't believe in heroes," she whispered.

20

JOLAN

Almira, Dainwood Province

When they were five leagues outside of Deepdale, Garret removed his cloak and stopped at a fresh spring to wash the dried blood off his hands and arms.

Back at the inn, he had stared at Jolan for a long time—hunting knife covered with gore and aimed at Jolan's face. Then he had sheathed the blade and, without explaining himself, helped Jolan pack his belongings and sneak out of the city.

The spring where Garret had stopped was about a hundred paces off the road, and hidden by two ancient Dainwood trees that had twisted around each other in a complicated pattern.

"We'll stop here for the night," Garret said, eyeing the western sky. "No fire."

Jolan nodded, but said nothing. They each found a comfortable spot beneath the trees and chewed on some dried beef while the sun went down. Jolan's right eyelid had been twitching since they left the inn, and his hands were shaking so much that it was difficult to eat his food.

"Was that warden already dead when you cut his throat?" Jolan asked after a while. He'd been running the question over in his mind the entire day, using it like a drumbeat to time their fast-paced flight from Deepdale. "The one I hit with the pestle."

"He wasn't breathing," Garret said.

"So I killed him, then."

"Does it matter?" Garret asked. "Your stone or my dagger, those men were dead the second they burst through that door."

"It matters to me."

Garret let out a heavy breath, then produced his pipe, packed it with tobacco, but didn't light it. Just sat with the pipe in his hand, rubbing at the wood with his thumb.

"You didn't tell me you were a fugitive," he said.

"You didn't tell me you were a murderer," Jolan shot back.

Garret narrowed his eyes but otherwise didn't respond.

"I am not an idiot," Jolan continued. "Lord Grealor hanging from a statue. Everyone talking about Lord Tybolt dead in Mudwall. It was you."

"That's right."

Jolan swallowed. "How many other men have you killed?"

"More than you," Garret admitted. "Less than others."

"Why are you doing this? Did they . . . wrong you somehow?"

"They wronged someone. And that someone hired me."

Jolan chewed on his lip for a moment. "You're an assassin."

"Is that such a bad thing to be?" Garret asked.

"Of course it is! You kill people for money."

"So does every warden in Almira. But your average soldier has done far darker work than me. You ever seen a village after some bloodthirsty wardens have ridden through it? Every man and boy killed, and killed messy. Every woman raped. Every girl, too, usually. You Almirans are known for that type of bloodlust."

"I saw what you did to Lord Grealor," Jolan said. "Looked like pretty dark work to me."

"He felt no pain," Garret said. "Most of the men I've killed never even knew I was in the same room with them. I once killed a prince while he was on a pleasure barge surrounded by soldiers and body-guards. None saw me. My work is clean."

"Getting bitten by a dragon doesn't seem very clean to me."

Garret seemed to think about that. "Well, life is unpredictable. But I'm the best at what I do."

"Being good at murder doesn't justify the act. You're still a hired killer."

Garret shrugged. "We all have our roles, boy. If I wasn't playing this part, someone else would."

"So, nothing's your fault?" Jolan raised his voice a little. "That's pathetic. This is what everyone does. They hide behind gods and titles and dragonshit excuses so they never have to actually stand for their crimes. Nobody can bear to look at themselves. Not honestly."

Garret thumbed his pipe a while, his face unreadable. Jolan couldn't tell if he was bored, uninterested, or about to stand up and cut his throat. "What about that apothecary?" Garret asked. "Do you take responsibility for burning it down?"

"After Morgan died, I didn't know what to do, so I just went back to the shop and waited. Lord Nimbu showed up after he'd fin-ished collecting his share of the oil from the dragonslaying," Jolan said. "He told me that I was trespassing on his land, and that he'd have me whipped if I didn't vacate by nightfall." Jolan swallowed. "He didn't deserve that shop, or the ingredients inside. So I put what I could into my pack, and burned the rest. It didn't get anyone killed."

"The flames didn't. But what about all the people in Otter Rock that an alchemist could have saved while working from that shop?"

"Nimbu was going to sell everything. Even if I stayed in Otter Rock, it wouldn't have mattered."

"Who's hiding behind an excuse now? You could have found a cure for that plague you talked about so much if you really wanted to. But instead you fled. And now there's nobody to help the people of Otter Rock."

"That doesn't justify what you've done."

"I didn't say it did. But I'm not trying to dodge responsibility for the lives I've taken. You are. And you're using sloppy logic to do it. Your Master Morgan wouldn't approve, I don't think."

"Fine," Jolan said, keeping his teeth together. "I take responsibility. I take responsibility for burning my *home* to the ground, and for killing that man back in Deepdale." Jolan tossed his dried meat onto the forest floor. "I take responsibility for saving your miserable life. Twice now. And I will feel guilty about all those things until the day I go on the long swim."

Garret blinked, but said nothing.

"And why haven't you killed me yet?" Jolan asked. "I healed you. Got you into Deepdale. But I'm not useful to you anymore. Why didn't you leave my corpse on the floor of that inn?"

Garret's eyelid flinched. "You're worth more to me alive."

"How?"

"In my line of work, easy access to a good healer is valuable. I know you now. And I know that you're a wanted criminal, which means you'll have plenty of incentive to help me again in the future, should I require it."

Jolan thought about that. "If you get yourself bitten by another dragon, it'd be easier to break into some alchemist's shop and threaten his family than track me down."

"Most people don't argue so hard against saving their own life, Jolan."

"I'm just pointing out sloppy logic when I see it, Garret."

They stared at each other for a long time.

"Well, you're a clever kid," Garret said. "I'm sure you'll figure out why you're still alive eventually."

Garret reclined against a tree stump. Closed his eyes. "I'm going to sleep now. One way or another, you and I will part ways tomorrow. I'll leave the particulars up to you."

Jolan watched Garret until his breathing turned regular with sleep. Then he dug out the alchemy supplies from his pack. There were enough ingredients to make a liquid poison that Jolan could soak in a rag and hold over Garret's face. The assassin would be dead in three seconds. Maybe five. Or he could brew something else entirely.

His choice.

21

GARRET

Almira, Dainwood Province

When Garret woke up, Jolan had placed three glass vials on a stone in the middle of their camp. All of the vials were corked and filled with the same reddish liquid. The boy was sitting cross-legged a few paces away, staring at the vials.

"The tonic I made for you in Deepdale will stop the dragon rot in your bloodstream, but the wound is still vulnerable. That's enough topical disinfectant to last three weeks," he said, refusing to look at Garret. "Apply to the wound three times a day, four if it stays humid like this. Keep your arm dry and change the bandage twice a day, every day."

Garret sat up. Checked his knife and his goatskin bladder. Everything was in order. Garret wondered if the boy had poisoned the vials while he slept. It was certainly possible.

"Which way are you headed?" Garret asked.

"Southeast." Jolan's voice was wary. "To the dragon warrens."

"Off to save the world?"

Jolan shrugged. Looked away.

Garret stood up. "It's north for me."

Jolan stood as well. "You've taught me a lot about the world, Garret. I'll remember it."

He nodded. "I hope you find what you're looking for, Jolan."

To his surprise, Garret meant it.

He watched as the boy disappeared into the forest. A twig snapped about a dozen paces off in the undergrowth, and then Garret was alone. He pulled a cork on one of the vials and applied the salve to his forearm. It burned for a moment, then went cool. Garret waited to see if the boy had killed him after all, but death didn't arrive. Just a few squirrels venturing down from the trees and picking around at his feet, hunting for some scraps of dried meat.

Garret smiled to himself. Realized he would miss the boy and his chatty company. It felt good, knowing Jolan would be down here looking for mushrooms and moss. Living the peaceful life that Garret had never known.

He gathered his gear and headed north. It was a long way to Flood-haven, but Garret did not leave a job undone. And there was one final bit of work waiting for him in the capital of Almira.

PART III

22

ASHLYN

Almira, Castle Malgrave

Ashlyn Malgrave sat on the throne and tried to keep her back straight. It was early afternoon, and she had been taking audiences with the lords of Almira for almost five hours. The small of her back was wet with sweat, her throat was dry, and a fly had been buzzing around her head for the past thirty minutes.

Her coronation was still a week away, but Ashlyn had begun holding court early. It was a good way for her to build favor and respect among the small lords of Almira, which she needed now that almost every Malgrave warden was outside of Floodhaven.

"Your Grace," said Crellin Nimbu. Ashlyn remembered watching the small lord ride into Floodhaven with his fresh lot of newly hired wardens. Now that he'd come into a fair amount of gold and soldiers, he was probably prowling Floodhaven for a wife. His handsome features and a perfectly trimmed goatee would help, but there was a rumor that he was fond of urinating on the women he brought into his bedchamber, which would not.

Nimbu knelt. "My family has always supported the Malgraves, even in the old days before your family had the throne. For generations, Blakmar has been the heart of Malgrave support in the northern Atlas Coast, in fact—"

"I am aware of your support," Ashlyn said, interrupting him. She had learned that lords would not stop listing their accomplishments during audiences—no matter how small they were—unless she forced them to. "What would you ask of me today?"

Nimbu paused and adjusted the collar of his jacket, which was bright yellow with black buttons. "My queen, I have a grievance regarding the apothecary in Otter Rock," he said. "According to your wishes, I hired an alchemist—Morgan Mollevan—into my service to help with the recent, uh, ailments of my people. I paid for his contract and provided him with three acres of land and a comfortable cabin for his business."

Ashlyn had ordered Nimbu to hire an alchemist five years ago, when it became obvious the sickness related to the invasive red-shelled snails wasn't going to leave the Blakmar province on its own. Hertzog hadn't stopped Ashlyn's request, but he hadn't supported her, either. So Nimbu had tried to shirk the duty.

"As I recall, you required quite a bit of convincing before doing any of those things. For how many years did I give you a discounted tax rate on your wool before you hired Morgan? One? Two?"

"Three, my queen."

"Three," Ashlyn repeated. She'd known that, of course. She just wanted to make Nimbu say it. "Continue, Lord Nimbu."

"Well, Morgan was killed by a dragon not long ago. Afterward, his apprentice—a boy named Jolan—stole the most valuable tonics and ingredients, then burned the apothecary down before disappearing. I have posted a bounty on him, but if the boy cannot be brought to justice, I at least expect recompense from the Alchemist Order. By right, I owned the contents of that shop after Morgan died."

Ashlyn had already heard of Morgan's demise. A terrible loss. She also found it interesting that Nimbu had fought tooth and nail to avoid hiring the alchemist, but now demanded reimbursement for the loss of the shop. But Ashlyn could not afford to test Nimbu's loyalty. He may have only brought fifty wardens into Floodhaven, but she needed all of them to fight for her if it came to that.

"The Flawless Bershad killed the Needle-Throated Verdun dragon after it killed Master Morgan, correct?" Ashlyn asked.

"Yes, my queen."

"Let's keep things simple, then," Ashlyn said. "The alchemists are a fragmented, decentralized order, which will make it difficult to obtain recompense for apprentices with tendencies toward arson. Instead, I will cover the loss. As per the laws of Almira, you owe the Malgrave Crown a third of your share of the dragon oil that you harvested from the Needle-Throated Verdun. No doubt you brought it with you today."

"I did, my queen. I wanted to deliver it personally."

"Take it back to Blakmar. Or, if you prefer, I will have a steward load it onto a trading galley with the next tide and pay you the current market's expected profit in gold today. Will that make things even?"

"Yes, my queen." Nimbu bowed, a smile spreading across his face. A third of a Needle-Throated Verdun's oil was worth far more than the inventory of a well-stocked apothecary. "The gold will do nicely."

"Of course, I expect you will use some of that gold to rebuild the apothecary and hire a new alchemist to replace Morgan Mollevan," Ashlyn added.

"My queen?" Nimbu asked. His smile disappeared.

"Since you went through the trouble of seeking reimbursement for the lost apothecary, I assume that your vassals found great value in the presence of a healer in Otter Rock." Ashlyn hardened her voice. "And you do not strike me as the sort of lord who would deprive his people of aid, especially when you have just come into a rather large sum of gold. Am I correct?"

Nimbu swallowed. His forehead had begun to sweat. "You are a very perceptive judge of character, my queen. The apothecary will be rebuilt right away."

"I'm glad we could come to terms, Lord Nimbu," Ashlyn said, making a mental note to check the construction's progress in a few weeks—she had an informant in the area who could send an update by pigeon. If someone didn't find an antivenom for those snails' poison soon, every village in Blakmar would be plagued with illness. "Thank you for coming to see me."

"The pleasure and honor is mine," Nimbu said. "I shall ask the gods to deliver you clear skies and warm sun for many moons."

As Nimbu departed, Ashlyn clicked her teeth together behind tightly pressed lips. Thought of her father's last words. She did not relish the idea of using steel to rule Almira, but gold worked just fine.

She touched the thread on her wrist. Ashlyn would have preferred to spend the rest of the day practicing with it in her tower, but the next lord was already approaching the throne. She settled in for a long afternoon.

23

BERSHAD

Skojit Territory, Razorback Mountains

When Bershad and Vera woke up, they washed themselves in the warm water.

"How many times have you used the moss to survive?" Vera asked, looking at his scars as she pulled her hair back into another tight bun.

Bershad ran some water over his left arm—feeling the ridge of a scar that ran from elbow to shoulder. A Thundertail's claw had done it years ago.

"Too many," he said.

Vera scooped some water into her hands and splashed herself in the face. "Back to the others today, then?" she asked.

"Yeah."

She nodded. Waded back to the shore—skin shimmering in the morning light.

"At least we got one pleasant memory from this mess," she said.

Vera hopped out of the water and began getting dressed. A minute later, her body was hidden once again behind the battered sharkskin armor. Bershad dressed, too. His back to Vera. They each took a few bites of the leftover fish while squatting around the remnants of the fire. Then they crossed the gentle river—leaving no evidence of the night before other than a charred mark in the earth.

The plants around them continued to thicken. The ground became so overgrown with moss and vines that it felt springy and strange to walk on. Bershad put on his mask, unsheathed the dragontooth dagger, and began hacking and cutting a path through the foliage for Vera to follow behind. Each swipe of his blade created a wet crunch.

"Jaguars are quiet, you know," Vera said after Bershad nearly cut a tree down by accident.

"I never was a very good jaguar," he said. "Wasn't a good lord, either."

"You are good at other things, at least," she said. Paused. "Lots of other things."

Vera pulled ahead of him—slipping between a set of massive thorn trees without so much as shaking the branches. She quickly became little more than a black flicker in the trees ahead. A few hours later, Bershad half-stumbled into a big clearing. Vera was sitting cross-legged on a flat rock. Sharpening one of her blades.

Vera motioned to the north. "The bridge is just ahead, along with the other two. I can smell Rowan's pipe."

Bershad nodded. Wiped his dragontooth dagger on each side of his pants and then sheathed it. Stared at Vera for a few moments. "Look," he started to say. "Last night . . ."

"Last night isn't something we need to talk about."

"It'd be dangerous, you and I going into Balaria and not knowing where we stand with each other," Bershad said. More than the sex, he wanted to know how Vera would carry things, now that she knew what his body could do.

Vera studied him. "I like what I see when I look at you," she said. "And I liked last night. But as you said—we are both out here doing work for a different Malgrave. Anything happening along the way is a stepping-stone best forgotten once our feet pass onward. That's where I stand. You standing somewhere different?"

"No," Bershad said. That suited him just fine.

———

The bridge was a decrepit structure made from blackened granite. When it was new, it may have been impressive—three humped arches hopping through the torrent of water below. But now it barely looked sturdier than the wood trunk that had collapsed beneath Rowan and Alfonso. Bershad ran his hand over the side and felt the bumpy, lichen-covered surface as they crossed.

"Who built this so far up the mountain?" Vera asked. "It wasn't Skojit."

"Alchemists. They've been delving inside dragon warrens for hundreds of years. The Balarians told me that the gray-robes used to hike this mountain in droves, collecting ingredients for their medicines and studying the land. The Skojit put an end to that, though."

"I see."

Rowan, Felgor, and Alfonso had set up a makeshift camp on the far side of the bridge. Felgor was napping beside a fire, using Alfonso's stomach as a pillow. Rowan was sitting nearby, smoking his pipe. Sword drawn and within arm's reach.

"Took your sweet time," Rowan said, pipe clenched between his teeth.

One of Felgor's eyes popped open, and he sat up. Smacked his lips together and rubbed both hands through his greasy hair. Looked them both up and down. Sniffed once.

"You two fucked."

Rowan raised an eyebrow but said nothing.

"How long have you been here?" Vera asked.

Felgor smiled, revealing his tiny teeth behind the scraggly beard. "'Might be a bit ahead of us,' he says." The Balarian did his best to mock Bershad's accent. "*Two days* we've been waiting. The path opened up a hundred yards past that crossing you two managed to destroy. Easy walking from there." He looked around the camp. "I'll be honest, though, things got a bit dull. Spent most of yesterday telling Rowan here about a butcher's daughter I knew back in Drummond County with the biggest—"

"And you two," Rowan interrupted. "How did you fare?"

Bershad shrugged. "Had some trouble, but we're only down a finger."

Rowan's eyes flicked to Bershad's hands and then Vera's. Lingered a while on the bandage covering the stump of her little finger.

"Do you know where we are?" he asked.

Bershad looked around. Got his bearings. The pathway cut north and led straight through a dragon warren, then to a mountain lake.

"Yeah," Bershad said. "I know where we are."

They reached the entrance to the warren by midday. It was a tunnel that went straight through the middle of the mountain. The passageway inside was obscured by green and red and purple plants. A stream trickled out from beneath the plants that was lined with an explosion of Spartania moss. Rowan immediately scooped some up.

The high peaks of the Razorback Mountains were an unusual place for a warren. Most of them formed in warm and damp places like the Dainwood. The alchemists still couldn't agree on why or how dragons built the things, but they'd found plenty of reasons to keep coming back. Most of the alchemists' precious medicines—from sleeping tinctures to cures for dysentery—were brewed with ingredients found only in the warrens. They kept their recipes secret from the rest of the world, and amassed fortunes selling their products to the sick and needy.

"Are you sure it's safe?" Felgor asked as Bershad began to cut his way through the thorn-covered undergrowth that covered the entrance. "It looks . . . prickly."

"Well," Bershad said as he hacked down a swollen vine that sprayed orange goo all over his chest and arms, "you've survived a dragon and a Skojit attack so far. Plant barbs should be pretty straightforward."

Felgor bit his lower lip and stared at the entrance for a few moments. Then he stepped behind Rowan and patted him twice on his chain-mailed shoulder. "Here's a strategy—no vines or hooked barbs of doom can get me so long as I have my dear Rowan-shield ahead of me."

"Can't you bother one of the others for a change?" Rowan asked, drawing his own dagger to begin clearing the growth.

"I prefer bothering you. That's what friends do."

"We're not friends, Balarian," Rowan said, although Bershad noticed he didn't say it with much conviction.

"Not as close as those two sparrows, maybe," Felgor said. "But I feel a definitive bond growing between us."

"Let's keep moving," Bershad said, then immediately stopped in his tracks. The noise of the warren had exploded in his ears—he could hear a thousand small animals and insects skittering around the loamy ground. But the rush of sound only lasted for a heartbeat before disappearing.

"Are you all right?" Vera asked him, putting a hand on his shoulder.

"I'm fine," Bershad said, blinking. It wasn't the same feeling he got when a dragon approached, so they weren't in that kind of danger. But it was still strange—nothing like that had happened when he came through the warren with the Balarians.

They trudged into the gloom. Bershad considered lighting a torch, but the high ceiling of the cave was riddled with small tunnels that led to the surface and allowed just enough sunlight to creep into the area that he could see where he was going. The air was thick and heavy—weighted down with moisture and filled with little insects that zipped from plant to plant. Shadows from taller, twisted trees loomed close on either side. As they moved farther inside the warren, the twitch and flicker of creatures fleeing their approach became almost constant.

"Just lizards and rats," he said after noticing the fear-filled eyes of his companions. Even Vera seemed alarmed by the shifting shadows.

"But not dragons?" Felgor asked.

Bershad shook his head. "Doubt it." He chopped through another engorged vine that blocked their path. Goo sprayed everywhere— purple this time. "There's still a few weeks before they start the Great Migration. And most breeds'll head for the warren in eastern Balaria."

That meant Bershad didn't have much time left to stop the emperor before he started his cull. They couldn't afford any more delays.

"Why's everyone so afraid of these things if there aren't any dragons in them most of the time?" Vera asked.

"Alchemists spread rumors about them."

"Them gray-robed fellows?" Felgor chimed in. "In Balaria they mostly do teeth pulling and tonics for cock rot. What do they care?"

Bershad wiped his brow to try and get the sweat out of his eyes, but mostly succeeded in replacing it with plant goo. "If you'd discovered a thousand gold mines just sitting up in the mountains—unguarded and unclaimed—would you go rushing to tell everyone they're not nearly as dangerous as they seem?"

"Huh," Felgor said. "Clever little con they've got working there. I'll have to remember that. Think we'll run into an alchemist up here? I do actually have a tooth that's bothering me."

"That's because you don't wash your mouth out at night like I showed you," Rowan said.

"All right, all right," Felgor said. "I'll try it tonight. You Almirans pick strange things to care about, though. Mud and lice in your hair. No decent road to be found in the entire country. But teeth! Your teeth, you keep clean. I will never understand it."

Ahead, the trickling stream they'd been following turned into a small waterfall. Moss-covered rocks rose on either side. Rowan nudged Alfonso forward, who sniffed the near bank and then studied the far side. His ears twitched a few times, and then he crossed the shallow water and began working his way up the other side.

"Is it wise to use a donkey as our guide?" Vera asked. She seemed amused more than angry.

"He's kept us alive this long," Bershad said. Splashing through the stream to follow Alfonso.

The donkey tromped up the cliff without trouble, but the humans in the party struggled on the slippery rocks. After they'd picked their way up the incline, things got rougher. The trickling stream disappeared inside a small cavern that only a baby could crawl into, depriving them of their path. Ahead, there was nothing but a wall of pricker bushes, thorn trees, and thick overgrowth.

Bershad glared at Alfonso. The donkey chewed on some cud and turned away, looking embarrassed.

"Might be we should try the other side?" Rowan offered.

"It'll be dark soon."

"It's already dark," Felgor said, waving his hand around in the gloom.

"What I mean is, we shouldn't be inside this thing when the sun goes down."

"Thought you said it wasn't dangerous," Felgor said.

"No more dangerous than a swamp or a fucking forest of needles," Bershad said. "Neither of which I want to deal with at night."

Bershad started to shove through. Hacking at the underbrush with one arm and flinging ruined foliage to the side with the other. After a few dozen paces, the foliage grew so thick he had to put his mask on to keep the thorns out of his face. As he crunched his dagger against another swollen purple vine, the violent blast of sound pummeled his ears again, but louder and longer this time. Pulses and thrums came from every direction. It was as if the heartbeats of every creature in the warren—from insect to rat to snake—were suddenly vibrating inside of his ears.

"What the hell?" Bershad said, tearing his mask off and leaning against a tree. He took a step forward, slipped on the mud, and fell.

"Silas?" Rowan asked, grabbing his arm. His voice sounded like a roar. "What's wrong? Gods, your nose is bleeding."

"Noise," Bershad muttered. "So much fucking noise. It's everywhere."

Bershad covered his ears but it just made things worse. He tried to take long, slow, deep breaths but nothing was working. His vision blurred.

"What do we do?" Felgor asked. "He looks like an opium-head going for the long swim."

The wild roar continued in Bershad's head.

"I think it's the warren," Vera said. "We need to get him out of here. Now."

Bershad felt hands underneath his armpits. His body was lifted and dragged a few strides. When they touched him, he could feel their panicked heartbeats as if they were his own. The wild choir of animal noise continued to rage from every direction. For the smallest of moments, just a flicker of time, all the noises combined into a harmonized swell of sound.

Then everything went quiet and black.

24

BERSHAD

Unclaimed Lands, Razorback Mountains

Bershad woke up on his back, staring at the clear blue sky. He listened for a moment, but his hearing had returned to normal. A light breeze. Distant birdcalls. His own pulse was alone inside his chest.

"How do you feel?"

Bershad propped himself up to find Rowan sitting on the ground across from him. He was holding a small glass vial with about a finger's width of dark green moss at the bottom. It was sprouting blue flowers.

"That what I think it is?"

"Yeah. I tried some from our stash of Spartania first, but it didn't help. I didn't know what to do. Your body was shaking and there was blood pouring out of your nose like a fucking river. You were gonna die. So, I pushed a little further into the warren. Found this beneath a gnarled tree, grabbed a handful, and shoved a bunch down your throat. It turned you around quick." He looked away. "I tried to go back and get more when I saw what it did, but I lost my way. So we just hauled you out of there."

"You saved my life, Rowan. That's what matters."

Bershad rubbed at his beard and looked around. The others had set up camp in a loose circle beneath a large oak tree. They were in a small valley that was surrounded by mountain peaks.

"How long was I out for?" Bershad asked.

"An hour, maybe."

Bershad flexed his hands. Blinked his eyes. He felt fine. Normal.

"Vera and Felgor took Alfonso to get water from down there." Rowan pointed behind Bershad. There was a large blue lake in the distance—Bershad could make out two figures hauling water from the shore. The donkey was grazing next to them.

"I've never felt anything like that before. Not in all the warrens I crawled around in as a kid, or when I came through here ten years ago."

"A lot's happened in ten years."

"Yeah." Bershad shook his head. "It felt like the world was . . . waking up around me."

"It almost killed you."

"If I stay out of warrens I doubt it'll happen again."

"You hope it won't. That's a big fucking assumption, Silas."

"Well, life's full of uncertainties."

Rowan looked at the vial of moss for a moment, then held it out to Bershad. "You should keep this with you from here on out."

Bershad hesitated. "I don't like using it unless there's no other choice."

"You're still fixing to kill an emperor at some point, yes?"

Bershad nodded. Otherwise all of this was for nothing.

"Well, this is the same shit that kid put in your leg back in Otter Rock. It makes sense for an alchemist to have some, seeing as they're generally the only bastards prowling around warrens. And it certainly stopped whatever was going on inside your head back there. Time might arrive where you're in a fix and this is the only way out."

Bershad was afraid of what the moss did to him, but he knew Rowan was right. If he did get in front of the emperor, Mercer would probably be surrounded by scores of guards. The moss would give him a chance, at least. He took the vial from Rowan and searched for a place he could keep it. He wound up tying the vial into a snarl of hair at the base of his skull where it'd be hidden and protected. All those years without a comb were finally useful.

"Vera knows about me," Bershad said as he secured the vial.

"I figured," Rowan said. "She'll carry it, I can tell. A woman like her is good for you."

"What kind of woman is that, exactly?" Bershad asked, glancing toward the lake. Vera and Felgor were heading back now—two big skins of water slung over Alfonso's back.

"Fierce," Rowan said. "Honest."

"Opposite of that Balarian pretty much, but I can tell you like him."

Rowan grunted. "He reminds me of my youngest, Po."

"How's that?"

In all their years of traveling together, Rowan almost never talked about his family.

"Always seeing the light side of a situation, no matter how rough." Rowan paused. Smiled. "Dishonest as a jackal, too. When Po was a kid, he convinced his older brother to cover his chores for a week by promising he'd show him a peephole on the girls' side of the local bathhouse. Wasn't no peephole, though, so he got his jaw busted when the week was up."

"Are they all back in Deepdale?" Bershad asked. "Your family."

"Yeah. They got families of their own now. My sons all work a mulberry orchard together outside the city, making plenty of money off the silkworms that live in the branches. I like that—the idea of them growing things instead of killing 'em like their old man."

"You miss them?"

"Course. But they understood why I had to do this."

"Your wife, too? You took a death sentence when you became my forsaken shield."

Rowan grimaced. "She went down the river ahead of me. Blood fever."

"I didn't know that. I'm sorry."

Rowan waved the sentiment away from him. "I have my debts to pay, same as you." He looked at Bershad. "Your father is the only reason I survived the Balarian Invasion. That means my sons wouldn't have gotten their peaceful life without Leon Bershad. Po and the rest can take care of themselves now, but you—" He smiled. "You still need my help."

"I guess I do."

Rowan stretched his feet out, watching Vera and Felgor make their way back. "Got to admit, traveling with 'em isn't so bad. Now that the shithead Grealor is dead, I'd say we make a half-decent crew. Even if we are a bunch of thieves and assassins."

Bershad didn't say anything—Vera and Felgor were almost back—but he agreed with Rowan. Bershad had always mistrusted large groups of people. Didn't make a difference if it was a castle courtyard full of highborns or a tavern packed with farmers and fishermen—they'd all boil down to a dirty mob given to cruel compulsion when things got rough. But Bershad couldn't summon the same jaded outlook for his two new companions. He liked them. Was on his way to trusting them, even.

"Not dead yet, eh?" Felgor said with a huge grin on his face.

Alfonso trotted over and licked Bershad's face with a happy kind of urgency, then wandered toward a field of berries to the left of the camp.

"That one was worried about you," Vera said, motioning to the donkey.

"Sure, sure," Felgor said. "Go ahead and pretend Alfonso was the only concerned party. I didn't think our ice-for-blood widow could look so distraught on a simple mission to collect water."

He beamed at Vera.

"Anyone ever told you that your teeth are the size of a six-year-old girl's?" Vera asked.

"Couple times, actually."

Vera sighed and looked at Bershad. "I'm glad you're all right. What happened?"

"Something in the warren messed with my head, that's all."

"And you said they were safe," Felgor said.

"No, I said there weren't any dragons inside of them."

"We were all in there for a while." Felgor sniffed a few times. "You think it could affect me, too?"

"Doubt it."

Felgor sniffed one last time, just to be sure. "Okay." He paused. "What's for dinner?"

Everyone insisted that Bershad rest at the camp while they looked for food. Rowan and Felgor went foraging while Vera went down to the lake alone to fish. Bershad got a fire going and stared into the coals, taking stock of his body. The world still sounded normal—he could hear some mice skittering around the camp, but he couldn't feel their heartbeats like he had before. As a test, he took out the dragontooth dagger and poked it into his arm. Watched the blood pool around the wound and drip down. His skin didn't close on its own, which gave Bershad an odd sense of relief. His ability to heal had kept him alive for all these years. But it also scared the shit out of him.

The others returned about an hour later. Rowan and Felgor had found a few dozen brown mushrooms, each one the size of a baby's head. Rowan threw them into the pot and turned to Vera. "What'd you find down by the lake? Fish?"

"Not exactly," Vera said. She dropped a leather sack next to the pot. The sack writhed and squirmed on the ground. "Crayfish," she explained. "They were all over the shore."

Felgor opened the bag with a finger and peeked inside. "I'd have preferred lake trout."

"I'd prefer a lamb shank dripping with brown gravy," Rowan said, grabbing the sack. "This is what we have." He looked at Vera. "Good work."

He dumped the crayfish into the mushroom-filled water and stirred.

"Fucking shells'll cut my gums," Felgor complained.

"Happy to eat your share for you," Bershad said.

"No, no," Felgor said quickly. "I want them."

After they finished eating the stew, which tasted a little like each of the crayfish had shit itself before dying, Felgor casually produced a full waterskin that Bershad hadn't seen before. He leaned back and poured a long stream of whiskey into his mouth. Swished it around happily for a moment, then swallowed.

"Ah," he said, smacking his lips. "That's the good shit."

Everyone stared at him.

"Felgor, where the fuck did you get that?" Bershad said.

"Found it."

"We're in the middle of nowhere. Where did you find a full skin of whiskey?"

"Down by the river when Vera and I were getting water," Felgor said. "Someone set up a dead-drop in the reeds, looked like."

"I didn't notice a dead-drop," Vera said.

"That's because your eyes aren't as sharp as mine, little spider."

Vera frowned. "I do not like that name. And how did you get into it without me noticing? I was with you the whole time."

Felgor smiled and took another drink. "I'm a thief, remember?"

Bershad studied the skin. It looked Balarian made. The soldiers who patrolled the pass must have hidden the whiskey there at some point, which meant there might be other supplies nearby, too.

"Tomorrow morning, you're going to show me this dead-drop," Bershad said. "For now, give me some of that, will you?"

Bershad took a long swallow of the whiskey. Felt it burn the back of his throat and warm his belly. He generally didn't feel the need to drink when he was in the wilds, but he'd nearly died in that dragon warren. Plus, they were relatively safe from harm for the first time in weeks. If there was a night to get drunk, this was it. He offered the skin to Vera when he was done. She took a long sip as well. Apparently, she'd come to the same conclusion as Bershad.

There was plenty to go around between the four of them. Felgor started slurring his words first, and spent an hour interrogating Rowan about his favorite types of women and, when that topic was exhausted, moved seamlessly into his favorite types of sausage and beer.

"I've never had this rain ale that you're glorifying to high hell," Felgor said to Rowan, pausing to burp. "But nothing beats juniper liquor with a bit of lime. Nothing. When we get to Burz-al-dun I'll show you—I know all the best taverns."

"Waste of time," Rowan said, a little louder than necessary. He was drunk, too. "Rain ale is the best. Tastes like, um. Tastes like . . ."

"Like a foggy morning," Bershad said. "Just after dawn."

"Exactly," Rowan said. "That's exactly right."

"Huh," Felgor said. "What does a foggy morning taste like?"

"Like rain ale," Vera said. She was on her back, staring at the stars. "Obviously."

"You're drunk, little spider," Felgor said.

"We're all drunk, thief."

"That is a fact," Felgor said, smacking his lips. "Quite a fix we've wound up in. Drunk next to some remote lake. We just ate a bunch of crunchy lake bugs for dinner. Vera's down a finger. And I don't know about all of you, but I haven't had a proper shit in days."

"Could be worse," Bershad said.

"How?"

"Yonmar could still be alive."

Everyone laughed. Vera passed the skin back to Felgor, and they kept passing it around until it was empty. Felgor passed out first, with Rowan not far behind. Both of them snored loudly. Bershad and Vera stayed up longer, sitting with the fire between them and not talking.

Just looking at each other and listening to the night.

25

BERSHAD

Unclaimed Lands, Razorback Mountains

The whiskey made everyone sleep past sunrise and then some. It was midmorning when Bershad woke up. His hangover was already gone, but the others were in rough shape.

"Up!" Bershad called. "Need to get moving."

"Not so loud," Vera muttered, then licked her dry lips. "Fuck, I'm thirsty."

"Pretty sure I'm dying," Felgor said, squinting at the sun.

"Well, before you die, think you can show me that dead-drop where you found the whiskey?"

Felgor burped, looked like he was going to vomit, then spat. "Yeah, yeah. It's this way."

They broke camp and walked down to the shore. Rowan and Vera drank greedily from the lake while Felgor retraced his footsteps and found the dead-drop.

"Here it is," he announced. "Nothing else in here, though."

Bershad unsheathed his sword and began to poke around the tall reeds that ruled the area. His sword made a soft sucking noise with each poke. He moved farther into the reeds and poked around for about five minutes until he reached a big hump in the mud. When he pressed his sword down, he got the hollow thud of metal on wood. Bershad bent down and pressed his fingers into the mud, tracking along the hump until he found the edge.

"Help me with this, will you?" he called to Felgor.

"What is it?"

"Just find the edge on that side and help me."

Felgor followed the same process as Bershad on the far side of the hump, then gave a little nod when he was ready. Together, they yanked a mud-caked boat free from its hiding place in the reeds. It was a Balarian dory—about ten strides long and large enough to fit four people, but the sides were warped and worn from years of muddy neglect. Beneath the boat there were four snail-covered oars.

"We'll use this to cross the lake," Bershad said. "The river on the other side will take us down the mountain to a larger river that leads into Taggarstan."

Felgor scratched his head. "That doesn't look very safe. Will it even float?"

"The other options are walking or swimming," Bershad said.

Felgor shrugged. "Boat it is."

They couldn't fit everyone, a donkey, and their gear on the boat. So, they pulled the saddlebags off Alfonso and, after the better part of an hour, managed to coax the donkey aboard with a handful of wild carrots Vera dug up. Alfonso clopped around the hull uncertainly, then wedged himself against the bow and fell asleep. The rest of them clambered into the boat, tried and failed to get comfortable, and then started rowing.

"I believe this is the very worst activity to do with a hangover," Felgor said after they'd been paddling for about twenty minutes.

"Fighting a battle is worse," Rowan said.

"You did that hungover?"

"Sure, if there isn't enough time to get drunk again first. Most of soldiering is waiting around for something to happen. The other bit is drinking and pushing people around in the mud. Stabbing them when you can."

"Sounds awful."

"No argument there."

On the far side of the lake, a narrow river flowed down the northern face of the Razorback Mountains. The current grew stronger as they descended, and the river was soon full of white rapids and swells that rocked them back and forth in the water like a sadistic child trying to drown a cat. It wasn't long before Felgor had stopped rowing so he could start vomiting and Alfonso was whining steadily, trying to stand but not being able to keep his balance and falling over again.

"I changed my mind," Rowan said when they reached a few moments of calm. "This is the worst thing to do with a hangover. Gods."

"Stay focused," Vera said. "And keep rowing. The key is to keep rowing."

The water cut through the mountains in jagged twists and switchbacks. The current dragged them from one side of the river to the other. They spent most of the time facing backward, rowing in different and desperate directions. Screaming at each other to try and avoid this rock or that massive swell of a current. By dusk, they'd been pinned against countless rocks and lost all except two oars. There was muddy water up to their ankles and Alfonso looked like he'd gone into shock.

But after they exited a narrow pass where they'd very nearly been bashed to splinters, the river widened around them and the journey turned into a relaxing float. For a while, nobody said anything, not wanting to celebrate before they were actually finished with the horrific descent. But just as the sun was setting Bershad looked back and saw the Razors in the distance behind them. Nothing but flat plain ahead.

"We made it," he said.

"That was the worst experience of my life," Felgor said.

"You didn't even get hurt," Vera said. "Although you still screamed plenty."

"Not everyone has ice water in their veins like you, little spider," Felgor said. "Or madness in their hearts like our famous dragonslayer over here. But a fair point. I guess it wasn't quite the number-one worst experience of my life. I once paid ten silvers for a whore who wound up having a cock."

Nobody said anything.

"A big one, too. Thick."

More silence.

"Well, doesn't anyone want to hear how that happened?" Felgor asked.

"If you tell that story," Vera said, "I will slit your throat and dump you into this river."

"Come now, little spider," Felgor said. "We all know that's not true. You're starting to give in to my charms just like Rowan." He splashed river water onto his face to wash some mud away. "So any-way, I pay this whore ten silvers because she's got the smoothest skin I've ever seen. Like fresh cream. And then we head upstairs to my room in the tavern . . ."

Bershad did his best to tune out the rest of Felgor's story, but more of the details slipped through than he would have liked.

They passed the Balarian checkpoint an hour after midnight. The sight of the thing finally got Felgor to shut up again. The entire north bank of the river was a stone wall, fifty feet high and black as a shark's eye. The wall stretched on for almost half a league, with nothing but a single steel portcullis in the middle to pass through. Two bra-ziers burned on either side of the gate and there was a small line of boats waiting to pass through. The metal helmets of sentries on top of the wall winked in the moonlight as they made rounds.

"Don't even think about trying to get through there," Felgor said as they rowed past the gate. "That tunnel lasts for four leagues and there are murder holes the entire way. No seal of passage, no heartbeat when you exit on the far side. They inspect every ship for freeloaders hiding amid the cargo, too. Anyone they find gets turned into a Balarian Por-cupine."

"A what?" Vera asked, not understanding the figure of speech.

"They shoot you with arrows," Bershad explained. "A lot of ar-rows."

Bershad rowed them past the long line of boats waiting to enter. Most looked like trading galleys meant for rowing up and down the flat rivers of the eastern lands.

"Who keeps all of this in place?" Bershad asked Felgor. "If Almira tried something like this, it'd go to shit after a moon's turn."

"Well, first of all, Almirans are fucking animals." Felgor smiled. "Second, Balaria is ruled by the Domitians. And they are a different breed of despot. Control over the masses comes natural to them. Emperor Elias Domitian built the border walls after his invasion of Almira failed. Kept the colonials and foreigners out. That seemed like a good place to stop to everyone except his son, Mercer. He's the one who cut Burz-al-dun up into districts, each one sealed by check-points that can only be passed with Balarian-made seals. Once the capital was tightened up, he spread the system to every city and high-way in Balaria. Whole thing's under his thumb, now. There's a story that he's got some massive room in the palace where he controls it all, but I call dragonshit." Felgor spat into the water. "I'd have found it."

"Hmm," Bershad mumbled, thinking of what Ashlyn had told him in Castle Malgrave. Balaria's checkpoint system might not collapse overnight if Emperor Mercer was killed, but his death would create enough chaos to prevent the dragon cull this summer.

The rest of the boats around the checkpoint had the look of military ships or pleasure cruisers. The military boats were outfitted with steel plates and carried archers' nests at the hull and prow. The pleasure cruisers were flat and large, adorned with silk cabanas and even from fifty yards away Bershad could smell the incense wafting across the water and the soft din of a harp being played.

"Rich Balarians come out here for slaves," Felgor said, following Bershad's eyes. "The shackle trade is illegal in Balaria, but you can bring in a slave you already own as long as you're willing to pay a tax the size of this morning's hangover. Which they all are, rich bastards. So they cruise around and pick up slaves in Taggarstan—concubines mostly—and then they float back."

"You seem to know a lot about it," Vera said.

Felgor kept his eye on the largest of the cruisers, as if he was hoping for a glimpse of a half-naked concubine that never came.

"What kind of thief would I be," he said after a while, "if I didn't know what those silky bastards were up to on their fancy boats?"

"Ever tried to rob one?" Bershad asked.

Felgor spat into the water and shook his head. "They're guarded tighter than a mouse's asshole and there's nowhere to run if you're caught. Only morons try to rob the actual boat. Best to wait until they're unloading and hit them at the docks. Docks are good places to rob people, especially in Balaria. The rich folk all have covered slips—kind of like a miniature house."

"I'll remember that," Bershad said.

They kept rowing until the wall ended against the side of a sheer canyon. The canyon tapered off to a height that Bershad thought would be climbable if they each had a pair of spikes and several lengths of good rope. Vera saw that, too.

"Why not scale the cliffs?" she asked. "Sneak across through the wilderness."

"There's a hundred leagues of desert up there," Felgor said. "Balarian soldiers guard the water and the road to Burz-al-dun. Only things that can cross that desert without getting caught by a patrol are vultures and dragons."

"That could be," Vera said. "Or it could be that you just want us in Taggarstan. Seems like a good place for a thief to disappear."

"You wound me, little spider," Felgor said. "Truth is, I'm quite looking forward to breaking into the Burz-al-dun palace again. Been a while since I had a good challenge."

"Just don't try anything foolish when we get there, Felgor. I will make you pay for it. Clear?"

"Clear," Felgor muttered. Then he turned away to watch the water.

————

They rowed through the night, sleeping in pairs while two others worked the remaining oars. By daybreak they could see the city. Taggarstan was built at the confluence of six mountain rivers. Some of them were barely more than streams, but others were sixty or seventy strides wide, which made the confluence a bloated circle of churning currents. Bershad glanced over the edge of the dory and saw the clear mountain water they'd ridden down from the Razors turn murky and brown as it mixed with the other rivers.

Taggarstan itself was a ragtag mess of planks and shacks and makeshift barges lashed together and anchored to form a semipermanent floating city and trading post. Beyond the city, the rivers combined into a deep, wide expanse called the Murakai River that flowed across a marshy plain until it reached Graziland—the distant realm in the east.

The Murakai's current was gentle, which meant there were hundreds of outlander merchants and smugglers digging their way out of the eastern lands every day, coming to Taggarstan to trade with the realm of Terra. Bershad shaded his eyes as they approached the city. They steered their dory beneath a wooden bridge with the painted white letters TAGGRST hung unevenly below it on slate squares.

"Seems they could use a new sign," Rowan said, yawning and rousing himself from the place he'd been sleeping, nestled between Alfonso and the hull.

The innards of the city were a maze of canals formed by interconnected barges that had been anchored in place. The smell of rotting wood and dead fish polluted the air. Flies and mosquitoes had already amassed overhead in a thick cloud even though it was only half an hour after sunrise. In the distance, they could hear the clatter and racket of a fish market.

"We should head to the market," Felgor said. "Get some breakfast, at least. Maybe some information."

Bershad had seen plenty of markets in his life. He'd stood outside perfume bazaars that only highborn ladies were allowed to enter, breathing in hard and wondering how such a thing was possible in the same world as Glenlock Canyon, where he had run his horse over so many corpses that the beast's legs and belly were still dripping blood hours later. He'd seen totem markets in the Gorgon Valley, where priceless gems, dried animal organs, and rare plants were organized by their alleged magical properties.

But Bershad had never seen anything quite like Taggarstan.

Every canal and alley led to the center of the city—a large eye of water where boats crammed themselves together like arrows in a quiver and then went about the business of selling their wares. Buyers ran across rope-and-wood bridges above the water and called down prices, haggled, complained, and then motioned for the boat to toss up whatever they'd bought while they dropped a bag of coins down in exchange.

Some boats were brimming with enormous fish that must have come from the deepest depths of the Great Western Ocean—their eyes were as big as Bershad's fist. Others carried river trout and tiny hens strung together at the fin or foot with a wire cord. The larger riverboats from Graziland came with hulls that sagged deep into the water because they were packed with as much opium as possible.

"So much trade on Balaria's doorstep. Why not conquer it?" Vera asked as they got closer.

"Because it's impossible," Felgor said. He was picking at his teeth with a splinter of wood from the boat. "There is no Taggarstan. Not really. It's just a bunch of rotting barges floating in the same place. If Balaria grabbed this spot, the riffraff would just cut the anchor lines and float their way downriver a bit, then start the whole thing over again. It'd be endless." He threw the splinter into the water.

Bershad steered the dory to an empty space along one of the canals before they entered the market proper. There was an old man with green vomit in his white beard leaning on a railing. He watched them through rheumy eyes.

"You own this spot?" Bershad asked in Balarian.

No response. He tried again in Ghalamarian. That just got the man to drool a little from the corner of his mouth.

"Pargos," Vera said from behind him while she strapped on her daggers. "That man is from Pargos."

"Can we tie our boat here?" Bershad tried in broken Pargossian.

The drunk's eyes slid over to Bershad. Eyed him up and down.

"Fuck if I'm gonna tell a dragonslayer what to do. Best watch yourself, though. Taggarstan don't have as many laws as other spots in Terra, but we still trim the necks of tattooed faces that linger too long."

He spat on Bershad's boot and then wobbled away, uncorking a ceramic jug tied to a string on his hip and taking a large gulp. Bershad figured that was close enough to permission.

"Felgor, do you know where the Seven Anchors is?" Bershad asked when the boat was secured.

"About that," Felgor said, lowering his voice. "You sure that you want to work out a deal with the vampire? Might be we can find someone else to do it."

"Why would we bother with that?"

"The vampire has a reputation," Felgor said. "And it's not a good one."

"That doesn't mean he can't help us," Bershad said.

"He's more likely to eat us than help us, Silas."

"What?"

Felgor hesitated, looking at each member of the group in turn. "For as long as Taggarstan's been around, three men have run it. Malakar Roth, Fallon Sicone, and Alto Yakun. Each of 'em have their own turf and operation. They make most of their money sneaking opium into Balaria, and smuggling refined dragon oil out. And it used to be, you couldn't smoke an opium pipe or throw a pair of dice in Taggarstan that didn't belong to one of them."

"Felgor, what does this have to do with eating people?"

"I'm getting there. Two years ago, the vampire shows up from who-knows-where, and starts stirring shit up. He spent a year recruiting pirates and criminals to his crew until he had his own little army. Then, a few months ago, he took Alto Yakun's entire operation down in a single night. Rumor is he ate the bastard's liver and heart, too."

"How do you know all this?" Vera asked. "You've been in an Almiran dungeon for weeks."

"Trust me, when you're in my line of work, this kind of news reaches every dungeon in Terra. The vampire is a sadistic bastard who we don't want to tangle with." Felgor stepped closer to Bershad. "There are other ways to get seals."

"Maybe. But this is the shortest way."

"It's a bad way."

"The shortest one usually is," Bershad said. "Look, I appreciate the history lesson, but we don't have time to find a nicer criminal forger. We finish the deal Yonmar set up and keep moving. Now where is the Seven Anchors?"

Felgor scanned the faces of the others and saw that he was outnumbered.

"Fine. Follow me."

———

Felgor led them down a series of narrow passages. Floating shacks and decrepit barges were lashed to the walkways. Bershad glanced inside a few windows only to find drunk people sleeping the morning away on thin, dirty mats. The people who were awake and going about their business looked like a criminal sort of fishermen who'd only do an honest day's work if the chance to rob someone didn't present itself first. Most people shoved and pushed their way down the alleys with no regard for the people around them, but they passed two men who received an inexplicably wide berth from the jostling crowd. They were shirtless and covered in weblike tattoos—as if a spider had been set free across their flesh. Both carried fishing knives and short swords. They had ceramic jugs of rice wine slung over their shoulders on a fishing line.

"Those two're with the Drunken Spiders," Felgor said after they'd passed. "Pirating outfit with their own private island up north. Dangerous bastards. Nobody fucks with them when they come to Taggarstan to do business."

They passed a tanned, topless woman who had rings through both nipples. She blew Felgor a kiss.

"Damn but I've missed this place," Felgor said.

They traveled through the makeshift city for almost an hour, shoving their way across narrow, planked pathways until reaching a small cove on the south side of town where seven boats were lashed together in the water.

"This is the Seven Anchors," Felgor said. "Name's pretty self-explanatory. The vampire doesn't control much of the city, but he is the fucking king of this setup here."

"Can we bring Alfonso inside?" Rowan asked.

"This is Taggarstan," Felgor replied. "We could bring a lion inside if we had one."

"Good," Bershad said, pushing past Felgor.

Inside, everything had been gutted and the seven boats were connected by wide, open-air bridges. Instead of individual rooms, the hull of the first ship was littered with colorful tents. Some only had enough space for a single person, but others were seventy strides across and filled with people and music. Felgor guided them through the maze of tents.

Most of the tents were filled with dancing women and dicing tables. Pretty standard as far as pleasure houses went. But the opium tents were something different. Bershad and Vera both glanced into a few that they passed. The first one had hundreds of tiny mirrors hanging from the ceiling by fishing line. Twenty naked men and women were lying on the carpet, staring up at the moving pieces. Another was lined with shelves of candles, and the floor was a huge basin of green paint. Three people were sitting naked in the paint, rubbing each other's skin and making swirling patterns.

"The vampire doesn't allow his men any opium," Felgor said. "Part of the reason nobody fucks with his muscle. But everyone else pays a pretty penny to use the tents. Nothing else like them in the world."

That wasn't true. The Morlang clan of the jungle nations kept craftsmen who did nothing but make opium tents. The drug was like a religion for them. Bershad knew about the tents because the Morlangs were also infamous mercenaries. When they hired out to foreign countries, they brought their tents with them. Bershad had trampled dozens of them in Glenlock Canyon.

They exited that ship and stepped onto another crude bridge that forked in two directions. Felgor pointed to the left, where a massive black war frigate sat anchored. It looked like a seaworthy vessel except for the wide and elevated platform that had been built on top of the deck.

"That's where the vampire'll be," Felgor said, then pointed down the right path where there was a tavern-boat with a swollen hull and several levels of jury-rigged rooms above the deck. There was a stone sign with BREAD, EGGS, MEAT scrawled across it. "And that's where we can get some damn good food before we deal with that crazy asshole. How about it? I'm starving."

"Not a bad idea," Rowan said. "Being honest, I'm feeling pretty thin myself."

Bershad hesitated. He wasn't exactly in tip-top shape, either. He looked at Vera, who nodded begrudgingly.

"Fine. Breakfast, then we go see the vampire."

The tavern-boat was dark and everything smelled like sawdust and seaweed. Almost every seat and table was filled with men who were drinking from ceramic jugs and plowing into plates of bread and eggs and meat. Bershad and the others shuffled through the crowd and found a spot at the end of the stained bar where there was room for Alfonso. Bershad caught the attention of the serving man behind the bar with a nod of his head.

"How much?" he asked in Balarian, motioning to his neighbor's plate of food and jug of wine.

"Three corals for the food. One for the wine," the man answered. He had a thick neck and big hands with silver hairs sprouting from his knuckles.

Bershad didn't have any corals, and he didn't know how much they were worth. So he removed two of the silvers from Yonmar's purse and put them on the bar. "Four of everything," he said.

The barman snatched the coins and walked away. He returned a few minutes later with food and wine and a fistful of corals for change. Bershad looked down at them.

"How badly did I just get ripped off?" he asked Felgor.

"You don't want to know."

Bershad shrugged, then dug into his plate of food. They ate in ravenous silence, all of them preparing their next bite of food before swallowing the current one. When his plate was empty, Bershad took a long gulp of his wine, which was warm and clear and tasted like rice. With so many people around, Bershad felt a burning desire to polish the rest of it off in a big gulp and order another one, but he resisted the urge. He motioned for the barman again. When he returned, Bershad pushed another silver forward.

"Do you know who the vampire of Taggarstan is?" Bershad asked.

Felgor opened his mouth, but Vera silenced him with a stare.

The barman frowned. "Where you from, lizard killer?"

"Far away."

The man grunted. "That's clear. Because everyone in Taggarstan knows who the vampire is. And they know better than to go around asking for him."

"Guess I'm the ignorant and reckless type, then." Bershad smiled, then passed two more silvers across the counter. Leaned in and spoke softly. "Is he on that black ship across the way right now?"

"Aye."

"What's it take to see him?"

The man rubbed a greasy hand through his dirty hair. "Seeing the vampire is done on the vampire's terms, lizard killer. So finish your wine and fuck off."

Bershad dug out five more silver pieces and laid them on the table. He wanted to know more. "Tell me what he looks like."

The man glared at the silvers like they were spiders. Then he sighed and scooped them up. "Bone-white skin. Red eyes. Moves like lightning with a blade and kills curious people for fun. Eats them after, some say."

Bershad felt the hairs on his neck prickle.

"Vergun," he said.

"Eh?" The barman squinted at him.

"You are describing a man named Vallen Vergun," Bershad said.

"Aye, Vergun the vampire. You're eating his eggs. Drinking his wine."

Bershad drained the contents of his jug in one long gulp, gripping the side with white knuckles.

"I want to talk to him. Right now."

The barman laughed. "Only reason you're gonna talk to the vampire is if you rack up a debt you can't pay or cause trouble in one of his taverns. And believe me, the conversation won't go your way."

"Fair enough."

Bershad drew the dagger from the small of his back and slammed the butt into the man's face. His nose snapped and he fell backward into the wall, holding his ruined face and bleeding everywhere.

"Go tell Vallen Vergun the Flawless Bershad is causing trouble in one of his taverns."

26

ASHLYN

Almira, Floodhaven

As the sun burned low in the west, casting an orange glow over Castle Malgrave and Floodhaven, Ashlyn prepared for her coronation. The voices of hundreds of people echoed up from the courtyard below, along with the smell of the sea. The lords of Almira were waiting for their queen.

She wore a gown of black silk that wrapped around her body five times—weaving across her breasts and arms in an intricate design that dropped down from her torso in a pattern of triangular slashes and precise angles of fabric. Servants had sculpted her long black hair into a series of rigid spires that stabbed upward, forming an onyx crown above her head.

"Did any more western lords arrive today?" Ashlyn asked a steward, who seemed very uncomfortable in Ashlyn's bedchambers. She had been stuck getting her hair shaped for the last five hours, and was unable to monitor the city walls herself.

"They have, my queen. More than fifty small lords of the Gorgon Valley rode through the gates today—they joined Cedar Wallace in his villa this afternoon and are now awaiting you in the courtyard with the others."

Finally.

"How many wardens?" Ashlyn asked.

"Pardon me?"

"The western lords—how many soldiers arrived with them?"

The steward consulted his ledger. Hesitated. "I'm sorry, my queen, but I only have a record of the lords themselves. They rode into the city alone."

Strange. Perhaps they had ridden ahead to arrive in time for her coronation, but Ashlyn wasn't going to ignore alternative possibilities. Wallace had promised his men by today; if he didn't deliver them, there was a reason.

"Ask Hayden and Shoshone to come in here," she told the steward.

The widows entered the room a moment later. Both of them were wearing their black armor and a plain sharkskin-leather mask that hid everything except their eyes.

"Cedar Wallace hasn't brought his wardens into the city, just his vassal lords from the Gorgon Valley," Ashlyn told them. "Something doesn't feel right."

"What do you think he's planning?" Hayden asked.

"If he's going to challenge me, now would be the time. If I'm killed or deposed before I'm officially coronated, it'll be far easier for Wallace to take power afterward."

"Wouldn't he have brought his wardens into the city if he was planning to rebel?"

"Not necessarily," Ashlyn said. "They wouldn't have been allowed inside the castle, and my wardens control all the vital positions within Floodhaven. Even if they had the numbers, they wouldn't have the advantage. But if they stay outside the city, I can't control them at all. As for lords—they're all welcome inside Castle Malgrave tonight. Wallace knows that."

Ashlyn chewed on her lip, her mind rattling through her options. She could have Wallace arrested right away, but that would turn his vassals against her and possibly start a civil war. She couldn't risk that this close to the summer solstice.

"My queen," Shoshone said, "if you suspect an assassination plot, we should postpone the ceremony."

"If I'm too vulnerable to attend my own coronation, nobody will sail to war for me. We just need to increase security. How many widows are stationed on the walls above the courtyard right now?"

"One hundred, my queen," Shoshone said.

"Bring half of them down into the crowd. I want a widow within sword's reach of any lord who claims allegiance to Cedar Wallace."

"That will make the nobles nervous," Hayden said.

"I want them nervous. If Wallace sees an opening tonight, I believe he'll take it. The best way to avoid violence is to design a single, inevitable outcome."

"Bringing half the widows off that wall leaves the entrances and exits to the courtyard vulnerable," Shoshone warned. "As it is, most of the castle hallways and corridors are unguarded right now."

Ashlyn chewed her lip. Shoshone was right. "Who else can we trust?"

"We could call Carlyle Llayawin off the city walls and into the castle," Hayden said. "I trust him and his men."

"No, if Wallace's wardens aren't accounted for, Carlyle needs to stay on the walls," Ashlyn said. Carlyle had spent years training to defend Floodhaven. He could stave off an attack of thousands with a few hundred under his command.

"Who, then?"

There was a silence. She needed Carlyle on the walls, but he could spare some wardens.

"Carlyle stays on the walls," Ashlyn said eventually. "But send word to him that I need fifty of his best archers back at the castle to guard the courtyard."

"Yes, my queen," Shoshone said.

"Shoshone," Ashlyn said. "Which of your widows is the best shot with a sling?"

"Me," Shoshone answered with no arrogance or pride.

"If I give the order, you will put a shot through Wallace's head. Understood?"

"Definitely, my queen."

"Good."

Ashlyn was prepared to make an example out of Cedar Wallace if he forced her hand.

"I'll make the preparations at once," Shoshone said, bowing and leaving the room.

When she was gone, Hayden took a step closer and lowered her voice. "Do you have the thread?"

"Right here," Ashlyn said, tapping her left wrist. "Thumb-knife, too."

"Good." Hayden scanned the room as if she might find Cedar Wallace hiding behind one of the curtains.

"It's all right, Hayden. I know the risks, I've prepared as much as possible. The only thing left to do is put on the mask and go down there."

Just like every warden wore a mask into battle, every Almiran king and queen was given a mask at their coronation, which they would then wear when they held court. Silas used to joke that the custom was invented so royalty could send someone else to handle court matters for them.

The best sculptor in Floodhaven had locked himself inside his studio and spent a month creating Ashlyn's mask according to her instructions. Most Malgraves, her father included, chose an eagle's visage. A mixture of tradition and practicality—that way their wardens didn't have to carve new battle masks.

Ashlyn would let her wardens keep their eagles, but decided to go her own way with the mask.

It was made from a block of Papyrian cedar that was painted white and carved into the shape of a Ghost Moth's face—oval eyes, gentle snout. A complicated scale pattern that reminded Ashlyn of a cracked-open honeycomb. The twin tendrils dropped from the snout and grazed her collarbones. They were festooned with silver rings and small circular mirrors that caught the light and sent it cascading around the room.

The sculptor had urged Ashlyn to let him sculpt something less troubling. Almirans carved their nameless gods into all shapes and animals, but almost never dragons. While only the most zealous worshippers clung to the belief that dragons and demons had roamed Terra before the gods and warm-blooded animals, honoring the great lizards was rare to the point of being vulgar. Ashlyn didn't care. She needed to show Almira that she was an independent queen who would not submit to the shackles of expectation and tradition. And she needed to begin convincing them the great lizards weren't their enemies. This was the start of that effort.

Plus, she had loved Ghost Moths for her entire life, and one of them had given her the thread on her wrist. Any other mask would have been a betrayal.

Ashlyn donned her mask. The spires of her hair slipped through small holes bored into the sides of the cedar, which smelled alive and fresh. The wood was shaped perfectly to her face. The sculptor may not have liked her design choice, but he had done excellent work.

The lords of Almira would all be wearing their masks at the coronation, too. It was tradition.

Ashlyn waited in the bedchamber so Carlyle's men had time to get into position. As midnight approached, an out-of-breath widow arrived at the door and spoke in Hayden's ear.

"We're set?" Ashlyn asked.

Hayden nodded.

Ashlyn took one deep breath in. Let it out.

"Let's go."

————

Out of habit, Ashlyn counted the stairs on her way down to the seaside courtyard. One thousand and fifty-eight. The trip from tower to sea was one of longest journeys you could make in Castle Malgrave, but it felt like mere moments to Ashlyn, whose head was swimming with anticipation.

The four high lords of Almira stood at the lip of a stone platform that overlooked the seaside courtyard. At the far end of the lawn a set of marble steps descended into the Soul Sea. Between the high lords and the water, there were seven large bonfires scattered across the lawn. Each bonfire was ringed by six human-sized mud totems wreathed in eagle feathers. Each totem also had enough sapphires pressed into the surface to buy ten vats of dragon oil. Ashlyn thought it was a shame to waste such wealth on useless decoration.

And, of course, there were hundreds of masked lords and ladies. The nobility of Almira.

It was extremely rare for all of the small lords to gather in Floodhaven at the same time. Under normal circumstances, nobles were frequently summoned to the capital, but always in small groups. The journeys were justified by the pretext of delivering tax payments or updating the Malgraves on their local needs, but the real reason was to keep the lords of Almira in a nearly constant state of movement, which made it more difficult to develop secret allegiances or spark rebellions in their homeland.

The system had worked for her father, but he'd never tried to invade Balaria. Ashlyn needed the lords to unite behind her.

They mingled with each other, drinking from long-necked wine bottles specifically designed for masquerades. Some of these small lords ruled over little more than a crossroads and a crumbling holdfast, others controlled multiple cities and thousands of acres of land. But all their webs of allegiance eventually led to one of the high lords, and then to her.

Among the sea of animal masks, Ashlyn located a group of wolves toward the back. These were the fifty lords who had arrived today and gone straight to Wallace's villa. Unlike the other guests, who had chosen silk garments for the warm evening, each wolf was wearing a heavy cloak across his shoulders. Strange. But Ashlyn took comfort in the fact that there was a widow standing near each wolf, as she'd ordered.

Everyone in the courtyard stopped what they were doing and looked up when Ashlyn appeared. Kira would have known each lord and lady by their mask alone—she was always keeping track of the latest fashions amongst the nobility. Ashlyn had always thought it was an impractical type of information to memorize, but in that moment, the value of seeing behind a person's mask became clear.

To her surprise, she found herself desperately wishing that her sister was by her side.

Ashlyn scanned the ramparts above the courtyard, where the silhouettes of her widows and Carlyle's eagle-masked wardens filled the space between each crenellation. With so many soldiers up there, and with such a powerful height advantage, she couldn't imagine that Cedar Wallace would try something.

Linkon Pommol subtly gestured for her to step forward. His thin frame was unmistakable, even with his turtle-shaped mask on. She'd chosen him as the speaker for her coronation. Ashlyn would have preferred an Atlas Coast lord with whom she had a stronger relationship—but the speaker had to be a high lord in order to hold authority with the nobility. Ashlyn was already planning to buck most traditions in Almira, but this was one that she needed to abide by. She moved to the edge of the platform so that everyone could see her.

"Lords and ladies of Almira," Linkon said, "I present the rightful heir to King Hertzog Malgrave. Queen Ashlyn Malgrave!"

It looked like an invisible wave crashed down over the people below as they fell to their knees and lowered their heads.

"All of you speak for Almira," Linkon continued. "Your voices are the voices of her farmers and her blacksmiths, her carpenters and butchers, her hunters and weavers, her wardens and men-at-arms. Speak now, on their behalf."

With eerie unison, the court of Almira began to chant. "Ashlyn Malgrave, we give you our castles. We give you our homes. We give you our rivers and our valleys and our forests. They are yours now. We ask that you watch over our shores and honor the nameless gods. That you guard the lives of our children. That you protect us from the demons that rule the darkness."

Ashlyn straightened her back and spoke loudly, knowing the mask would muffle her voice. "I accept your castles and homes. I accept your rivers and valleys and forests. And I accept the burden of protecting your shores and your children. I will honor the nameless gods, and defend you against the demons in the dark." Beneath the mask, Ashlyn cringed. That line was another tradition she had to abide by. "I will not fail you."

"Ashlyn Malgrave," the courtyard spoke in unison, "we name you our queen."

Ashlyn bowed, deep and low. It was supposed to be the last time she ever bowed to anyone. "Rise, Almira," she said.

It was customary for the new ruler to address their subjects—usually with vague promises of honor and riches and glorious victories in the years to come. Ashlyn, on the other hand, needed to justify the army she was gathering. She cleared her throat again.

"I ascend the throne of Almira during a difficult time," Ashlyn said, keeping her voice loud and clear. "The death of my father was a tragic loss. And earlier this spring, the treacherous Balarians stole my sister from her bedroom and took her across the Soul Sea where she lies imprisoned behind their borders."

Some of the smaller lords—whose lands were so remote they'd been unable to keep up with current events—gasped and cursed at this news.

"There has been unrest and bloodshed in Mudwall," Ashlyn continued over the noise. "And Elden Grealor, high lord of the Dainwood, was killed in his own city. His sons squabble over the right to rule while other smaller factions have risen to sow the seeds of discord and chaos through the countryside."

Ashlyn saw no reason to identify the Jaguar Army by name, but they were definitely the ones fomenting unrest in the villages of the Dainwood. It was a problem, but like so many things, it would have to wait.

"My lords, this divided Almira is not who we are. We are stronger than this!"

There was a ripple of agreement.

"I have given Balaria a choice," Ashlyn said. "Either return my sister to her rightful home a week before the midsummer solstice, or face the wrath of Almira." She licked her lips. "My lords, you have brought your most ferocious warriors with you to celebrate my coronation. And surely you have noticed the fleet of ships that sits in Floodhaven harbor. If the emperor of Balaria does not heed my warning, I ask that you and your wardens sail to war with me!"

Some lords cheered and cried out happily. Others looked more hesitant. Ashlyn knew that most would follow their high lord's lead. It was time to put her work to the test.

"Lord Linkon," Ashlyn asked, motioning to the skinny lord. "What say you?"

Linkon turned to face the crowd below the platform, so they could hear.

"I will gladly ride to war to avenge the kidnapping of Kira Malgrave!"

His turtle-masked vassals howled support.

"Lord Korbon?"

"I support you with all of my heart, and all of my swords!" he growled from behind his goat's mask. Since nobody could see his nervous eyes and twitchy nose, Korbon managed to rally more cheering than Linkon.

"Lord Brock." Ashlyn motioned to the high lord, who was leaning against a wooden cane to keep himself upright. "Do I have your support?"

Yulnar Brock straightened up as best he could—badger mask rising a few inches.

"As all of you can see, I am nearly too fat to ride a wench, let alone ride to war."

The crowd laughed.

"But I have eleven sons. All of them strong and powerful and stuffed full of fire, instead of gout, like their father." He paused to catch his breath. "Each of my sons have promised me that their boots will be the first to fall on Balarian sand. Their swords the first to spill dirty Balarian blood!"

That released a torrent of cheers. Ashlyn waited for them to die down. The final lord was the most important. She needed the full support of Cedar Wallace and his newly arrived vassals, and she needed it tonight. Ashlyn glanced at the widows on the walls one more time and found Shoshone, who gave her a subtle nod. She had already unwound her sling from her thigh.

"Lord Wallace," Ashlyn asked, turning to the man in the wolf mask. He was wearing a heavy cloak, just like his vassals. "You were the most celebrated hero of the Balarian Invasion. They say you personally slew a hundred men at Black Pine. Will you join me in this fight for Almira's honor?"

For a moment, the wolf didn't move. Then he took one step toward her on the platform and slowly removed his mask. Ashlyn's stomach dropped when she saw the look of satisfaction on his face. The curl of a smile on the edge of his lips.

"No."

"You would abandon your country in a time of war?" Ashlyn asked, giving him another chance. She couldn't kill a high lord in public for a single, terse refusal.

"I abandon you, Ashlyn Malgrave," he said. Then he turned to the lords and raised his voice. "Look at what this half-breed has tricked you into doing! She's convinced you to load your wardens into a bunch of Papyrian ships and sail to a war you didn't start, and don't need to fight!"

A shudder of doubt rippled through the courtyard. The wolf-masked lords scattered through the crowd, forcing the widows shadowing them to spread out, too.

"Ashlyn sits in her tower, twisting our country into ruin. Obsessing over dragons and plotting a petty war against the Balarians while Almirans are being torn apart on their own bloody land!"

"What is the meaning of this, Wallace?" Linkon asked, his voice muffled and weak behind his turtle mask. "You are committing treason!"

"Stay out of this, boy." He spread out his arms. "Anyone who stands with Ashlyn Malgrave stands against me. Each of you must decide. Right now."

"No, Lord Wallace," Ashlyn said. "It was you who had the choice—obey your queen or face the consequences. And you have decided." She looked up to Shoshone. "Do it."

Shoshone whipped a shot from her sling toward Wallace so quickly that Ashlyn didn't have time to turn her gaze back down before it connected. But the sound that followed the impact wasn't the wet smack of lead shot hitting flesh. It was a metallic thump. When she turned back to Wallace, he'd slung a reinforced steel shield from underneath his cloak and raised it over his head, deflecting Shoshone's shot. It looked like he'd sawed off pieces of the shield so it was small enough to fit beneath his cloak without being noticed.

The lead ball was lodged deep in the shield's steel. Wallace was still smiling at her—dark eyes gleaming from the torchlight.

"Again!" Ashlyn ordered.

Before Shoshone or any of the other widows had a chance to fire their slings, Wallace lowered his shield and jumped into the crowd of lords. Everything turned to chaos. The lords were pressed too closely for anyone to risk firing at Wallace again, and the wolves had spread out too quickly for the widows in the crowd to reach them.

Ashlyn watched in horror as the wolves produced short-swords and shields from behind their heavy cloaks, too. They'd known how this night would end. And just like Ashlyn, they'd prepared.

"Get behind me," Hayden said. A circle of leathered bodies flowed around her. The widows drew their blades.

After the wolves had scattered across the lawn and separated from the widows who'd shadowed them, Wallace's men began to regroup toward the platform, shoving unarmed nobles out of their way—one of whom went crashing into a mud totem, knocking it over and spraying sapphires and feathers across the grass. A wolf tossed Cedar Wallace a sword. Before the courtyard had emptied enough for the widows above to have clear shots with their slings, Wallace and his men locked their shields into a tight formation.

Linkon moved closer to Ashlyn. Even with his turtle's mask on she could tell he was terrified. Lords Korbon and Brock fled the courtyard, surrounded by a small retinue of their wardens.

"My queen, we need to get you out of here," Hayden said, keeping her eyes on Wallace's approaching men.

Ashlyn clenched her jaw and tightened her fist. If she tried to run, her widows would make protecting her the priority, which gave Cedar Wallace a better chance of escaping. She couldn't allow that to happen. This needed to end here.

"No. Kill them all."

Hayden's face twitched. She hesitated.

"Hayden!"

"Slings!" Hayden shouted. A whooshing sound filled the courtyard as every widow surrounding Ashlyn raised their slings, whirled them three times over their heads, and released.

Normally, a wardens' shield wall would be near-impenetrable, even to a widow's sling. But Shoshone and her widows had a height advantage, and Wallace's wardens had all sawed down the size of their shields to smuggle them into the courtyard. There were gaps, and the widows found them. One wolf didn't get his shield in place fast enough. His mask exploded and he fell to his knees, blood spraying across the stones where Ashlyn had been made queen five minutes earlier. Ten more men fell as the widows above found more gaps between the shields. If the wolves stayed where they were, they'd all be dead in two or three more volleys.

"Charge her!" Wallace snarled.

The shield wall broke apart and the wolves rushed at Ashlyn. Half the widows dashed forward to meet them—blades flashing in quick arcs. The widows dodged and parried the men's heavy blades, but it seemed like most of their sword strikes and dagger gouges were blocked, too.

Now that Wallace's men were in the open, Ashlyn waited for the slings and arrows from above to end the fight. But the shots stopped. Ashlyn looked up and saw the eagle-masked wardens attack the widows from behind. Swords stabbing and swinging. One of the eagles grappled with a widow who was trying to fire another shot into the courtyard and both of them wound up going over the wall. The other widows on the wall dropped their slings and drew blades to defend themselves against the attack.

Ashlyn couldn't believe that Carlyle's men had betrayed her, but there was no other explanation. Without their help on the walls, Ashlyn had lost her advantage. She unwound the dragon thread from her wrist. She wasn't letting Cedar Wallace out of this courtyard alive.

"The cunts are too fucking quick," a wolf snarled as he hacked at one widow and missed. "Just shove the bitches off!"

A moment later he swiped his round shield in an arc and knocked two widows off the high platform. They landed gracefully on the grass, but then had to run back up the stone stairs to rejoin the fray. The other wolves followed suit, shoving and swiping with their shields instead of attacking with swords. A gap formed in the widows' line, and Cedar Wallace came pouncing through it.

He rushed directly at Ashlyn, but Hayden bolted forward and caught his sword with her own. Their blades flashed together once, twice, three times. So fast Ashlyn could barely follow the movement.

"Get the queen to the tower!" Hayden shouted when they broke apart for a moment.

Before Ashlyn could protest, a pair of strong hands lifted her by the shoulders and rushed her backward so quickly it felt like she was being carried by a powerful ocean current. The last thing Ashlyn saw before being whisked through a narrow hallway was Cedar Wallace slashing a widow's throat open when she tried to attack him from behind.

Everything became a blur of stone floors and torches as Ashlyn was taken through the castle. There was shouting. The widow who'd grabbed her was breathing heavily.

"We have to go back," Ashlyn said.

"No, my queen," she huffed.

"I give the orders, and I order you to let me—"

"Hayden is following your orders, my queen," the widow said, keeping Ashlyn moving. "There were too many of them to protect you and kill Cedar Wallace at the same time. With you safe, Hayden and the others can finish the wolves. It'll be—"

They turned a corner and Ashlyn felt a splash of hot liquid hit her face. She turned to see a crossbow bolt in the widow's throat. There were two wolves waiting farther down the hall, one of them already rewinding his crossbow. They stalked toward Ashlyn.

"Looks like the little dragon queen is all alone," said the wolf on the left, who had a pale white mask.

"No Papyrian bitches around to cause trouble, either," said the brown mask on the right. "Might be we can have a little taste before we gut you."

Ashlyn knew what needed to be done. The two wolves approached, confident and relaxed. They didn't even have their blades up.

"Please," she said, letting her voice quiver and raising her hands.

"Please, what?" the white mask jeered, then looked at his friend. "Suldur, you want her first or second?"

"All yours, Owan. I'll hold her down."

Ashlyn didn't move. She needed them close.

"Bet you're wishing Hayden was with you right now," Owan said as he wrapped a hand around Ashlyn's throat. He didn't squeeze, just held it there for a moment. The cold metal of his glove prickled Ashlyn's flesh.

"Thing is," Ashlyn said, "Hayden always said it was easier to protect me if I could protect myself."

Ashlyn flicked her wrist in the practiced motion she'd made a thousand times, releasing the thumb blade into her hand. She slipped it beneath the white wolf mask, felt it sink deep into the flesh of his throat. The blade was so sharp, it was as easy as pushing a pin through a piece of paper. The wolf stumbled backward, dropped his sword, and put both hands against his throat as blood flooded around his fingers.

"Owan?" Suldur asked, too surprised to move.

Ashlyn sliced her palm open with the thumb blade—pushing the steel far deeper than she ever did when she practiced—and ripped her bleeding hand down the thread. Felt the lightning fill her hand. She focused on the two men's chests. Pretended they were mortar seams.

"What the hell is—"

Ashlyn released two jagged arcs of lightning. Both men went rigid—smoke pouring from behind their masks. The wooden edges turned black and singed. When she stopped, they dropped to the ground like anchors from a ship.

Ashlyn pushed her back against a wall and slowly slid down to the floor, keeping her eyes fixed on the two dead wardens. She could smell their cooked flesh and burnt hair. The thumb-knife had turned so hot it left a blister on her wrist. The small metal hooks that kept her dress together were smoking around singed fabric.

She couldn't stay there. Ashlyn pulled herself together, snatched a dagger from one of the dead wardens' belts, and moved down the hall until she reached another corner. She pressed herself into an alcove so she had a view of both ends of the hallway, a dagger in one hand and the thread in the other. Heart hammering. If a warden came around either side, she was ready to kill them.

But it was five widows who found her.

They took Ashlyn back to the Queen's Tower. Within minutes, the room was packed with widows. All of them had their weapons drawn and kept their eyes shifting between the doors and windows and shadows. Linkon Pommol was the only high lord who hadn't fled the castle. He sat on a sofa across from her and said nothing. His skin was bone pale. Eyes wide with panic.

"What happened in the courtyard?" Ashlyn asked. "Malgrave wardens betrayed us?"

"It wasn't Malgraves on the ramparts," a widow said. She was bleeding from the forehead and wrist. "Wallace's men intercepted them on their way to the castle. Murdered them and took their masks."

"Are any of them still alive?"

"No," the widow said.

Ashlyn was stopped from asking another question by sounds lower in the tower. Doors opening. Footsteps in the stairwell. Hayden burst through the door with her sword still drawn. There was fresh blood on her face, and even more gore on her blade. It dripped onto the pristine carpet at her feet.

"You're safe," Ashlyn said, standing. She resisted the urge to cross the room and hug Hayden.

"The castle and courtyard are secure, my queen," Hayden said. "We killed almost all of the wolves."

"Almost," Ashlyn repeated. "What happened?"

Hayden wiped some blood away from her lips. "When Wallace saw that you were out of reach, he fought his way to the back of the courtyard. There was a boat there waiting for him. He escaped."

Nobody said anything for a moment. Ashlyn stared at her dragon's mask. Blood was splashed across the left cheek. A splinter from the wolf's mask was lodged on the dragon's snout.

"My queen," Hayden said. "What are your orders?"

Even if she'd killed Cedar Wallace, the fact that the attack happened at all was catastrophic. Instead of shoring up power and authority to launch an attack on Balaria, she'd nearly lost her life. If she didn't make smart decisions now, she would lose Floodhaven, Almira, and everything else.

"Empty the castle, then seal it. That way, we don't need so many widows guarding it. Then send two widows to Carlyle Llayawin on the walls," she said. "Tell them to be prepared for an attack from outside, but also from within. They have permission to kill any warden who threatens them. It does not matter what type of mask they're wearing."

"Yes, my queen."

"Then I want every lord that was at my coronation found and visited by a widow. Tonight."

"What message should they deliver?"

Ashlyn paused. Wallace hadn't organized this attack alone. At least one other lord had helped him. But starting a witch hunt now wouldn't get Ashlyn to the place she needed to be. She needed to build confidence, not spread fear.

"Tell them that Cedar Wallace has fled the city like the coward that he is. His assassins are dead. Tell them that Ashlyn Malgrave is alive. And she is their queen."

27

BERSHAD

City of Taggarstan

The barkeep that Bershad had hit in the face left the tavern with a bloody rag pressed against his nose. After that, everyone else cleared out. Nobody wanted to be around if the vampire was getting involved.

"I am assuming you and Vallen Vergun know each other?" Vera asked when the room was empty.

Bershad nodded. "It was his army I massacred at Glenlock Canyon."

"And what are you planning to do when you see him, exactly?" Vera asked.

Bershad glanced at Rowan, who had a concerned look stitched to his face.

"Kill him," Bershad said. His old life was dead and gone—nothing would change that—but that didn't mean Bershad was going to pass up a chance to remove that pale bastard's head from his body.

"In case you've forgotten, we need to make a deal with this vampire to get our seals," Vera said. "Hard to make deals with dead men."

Bershad didn't say anything. Just reached around the bar to get another jug of wine. Drank half of it in one gulp. He knew Vera was right, but in that moment—with so much ancient rage boiling back into his blood—he was having trouble summoning concern for kidnapped princesses or doomed dragons.

"The three of you need to leave," Bershad said.

"We should all leave while we still have a chance," Felgor said. "This is a bad, bad situation we're in."

"I agree," Rowan said. "It's a pretty big coincidence that the man we need to see is the same man Bershad has such history with." He put a hand on Bershad's shoulder. "I say we get out of here and find another way into Balaria."

"And I say we pay him with the emerald egg, take our seals, and finish the job we came here to do," Vera said. "No reason for any-one to draw steel."

"Yes, there is." Bershad turned to Rowan. "Get them out of here. Wait for me by our boat. If I'm not back with the seals by nightfall, Felgor can try his luck with another forger. Do not come looking for me."

"Silas . . ." Rowan started to say.

"No arguments. Get out of here, all of you."

Bershad rubbed Alfonso's muzzle once, then patted him on the butt so he'd follow Rowan out the door. Felgor followed, shaking his head. Vera stopped at the door.

"Ashlyn Malgrave didn't send you out here for vengeance."

Bershad drank from the horn of ale. Didn't look at her. "Go, Vera."

The tavern stayed empty for half an hour. Bershad drank and waited.

Eventually, two men came through the main door. One of them was twice the size of a normal person. He had pale skin, an ox-like neck, and hands the size of cooking pots. Taller than Bershad by half a head, and almost twice as thick in the chest. His eyelids were tat-tooed with a second pair of eyes, something Lysterian mercenaries did to show they were always ready for trouble. There was an enor-mous two-handed sword slung over his back—the grip extended past his head and the tip of the blade nearly reached the floor.

The second man was shorter than Vera—all sinewy muscle and bone. His skin was dark and covered with tattoos. His long black hair was braided and tied into a big knot on the top of his head. He had weasel-eyes that darted back and forth among everything in the room.

"Heard you smashed Barlow's face," the skinny one said.

"He the one that pours wine in this shithole?" Bershad asked.

"Yup."

"Then you heard right."

"I'm Liofa. That's Devan." He jerked his head toward the big man.

"Don't bother trying to get past us." Liofa twirled one finger in a circle. "Got the place covered."

"If I wanted to run, I'd have done it already," Bershad said. "Did Barlow tell you who I am?"

"He told me who you said you were." Liofa spat on the dusty floor. "Let me see your arm, dragonslayer."

Bershad took a few steps forward so he was closer to a torch. Then he pulled his sleeve up, revealing the dozens of dragons tattooed to his skin. No other dragonslayer in the world had even half as many marks, leaving little doubt about Bershad's identity.

Liofa whistled. "Right. The boss would like to invite you to the *Black Fox* for an early lunch."

Bershad grunted. Spat. "Let's go."

Devan led them across the floating bridge to the *Black Fox*. Liofa followed three paces behind them, whistling. Bershad glanced down the bridges that led to the main part of Taggarstan and saw they were all blocked off by armed men who were staring at him. When he reached the *Black Fox*'s hull, Devan pointed to a wooden spiral staircase that crawled up the side, leading to the raised platform above.

"You first, lizard killer," he said.

The platform was at least three hundred strides across. Half of it was covered by a pavilion made from human skin. The different sections of people-shaped leathers were lashed together with strands of red-and-white silk that fluttered in the afternoon breeze. Bershad had seen the pavilion before. The smell of perfumes floated through the air, but there was something else mixed in with the eucalyptus and rosemary.

Blood.

Devan moved past Bershad and nodded at the two guards who stood on either side of the tent flap, both of whom wore expensive breastplates and carried well-made swords. They opened the flap and the smell of death poured out.

"Takes some getting used to," Liofa said.

"Inside," Devan growled. Nobody bothered to confiscate his weapons, but they both followed him into the tent.

There were four impaled men inside—one in each corner. The wooden spear had gone through their asses and now sprouted from their mouths like a thick, red-stemmed plant. The floor was covered with more leathered skins cut from human flesh.

A man with bone-white skin was sitting at a large circular table in the middle of the room, eating a bloody piece of unrecognizable meat.

"Hello, Silas," Vallen Vergun said from his seat. "It's good to see you again."

Vallen's long hair stretched down to his waist in a silver streak. The pallor of his gaunt face would have made more sense on a dead man. But Vallen's eyes were the most unsettling thing about him—bloodred orbs set in deep sockets.

"Heard about that whole exile thing," Vergun continued. "Tragic."

"I'm sure you're overcome with sadness," Bershad said.

Vergun smiled and set down his knife and fork. Steepled both of his hands in front of his face. "I'd ask what you're doing in Taggarstan, but I've been expecting you for quite some time." He studied Bershad. "Although I was also expecting Yonmar Grealor. Where is he?"

"Yonmar got shot in the face with an arrow on the way here," Bershad said. "Bad luck."

"I see." Vergun didn't seem surprised. "Liofa, Devan. That will be all for now."

The two thugs left.

"So. Forgeries and cheap taverns in this mosquito-infested shithole, is it?" Bershad asked when they were alone. "Pretty long fall from commanding your own mercenary company."

"To the contrary, I have more killers working for me now than I ever commanded under Wormwrot Company. They're just a bit more spread out. And I'm far wealthier and more powerful than I was fourteen years ago. Take my arrangement with Grealor, for example. He agreed to deliver an item of peerless value to me in exchange for the forged seals of entrance to Balaria. Creating those seals is a very difficult and expensive process. Many people in Taggarstan claim to sell forgeries, but they're almost always detected at the gate and the unlucky travelers are turned into porcupines. Mine, on the other hand, are flawless. Just like you, Silas. And because they're so good, I turn a rather incredible profit on them."

Vergun sneered. Seeing him again made Bershad want to kill him even more, but he also needed a way into Balaria. He took out the emerald egg.

"I want those seals."

Vergun smiled. Licked his upper lip once.

"Ah, so that wasn't lost. Good. But I'm not sure you understand the situation that you're in. I don't have a seal for you."

"What do you mean?" Bershad asked.

"Seals come with physical descriptions," Vergun explained. "Balarians are a thorough people—they love bureaucracy far more than they love their machine god. That's the real reason the emperor has managed to keep his border sealed so tightly for so long. Anyway, I have one seal for the dead lord, Yonmar. One for a short woman with black hair. One for a native with very small teeth. Fake names all around, of course. There's no mention of a tall Almiran with blue bars on his cheeks. Or an old man and a donkey, for that matter."

Bershad chewed on that. It had never made sense that the Grealors were so eager to help lift his exile. Bershad was the rightful lord of the Dainwood—if he was alive and free, he was a threat. But if the Grealors got rid of Bershad while also helping the Malgraves, they won favor and solidified their position at the same time.

"The egg wasn't the only way that Yonmar was paying you," Bershad said. "He also agreed to deliver me."

"I'm impressed," Vergun said. "Subtle tactics were never your strong suit in the past. I'm curious, you must have found out I was the one selling the seals, but you came to me anyway. Why?"

"Same reason you wanted me here in the first place," Bershad said. "You and I have unfinished business."

"Yes."

A weak breeze moved the rusty, putrid smell of blood and bodies through the tent.

"I think you'll make a lovely addition to my tent decorations. I have a special place picked out to display those tattoos of yours." Vergun motioned to the impaled man in the corner. "You've proven yourself to be a difficult man to kill—I've been looking forward to seeing how long you'll survive with a pole through your asshole."

"And I suppose you're planning to call your henchmen back in here after our talk to hold me down while you do the pole ramming?"

Vergun smiled. "Something like that."

"Give it a try."

Vergun made a tsking sound. Shook one finger.

"No, no. Killing you here would be a waste. And far too quick, I think. We'll do this my way. On my terms."

Bershad drew his dagger. "We'll do it right now."

"Take one more step, and I will impale all of your friends while you watch," Vergun said, holding up a hand.

Bershad stopped. Frowned.

"You thought they got away? Silas, please. Not only did I know what they looked like already, but you morons wandered onto *my* ships. I own the eyes of every person you passed. Your friends barely got halfway across town before my men stopped them." He jerked his chin up. "They're just outside."

Bershad tightened his grip on the dagger. "You're bluffing."

"Was I bluffing when I said I'd hang those Almirans from the cottonwoods?" Vergun asked. "Sheathe that thing, or your friends die."

Bershad cursed himself. He'd walked right into Vergun's trap.

He shoved his dagger back into its sheath. Vergun smiled and stood up.

"After you," he said, beckoning back outside the tent.

Vera, Rowan, and Felgor were on the deck. Their wrists were bound. Mouths gagged. Rowan was bleeding from a gash in the side of the head and Vera's left eye was swelling from a blow to the face. There were twenty men with drawn weapons standing on the deck now, too.

"Excellent work," Vergun said, following Bershad out of the tent. "Any trouble?"

"They didn't come along easy, but they came," said one of the men. "We stowed the donkey down below, in the hold. Oh, and the widow killed Pollar and Roy."

"Nothing like an angry widow to help cull the herd a bit." Vergun shrugged. "Pollar and Roy were weak."

"Not that weak," the man muttered, mostly to himself. Then he eyed Vera. "But you said to keep 'em alive."

"Indeed I did. Do you know why?"

The man shrugged.

"I could kill the lot of you right now," Vergun said, pacing up and down the deck. "But that would be such a wasted opportunity with nobody here to watch. Tragic, really. Some might not even believe I truly killed the Flawless Bershad. I can't have that."

Vergun pressed his lips together.

"You see, I've had a good run these last few months. Everything that once belonged to Alto Yakun now belongs to me. But Yakun was a weakling. His heart was full of fat and pus. Killing him was too easy to earn the deference I require. On the other hand, if I kill the Flawless Bershad in a duel while half of Taggarstan watches, that's something Malakar and Sicone will remember. And respect. In Taggarstan, respect is the only currency that matters."

Bershad gritted his teeth. "Get to the fucking point."

"Very well. You and I go into a chalk circle. I always liked that Almiran custom. If you beat me, my men will give you the seals and let you go free. A deal is a deal, after all. But if you lose . . ."

Vergun trailed off. Motioned back inside his pavilion, and the impaled men.

Bershad looked at Rowan, Vera, and Felgor. Tried not to linger on their eyes.

"They have nothing to do with this. Give me your word you'll let them go, either way."

Vergun smiled. Red eyes beaming with sadistic joy.

"There are no agreements between men and demons. But despite appearances, contracts are honored in Taggarstan. My deal with Yonmar Grealor stands, even if he has fallen. So long as you do what I ask—and your friends don't try to cheat—they will not be harmed."

Bershad nodded. "When do we do this?"

"Midnight."

––––––––––

"There has to be another way," Vera said.

She was leaning against the railing on the deck while Bershad got ready. They'd taken her daggers and Rowan's sword, but removed their bonds. They were surrounded and outnumbered, no need for restraints. It was almost midnight. Vergun's men were the only people on his ship, but word of the duel had clearly spread across the city. A dozen boats were floating nearby, all of them sagging under the weight of spectators.

"There isn't," Bershad said.

He'd donned all his armor except for the jaguar mask, which hung on his hip. He was fooling with a ring of steel on his left glove that had gotten bent somehow. It would screw with his grip.

Rowan was sitting cross-legged on the deck with a grim look on his face, making a mud statue and decorating it with bark from a Dainwood tree. Bershad hadn't seen Rowan build a totem in fourteen years, right before Bershad went to kill his first dragon. He threw

Bershad a worried look, but didn't say anything. Rowan knew there was no point.

"I've heard he's the best sword on this side of the Soul Sea," Felgor said. "I mean, people tend to exaggerate, but still."

"I know how to use a sword, too." Bershad winced as he tried to bend the ring back into shape by pressing it against his palm. "And this is the only option."

"We can jump," Vera suggested, looking out over the railing. "They'll lose us in the dark. Everyone can swim, right?"

"So, we abandon Alfonso, who's somewhere belowdecks scared out of his mind, and then what?" Bershad asked. "We steal some fisherman's boat and sail for Balaria? Figure we can cross the border with a smile and a wave? Or maybe we just head farther east and forget this whole fucking thing?"

Nobody said anything. Bershad went back to the metal ring.

"It will be midsummer soon. Our time is running thin." He kept his eyes on the glove. "My job was to get all of you over the mountain and into Balaria. That's what I intend to do."

Bershad gave up and tore the ring off the glove. Tossed the metal into the water.

Vera put a hand on his arm. "They didn't take my slings. And I have one lead shot behind my breastplate. If he gets the upper hand, I can take him down," she said softly.

"No. That'll just get you killed, too. If I die, keep Rowan safe— he'll take care of the donkey." He hesitated. "And when you get to Burz-al-dun, give some serious thought to killing the emperor of Balaria for me, will you?"

"What are you talking about?"

Before Bershad could respond, Vallen Vergun came out of his tent wearing black from head to toe. His coat, gloves, and boots were reinforced with steel strips and studs, but otherwise he was unprotected. Vergun had always preferred to be light on his feet.

There wasn't time to explain more to Vera. Bershad gave her one final nod, then walked toward Vergun. He spat, unhooked the jaguar mask from his hip, and cinched it around his face. Felt the familiar pressure against his cheekbones and nose.

The moon was full, so there was plenty of light to see a large chalk circle etched into the middle of the boat's deck. Vallen Vergun drew his steel—a Balarian-made falchion with a single edge and a bat on the pommel. There was a red silk scarf wrapped around the cross guard that shimmered in the breeze. It was the same weapon Vergun had carried in Glenlock Canyon. Bershad drew his sword and stepped into the chalk circle.

"Tonight, the Flawless Bershad and I will engage in single combat," Vergun said, speaking loudly so the spectators on the closest ships could hear him. "If the exile wins, he and his friends get their seals and go free. If the exile falls, I'll turn him into the most famous tent decoration in the realm of Terra!"

That got a roar of excited cheers from the ships. They didn't seem to care who won, so long as they got to see some blood.

"Ready, Silas?" Vergun asked.

"Let's just get on with it."

Vergun smiled, then dashed forward on graceful feet. Three attacks came in rapid succession. High. Low. High. Bershad parried each one and went for a counterriposte, but Vergun skipped backward and dodged the blade.

Bershad always figured the best kind of duels were the short ones. When it came to long, drawn-out affairs, the man who practiced the most usually won. Bershad had barely touched a sword in fourteen years. Vergun had probably trained hard with one every day for decades.

So Bershad bulled forward, sword cocked back near his hip so it was ready for a quick jab. Vergun slipped to the left, which was exactly what Bershad wanted. Instead of stabbing at a moving target, Bershad rushed inside of Vergun's sword-reach. Vergun managed a weak attack that glanced off Bershad's shoulder, but caused no real harm.

Bershad grabbed Vergun's wrist with one hand, then bashed his face with the pommel of his sword. Yanked him forward by the wrist, kneed him in the stomach, and then shoved Vergun backward. That was almost the end of it. A fifteen-second fight. All he needed to do was stab Vergun through the heart.

But all Bershad stabbed was air. Vergun spun around and crunched the falchion into his rib cage. Bershad grunted. Felt his lamellar breastplate crack and the bones beneath break. He went down on one knee.

Vergun slammed the bat-shaped pommel into Bershad's forehead. His vision went white, then hazy and full of spots. He tried to push himself up and regain some balance, but Vergun swept his legs out from under him with a scything strike that tore a big chunk of meat out of Bershad's calf. Vergun kicked him twice, then pinned him to the ground with a boot pressed to his chest. Blade pointed at his throat.

"Well, that wasn't very satisfying," Vergun said. "Care to yield? If you beg, I'll finish it clean. No more pain."

Bershad drew his dragontooth dagger from the small of his back and tried to ram it through Vergun's knee. He wasn't done yet.

Vergun skipped back again, laughing a little while Bershad pushed himself up. Sword in his right hand, the dagger in his left, held in a reverse grip. His left leg was useless now. The crowds on the boats were snarling and cheering for more violence.

"You've lost," Vergun said, panning to the left. "Continuing will just make it worse."

"You talk too much, Vergun. Anyone ever told you that?"

"Not lately."

Vergun darted behind Bershad and stabbed him in the back, then shoved him onto his knees again.

"Let me ask you something, Silas. Seeing you again has made me ruminate on Glenlock Canyon a bit today." Vergun circled him. "Why'd you decide to charge me after I'd strung all those Almirans up at the mouth of the canyon? I was ready to negotiate terms."

Bershad didn't answer.

"Now that you're a legendary lizard killer, I doubt people ask you. Manners and all." Vergun's voice moved closer, then farther away. The bastard was pacing again. "Out here in Taggarstan, where Hertzog Malgrave's name doesn't carry weight, people justify it for you. Bad information. Threatening mercenaries. Like that. Some people even say I killed the hostages first, then you charged. It's funny how that works, isn't it? Heroes and villains morphing out of the same people based on rumors and reputations and the simple passage of time. But you and I both know the truth."

He kicked Bershad in the stomach, then the face. Bershad felt the pain and anger welling up in his chest like a storm.

"Answer me!" Vergun snarled, voice filling with fury.

"Because I'm an evil bastard!" Bershad hissed from the ground. He struggled to his feet, head pounding. Leg bleeding. "But at least I stayed until the job was done. You're the one who ran. Abandoned your soldiers in that canyon." Bershad winced as he stepped forward. "I might be a demon with a shit-coated heart, but you're a fucking coward."

After the last word left Bershad's lips, Vergun snarled, then bolted forward, feinted low, and came in for a high attack. Bershad got his dagger up, but wasn't strong enough to hold a parry. Both blades wound up hitting Bershad's mask, cracking it more and twisting the eyeholes around so that he couldn't see.

Vergun kept hitting him. He was using the blunt edge of his sword—not trying to kill Bershad, even though it would have been easy. He started breaking bones.

His right arm first, at the elbow and the wrist and shoulder. Bershad dropped his sword and grunted.

"Beg for mercy," Vergun said.

"Fuck yourself," Bershad snarled from behind his mask.

Vergun crushed his left kneecap, then his ankle.

"You will beg before the end!" Vergun said. Louder.

Bershad dropped the dagger. Ripped his mask off. The cold night felt good on his skin—like a breath of air feels to a drowning man. "Not happening."

"I will break every bone in your body," Vergun said.

Bershad glanced at Vera, who stood outside the circle. She was shaking her head slowly. One hand clamped down on the ship's railing. She looked like she was going to be sick. Bershad turned back to Vergun.

"I got plenty of 'em left." Bershad coughed up some blood.

Vergun growled. Attacked. Broke Bershad's left hand, then his collarbone. Bershad hit the deck with his forehead.

"Beg, you piece of shit!" Vergun shouted, spit glowing in the moonlight. "Beg!"

"No."

Bershad grabbed his sword and tried to use it as a brace to stand up, but fell over. As he was trying again, Vergun sheathed his falchion, walked over, and snatched the sword from underneath him, sending him back on the ground. He tested the blade's balance.

"Papyrian trash," he said, tossing it out of the chalk circle. Then Vergun stepped on Bershad's other hand and took the dragontooth dagger.

"This is a little more interesting." Vergun tossed it from one hand to the other a few times. "If you won't beg for your own life, per-haps you'll beg for another? I'm a man of my word, so I won't harm your friends. But . . ."

Vergun trailed off. Flipped the dagger a few more times, then turned to Liofa.

"Bring out that donkey."

Bershad's stomach filled with acid panic. Liofa disappeared. Vera tried to come into the circle, but Devan stopped her with a huge hand on her shoulder. Rowan just stood where he was, grinding his teeth together. A few moments later, Alfonso clopped out onto the deck, lured to the center of the circle by an apple in Liofa's hand. Vergun inspected the donkey as if he was going to buy it.

"The last mount you'll ever ride. That's how it goes, right?" he asked Bershad.

"Touch the donkey and—"

"And you'll do what?" Vergun cut in, moving toward Alfonso and flipping the dragontooth dagger into a reverse grip. "Grow new legs and hands, stand up, and kill me? Doubt that." Vergun looked down at Bershad. "Now. Beg for mercy, Silas."

If Bershad could get to the vial of moss in his hair, there was a chance. But when he slumped onto his left side and tried to reach behind his head, he could barely lift his right arm.

The crowds on the ships had gone silent. Bershad felt the bile and panic rising in his chest.

"I will not ask again."

Bershad tried to reach the vial one more time, but there was no point. Both his arms were ruined.

"Mercy," Bershad muttered.

"A little louder, please. I'm not sure everyone heard you."

"Please," Bershad said, raising his voice. "Kill me if you want. But don't hurt my donkey. Please."

Vergun grinned, red eyes wide with glee. "Thank you, Silas. I needed that, I really did." He licked his lips. Considered the dagger for a moment. "Remember what this feels like."

Vergun jammed the dagger into the top of Alfonso's spine, right where it met his skull. The donkey whimpered once and then crashed onto the floor of the dock. Vergun spat on Alfonso's corpse and then kicked the butt of the dagger deeper into the brown hide.

Bershad screamed. Tried to push himself up and felt the bones in his wrist snap—the pain blinding and hot. "No," Bershad screamed into the wood. "Not him. Not . . ."

Vergun drew his sword again. "And now, my dear Silas, I think I'll give you some of that mercy you asked for." He took a step toward Bershad. "I'll see you in whatever wretched afterlife waits for us."

Bershad knew he'd fucked up. He knew he'd betrayed his promise to Ashlyn by getting himself killed. But in that moment, with the wrath boiling up to his eyes, this felt like the death he deserved.

"Wait!" Rowan called in a gruff voice that carried through the night. Everyone turned to him. There were tears in his eyes. A look of pure anguish on his face. "Just wait a second."

"What is it, old man?" Vergun snapped.

"Put Silas's debt on me. I'll carry it."

"No," Bershad grunted. "I won't let you—"

Vergun kicked Bershad in the stomach, silencing him.

"Don't be ridiculous," Vergun said, keeping his eyes on Bershad.

"There's a way of doing things!" Rowan barked, loud enough for everyone to hear. He stepped forward. "Even for criminals. Even for monsters like you, there's a way of doing things. I will stand for Silas Bershad."

That got Vergun's attention. He looked at Rowan.

"You weren't in Glenlock Canyon, but I know who you are," Vergun said. "Rowan, isn't it? Leon Bershad's man during the Balarian Invasion."

"That was a long time ago."

"Even so. Silas obviously isn't much with a sword, but I've heard different about you. Might be you're thinking now that I'm a bit tired, you have a chance."

"Might be I do. But do you see a sword in my hand, asshole?" Rowan growled. "I said I'll carry the debt, not fight you." He looked at Bershad. "Take my life instead of his, that's the offer. Just swear you'll give them the seals and let them go when it's done."

Vergun squinted at Rowan, as if he suspected a trick. "You sure about this, old man?"

"Yes."

"Well." Vergun glanced at Bershad. "Silas is dead anyway. Even the Flawless Bershad can't come back from what I just did to him. This way he can die crippled, with the knowledge he got his friend killed, too. I like that idea. I like it very much. Almost makes up for

Wormwrot Company." Vergun raised his voice, speaking to everyone again. "This man is willing to stand for Silas Bershad's defeat in
the chalk circle tonight! All of you know that I'm not much for tradition, but I respect the old ways. I accept your offer, Rowan."

Vergun patted the blade of his sword.

"Say when, old man."

"Just give me a second with him," Rowan said, stepping to the
edge of the circle.

Vergun weighed that carefully, but eventually nodded. "Try anything stupid and everyone dies."

The deck was silent as Rowan crossed the chalk outline and knelt
next to Bershad.

"I'm sorry, Silas."

"Don't do this," Bershad said. "Leave me. Just get Vera and Felgor
out of here."

"That's what I'm doing. Saving them and saving you."

"I'm already dead."

"You're not. And you know it."

Bershad swallowed. His mouth filled with the metallic taste of
adrenaline and blood. "I won't keep going if you and Alfonso are
gone. There's no fucking point."

"Of course there's a point. You and me wandering around the wilderness for fourteen years killing dragons was the useless work. But
what you're doing now—what you're going to do when you get to
Burz-al-dun—that matters. I haven't been looking after you all these
years to see you piss away that chance. There's greatness in you, Silas.
You've been hiding it for years, but you can't fool me." Rowan
smiled grimly. "Now let's have that shell you've been saving."

Bershad didn't know what to do. Everything hurt. He opened his
mouth to try and protest but choked up. Couldn't get the words
out.

Rowan put a hand on Bershad's shoulder. "It's all right, Silas."

He reached behind Bershad's breastplate and took the blue-and-
yellow seashell that Bershad had carried next to his heart for fourteen years. He thumbed it with his worn and scarred hand. "Alfonso
is ahead of me, but I'll catch up with him downriver. That donkey
always was a slow swimmer." He paused. Swallowed once. "When
I get to the sea, I'll find your father. We'll wait for you there. But I
better not see you again for a long time."

Before Bershad could respond, Rowan stood up and walked across the circle.

"Get on with it," he grunted to Vergun, then put the seashell into his mouth.

"Boss," Liofa said, stepping forward with a sneer. "If the old man stands for the exile, there's no need to bloody your sword with his life."

"A fair point." Vergun shrugged. "Devan, take care of this for me."

Devan stepped forward and drew the massive sword from his back, smiling as he moved toward Rowan with a dirty grin. Rowan didn't flinch. Just stood there, waiting.

Vera tried to stop it, but Felgor held her back with a surprising amount of strength. Bershad tried to get up again, felt his knees and feet snapping from the effort. He screamed. Fell again.

Bershad closed his eyes just before Devan's sword connected. But he still heard the sound of steel hitting flesh. And everything after.

PART IV

28

VERA

Balaria, Lorong River

The Lorong River cut through the yellow sands of southern Balaria like a knife. Vallen Vergun's cargo cruiser moved at a swift pace. Their captain—a drunkard named Borgon who had a jug of rice wine in his left hand at all times—explained that he'd been running boats up and down the Lorong for twenty years, and knew all her secrets.

Bershad was holed up in a cabin belowdecks. Wrapped in rough-spun bandages and alternating between sleeping, mumbling for rice wine, puking, and sleeping again. They'd been in Balaria four days. Getting past the checkpoint had seemed easy compared to the Razorbacks and Taggarstan. After the mess on the *Black Fox,* Vergun had set them free, as they'd agreed, and given them the three forged seals, which were metallic discs with physical descriptions etched on one side, and a series of small holes on the other. To add insult to injury, Vergun had offered them passage into Balaria with Devan and Liofa, who were making a smuggling run. Vera had figured that Vergun just wanted witnesses when Bershad died—or people to kill him if he managed to survive—but she wasn't in a position to turn down a ride into Burz-al-dun. She needed to get to Kira as soon as possible.

When they reached the checkpoint, the border agents scrutinized the description of their faces and ran the discs through some kind of machine that she didn't get a good look at, but everything checked out. Then the agents spent four hours inspecting and digging through their cargo, going so far as to lead three hounds through the holds, sniffing for contraband. They didn't find anything.

Bershad used Yonmar's seal. The agents had been suspicious of a man wrapped in bandages and seeping blood and pus. But it was easy to see by the exposed bones and splayed tendons in his leg that the wounds were real. Vera told them he was a minor lord from Ghala-mar heading to Burz-al-dun for medical treatment of a contagious skin disease. That wasn't quite enough to dissuade the agents from unwrapping the bandages on Bershad's face, but Vera had spent two hours stitching bloody pigskin over his tattoos to hide them. The sight of his mangled face convinced them that her story was true.

Vera wondered if scaling the cliffs and traversing the desert would have been the easier path to Burz-al-dun after all. Bershad was crippled. Alfonso and Rowan were dead. Vera hadn't known the old Almiran for very long, but she'd liked him. He was loyal and fierce—protective of Bershad and Alfonso until the very end. She missed him already.

Vera watched the Lorong River for a few more moments, picking at the stump of her lost finger. The tip still itched somehow, even though the digit was up in the Razorback Mountains. Then she went belowdecks to check on Silas. His wounds were catastrophic—a normal man would never walk or hold so much as a cup again. But she knew how to heal him. Problem was, finding moss on a ship traveling through a desert had proved difficult. She was running out of time.

Vera waited until everyone's attention was elsewhere, then slipped into the cargo hold. The belly of the cargo cruiser was far larger than Vera had thought possible for a river craft. The ship had four big cargo chambers. It had taken Vera three days to search them, mostly because she had to do it when nobody was paying attention to her. All she'd found was wheat, mushrooms, and salted pork. Useless. Vera had been about to give up on finding anything that would heal Bershad when she noticed a finger-sized hole in the far corner of the chamber. When she stuck her finger inside and lifted, it revealed a trapdoor that led to a secret compartment filled with oak casks. Vera had wanted to explore it right away, but Liofa had come down into the hold and she'd been forced to sneak away.

But now she was alone, and this was her last chance. She took a breath, opened the trapdoor, and ducked inside.

She crawled to the closest cask and pried it open with one of her daggers. Then she smiled in the dim light of the secret hold.

The top of the cask was packed with a thick layer of wet moss. She scooped it away to reveal dozens of opium vials beneath. They must use the moss to hide the scent of the opium from the hounds. Perfect.

———

Bershad's quarters smelled like a septic pit. Full of infection and rot and shit. Vera had removed the pigskin from his face and arms on the first day, but he didn't look much better for it. When she entered, he opened one eye, which was rimmed with a yellowish crust.

"Wine . . ." he muttered. "Wine or just . . . fucking . . . kill me."

Those had been his only requests since he regained consciousness.

Vera closed the door, then set down the opium cask she'd stolen and pried it open.

"Fuck your wine. And fuck an easy death, too."

She started removing the spoiled bandages from the worst of his wounds. His crushed legs and arms. His broken ribs. The shattered collarbone that broke through his skin in three places. She cleaned each wound with boiled water, then started caking them with the moss.

"This is all I could find," she said.

Bershad tried to struggle when he realized what she was doing, but he was too weak to stop her.

"I don't want it, not again," he muttered. "Let me die."

"I need you alive," Vera said as she pressed a wet lump of moss into his ribs. A long ribbon of black, infected blood spurted out. "And life's full of disappointments, remember?"

Vera needed another killer when they got to Burz-al-dun if she was to have any hope of getting to the princess. Vergun had given them the seals and told his men not to harm her or Felgor, but Vera didn't expect them to listen. She had a fight coming.

She wasn't sure the moss would be enough to fix this—it was far worse than the arrow wound in his thigh. So, she made up for it with quantity, packing each wound with a thick layer of moss and wrapping it in a fresh silk bandage.

"Wine, at least," Bershad muttered when Vera was finished. "Please."

She hesitated, but eventually placed another clay bottle of rice wine next to his cot and left. Bershad took it with shaking hands and drank deep.

————————

Back on the deck, Liofa and Devan sat together near the stern, roasting a small quail over a fire pit and watching her. As always, Devan kept his massive two-handed sword within arm's reach.

"Had a change of heart, Papyrian?" Liofa called.

They'd spent the majority of the four-day journey asking to fuck her. Liofa had insisted that there was no pleasure like having two men inside of her at the same time. It had been a large struggle not to kill him. But now wasn't the time.

"Where's Felgor?" Vera asked.

Liofa squinted at her. Smiled. There was a piece of meat that had been stuck in his crooked teeth for two days. The silence dragged on—the two idiots probably thought it was filled with sexual tension—and then Devan gave in. Jerked his head toward the bow of the ship.

Felgor was perched on the back rail, whittling a piece of wood. The shape wasn't anything Vera recognized. Like a deformed ox-horn.

"Still working at that?"

"Will be for some time," Felgor said without looking up. He'd been sullen and angry since Taggarstan.

"But you won't tell me what it is?"

"I did tell you. It's a key to the palace."

Vera leaned out over the gunwale and watched the river. She could see the shadows of two large pike tracking them down the river.

"He gonna die?" Felgor asked, interrupting Vera's thoughts.

"I'm not sure."

"What happens if he does?"

Vera paused. "Getting to Kira is still the priority."

Felgor finished shaping a curve in the wood, then lowered the carving. He stared at the water.

"That bald bastard killed Rowan." He turned to Vera, and she could see tears in his eyes. "You aren't going to do anything about that?"

Vera bit her lip, remembering the image of Devan standing over Rowan's body and smiling.

"We need them to get into Burz-al-dun."

"So we do it then?"

"There's no 'we' involved."

"I can help you," Felgor pressed. "I can fight."

"I've seen you in a fight, remember? You'll just get in my way."

He didn't say anything.

"I'm serious, Felgor. Stay out of this. I need you alive to get into the palace."

Felgor dropped his head. Started whittling again. "I miss the old man and that donkey. Rowan said he'd teach me how to use that rabbit bow of his. I was . . ." He swallowed. "I was looking forward to that."

"I miss them, too," Vera said. They sat in silence for a while. She looked at the sun—it was late afternoon. "I need to talk to the captain. Find out where we are."

The captain's cabin was built near the bow of the ship, where it was easy to see the river ahead through a dirty window. Captain Borgon only left his cabin to get more rice wine. His cabin reeked of alcohol and piss. There wasn't a door, but Vera knocked on the wall beside the opening before coming inside. Borgon was leaning back in a chair, sleeping. He cracked a jaundiced eye at the sound of fist on wood.

"Told you not to come in here," he growled.

"How long until Burz-al-dun?"

"By Aeternita, you are a pest." Borgon woke up a little more. Rubbed a hand through his mangled, dirty beard. He was one of those men who looked like he'd seen seventy summers, even though the reality was probably closer to forty. His skin was sallow and blotchy, fingernails yellow and cracked. He burped constantly.

"Do not make me ask you again." Vera crossed her arms.

He licked his lips and scratched his beard some more. Borgon was an asshole. But he was smart enough to use caution around a Papyrian widow.

"A fortnight, I'd say."

"That long?"

Borgon sighed. "You dig an answer out of me, then fuss about the quality. If you don't like what I have to say, feel free to chart your own course." He motioned to the wrinkled and stained charts on a table in the corner of the cabin. "I am happy to abide. Always wanted to ground a ship in the middle of the desert. Dying of thirst sounds fun."

Borgon leaned back in his chair again and closed his eyes.

Vera glared at him, but the captain started snoring lightly in an almost unbelievably short period of time. She left the cabin and jumped down to the prow, where there was a small subdeck meant for one person to sit and fish when the boat wasn't moving. It was a good spot—anyone approaching from behind pressed on some loose boards and created a squeak that warned of their approach. Vera stayed there until the sun was just an orange sliver over her right shoulder.

As dusk settled in, she noticed a large group of dragons winging their way east. It was too dark to make out the type, but she figured it was a fully grown female leading her juveniles to the warrens in the east. Vera had never had the time to take much interest in the dragons of Terra, but everyone knew about the Great Migration that occurred every five years. Soon this entire sky would be filled with dragons.

Once it got dark, Vera went belowdecks and checked on Bershad. When she opened the door, the putrid smell of rot was gone. Replaced by the rich, loamy scent of earth and forest. The air was sticky and hot. Bershad was awake—his eyes clear and glowing bright green in the dim candlelight of the cabin.

Vera untied the bandage around his collarbone. Moved the moss out of the way. The wound was still open, but the snapped bone had started knitting itself back together. All evidence of infection had disappeared.

"Black skies," she whispered.

Bershad looked at her with burning eyes that Vera didn't recognize.

"You should have let me die," he said.

29

BERSHAD

Balaria, Lorong River

The moss did its work, but the labor of healing was not gentle or fast. Bershad ground his teeth and gulped rice wine while his body knit bone and flesh back together one fiber at a time.

For days, every moment was a blurry mess of pain and nightmares. His only relief was the few precious seconds each time he woke up when he didn't remember what had happened. His first instinct was to look around for Alfonso and pat his muzzle. Find out what Rowan was cooking for breakfast. Then the memories of their dead bodies on that deck came flooding back to him, and he sank into a thick and miserable darkness.

Bershad whispered curses to the nameless gods. He longed for the death that refused to arrive.

Days later—he couldn't be sure how long—Bershad awoke gasping from a fever dream where the women and children Vergun had hung from the trees outside Glenlock Canyon had cut themselves down and stalked him through the forest. Their glowing red eyes cut through the darkness. They muttered to him, mouths filled with bloated black tongues.

Vera was in his cabin—sitting in a chair on the far side of the room. She had taken her boots off and looked like she'd been watching him for a long time.

"Does it hurt?" she asked.

"What do you think?" Bershad growled. He spat off the side of the bed and rummaged around for a bottle of rice wine that wasn't empty. Didn't find one.

"You need to stop drinking."

"Growing bones all day would make you thirsty, too."

"It goes slower when you're drunk," she said. "I have been watching. We'll reach Burz-al-dun in less than a week and you need to be ready."

He fell back into his sweat-stained mattress and looked at her through half-closed eyes. "You should leave me down here. Slip away with Felgor and find your princess. Let me die in this shithole." He rubbed his throat.

"If you rot away on this ship, you'll leave our work unfinished."

"Good. Everything I've done in my life has ended with the blood of innocents. Glenlock Canyon. All those dragons. And now I got my donkey and my only friend killed. The longer I live, the more people I'll hurt."

"I feel responsible, too," she said. "We should have listened to Felgor and found another way into Balaria. And on the deck, I should have . . ." She trailed off. "We all had chances to prevent it, but there's nothing to do except move forward."

"I can't. Not after all this."

Vera looked at him for a long time. "You've been muttering about Glenlock Canyon for days. What really happened there?"

Bershad frowned. "Thought you didn't care about my past."

"Unless it was going to fuck with my future. And it's starting to."

Bershad didn't say anything.

"Why did you order that charge, Silas?"

Bershad had been lying about Glenlock Canyon for fourteen years. But down in the hold of that ship—with a head full of nightmares— the truth seeped out of him on its own.

"Hertzog Malgrave didn't send me to negotiate new terms with Wormwrot Company. He sent me to kill them all. Being honest, I didn't have a problem with the order. Vallen and his men were bastards, and they'd been leeching off the people of the Dainwood for years. But I screwed it up. My attack was sloppy, and Vergun slipped away with most of his men. I pushed his retreat back toward Glenlock because there's no way out of the nearby box canyon, but he rode through the town and took hostages before I cornered him. Strung them up in a line at the mouth of the canyon. All those women. Children, too. They were so scared."

Bershad paused. Talking about it made his chest and throat tight.

"Glenlock isn't far from Floodhaven. I sent a letter to the king telling him Vergun had taken hostages, but all I needed was time and some gold for ransoms, and I could save them. I thought I could fix it. But Hertzog sent me a letter back telling me that my father had been arrested for treason." Bershad swallowed. "He also said that if I completely destroyed Wormwrot Company that day, he would pardon my father. Send him to a country across the Soul Sea and let me rule the Dainwood in his stead." Bershad pressed two fingers against the wound on his wrist. Gritted his teeth at the pain, and at the memory. "So I did it. I traded hundreds of innocent lives to save my father. But Hertzog killed him anyway."

"The king betrayed you."

"I betrayed myself. My father wouldn't have wanted it, but I was afraid of losing him." He paused. "I can still see their bodies swaying in those trees when I close my eyes. I deserve what happened to me."

Vera didn't speak for a long time.

"Protecting Kira was not my first assignment as a widow," she said eventually. "A day before I returned from my training on Roriku, a group of pirates kidnapped one of the empress's cousins. She was just a little girl who'd been playing by the ocean, collecting shells.

They snatched her. My ship was heading to the capital, but I was diverted and tasked with getting the girl back. I was eighteen years old, just like you were. Strong. Confident. Reckless. I snuck onto the ship at night and found the girl. Thought I could fight my way out with her, too, but . . ."

She looked down at her hands.

"You can have black deeds and mistakes in your past without being rotten down to the core. You can keep moving through this world, even if there is no redemption for the things you left behind you. That child's life taught me that lesson. Rowan understood it, too. He saw something bigger in you, swimming beneath all the guilt you carry. And he sacrificed himself so that you could keep on going. It is time for you to stop hiding your true nature and start using it for something worthwhile. Otherwise Rowan died for nothing." Vera leaned forward. "Do not forget the promise you made to Ashlyn Malgrave. And to me."

"I haven't forgotten," Bershad said.

"Good." She pulled her boots on and stood. "There's something else, too. Devan and Liofa are on this ship with us. So stop drinking. Once you're healed, we will kill them."

Vera left. Bershad stared at the ceiling. He felt something different inside his body as he healed. There was a restless energy tangled up with his pulse, like an animal scratching against a cage. Bershad could feel the movement of the boat and then a thousand movements beyond that—the electric crackle of fish heartbeats swarming outside the hull. The vague, magnetic pull of dragons in the distance. The only other time he'd felt something similar was right before he'd passed out in the dragon warren at the top of the Razorback Mountains.

Vera didn't fully understand what she was asking him to do. If he dropped all the chains and removed all the masks, Bershad didn't know what he'd find underneath. It might be just as destructive as the emperor's cull of the dragons. It might be worse.

But she was also right. He'd made promises. And one way or another, Bershad wanted to watch the life drain out of Devan's eyes before the end. He threw the last, half-full jug of rice wine across the room, where it shattered. Then he scooped another handful of moss from the cask Vera had found and pressed it into the worst of his injuries. Lay back and let the pain of healing consume him. Tried to clear his head. He remembered the glass vial of warren moss Rowan had given him. Checked his hair to make sure it hadn't broken. He could eat it now and heal the wounds in a few seconds, but he resisted the temptation.

If Bershad used the vial now, he wouldn't have it when he found the emperor in Burz-al-dun.

30

ASHLYN

Almira, Castle Malgrave

"What do you mean there's been no word?" Ashlyn asked Godfrey. The pigeon shit on his shoulders was particularly thick that day.

"I'm sorry, my queen. I have sent two versions of the messages you requested every day. Two to Mudwall and two to Deepdale, all of them ordering every Malgrave warden back to Floodhaven immediately. There have been no responses."

One or two birds could get lost, especially on the long flight down to Deepdale. But it had been seven days since Cedar Wallace had disappeared. Twenty-eight messages had flown from Floodhaven since then—she'd nearly emptied her dovecote with the task. The only way that many birds could fail to arrive was if someone was systematically shooting them down. But that meant Wallace had surrounded Floodhaven with hidden archers before trying to assassinate her and given them orders to shoot any pigeons that flew out of the dovecote. Cedar Wallace was unmatched when it came to battle tactics, but this level of forethought surprised her.

"Maybe the sentinels will turn something up," Ashlyn muttered. After it became clear the pigeons weren't working, Ashlyn had dispatched two score of sentinels to deliver messages on foot. She expected them to return before nightfall.

"If you don't mind me asking, how are things in the city?" Godfrey asked, lowering his head.

Ashlyn looked at him. "Order is being maintained."

After the attack at her coronation, Ashlyn sent ships along the coast and wardens into the woods to search for Cedar Wallace, but he'd disappeared. She'd also instituted a curfew in the city. Carlyle Llayawin and his remaining wardens had volunteered to guard the walls on their own—the last time she'd taken his report, the man looked like he hadn't slept for days. Linkon Pommol's wardens had continued to help patrol the streets, but Korbon and Brock had cordoned themselves off in their respective compounds inside the city and surrounded themselves with their sworn wardens. They might not have tried to slash her throat open like Cedar Wallace, but it was clear they wouldn't be rushing to support her anymore, either.

"What about from the far side of the Soul Sea?" Ashlyn asked. Bershad could have reached Burz-al-dun by now. "Any news?"

"Signs of the Great Dragon Migration are picking up all across Terra—many of the adolescents have already journeyed east. The mothers and their juveniles will fill the skies within a few weeks."

Ashlyn nodded.

"No other news?" Ashlyn asked.

The steward hesitated. Coughed. "Nothing new, my queen. Our informants in Ghalamar continue to report crop shortages and refugees. Riots in the major cities. But that has been going on for quite some time. Northern Lysteria is still rumbling with rebellion, and the viceroys are scrambling to quash it. Balaria is quiet as always."

Ashlyn nodded. Balaria was like a locked safe when it came to information, but the death of an emperor would have slipped out. She had to assume Bershad had either failed or been delayed to the point that his mission wouldn't matter.

There was a quick commotion outside the dovecote. Hayden stepped between Ashlyn and the door. Hand on her sword. But it was Shoshone who came through.

"My queen, there's an update from the ramparts. Riders approaching."

"The sentinels?" Ashlyn asked.

"Unknown, but I figured you'd want to meet them as soon as possible."

"Yes, thank you." Ashlyn turned back to Godfrey. "Keep sending messages. We *must* get word to our wardens in Deepdale and Mudwall."

———

It was nearly dark by the time they reached the outer wall of the city. Ashlyn hopped onto a platform so she could get a better view. Carlyle Llayawin was already there, looking both exhausted and determined.

"High-Warden Llayawin," Ashlyn said. "Have the sentinels come inside the walls yet?"

"No, my queen. They stopped in those trees for some reason."

Carlyle pointed. Ashlyn followed his finger, waiting for her eyes to adjust to the gloom. The chorus of summer insects had begun—locusts and crickets screaming into the fading light. The small, glowing flashes of fireflies pulsed amongst the trees. After a few moments, Ashlyn started noticing larger movements in the trees.

"They're definitely soldiers," Ashlyn said. "But I can't make out their colors. Why would our sentinels wait in the trees?"

"No idea, my queen," Carlyle said. "It's not protocol. I was about to ride down there with a score of my wardens. Find out what's keeping them."

"No, don't do that," Ashlyn said.

Something wasn't right. She scanned the tree line more carefully, but it was too dark to see much besides the silhouettes of moving bodies between trunks. From the corner of her eye, Ashlyn caught the flicker of two pigeons being set loose from the dovecote. Godfrey following her instructions.

She watched the pigeon that headed west. It stayed high above the tree line like she'd trained it to, but just before it was about to pass from sight, an arrow shot up from the top of the tallest tree and speared the bird through the heart. Ashlyn's eyes widened.

"Close the gates," she ordered.

"My queen?" Carlyle asked. "But our sentinels won't—"

"Those aren't our sentinels. Close everything as quickly as possible. Get all of your wardens up on these walls and prepare for an attack. Now!"

"Right away!" Carlyle barked off quick orders to the men on the rampart, then he ran down the stairs to inform the rest of his men. Soon after, the sound of Floodhaven's gates creaking closed echoed from below.

"My queen?" Hayden asked, stepping closer.

"It's Wallace," Ashlyn explained. "He's trying to bait me. If I'd sent more wardens outside to check on the sentinels, he would have surrounded and slaughtered them. Probably tried to rush the gates afterward and avoid a siege."

"But I don't see any of Wallace's men," Hayden said, turning back to the wall.

"Trust me, they're out there."

As if the men in the trees could hear her, hundreds of campfires were ignited against the tree line, illuminating the trunks with an orange glow. The rough shadows of the wardens were easy to see now, along with the red-and-white colors of Cedar Wallace on their chests. If there was any question as to who was out there, a massive banner with Wallace's colors had been erected above the main road leading to the city.

No sense hiding now that Ashlyn had closed the gates.

The fires provided enough light to better make out the movement between the trees. Dozens of objects were swaying like long grass on a breezy day.

"What is that?" Hayden asked, noticing them as well.

It took Ashlyn a moment to realize the answer. When she did, her mouth went dry and her pulse quickened.

"Malgrave wardens," Ashlyn said. "They've hung them from the trees."

"Looks like almost a hundred men," Shoshone said. "So it's not just the sentinels you dispatched."

Ashlyn kept watching the swaying men. In the firelight, she could make out the green plumes of high-wardens.

"Those are the officers that my father sent to Mudwall," Ashlyn said. "And the ones that I sent to Deepdale. Cedar Wallace killed them all."

If the officers were dead, that meant Wallace had destroyed both armies.

"And judging from the number of fires, there are at least ten thousand of Wallace's wardens out there," Ashlyn said, doing a quick calculation in her head. "Possibly more."

So, Wallace's vassals had brought their wardens after all. They just hadn't taken them inside the city.

"Should we call an alarm to our other wardens?" Carlyle asked.

"Not yet." That would just cause a panic. "Now that we've closed the gates, Wallace won't attack," Ashlyn said. "He doesn't have the numbers to storm our walls. But he knows I don't have the wardens to risk fighting him in an open field. He'll have brought catapults with him. He plans to dig in for a siege."

"We have ships," Shoshone said. "We can resupply by sea."

"That will take too long," Ashlyn said. "Floodhaven is at four times the normal capacity because of my coronation. We'll be out of food in a few weeks, which is probably half as long as it will take the lords and wardens behind our walls to rebel."

Never mind the fact that she planned to send the navy to war in half a moon's turn. Godfrey was right—the Great Dragon Migration was gaining momentum with each passing day. According to her latest tally of sightings, and calculations based on previous years, this migration would reach full force anywhere from nineteen to twenty-seven days from now.

"Rider!" a warden shouted from farther down the wall.

"How many?"

"One! It's just one. Heading for the main gate."

Ashlyn scanned the tree line until she saw the figure, riding slumped and messy atop a horse that zigged and zagged in different directions.

"Do we fire?" an archer called.

"No," Ashlyn said, keeping her eyes on the rider. "He's already dead. Use the northwest postern gate to get him inside." That gate could be opened and closed quickly. "Bring his body to me."

————

It was Uylnar Went—high steward of Mudwall. The man whose letters Ashlyn had been waiting to receive. Cedar Wallace had slit Uylnar's throat, then lashed his boots to a horse and sent him galloping into Floodhaven with a letter nailed to his chest. Hayden grunted as she removed the nail, which had been hammered straight through his body. Passed the paper to Ashlyn. She tried to ignore the blood as she read.

Ashlyn Malgrave,

You are queen of Almira no longer. I have killed the wardens you sent to Mudwall. I have killed the wardens you sent to Deepdale. The Gorgon Valley is mine. The Dainwood is mine. Everything else will follow.

My catapults will begin to fire at dawn tomorrow. Surrender Floodhaven to me, and you may live in exile. Make me root you out of that precious Queen's Tower, and I will let each one of my wardens have a turn before I cut off your head.

Cedar Wallace, *King of Almira*

Ashlyn stared at the paper, squeezing her left fist so hard that the dragon thread crackled against her skin and started to smoke.

"What are your orders, my queen?" Hayden asked.

"Tell the men to prepare for catapult fire at dawn."

31

VERA

Balaria, Burz-al-dun

The skyline of Burz-al-dun rose in the distance. Since midafternoon the day before, the sandy desert had been giving way to small bushes and brown reeds along the shore. Overnight the stunted growth had transformed into olive groves and lemon orchards. Vera spotted a few small herds of queer, hooved creatures. They had brown hides and two long horns that spiraled up from their heads in black-and-white rings. They were grazing in the shade of the lemon trees.

"Quite the sight," Borgon said from behind Vera. "When I was a boy, you started seeing the orchards and gazelles two days before you caught sight of the Clock." He scratched his head.

"What changed?" Vera asked.

Borgon shrugged. "Balarian government killed all the dragons in the area we just passed. Everything went crazy after that. Monkeys turned vicious—killed and ate everything except the cactus. Then we got hit with a drought that wouldn't quit. Turned everything to sand and it never turned back. Been a long run of bad luck, that's for sure. Only reason these orchards aren't dried up and dead, too, is because of the irrigation pipes running from the heart of Burz-al-dun to here."

"Too bad," Vera said. She didn't have sympathy for the Balarians. In her experience, long strings of bad luck were preceded by men making a long series of bad decisions.

The sea was close. Vera could smell the salt in the air. She had been watching the city from the bow of the ship since dawn, marking the growth of the towers with her thumb as they drew closer. Vera had seen many cities in her life, but this one was by far the largest and tallest. Himeja, the capital of Papyria, was just a cluster of stone and cedar huts in comparison.

Burz-al-dun dominated both banks of the Lorong River, but the two sides looked very different. The western buildings were made from gray stone and wood—taller than she thought possible, but otherwise not so different from the buildings of Floodhaven. The other side, however, was like nothing Vera had ever seen. The buildings were made from red and white and cream marble blocks that glinted in the sun, all of them neatly ordered and sturdy. Steam rose from countless tin chimneys. The massive towers were festooned with copper pipes and geared scaffolding that lifted platforms up and down the high levels.

"What are those for?" Vera asked, pointing at the scaffold.

"Now you see why they call Burz-al-dun the Clock," Borgon said. "They're for the rich bastards living in those towers—food and drink and whatever else them fat cats want goes up, and they never even leave their sofas. Fresh water comes in and out of those copper pipes, too. Quite the setup."

Vera had heard rumors that Burz-al-dun was home to marvelous luxuries, but she'd imagined plush rooms and swarms of servants. Not a city dominated by metal and machines.

A massive domed building came into view. It was so much larger than the other buildings that it had to be the Imperial Palace. There was an enormous gear sprouting from the middle of the dome— halfway exposed and as wide as an avenue. It moved in a slow, deliberate circle.

"What is that?" Vera asked, pointing. She had never seen anything like it.

"Ah, that's the Kor Cog. She powers the whole city. Lights, heat, water, and checkpoints are all fueled by the big bitch." Borgon picked at a scab on his ear. "Got to think it'd cause a racket at night."

Vera wanted to ask more questions about the Kor Cog, but was stopped as they came upon the longest bridge she had ever seen. It stretched across the river, connecting the halves of the city.

There were two levels. The bottom was dark and dirty, dominated by foot traffic. The open-air top was filled with carriages and litters. The rich and privileged above, and the peasants down in the shadows. That, at least, was familiar.

Far more noticeable, however, was the statue in the middle of the bridge. Aeternita.

She was at least one hundred strides tall, and made entirely of steel. Her arms were outstretched, body naked, but halfway covered by her streaming hair. As they got closer, Vera could see that the locks of hair were made from a river of small clocks, gears, and carved steel bits.

Borgon squeezed the copper clock hanging around his neck as they passed beneath the bridge, but said nothing.

On the far side of the bridge, they began to pass quays and boat slips. A flock of seagulls clucked nearby, and the faint sounds of sailors and dockhands drifted across the water. The quays were crowded but orderly.

Vera sniffed and frowned. Something was out of place.

Every other port city in the realm of Terra reeked so badly you'd have thought the buildings were mortared together with shit. But this place was laced with the piney smell of burning dragon oil, wafting over the water along with the dockhands' voices and the salty sea air. Masking the stink of thousands of crapping peasants was no small thing. Replacing it with the most valuable substance in the world was quite another.

The river widened beyond the bridge as they approached the harbor. Massive trading galleys destined for the Soul Sea mingled with riverboats and barges.

"Where do we go from here?" Vera asked Borgon. "One of those slips?" Vera pointed to the western shore where long docks poked out into the water.

"No. Ours is on the shiny side of town. It'll be gated and covered, like one of them over there." Borgon pointed to a tall rectangular dock with a metal roof that looked more like a miniature warehouse. "Vallen always makes sure we have our privacy. Nobody without the proper seals can even come near."

"The seals control movement inside the city, too?" Vera asked.

"The seals control everything in Balaria. Where a man can live. What kind o' work he does. Whether or not he can even leave the city." Borgon ran a hand through his messy beard. "A sewage worker living in the slum of the Clock won't ever stray more than a few blocks from the spot he was born 'cause o' the seal checkpoints." Borgon motioned to the western bank, where a tall metal gate rose up from between two sagging stone buildings.

"Seems like a lot of freedom to give up."

Borgon shrugged. "Depends on how you look at it. That sewer worker might be stuck in a slum, but the slums of Burz-al-dun smell like pine and dragon oil instead of pig shit and trash, like every other city in Terra. Ain't been no plague in decades. Might be there's famine and crazy monkeys outside the city, but nobody in the Clock goes hungry. Plenty are willin' to call that a fair trade." Borgon spat into the water. "Still, making port in the ole Clock always puckers my ass a little. It ain't natural."

He ambled away, back to the pilot's cabin.

Vera had always assumed the stories about Burz-al-dun were exaggerations passed down from the mouths of merchants until they became outright lies. But she'd been wrong. The stories didn't even begin to capture the magnitude of innovation in the Balarian city.

Vera made her way to the rear of the boat. Liofa saw her coming and cut her off.

"Going to see the gimp?" he asked, smiling. He had redone the strange braids in his hair.

Vera waited for him to move. He didn't.

"Vergun's done things like this before," Liofa continued. "Crippled a man and then left him alive to torture more. Once he cut off all a man's fingers, pickled them, and sent the poor bastard to catch a marlin. Can you imagine that, fishing with just your thumbs?"

Vera didn't say anything.

"Anyway, when the man came back empty-handed—or so to speak—Vergun fed the guy his fucking fingers. Then had him describe all the flavors. Even to me, that one seemed a little strong."

"Why are you telling me this?" Vera asked.

"It's a funny story." Liofa's mouth smiled, but his eyes didn't. "But the thing is, that man with no fingers had a brother who came after me and the vampire for that little trick. Tried to kill us with a pitchfork. Couldn't blame the man for his reaction. Family is family. But you and the Balarian seem to be handling that old man's death awfully well. Makes me wonder."

"I barely know Bershad, and the man you killed was a stranger," Vera lied, letting her hand drift a few finger-lengths closer to the grip of *Kaisha*. "I'm just trying to get into the city."

"I see. Guess you're smarter than you look." Liofa leaned in closer. "Because we have seven men waiting for us when we dock. Hard men. And I cut that brother's intestines out and strangled him with them. I'll do the same thing to you if you try anything stupid."

Before Vera could respond, he slapped her on the shoulder and strode off in the opposite direction.

Vera went down the hatch into the lower cabins. When she was five strides away from Bershad's door, her nose picked up the fertile smell that had become familiar to her. It was a good thing that the others never came down to this part of the ship. A miniature rain forest belowdecks would have caught their attention.

Bershad was sitting on the floor, leaning against the far wall. He was naked except for a deerskin breechcloth and picking at the brownish-green bandage on his right hand. A lot of his wounds didn't even need bandages anymore—the only evidence of his ruined wrists and ankles were rings of pink flesh and fresh scars. Even though Vera had watched his healing progress day by day, it was still incredible to see.

Bershad looked up at her. His eyes were different. They seemed to smolder inside of his skull.

"Are we in the city?" he asked.

Vera nodded. "Heading to some kind of covered dock."

"Devan and Liofa are up there?"

"Yes."

Bershad flexed and relaxed his hand. Started to unwrap the bandage, saw what was beneath, and left it alone.

"What are you thinking?" Vera asked.

"That neither of them have much longer to live."

"Liofa said there would be seven men meeting them at the dock."

Bershad stopped flexing his hand for a moment, then started again. "We beat worse odds with the Skojit."

"No, that was six men. This'll be nine, including Devan and Liofa. Those Skojit were out in the open and we had the element of surprise. And in case you forgot, you hadn't just spent two weeks on a moldy bed regrowing dozens of broken bones."

"I'm fine."

"You're better than you were," Vera said. Then she went over and pressed two fingers against Bershad's collarbone. He hissed in pain. "But that doesn't mean you're ready for a fight like this."

"I'm not letting those two bastards get away."

"Neither am I. But if we're that outnumbered and you're not fully recovered, we need to be smart about this."

"You have a suggestion?"

Vera looked around the room, a plan forming in her head. Devan and Liofa still thought Bershad was crippled and dying in the hold. They could use that.

"We'll put your old, dirty bandages back on," Vera said, squatting in front of Bershad so she could draw a rectangular diagram on the dusty cabin floor. "Judging from the other docks I saw on the way in, it'll be a large room about this shape. Tall. Two or three stories to fit cargo crates. If you get down close while they're unloading, I can get to a vantage point higher up on the ship, either bow or stern, depending on where the door outside is. You draw them all to one area that's as far from that exit as possible. I'll start taking them down. You deal with any stragglers."

Bershad stared at the diagram for a moment, then stood up. Wincing again from the effort. "Get the bandages."

32

BERSHAD

Balaria, Burz-al-dun

Vera's plan wasn't perfect, but it was the best chance they had. She'd already made sure that Felgor was out of sight and would stay that way. The rest was up to them.

As their boat was docking, Bershad rewrapped the half-healed parts of his body with old bandages that reeked of earth and blood until he looked more like a freshly exhumed corpse than a man. Now that he was moving around, he realized how injured he still was—every time he shifted his weight he could feel the places Vergun had broken his bones. The delicate flesh around the worst of his wounds threatened to split open at any time. He wouldn't be able to last long in a prolonged fight.

The boat stopped moving. A few men shouted to each other as they tied it to the dock. Bershad and Vera waited until they heard a large gate closing, then they slipped out of the hold and looked around. The boat was docked in a dim, enclosed building. The harbor was completely obscured by a thick metal gate that dropped into the water, preventing any natural light from getting through. On the other side, there was a wooden gangplank leading from the boat to a stone quay about the size of a small courtyard. Devan, Liofa, and seven armed strangers were standing on the quay. One of the strangers was a fat man wearing a leather vest covered with silver rings. He was inspecting one of the opium casks. Liofa was doing the same with a squat ceramic barrel. He opened it and dipped the tip of his knife inside. Scrutinized the blade.

"What do you expect to accomplish from that?" the fat man asked, looking up from his work.

"Checking to see if it's refined. Oil's got a greenish tint after them engineers work on it."

"We ever brought you dragon oil that wasn't?"

"No. But nobody's cheated you till the first time they cheat you." Liofa glared at the fat man for a moment, then wiped his blade off on his shirt and resealed the barrel. "This is ready to go."

"Not so fast," the fat man said. "You're missing some poppy, friend."

Liofa frowned. "The fuck I am."

"Count 'em, then."

Everyone was distracted by the missing opium cask, which was the best shot they'd get.

"Ready?" Vera whispered.

Bershad nodded, then started hobbling toward the gangplank, using his sheathed sword as a cane and clutching a half-empty bottle of rice wine against his chest. Vera moved to a vantage point above the pilot's cabin of the boat.

"Who the fuck is that?" asked the fat man. "Is the vampire selling lepers now, Liofa?"

Everyone looked at Bershad. He groaned, spilling some rice wine and drooling as he walked.

Liofa cursed. "This is all we need," he muttered. Then louder, to Devan, "Get the gimp back in the fucking boat. How is he even walking?"

Devan turned, face darkening into a dirty grin. He put a hand on the massive broadsword on his back, but didn't draw.

"You still alive, lizard killer?" he growled. "Figured I'd be scraping you out of that hold with a shovel."

Bershad kept moving down the gangplank. Devan, Liofa, and the fat man were all too close to the boat for Vera to have a clear shot. The other six smugglers were watching, but not getting any closer.

Devan's smile faded as he realized that Bershad wasn't stopping. "Get back in the fucking boat, dead man."

"You're the dead man, asshole," Bershad said, getting close and slamming his palm into Devan's bare chest. Pain shocked up his forearm from the impact. Devan barely moved. "Now draw your fucking sword!"

That got the smugglers' attention. The four who'd been spread out inspecting crates started moving closer to Bershad, eyes hungry with the promise of a fight. The two guarding the door put their hands on their blades, but didn't move.

"Telling you for the last time," Liofa said, knuckles tightening around his weapon. "Get. Back. On. The. Boat."

"It's all right, Liofa." Devan drew the sword from his back and held it casually by the cross guard in one meaty hand. "This one can die same as that old man." He smiled. "Like a cowed bitch."

Bershad had promised to wait for Vera to make the first move with her sling. She had the better view and would know when the time was right. But now that he was within sword's reach of the man who'd killed Rowan, his blood was rising. He couldn't wait.

He coiled his body. Drew the blade and made a sweeping attack. Devan just barely managed to raise his sword for a clumsy parry, then fell backward on his ass.

"What the fuck are you idiots doing?" the fat man shouted. "Stop this—"

Bershad ran his sword across the man's belly. His skin opened and an enormous layer of fat split apart, blue guts dropping all over the quay. Bershad slammed the pommel of his sword into Liofa's face, then tried to stab him in the heart. But Liofa twisted away, ducked behind a crate, and disappeared into the building's gloom.

Devan was on his feet again. Sword raised in a high guard. There was a gash in his ribs where Bershad had knocked the huge blade into Devan's body from the first attack.

Two smugglers rushed Bershad from the right. There was a quick whooshing sound, and one of their heads exploded in a cloud of bone shard and brain. The other smuggler fell over, holding one hand to his temple, blood pouring between his fingers. Vera's shot must have gone through one skull and hit the other. The four remaining men—including the two by the door—sprinted toward Bershad. Vera took a shot with her sling but the stone banged harmlessly into a wood crate. She cursed from the boat.

Bershad spat out a low growl and charged Devan.

They met on the stone quay in a flurry of blows. Devan's sword was twice the size of a normal weapon but he swung as if it weighed no more than a kitchen knife. Every time Bershad parried a strike, it felt like his wrists were going to snap apart. Devan grunted and heaved a powerful downward attack that took all Bershad's strength to block—the skin around his collarbone tore open, sending shocks of pain across his chest.

If he kept trading blows with Devan, Bershad was a dead man. So, he snarled and bulled forward—close enough to smell Devan's hot breath—kneed him in the balls, then head-butted him. Blood and little chips of bone sprayed out Devan's nose and down his chest. He dropped his massive sword, dazed and vulnerable. Before Bershad could finish it, someone tackled him.

He hit the stone floor and felt the wind go out of him. Ribs crunched and cracked. Someone raked a blade across his back. Another kicked him. Bershad rolled over just in time to catch a machete coming at his face. The serrated metal sunk deep into his hand, striking bone. He howled and cursed, then pulled the smuggler down on top of him. Bershad snarled and bit into his cheek—a rush of warm blood filled his mouth. The man screamed and recoiled, drew a pickaxe from his belt, and was about to slam it through Bershad's forehead when the back of the smuggler's skull blew apart in a storm of pink mist.

Bershad grabbed the pickaxe and crunched it into the other man's foot, pulling him to the ground. He ripped the pickaxe free and thumped it into the bastard's chest three times, feeling bones snap and break. More blood sprayed across Bershad's forearms and face.

Bershad kept the pickaxe in his hand as he stood up to face the last smuggler, whose hair was waxed into four large spikes. There was so much blood on Bershad that it dripped off him like water from a heavy rain. The man was holding a machete, hands shaking.

"Fuck this," he muttered, then turned and ran toward the door.

He didn't even make it halfway to the exit before Vera put a hole in his skull. He collapsed on the stones and started twitching.

Bershad turned back to Devan, who'd picked up his sword again. But it hung heavy in his hand now. Blood was pouring from his ruined nose.

"The fuck are you, lizard killer?"

Bershad flipped the pickaxe around so the spike was facing out. Moved forward.

"What are you?" Devan shouted.

Bershad just kept walking. Every step burned with agony.

When Devan brought his sword back to attack, Bershad jammed the pickaxe through Devan's wrist and left it there. Punched him in the throat. His eyes bulged to the size of chestnuts and his cheeks turned deep red. Bershad stabbed him in the stomach with his sword, twisting the blade inside Devan's guts and feeling them churn.

"This is for killing my friend, asshole," Bershad hissed.

He ripped the sword out of Devan's chest and slammed it down on the top of his head so hard that he split his skull in half, lodging the blade in the middle of his collarbone.

A moment later, Bershad heard footsteps from his left. He turned to see Liofa charging, sword raised. He was coming from behind a stack of crates so Vera wouldn't be able to get a clean shot. Bershad tried to pull his sword free, but it was stuck in Devan. Liofa rushed forward—his blade aimed at Bershad's heart.

At the last moment, a dark blur slammed into Liofa, driving him into a shipping crate.

Felgor.

They fell to the ground and started grappling. Liofa snaked around Felgor's body and got the upper hand. He was just about to slit Felgor's throat when Bershad got to him, grabbed Liofa by the back of the head, and slammed it into the quay again and again.

"Rat. Fucking. Bastard!" Bershad screamed as he pounded the last ounce of life from Liofa's body.

When it was done, Bershad sat back on his haunches, breathing heavily and looking around. Trying to push the animal rage in his body back down. He wanted more men to kill—anything to slake the bloodlust that had consumed him—but everyone was dead. Felgor had scooted away from him and was trying to wipe Liofa's blood and brain off his face.

There was movement from the ship. Vera came down, sweat on her brow and sling in her hand.

"What the fuck happened to waiting for my signal?"

————

Bershad needed time to calm down after the fight. He sent Felgor and Vera outside to figure out where they were. While they were gone, he pulled off his soiled bandages and dug up some more moss from one of the opium casks. Stuffed it into the new wounds on his hand and back, plus the old ones he'd reopened during the fight. He wouldn't be at full strength for a few days, but the moss was enough to keep him moving.

When that was done, he packed the smugglers' corpses into a large cargo crate, then washed his face and arms in the water. Vera and Felgor came back just as he was about to deal with Devan's and Liofa's bodies, which were still lying where he'd killed them—faces broken and ruined.

"So?" Bershad asked.

"We're in the theater district," Felgor said.

"Do you know how to get to the palace from here?"

"Yeah. We're pretty close. As long as our seals have the right checkpoint codes, we should be fine."

"Codes?"

"You'll see," Felgor said. "There's something else." Felgor held up a wrinkled piece of painted canvas. "Found this posted on the street outside."

"What is it?"

"They spread these around when there's going to be an event open to the public. This one's down in the central garden district the day after tomorrow." Felgor hesitated. "It's a wedding."

Bershad grabbed the canvas from Felgor. The writing was in Balarian but the image of a marriage cape was painted clearly. And Kira Malgrave's name was drawn in large, black letters.

"Shit," Bershad muttered. He passed the fabric to Vera who looked it over.

"We'll wait here until nightfall," she said. "Then we're going into that palace."

The covered dock was small, but quiet. Vera squatted in a corner and sharpened her daggers. Felgor sat as far away from Devan's and Liofa's corpses as possible. Bershad checked and rechecked his armor, then put it all on. Looked back at the boat. The captain was still hiding in his cabin. Bershad could leave for Taggarstan right now if he wanted. Head back to kill Vallen Vergun.

"I wouldn't stop you," Vera said, watching his eyes and guessing his thoughts.

"What?"

"If you want to go," Vera said, "I understand."

Bershad looked at his hands. He didn't feel better now that he'd killed Devan and Liofa. Rowan and Alfonso were still gone. Nothing would change that.

"No," Bershad said. "You were right. The only thing to do now is move forward."

"Good," Vera said. "But if you're coming into the palace, I need to know you're not going to do that again."

"Do what?"

"Lose your fucking composure. You were . . ." She trailed off, looking at the bloodstains all over the quay. "Like some kind of animal. If you do that in the palace, you will get us all killed."

Bershad swallowed. "It won't happen again. I promise."

At least, not until he found the emperor.

"There's something else I need to ask you about. What you said to me back in Taggarstan, just before the fight."

"I didn't come to Balaria to save Kira."

"That's clear," Vera said. "Why do you want the emperor of Balaria dead?"

Bershad hesitated. Tried to think of a way he could explain it.

"You told me once that if you were like me, you'd use the strength to protect the people you care about. I've lost so many people in my life. A family. A lover. And now my only friend." Bershad pushed down into the wound on his hand. Winced at the pain. "The emperor wants to destroy the last things in this world that I still care about. If there's a chance I can stop him, I have to take it."

Vera looked at him for a long time. "I trust that." Vera wiped a strand of dark hair behind her ear. "But you're wrong about one thing. Rowan wasn't the only friend you have left." She motioned to Felgor. "There's him. And there's me. Might be we didn't start off with much between us, but things have changed. For me, at least."

They'd changed for Bershad, too.

"Rowan liked you both," he said. "Up in the mountains, he told me that a woman like you was good for me. Took a while for me to realize why that was. We're all outcasts, one way or another, walking a path along the fringes of this world." He looked at Vera. "I'll help you get to Kira. But then I have to go my own way."

Vera nodded. Stared at him a while. "I wish things were different."

"Me, too."

Bershad looked back at the boat. "There's something I have to do before we leave."

"What?"

"Send a message back to Taggarstan."

He used one of the machetes to hack Devan's and Liofa's heads off, gathered the pieces, since Devan's had been sliced in half, and carried them by their hair to the pilot's cabin. He found Borgon hiding underneath a table of crumpled, dirty maps.

"Get out from under there," Bershad said.

Borgon obeyed, staring at the heads. "I saw them bring you onto the boat," he said, looking at Bershad through jaundiced eyes. "Never seen a man with that kind of damage done who was still breathing a day later. But you're . . ."

Bershad took a step forward. Borgon took a step back. "After we leave, you're going to bring these back to Taggarstan." Bershad dropped the heads, and snatched Borgon by the collar. "You're going to tell Vallen Vergun what you saw me do. And you're going to tell him I'm coming back to do the same thing to him. Tell him that the Flawless Bershad wishes him sweet dreams while he waits."

When he came off the boat, Bershad noticed Felgor was still in the corner of the dock, massaging his hands together. There was a small pile of dried, crusty blood between his feet from where he'd rubbed it off his skin and let it fall.

"You saved my life," Bershad said, coming over and sitting next to him.

"Did I?" Felgor asked, looking up. "Would it even have mattered if he'd put that sword through your heart?"

"Yes."

"You're fucking terrifying, you know that, right?"

"Why'd you save me, then?"

Felgor went back to his hands. "When we started, I just wanted a way out of this mess. But I guess you could say my perspective changed somewhere up in those mountains. I couldn't just let the bastards kill you, not after what you've done for me. Or after what happened to Rowan." He paused. "Whether you're a demon or a dragonslayer or something else entirely, you're also my friend."

Bershad looked at Felgor. "I'll make sure you live through this mess. If you get us into the palace, you'll be done. You've earned that."

Felgor nodded.

"I found something for you," he said after a while, and passed Bershad a small metal tin. "Nicked it from a theater troupe's setup while Vera and I were having a look around."

Bershad opened it. It was a makeup tin—looked to be about the same shade as Bershad's skin.

"For the bars on your face."

Bershad nodded. "Rest up," he said. "We leave in an hour."

33

BERSHAD

Balaria, Burz-al-dun, Theater District

Even in the thick of night, Burz-al-dun was alive. Bershad had never seen anything like it. The cobblestone boulevards and avenues were lit by hundreds of copper lanterns—all of them burning dragon oil—that allowed people to carry on with their night's business.

Almiran lords could burn as much dragon oil as they pleased. It was a luxury of the nobility, just like their thousand-acre farms and their armies of wardens. But the notion that a city would burn hundreds of gallons of dragon oil every night for public use was verging on an unfathomable kind of extravagance. It would be like buying a fleet of ships every day, setting them on fire each night, and doing the whole thing over again each morning.

The three of them walked in single file. Felgor led the way, carrying a lantern that he'd plucked from the wall. Bershad wasn't sure if that was legal, but nobody had stopped them. Along with the makeup tin, Felgor had stolen an ostentatious jacket for himself—all colorful slashes and white frills—and two almost equally flamboyant cloaks for Vera and Bershad that hid their weapons, faces, and armor. Bershad balked at the garments, thinking they would draw attention, but Felgor insisted.

"I grew up 'round here," Felgor said as they walked. He waved a hand toward a group of five boys who were perched along a low wall off to the side, scanning the crowd. "Just an urchin like one of them who got into the theater district on a work seal to pick up trash or shovel horse shit for the rich folks come to see a show. Most of those boys'll probably just keep on watching all their lives. Jealous of the nobles and the rich merchants, but lulled to sleep by steady food and the warmth of endless dragon oil. Living their whole life never breaking routine. But one of 'em just might realize the truth."

"What truth?" Bershad asked.

"The Clock's rules and laws look unbreakable when you're standing on this street looking up at the high towers, but they're not." Felgor smiled. "Nothing's unbreakable. And once a kid from the slums across the river realizes that, he's the one with the power, 'cause he's got nothing to lose. Only a matter of time before he starts slipping checkpoints and causing trouble."

"Speaking of checkpoints," Vera said. "How many do we have to cross?"

"Some good news there. Just one. First we need to cross this district, which is big. Balarians like their theater. On the far side, there's a checkpoint that leads to a shit-ton of fancy villas and manses near the palace. Yonmar actually set this part of the deal up pretty well, even if he was an asshole."

"There's no checkpoint leading into the palace?" Bershad asked.

"There are nineteen checkpoints leading into the palace, but we're going a different way." He turned around, the torchlight reflecting off his small teeth. "Trust me, you'll like it."

The buildings rose on either side, the shortest still twice as tall as an Almiran holdfast. The sides of each building were wreathed with copper pipes and pulley systems. Noises rang from the taverns and alehouses they passed—laughter and music and mugs clanging together. They crossed a wide bridge and were met with a throng of people who were pushing toward an open-air amphitheater built down by the water. All of them wore the same style of silk tunic and neat, closely cropped hair.

"Should have trimmed this up," Felgor said, running a hand through his shaggy hair. "Long noses and short hair, that's how you can spot a Balarian. Oh well."

Below the rows of seats, a massive paper dragon sailed around the stage—red and glowing from candles inside of its belly. Naked dancers who were painted pitch-black moved the thing forward with small handles made of wood. Every once in a while a dancer near the head blew a stream of blue flame from her mouth. A young boy began singing something in Balarian. His voice was a high, clear falsetto. Bershad didn't catch all of it, but he understood enough.

It was a song about him. The seventeenth dragon he'd killed along the northern coast of Almira.

"Perfect," he muttered, pulling the hood of the cloak tighter around his face.

There were street vendors set up at the mouth of the amphitheater, selling admission, food, and bottles of wine. Felgor stopped at one and filed into the back of the line. Vera jabbed him in the ribs with two fingers.

"The fuck?" she hissed. "We've no time for this."

"I'm hungry," Felgor said. "And I've not had a cranberry tart in two years. If I'm gonna die tonight, I want to have a treat first. C'mon. Blend in, watch the show a while." He turned to Bershad. "Just don't ask him what happens, he'll ruin it."

"Everybody knows what happens," Bershad said.

While they waited in line, Bershad noticed that almost every Balarian around them was wearing a clock around their neck. The gentle, metallic ticking made his skin crawl.

When it was their turn, Felgor bought four cranberry tarts and a jug of wine from a man with such a sharp nose it could have been a dagger. He doled out the tarts—keeping two for himself. They watched the show until the actor playing Bershad appeared—he was a seven-foot-tall giant with bulging muscles and a stupidly long spear. He began a long, intricate dance that was mixed with a song about his glorious duty as a dragonslayer to save the people of the town.

"Let's get the fuck out of here," Bershad muttered.

Just as he'd gotten everyone moving, there was a commotion in the crowd. Bershad panicked for a moment before he realized people weren't pointing at him, they were pointing at the sky. There was a group of dragons flying overhead—a Blackjack mother leading a dozen or so juveniles east, their reptilian silhouettes flashing in front of the moon. The crowd oohed and aahed, pointing excitedly.

"Why all the fuss?" Bershad said. "You can't go more than a day or two without seeing a Blackjack in the Dainwood."

When Felgor didn't respond, Bershad looked down to find him gawping at the sky just like the other Balarian citizens.

"Felgor."

"Huh?" He looked down. "Oh. Well, this ain't the Dainwood. Pretty much the only time a lizard's seen flying overtop Burz-al-dun is the days and weeks leading up to the Great Migration," Felgor explained. "Even then, it's rare. I never saw one when I was living here, but when I was eleven, a Red Skull flew directly over the house while I was taking a shit. That's what my older brother said, anyway. But he's a known fabricator." He paused. "If they're flying overhead, the migration must be getting real close by now."

"Very close," Bershad said, reminded of what he'd come to Balaria to do. "Let's keep moving."

They continued pushing east. Felgor took large, greedy pulls from the wine. The crowd started to thicken on the left side of the street—it looked like washerwomen and cooks, mostly. But Felgor guided them to the right side, where there was hardly anyone.

"Won't we stand out?" Vera asked, adjusting the weapons she had hidden behind her cloak.

"Nobody's gonna mistake us for the hired help." Felgor motioned to the line of servants on the far side of the street. "Anyway, if Vergun made our seals properly, it won't matter." Felgor drew his metal disc from his pocket. Bershad and Vera did the same.

The seal was no larger than a tea plate. Made of smooth, gray metal. One side had a complicated series of holes, the other had a physical description etched in Balarian. That was a problem for Bershad. The makeup hid his blue bars, but it didn't turn him into an entirely different person. And he didn't share a resemblance with Yonmar.

"What about the description on mine?" Bershad asked.

"I asked the same thing back on the boat," Vera said. "He ignored me."

"Will you two just relax? This isn't my first time slipping a checkpoint. Just make sure the dragonslayer goes last. And give me more of that wine."

Felgor took four or five long gulps and cast the jug aside. They turned a corner on the avenue to find a massive metal fence blocking the road. It was built from dozens of thick bars that were made of the same gray metal as their seals and crisscrossed each other in a geometric pattern. The fence rose all the way to the top of the adjacent buildings—two hundred strides at least. There were narrow gates on either side of the street, and two sentries shuffling people through. Some kind of metal contraption was set up next to each gate. Four copper pipes ran out of each machine, then disappeared beneath the street.

"So this is a checkpoint," Bershad said.

"Yup," Felgor said. "Remember, Silas goes last."

They lined up on the right side of the street behind three nobles who were all wearing extravagant attire that practically matched what Felgor had stolen for them. Finally, Bershad understood. Each noble gave his seal to the sentry as he approached the gate. The sentry then placed the metal disk in the strange machine and turned a crank on the side, which caused the machine to whir, release a puff of steam that smelled of dragon oil, and click in a quick series before spitting the seal back out. The sentry then took the seal, read the description, eyes darting between the metal plate and the man's face, and returned the seal to the noble, who was allowed to move on.

Felgor approached confidently, handing his seal over.

"Lovely show, must say." He burped. "Just capital really! Just . . ." He swayed a little, but collected himself.

The sentry eyed Felgor for a moment, read the description one more time, then handed back the seal. Felgor took it and lingered on the other side of the checkpoint. Gave a reassuring nod to Vera and Bershad.

Vera passed through without incident, and it was Bershad's turn. He eyed the guards, deciding he'd kill the one on the left first if things went sour because he kept his hand near his sword at all times. Usually that was the sign of a capable fighter. Bershad's seal passed whatever test the machine performed and spat it back out. The sentry raised it to his face to begin reading the description.

And Felgor vomited all over his shoulder and cheek—red wine and cranberry tart spraying everywhere.

"Fucking hell!" the sentry shouted. "What's wrong with you?"

"Apologies," Felgor muttered. "Had a bit too much of the wine I—"

Felgor vomited again, splashing the sentry's boots.

"A bit too much?" the sentry asked, wiping at his face and neck. "My shift's not over for another six hours." He handed Bershad his seal. "Take your drunk friend and move along."

The sentry turned to the next person in line and waved him forward. "Fucking nobles," he muttered under his breath when he thought Bershad was out of earshot.

"You see?" Felgor said after they'd turned a corner. "Every law is either breakable or avoidable."

———

After the checkpoint, the city became quiet and calm. The massive buildings gave way to sprawling estates hidden by low walls.

"These neighborhoods don't come cheap," Felgor said. "Only the richest of the rich can afford to live in a place like that." He motioned to the high white courtyard walls and ornate roofs that bordered the small road they walked on. "I pulled some good scores in these houses when I was a kid. You would not believe the amount of silver and gold plates rich people keep in their houses. How many fucking plates does one family need?"

They walked for a long time. Bershad figured it was an hour after midnight. Maybe later.

They had to get themselves inside the palace and hidden before the sun came up.

"Felgor, how much longer till—" Bershad's voice caught in his throat. They'd turned a corner, and just like that, the palace was in front of them. The massive dome was so large it could have been dropped over most cities and snuffed them out. There was a ring of towers encircling the dome that seemed small in comparison, but still loomed over everything else. An immense, steel-plated wall divided the palace from the rest of the city.

"It's still farther away than you think," Felgor said. "Another league, almost. Bitch is so big she screws with your head."

Bershad squinted—something was moving along the middle of the dome.

"Is that . . ."

"A massive gear?" Felgor said. "Yeah."

"That drunk river captain told me it powers the city," Vera said.
"Yeah."

"How?" Bershad asked.

"No idea."

For a few moments, all three of them just looked at it.

"How are we going to get over those walls?" Vera asked.

"We're not," Felgor said. "Follow me."

They wound their way through the streets. A few times, the orange light of a sentry's dragon-oil lantern lit up the walls from around the corner, but Felgor was watching closely and they ducked into a side alley or behind some bushes to avoid the possibility of getting their seals checked again. The one time they seemed truly cornered, he sprung the lock on a garden gate with a few snaps of a metal pick and pulled them inside.

"You've got your dragons," he whispered to Bershad as they waited for the sentry to move on. "I've got my locks."

They reached the base of the wall surrounding the palace. These houses were larger than the ones they'd passed earlier—practically palaces themselves by most cities' standards. They rose out of red, perfectly laid brick or pale marble.

"These are for the really big dicks," Felgor said. "Generals, senior ministers. Like that. They spend their days in the palace, so they get the nice houses nearby. Saves them a carriage ride, I guess. And it's going to save us quite a bit more than that." He led them down a narrow pathway between two houses. It was so thin that Bershad had to turn sideways and scrape through.

In the back, there was a small yard with a white tree. Felgor made his way to the base of the tree, took three measured paces to his right, and then began poking at the ground with a finger.

Jab, jab, jab.

On the third strike, he left his finger in the ground and smiled.

"Still there," he whispered. Then he pulled up and a rectangular patch of grass peeled away from the earth as if it was on a hinge. It took Bershad a moment to realize it *was* on a hinge. Felgor had opened a trapdoor that led into a dark tunnel.

Felgor grinned at Vera and Bershad. "The people who live here don't even lock the thing," he said. "My guess, it was forgotten generations ago. Only reason I know about it is 'cause of a spot of luck. Right place, right time, if you know what I mean."

"Where does it lead?" Bershad asked.

Felgor grinned even wider. "My friends, every scrap of royal shit and noble piss flows through this sewer pipe. All we need to do now is backtrack."

———

The sewer was cramped and hot and smelled like shit had been baked into the walls. Felgor continued to lead the way—carrying the lantern and shuffling along a narrow track of decaying brick that ran next to the trickling shit river. There were also dozens of copper pipes running along the ceiling that would twitch and shudder occasionally.

A turd floated by them. "Some noble performing the late-night deed," Felgor observed. "Think he had chicken or lamb?"

"Quiet," Vera hissed.

Felgor ignored her.

"This is nothing, though. First time I came in, it was just a few hours after a wedding. Some cousin to the emperor, I think. You should have seen the crap. River was damn near overflowing. I must have thrown up four, five times."

Bershad thought about the rows and rows of dragon-oil torches on the avenues—the roasting candy and treats that filled the theater district. Beauty and comfort above, crap below. Every three hundred strides they'd reach a cistern room that branched off in two or three or sometimes five directions. Felgor never hesitated at the crossroads—just guided them along with instinctual confidence. It was hard not to be impressed.

"Right place, right time, you said?" Bershad asked after he'd led them through the seventh cistern. "What's the right place, exactly, to learn your way through all this?"

"Oh, people in my line of work love sewers. You head back into the city"—he waved behind them—"you'll find tiny towns built inside the larger cisterns, all full of people who refused to live by the law of the seals. Rebels and reprobates can make a fine life down here. Some of 'em don't come to the surface for weeks or months at a time. Easy to move about underground back there. But here"—he tapped on the stone wall—"there's only a handful of ways into the sewers below the royal palace. The main tunnels are barricaded with mortar and steel. No way through without a score of men pounding night and day. Or a wizard, I guess. I don't believe in shit like that, but I didn't believe you'd ever walk again, either." He glanced at Bershad. "So maybe my perspective's been updated a bit."

"Who told you about this sewer?"

"Nobody," he said. "At least not on purpose. I was casing the house—hanging upside down above a bedroom window trying to see if it was worth breaking into. Eavesdropping in the literal sense, you could say. I overheard the minister who lives there—at least the one who used to live there—ripping into his servant about how the air near his favorite tree always smells like shit. His tone was quite nasty."

"And you put two and two together, just like that?"

Felgor scoffed. "Fuck no. I robbed the place a few days later and then spent a month in whiskey. Nearly forgot the whole damn thing till a barmaid I fancied took me back to her spot in a cistern-town. She found the entrance by sniffing for shit in that haze of dragon oil this city's filled with. Old Felgor put it together after that. Lucky, but luck only got me part of the way, same as anything else. Took three nights of plodding around in that yard to find the grate and get it open. And once I got down here, it was months before I got all this figured out. Months."

Felgor squinted and smelled the foul air again.

"Best keep our voices down from here on out. We're underneath the living quarters," he whispered.

"You're the only one talking," Vera hissed.

After a few more turns, Felgor began stopping at the chutes they passed on the wall. Each one had a small metal plate with a few markings scraped into it. The thief held his lantern inches from the metal and puzzled out the writing on each one. On the fifth panel, he passed the lantern back to Bershad. "Aye, this is it." He produced a metal rod and a wooden carving from inside of his coat. The rod was about three feet long, and Felgor attached the wooden carving to the tip.

Bershad looked up at the metal chute. Most of them had been narrow—no wider than a child's shoulders across—and full of corrosion. But this chute was newer and larger. Almost the size of a man's shoulders.

"This one is different," Bershad said.

"I checked every one of these chutes back when I was first exploring. None of 'em are as big as this one."

"Why?"

Felgor shrugged. "Can't say for sure, but my guess is that the person frequenting the toilet above was prone to taking massive shits and clogging the thing up."

"They'd widen an entire shit-pipe just for one person?"

"When you see where this leads, it'll make more sense. Hold the lantern up higher. Yeah, just like that."

Felgor raised his odd spear and wedged the carving into a hole beside the chute. About half of it disappeared into the hole right away. Then, Felgor moved the rod back and forth. Every few seconds, something would slip and the rod would push forward another inch.

"How long did this take to figure out?" Bershad asked after Felgor had been working for about five minutes.

"Don't ask. Just be thankful they don't use seal locks on sewer chutes."

The last tumbler released, and the chute sprang open with a metallic clang. A few turds dropped down to the sewer, nearly catching Bershad in the face. He looked up the narrow tunnel and only saw darkness.

"Right, then. Biggest man goes first," Felgor said, looking at Bershad. "If you get stuck in there, I don't want to be ahead of you."

Bershad yanked off his cloak, took another look at the narrow hole, and removed his armor, too. Left it in a heap. He swung his sword around his waist so that it sat against the small of his back. Then he pulled himself into the chute. His fingers slipped a little on the sides.

"Breathe as little as possible, and try not to fall," Felgor called to him.

"Fuck yourself," Bershad grunted.

The shit-pipe was so narrow Bershad barely needed to hold himself up—his shoulders were wedged tight against the stones. The climb became an exhausting series of agonizing leg presses that inched him up one putrid stone at a time.

Getting Kira out of the palace was going to be interesting. The notion of running through the halls—covered in shit and piss—snatching the princess, and then cramming her down a toilet didn't seem realistic. But that was Vera's problem.

After what seemed like the better part of an hour, Bershad squeezed himself around a slight curve in the chute and saw some light above.

The sides of the wall near the top were completely caked in shit. Bershad had to stifle his urge to vomit several times. But finally, when he reached up with his tired, aching arm, he found cool air above instead of another warm stone.

He pulled himself up and clambered out of the toilet as quietly as he could. Looked around.

It was the biggest privy he'd ever seen. At least fifteen strides across. The toilet he'd come out of was made of ivory, the edges painted with gold leaves. One entire half of the room was a massive tub. Cedar wood on the sides and mother-of-pearl at the bottom. Moonlight poured in from a skylight in the ceiling.

Felgor's grubby hand popped out of the bowl, and the rest of him soon followed. Vera was right behind him. Felgor crossed the room and started to fiddle with an unlit sconce on the wall. He released some hidden latch and a panel of the wall popped out.

"Secret passage?" Bershad whispered.

"Linen closet," Felgor whispered back. "Although, might be we want to wash some of this shit off before we spend the night crammed in there."

Bershad frowned. "We've got no time to fetch water."

Felgor smiled. "You mud slingers and your old ways. Observe." Felgor moved over to the tub and fiddled with a copper handle Bershad hadn't noticed before. There was a distant thumping noise, and then a stream of water began flowing from a faucet.

Felgor cupped his hands to collect some water and then splashed it on his face and arms.

Bershad had never seen anything like this before.

"If your shamans would cut back a bit on the mud statues and orgies, I'm sure they could figure it out as well," Felgor said. "Might even learn how to properly pave a road while they were at it," he mumbled under his breath.

Bershad frowned, and then pushed Felgor out of the way so he could wash the shit out of his hair.

When they'd all cleaned up as best they could, Felgor returned to the linen closet and shifted a few fresh towels out of the way, revealing a compartment about two strides across and six strides deep. He disappeared inside it.

Vera and Bershad looked at each other.

"After you," Bershad said. She scowled and went inside. He

squeezed in after her, then stacked the towels back in front of the door so they were more or less hidden.

"Get comfortable," Felgor said. "Morning shifts for the servants are starting soon, so we're stuck here till nightfall."

Bershad leaned back and tried to rest, but clutched his sword tight. He wondered if Emperor Mercer ever used this bathroom. In a way, it would be a fitting end for Bershad to have walked all these miles, struggled against so many obstacles, just to jump out of a linen closet and stab an emperor on the toilet.

But the emperor never came. Bershad was glad for the extra time to let the moss in his wounds do its work. Eventually, he fell asleep. But Vera woke him up.

"Your nightmares are too loud."

34

BERSHAD

Balaria, Burz-al-dun, Imperial Palace

The room outside the linen closet stayed empty most of the day. Once, a wheezing man came in and performed what sounded like a deeply painful bowel movement. A servant entered a few minutes later to light a dragon-fat candle. She didn't go for extra linens.

Felgor passed around a few morsels of cranberry tart he'd been keeping in his pocket. He must have stolen extras. Once night fell, the sounds of movement and activity in the adjoining chambers faded away.

"Where the fuck are we?" Bershad whispered.

"One of Emperor Agriont's old chambers," Felgor whispered back. "He kept his favorite mistress here, apparently. He was a large man. Hence the big shit-chute, I think."

"How far are we from Kira?"

Felgor shrugged in the darkness. "Depends on where she is." He paused, scratching his dirty beard. "But, if I was gonna stash an Almiran princess, most likely I'd put her in the eastern wing. There are some nice, private tower apartments on that side, as I recall."

"Fine. Let's go there first."

Felgor found a small latch in the darkness and released it. The panel popped open with a soft click.

They left the privy in their familiar line: Felgor at the front, Bershad in the middle, and Vera in the rear. The chambers outside were lavish, even compared to the best rooms in Castle Malgrave. Plush carpet covered the floor. Detailed tapestries hung from each wall. There was an array of wooden furniture covered with soft cushions scattered throughout the room—long couches and oddly shaped chairs. And there was none of the customary gloom that came with Almiran castles. The entire southern wall was two massive windows—glass from floor to ceiling. Moonlight poured in.

Outside the windows, the dome of the palace still rose above them. That meant they were inside the ring of towers that bordered the dome, looking in. They had a better view of the Kor Cog now, which was churning at a steady pace. Bershad and Vera both watched it—enthralled by such a large piece of machinery. Felgor snapped them out of the trance.

"Right, so that's where we're headed," Felgor said, pointing to a group of three towers on the far side of the ring. They looked almost dainty compared to the massive dome. "If we stick to the servants' passages, there shouldn't be any guards. They generally stay in the rooms and hallways that have valuables—trying to prevent 'em from being nicked in the night." He paused. Seemed to think that statement over. "All the same, best be ready to kill anyone we see."

Felgor moved toward the corner of the room, away from the main door, and fiddled around until he found another hidden latch. A small door popped open—just like the linen closet—and Felgor went inside.

They wound through a long series of narrow, unadorned passageways that were empty except for copper pipes running along the ceiling. It wasn't much different from the sewers except there was a lot more headroom and everything smelled like rosemary.

Eventually, Felgor motioned for them to stop and crouched down. He fiddled with a latch and popped open another door. Peeked outside. Closed it again.

He motioned to Vera and Bershad, then whispered. "Two sentries, twenty paces outside this door. One of them is more or less facing you straight on, the other is angled down the other side of the hallway." He paused. "They need to die *very* quietly if we don't all want to get arrested in the next five minutes. Every room down that hallway has a guard posted inside."

"No other way around?" Vera whispered.

Felgor shook his head. "Only one way into the eastern towers. One way out, too."

Vera nodded, then unstrapped the short sling from her thigh. Loaded a shot into it.

"How fast can you cover twenty paces?" she asked Bershad.

"Fast enough." He unbuckled his scabbard and drew his sword carefully so it didn't make any noise. Nodded to Felgor.

The thief opened the door and slipped out of the way. Bershad sprang forward, keeping low and making long, quiet strides. The sentry who was facing them squinted, trying to figure out what the sudden movement was about. When Bershad had covered half the distance the sentry's eyes widened and his mouth opened to let out a cry.

Then his face caved in.

The sentry's body quivered and fell to the floor with a metallic clatter. Luckily, he fell facedown so that when the second sentry turned to see what had happened, he didn't see the damage from Vera's sling. He didn't look down the hall, either.

"Thorin?" he asked. "What's the—"

Bershad grabbed the sentry's face and shoved it into the wall. Then he took a quick step back and cleaved the back of his head off with an upward swing of his sword—it was the only killing stroke he could manage in the narrow hallway. The sentry fell onto his back. Bershad knelt and pressed a hand over the sentry's mouth, just in case he somehow managed to scream without the back half of his brain.

He didn't.

Felgor had already fished out a set of keys from the other sentry and was trying them in the lock. Vera was pulling the first body by the arms toward the small passageway they'd come from. Bershad did the same with the man he'd just killed. As he dragged him, he noticed there was a coin-sized clock embedded in the man's bracer. It was still ticking. After he'd hidden the body, he returned for the back of the man's skull and tossed that into the passageway, too. Closed the door.

Felgor had the apartment door open. There was a spiral staircase on the far side—bars of moonlight shining across the floor every few feet from narrow windows on the walls. They went inside.

The tower was a honeycomb of hallways, but all of them were deserted. Once they'd risen a few flights, it seemed like everything was a door leading in a different direction. Felgor took a look at each lock, but moved past each of them. Snorting and shaking his head. When they got to the top, they found a gilded oak door with dozens of ticking clocks pressed into the wood. Felgor squatted down next to it, ran his finger over the gold plate of the lock, and then pulled out a small hook and wire from his coat.

"She's through here."

"You're sure?" Bershad asked.

"Every lock is a story. This one's all about a princess who doesn't want unannounced visitors. No other reason to have something so complex."

Felgor fiddled with the lock for a few minutes.

"Tough little bitch," he muttered at one point. Then there was a soft click and the door opened. Felgor stood aside and held out a hand. "Time to play the hero," he said.

The door led into a hallway that was actually an enclosed bridge leading to a separate tower. Bershad walked across and tested the door on the other side. It was open. He went back.

"Get out of here, Felgor," Bershad said.

"What?" Felgor asked.

"What if Kira isn't in there?" Vera asked.

"She's in there. The bedrooms of royalty have the same feel on both sides of the Soul Sea. You've done your part, Felgor." Bershad turned to Vera. "And we keep our promises."

Vera hesitated, but eventually nodded.

"You're free, Felgor."

Felgor looked at them. "Thank you, both of you. I know what Rowan would say." He swallowed, face turning serious. "Try not to die, eh?"

And with that, the Balarian thief bowed and slipped into the shadows.

Vera and Bershad crossed the bridge and opened the door. Inside, there was a circular room with a massive round bed placed in the center and a large trunk sitting against the far wall. The ceiling was glass. Moonlight touched everything.

A woman slept in the bed—Bershad could see the sheen of her black hair and the curve of her hip beneath the silk sheets. One arm dangled off the edge. His eyes flicked across the room, looking for sentries or doors. He saw neither, so he stepped inside.

It was the middle of night, but the moonlight made it easy to see her face. Bershad had only seen Kira as a child, but there was no mistaking a Malgrave face.

"Wake up, Princess," he said.

Kira had high cheekbones and full lips. Where Ashlyn had gotten the severe, calculating look of her father, Kira had the wild beauty of her mother. She stirred in the bed, opened her pale turquoise eyes, and blinked.

"Hello. You must be the Flawless Bershad."

She propped herself up on one arm—the silk sheet slipping off her skin and revealing her breasts. She made no move to cover herself.

"How do you know me?"

"You're the most famous person in the realm of Terra," she said. "And my sister always said you were the only one she could rely upon in a real pinch. I'm betting she sent you here to rescue me, right?" she asked.

"Something like that," Bershad said.

"I don't need rescuing. I never did."

Bershad looked around the room. "Where are your clothes?"

Kira waved a hand through the air. "There are a few dresses in that chest. I rarely put them on these days." She smiled. "Ganon prefers me without clothes."

"Cover yourself up, Princess," Vera said, moving around Bershad. She kept her voice quiet, but Kira moved the sheet over her chest as though she'd been screamed at.

"Vera?" Kira asked. "What are you doing here?"

"What do you think I'm doing here?" Vera hissed, kneeling beside the bed. "You were kidnapped, do you think I would just leave you to the mercy of the Balarians?"

"I wasn't kidnapped, Vera." Kira rolled her eyes. "I ran away to marry Ganon!"

Vera blinked once. Her face turned red for a moment, then returned to its natural color through what appeared to be sheer willpower.

"Princess," Vera said. "I have traveled hundreds of leagues through wilderness and danger to rescue you. I have killed dozens of men. And you're telling me that you left of your own volition?"

"Well, yes. I'm sorry for the trouble, but really I'm doing just fine. After I marry Ganon, I'll be wife to the heir of the Balarian empire. I'm not chained to some backwater, muddy country of savages anymore. Burz-al-dun is civilized and modern and powerful. This is where I want to be. Where I belong."

"You're sorry for the trouble," Vera repeated.

"That's right."

Bershad balled his hand into a fist and resisted the strong urge to slap Kira. But there were more important things for him to worry about. He wondered if the emperor's chambers were nearby.

Vera put her hand on Kira's jaw. Squeezed ever so slightly.

"If you ever do something like this again, I will kill you myself," Vera whispered. "Do you understand?"

Kira's faced scrunched up. All at once, the young woman melted into the child.

"Yes, Vera."

"Why didn't you tell me?" Vera asked.

"You'd have stopped me."

"I'd have tried," Vera admitted. "But I'd have gone with you, too. If that's what you really wanted. I can't protect you—"

"If you're not with me," Kira finished, rolling her eyes. "I remember. But right now what I really want is to stay in Balaria. There's nothing for me back in Almira."

Vera looked at Kira for a long time. Bershad could tell she was conflicted—battling her frustration with Kira against her duty to protect the princess.

"Then I'm staying with you."

Kira looked wary, as if she suspected a trick.

"It's not like I can sneak you out of the castle in the middle of the night if you don't want to go," Vera continued. "You have royal Papyrian blood in your veins, which means my job is to protect you no matter where you are. And no matter who you marry."

Kira smiled. "You always were a pragmatist. I've missed you, Vera. More than I expected."

"I missed you, too, Princess. I was so worried, I . . ." Vera swallowed. "I'm glad you're safe. And I won't leave you unprotected again."

Vera hugged Kira. The tenderness looked foreign on a woman who'd killed so many people.

Bershad cleared his throat. "The emperor might not be so accommodating to a widow who snuck into his castle and killed his men."

"That won't be a problem," Kira said. "I can convince Ganon of anything, and Ganon will convince the emperor to let you stay with me." She smiled. "This will be wonderful, Vera! I'm sure of it."

Vera nodded, then turned to Bershad. "You need to leave, Silas."

Bershad glanced toward the door.

"You sure you'll be okay?" he asked.

"I'm sure," she said. "Whatever you do next, I won't stop you."

Bershad put a hand on her shoulder. "Take care of Kira. But take care of yourself, too."

"I will."

Bershad headed for the door, but before he reached it, the high, delicate sound of a calling-bell rang through the chamber. He turned around and saw Kira's free hand wrapped around a small string that dangled from the ceiling near her bed. It was attached to the bell she used to call servants. The mischievous smile was back on her face.

"Oops," she said.

Instead of a servant or two flitting into the room—ready to help Kira get dressed or fetch her some breakfast in bed—a score of soldiers in full armor streamed through the door a few seconds later. Bershad had six spears pointed at his throat before his sword was halfway free from its sheath.

"Put down your weapons," said one of the sentries—a sergeant by the looks of him. "And you'll get to leave this room alive."

Bershad considered the eyes of each man and found grim, hardened faces. He lowered his sword onto the ground.

"You, too, Papyrian."

"Black skies," Vera hissed, then dropped her daggers.

"They're not to be harmed!" Kira piped. "Ganon said—"

"I am aware of my orders, Princess," the sergeant said in a less-than-reverent tone. "You can go back to sleep. Thank you for your assistance."

Bershad noticed that all the sentries with spears at his throat were stealing glances at Kira's naked body while the sergeant talked to her. He moved his fingers to the base of his scalp and felt the glass vial

he'd tied there back in the mountains. Still intact. He started to un-
tie it from his hair, but before he could finish the sergeant turned
back to him.

"Bind their hands," he said.

A sentry circled Bershad, then pulled his hands behind his back.
As he tightened a pair of irons around his wrists, the sergeant came
closer and looked at his face. The makeup had washed off his cheeks,
making his blue bars easy to see again.

"You're the Flawless Bershad," he said.

"That's right," Bershad said.

"Thought you'd be bigger."

One of the other sentries glanced at him sideways. Probably
because Bershad was already the tallest person in the room by half a
head.

"Sorry to disappoint. What happens now?" Bershad asked.

"The emperor wants to see you," the sergeant said. "Can't pre-
dict your future much beyond that."

Someone yanked a burlap sack over his head. Bershad didn't
struggle—they were taking him where he wanted to go. He smiled
to himself. After all these leagues of pain and trouble, he'd finally
gotten a stroke of good luck.

"No!" Vera started to shout when they tried to take her away, too.
"I must stay with the princess—"

The thud of someone punching her in the stomach filled the room.
Vera groaned and then there was a splattering sound of vomit hitting the floor.

"If you touch my widow that way again, soldier, I will have you
killed." Kira gave the order with such authority that it took Bershad a moment to realize she was the one who'd said it. "Vera stays
with me."

The room was silent a moment as the sergeant weighed his options.

"Fine," he said. "The widow stays with the princess. The Flawless Bershad comes with us."

———

The sergeant prodded Bershad through the castle with the butt of a
spear. After several minutes of shuffled walking, they led him into a
room and sat him on a cushioned chair. Four strong hands held him
down by the shoulders, then someone unlocked his wrist irons and

immediately replaced them with two thicker wrist clamps that weren't connected to each other.

"I'm not that dangerous," Bershad said. Nobody responded.

A few doors opened and closed. They left the sack over his head, but Bershad could hear the intermittent sniffing of a man behind him.

"Think I can get any breakfast?" Bershad asked.

"No talking. Don't make me gag you," the sentry said. "Because I will, but I'll beat you till you piss blood first. Clear?"

Bershad just grunted.

There was nothing to do but sit and wait. Seemed like Vera would be all right with Kira. Bershad wondered where Felgor was by now, too. Probably blind-drunk in a tavern, enjoying his freedom. Good. The clever thief deserved to survive this mess.

After a long time, Bershad heard a door open behind him. A large group of people entered, judging from the number of footsteps he heard. There was some rearranging of chairs, then the sack was pulled off his head. Bershad squinted in the morning light. Surprised at how high the sun was already.

He was sitting in another lavish room, although this one looked like an office instead of a bedchamber. The chains on his wrists were connected to two steel plates that had been bolted to the floor. He could move his arms, but the chains were too short for him to put his hands together. There was a long series of bookshelves on the wall in front of him and a massive map of Balaria and her colonies to the right. Seven soldiers were spread out along the edges of the room. They wore ornate, steel-plated armor and each carried a sword and spear. Bershad could hear the clocks on their bracers ticking.

A polished ebony desk was in the middle of the room. There were two men on the far side of it.

The first was sitting. He wore a simple but expensive set of dark blue silk robes. He looked like he was about forty years old, but his dark hair and close-cropped beard were littered with silver strands, which made him look older than he probably was. His eyes were a gray so pale they almost looked translucent.

The second man stood behind the first. He was a spindly old man who looked more like a dying tree than a person—his face was gaunt and his limbs and finger joints were knotted. His beard and long gray hair were twisted into a wild array of branchlike shoots that were held together by oil and twine. He was wearing a strange jacket made from green leather, and he had a look of intense curiosity on his weathered face.

"The Flawless Bershad," the seated man said in Almiran. "Defeated by a naked girl and a bell."

"In all fairness, it was the armed soldiers that forced the issue."

"I'm told they were afraid to go in there. Twenty veterans and your name still got them pacing about and pissing from the nerves." The man leaned forward on his desk and squinted at Bershad with those unsettling eyes. "Is that shit in your hair?"

Bershad tried to run a hand through his hair, but was stopped short by the chain on his wrist. He kept his hand there for a moment and tried to gauge whether he could lower his head and reach the vial in his hair. It would be a stretch.

"I expect it is," Bershad said. "Sorry about that."

The man leaned back again. "You are a long way from home, exile." He spoke Almiran with the sterile pronunciation you can only achieve from hundreds of hours under a tutor's instruction.

"Exiles don't have homes." Bershad studied the man. "You're the emperor, aren't you?"

He smiled, revealing a set of perfect white teeth, except for a silver one off to the side. "I am Mercer Domitian. Emperor of Balaria, commander of her military, and overlord of her colonies."

"Impressive titles," Bershad said, feeling his pulse quicken.

He'd made it. After crossing the sea, the mountains, and a desert. After taking lives, losing his best friend, his donkey, and snapping his bones to pieces, he'd found the man he came to kill. Bershad noticed the seam of a scar running down Mercer's jaw—well covered by his beard but not invisible. Could have been a battle wound, or he could have just fallen down some palace steps by accident as a child.

"And this is my royal engineer, Osyrus Ward." The emperor motioned to the old man behind him. "He is very excited to meet you."

The old man wet his lips with his tongue. "Tell me, exile, how long ago did that injury occur?" He pointed to the place where Bershad's collarbone had broken the skin. The moss had rubbed away during their journey to Kira, revealing the pink skin beneath.

"What do you care?"

"It appears to be several months old," Osyrus Ward said. "But I believe it happened much more recently. Two weeks? Maybe three?"

"Fuck off."

Osyrus Ward smiled. "What do you use to speed up your healing process?"

Bershad felt his stomach turn.

Osyrus paused, lowered his voice. "Moss, perhaps?"

Bershad didn't know what to do. He'd been asking people about unnatural healing for years and gotten nothing for it except idiot prophecies from backwater shamans. This was the worst possible time to finally meet someone who knew what was happening to his body.

"Do you know what the moss means?" Bershad asked.

Osyrus Ward smiled. Turned to the emperor. "That is all I need for now, Emperor. I know you have much to discuss with our guest. However, when you are done speaking with the exile, I would very much like to have some time alone with him."

"That really depends on the exile," the emperor said, keeping his eyes on Bershad. "That will be all, Osyrus. We'll speak later."

Osyrus Ward bowed even though nobody was looking at him. Instead of moving toward the door, he turned and walked to the wall of books. He lifted a latch hidden on the inside of a shelf. Something released deep inside the wall, then an entire shelf rolled to the side, revealing a winding staircase down. Osyrus went inside and disappeared just as the books slipped back into place.

"The man loves that passageway," the emperor said. "Took a year to build it and cost a fortune, but before my father died he told me that keeping Osyrus Ward happy was the key to a long, healthy rule of Balaria. I have found that to be accurate advice thus far."

Bershad shifted a bit, but didn't say anything.

"That's not what we're here to talk about, though," Mercer continued. "We're here to talk about your presence in my palace."

"I can explain that, actually," Bershad said. "That Papyrian widow got me drunk and drugged me back in Almira. I woke up in a bathroom of this palace and was just wandering around looking for the exit. Total misunderstanding."

There was a pause. Mercer's eyes didn't move from Bershad's face.

"You're funny," Mercer said, although he wasn't smiling. "Under different circumstances we may have been good friends. You could have told me stories of your heroic endeavors while I served you expensive wine and tender meat. Maybe arranged for a servant girl to fuck you senseless before you passed out."

"Sounds nice."

"It does," Mercer agreed. "It really does. But, under the current circumstances, I don't see a living legend full of interesting stories. I don't see the man who slew a Green Horn in Levenwood one morning, and then rode to Vermonth and killed a Thundertail that same afternoon. Nor do I see the young lord who got a bunch of innocent people killed in Glenlock Canyon and got himself exiled." He paused, scratched at his beard—just under the spot where the scar lay almost hidden. "I see an intruder who murdered two of my sentries and then attempted to kidnap my brother's bride-to-be, on the eve of her wedding, no less."

"Well, to be fair, I was under the impression you assholes had kidnapped her first. This was meant to be a heroic rescue type of thing."

Mercer seemed to consider that. "Nonetheless, we have a problem."

"Yeah," Bershad said. "We do."

"There are essentially three options. Would you like to hear them?"

Bershad lifted his wrists until the iron locked. "It's not like I can get up and walk out on you."

Mercer nodded. "Option one. I cut off your head and send it back to Almira in a pinewood box. That's the simplest option and"—he leaned forward, as if confiding a secret to a friend—"if we're being honest here, that's my preference."

He waited for Bershad to react. Bershad just sat there.

"Option two. I turn you over to Osyrus Ward, who always has use for 'live specimens,' as he calls them. And the old man is particularly interested in you for some reason. Says he's been keeping track of you for a very long time. So this is a tempting option as well. Like I said, keeping Osyrus happy is a good way to keep ruling Balaria."

Again, Bershad said nothing. He tried not to let the notion that Osyrus could answer the questions that had plagued him for years—and he was waiting down a flight of stairs—distract him from the job at hand. One thing at a time.

Mercer released a weary sigh. "And option three. Truly, this is more my father's idea than mine—he never could abide a wasted as-set. Even from the grave he manages to influence me. Fathers are irritating that way, don't you think?"

Another silence. Mercer dangled one arm across the back of his chair.

"Option three is I put you to use."

"What, as a servant or something?"

Mercer stared at him. "No. Not as a servant or something."

"Good. Because I don't think I'd be so good at that. A cook, maybe I could manage. Rowan made a pretty decent stew and I picked up the ins and outs of it over the years—"

"Do you think I'm just going to let you walk out of here after what you tried to do?" Mercer interrupted. "You have lost. The fool's errand that brought you here is worth less than the shit in your hair. Kira never wanted to leave in the first place."

Bershad thought back to the look on Kira's face when she rang that calling bell. It wasn't fear or anger or contempt. It was convic-tion.

"How'd you know I was coming?" Bershad asked.

Mercer smiled. "What makes you ask that question?"

"A servant's bell usually brings servants. Kira's brought soldiers."

"Ah." Mercer steepled his hands. "I could tell you, but I think you can figure out the answer for yourself."

Bershad thought about that. "Garwin survived the Red Skull at-tack at Argel."

"Correct. The baron sent word from the rubble of his city as soon as you headed into the mountains. There wasn't much reason to bother hunting you down when it was unlikely you'd survive the journey through the Razors. And if you did, I knew where you were headed. Right down to the room. I certainly applaud the feat, though. It was very well done."

Bershad clenched his jaw—it pissed him off to be manipulated that easily. Made killing Mercer a lot more attractive. But before Ber-shad made his move, he wanted to be sure that Ashlyn was right about the man.

"What use for me did you have in mind?"

"The people of Almira love you. The Flawless Bershad. The De-stroyer of Dragons. You've killed, what, fifty-two lizards? Fifty-three?"

"Sixty-seven," Bershad said. "I've fallen behind on the tattoos."

"Sixty-seven. How very impressive," Mercer said, looking the opposite of impressed. "What would you say if I told you that I've developed a weapon that makes dragonslayers obsolete?"

"I'd say you're delusional."

"Far from it." Mercer pointed to the map on the wall. "Do you see those red areas? Those are the last remaining dragon warrens in Balaria and her colonies."

It was a similar map to the one Ashlyn had shown Bershad in her castle. Tanglemire was by far the largest red mark, but there were half a dozen smaller ones sprinkled throughout the Balarian colonies.

"Not many left," Bershad said.

"Perhaps not, but Tanglemire is still massive. Far too large for a dragonslayer to wander in and accomplish anything besides a quick death. But I have designed a new kind of ballista that will make short work of the dragons who will soon be arriving for the Great Dragon Migration. The machines are reloaded with a pressurized charge rather than a hand crank, which allows them to kill a dragon every thirty seconds. I've built hundreds of them."

"Where are they?" Bershad asked.

"Not far from here," Mercer said.

Bershad looked at the map. There was a good highway leading from Burz-al-dun to the warren, but judging from the number of checkpoints marked on the map, it was a long journey. Midsummer was less than three weeks away.

"If they're in the city, how are you going to move them across Balaria so quickly?"

"Ah, of course something like this would be impossible in your country. You would have needed to start moving the ballistas a year ago. But a straight, paved road can do wonderful things. Plus, there's a royal wedding tomorrow. Quite the affair—ministers and generals have come from all over the empire to celebrate. And each of them brought a retinue of porters with them. After the wedding, I'll update the porters' seal codes so they can travel across the country and move the ballistas into position. Using a celebration for ulterior motives is hardly a unique idea among rulers." He smiled to himself, as if that was the punch line to some private joke. "It is certainly a logistical undertaking, but my seals make it easy."

"Why bother with ulterior motives and secrecy? Thought you had absolute control over your people and all that crap."

"First, nobody has absolute control over anything," Mercer said. "Second, killing the great lizards en masse has never been possible until now. The very notion is inconceivable to the people of Terra. I do not want to waste time convincing the small-minded bureaucrats of Balaria that this will work. They don't need to understand my methods—they just need to execute my orders. In my experience, it's more productive to simply demonstrate a paradigm shift of such magnitude. I used the same strategy with the seals."

"You and those fucking seals," Bershad said.

"You don't like them?"

"They've caused some problems."

"Well, seeing as you are an intruder in this country and this palace, that's part of their job," Mercer said. "My father developed the original apparatus, but he only envisioned them as a way to seal the Balarian border against resource-leeching foreigners, hence the name. Those early iterations only included a physical description and a fixed pattern of punched holes. Crude, but effective, so far as it went. But I saw their full potential. I updated the design to include a series of internal gears that rotate through multiple hole patterns in a specific sequence. You wouldn't understand the particulars of the mechanism, but the result is a system for controlling travel privileges for every citizen of Balaria. I can adjust access to the different districts of the capital and—more relevant to this conversation—access to the highway checkpoints all through the country, anytime that I please."

"You seem awfully proud of yourself."

"It is my legacy."

"What happens to your precious legacy when you die?" Bershad asked. "Or did you design a mechanism to prevent that, too?"

"The relentless passage of time is one of the few certainties in this life. Aeternita claims us all eventually. And while my younger brother Ganon certainly knows how to entertain the ministers, I sometimes fear he lacks the fortitude to carry on my work." Mercer shrugged. "But I'll address the consequences of my death when it becomes a more pressing issue." He motioned to the sentries in the room. "As you can see, I'm quite healthy and well protected."

Bershad grunted. If the emperor died in this room, the dragon cull died with him.

"It's all very interesting," Bershad said. "But it doesn't sound like you need my help. Why tell me all of this when you've kept it a secret from your own people?"

"I don't need your help to clear out Tanglemire." Mercer licked his lips. "But there is one last place in this realm with an abundance of dragon warrens. I believe you are quite familiar with it."

Bershad narrowed his eyes. "The Dainwood."

"Yes. I want you to cross the Soul Sea and help me cull those warrens."

"Not sure if you've heard, but King Hertzog and I aren't on the best of terms."

"Hertzog Malgrave is dead," Mercer said. He paused to let that sink in. "He died of a lung ailment not long after you left Almira. Ashlyn Malgrave is the queen now."

Bershad hesitated. "I'm not on the best of terms with her, either," he lied. If the emperor knew how close he was to Ashlyn, or the reason she'd sent him here, the conversation would be over and a lot of swords would be drawn.

"No matter. If Ashlyn had accepted my marriage proposal she would have become the most powerful woman in Terra, but she has taken a different path. I do not expect her to rule Almira for very long."

"You're going to overthrow Ashlyn because she wouldn't marry you?"

"I don't have to overthrow her myself," Mercer said. "The high lords of Almira are doing that for me. They just needed a little push. All I had to do was slip a disgruntled lord a name before I left your muddy country, and the mechanisms of politics and greed took over. That lord hired Garret the hangman to carve instability across your homeland. And Garret never leaves a job undone. In that way, he is one of the most reliable tools in Terra. His work has already put Ashlyn's reign on the precipice of disaster. While we are talking in this room, she is under siege at Floodhaven. Cornered. Desperate. Out of options."

Bershad frowned. He'd been imagining Ashlyn safe in her observatory this entire time, studying dragons and mapping out their migratory patterns. Instead, she'd taken control of a country that was halfway turned against her. The news was a shock.

"How do you know all of this?" Bershad asked.

"Ashlyn Malgrave isn't the only person who can train a pigeon to cross the Soul Sea. After that, all you need is a literate pair of eyes on both coasts. And I have plenty of those."

Bershad stayed silent. He wished Mercer was lying, but it didn't seem like he was.

"After Ashlyn is deposed, Kira will have the strongest claim to the throne," Mercer continued. "Who better to escort her back home than the most famous hero the realm of Terra has ever known? Hertzog may have hated you, but the other lords will embrace you, especially since the commoners love you so much. You can ensure a peaceful transition of power, and then you can ensure that Almira never needs to put another pair of blue bars on a man's cheeks. After the dragons are gone, what would be the point? You can bring Almira into the modern age."

"Modern age? Your country is nothing but desert between here and the border. Owning the world doesn't mean anything if you've turned it to shit in the process."

Mercer narrowed his eyes. "You sound just like her."

"Who?"

"Ashlyn Malgrave. Droning on about the importance of preserving dragon populations." Mercer waved a hand through the air like he was swatting away an annoying fly. "Meanwhile, her country is beset by disease, poverty, and rebellion. I cannot believe she could be so ignorant of the greater good. Did you know that only five in ten commoners born in Almira live to see their second summer? In Burz-al-dun, that number is nine in ten. There is no hunger in this city. No disease. Everyone has a job and everyone has a place. Even the lowliest pipe setter enjoys the luxuries of dragon oil on my streets and in their homes. Providing these comforts at the expense of some reptiles does not make me a villain."

"You can sit here and tell yourself that you're slaughtering the great lizards to keep your people comfortable, but we both know that's a lie."

"Is that so?" Mercer said, mouth tight.

"You're doing it because you need more oil to stay in power. You've destroyed all the other warrens, and now you're starting to panic because without the fancy lanterns and mechanical gates, your little system of control in Burz-al-dun might not work so well. Might be your precious mechanism of control falls apart on you."

"You cannot improve the world without control over it," Mercer said. "Ashlyn Malgrave doesn't understand that, which is why her city is under siege right now and Burz-al-dun is not."

"Might be you're right," Bershad said. "But killing the dragons in Tanglemire will solve one problem and create a thousand more down the line. You'll destroy Terra."

Mercer smiled. "I won't deny that the dwindling numbers of dragons has had an impact on my empire. There have been crop shortages in Lysteria. A grain famine in Ghalamar. And those damn monkeys went insane and tore apart the southern lands. But such is the cost of progress, and the oil I get from the Tanglemire cull will guarantee my dominion, but it will also open the doors to far greater advancements. Things you can scarcely imagine, exile. And I refuse to hunch down beneath the yoke of human plight and misery because I am afraid of disrupting the natural order of things. Burz-al-dun is a bastion of health and prosperity. A single, bright light in the dark. Don't you want to see these achievements brought to Almira?"

"Not really." Bershad shrugged. "I spent some time in your city. Not for me. So how about you take your third option and stick it up your ass?"

Mercer's face twitched.

"I'd have thought you'd be uniquely sympathetic to eliminating the creatures that have caused you so much strife, but I don't need to change your mind, exile. If you won't help me, I will simply kill you and move forward with my plans."

Bershad knew it would be safer to go along with the emperor's plot for a while. Gain his trust, then snap his neck when the opportunity arose. But he'd never been much for subterfuge and deception. Or patience. He had a chance now. He was going to take it.

"Kill me then," Bershad said. "Because I wouldn't even help you up from your fucking chair."

"Pity." Mercer stared at Bershad with his eerie gray eyes. Behind him, the sun was casting an orange-gold sheen over the looming buildings of Burz-al-dun. "I had such hopes for you. But you and Ashlyn Malgrave are both clinging to an ancient world that will soon cease to exist. She will fail as the queen of Almira, just as you've failed your mission to rescue Kira."

"See, that's where you're wrong."

Emperor Mercer raised an eyebrow.

"I didn't come to Balaria for Kira." Bershad loosened his shoulders. "I came for you."

For the first time since the conversation started, the emperor of Balaria looked confused.

Bershad jerked his arm up as hard as possible. Felt his shoulder snap out of the socket. It gave him just enough reach to tear the vial of moss from his hair, rip the cork out with his teeth, and drink the contents. The loamy flavor filled his mouth. A warm strength radiated from his bones.

The emperor stood up from his chair. The sentries around the wall were too surprised to move.

"What are you doing?" Mercer said, face twisted into confusion and disgust.

Bershad looked at him and smiled. Felt his shoulder sink back into the socket with a satisfying click. All of the lingering wounds from his fight with Vergun repaired themselves in seconds.

"Choosing a fourth option."

Bershad heaved both arms over his head, except this time, instead of being stopped by the chains, he pulled the iron links out of the floor with a splintering snap. He swung one chain into the nearest sentry's head, turning his face to red slop. Whipped the second chain toward the emperor. Mercer managed to tumble backward just fast enough so the scrap of iron dug into the leg of his chair instead of his chest.

Bershad stood up. Pulled the chains off his wrists. But before he had a chance to do anything else, three spears jolted into his body from different directions. He went down on one knee. Snapped a spear shaft with an open palm, tore the point out of his stomach, and rammed it under the chin of the soldier who'd stabbed him. The spears in Bershad's back twisted, but he ignored the pain and reached for the sword of the man he'd just brained. Drew it and flashed it across the throats of the other two men who'd stabbed him.

"Protect the emperor!" one soldier yelled.

"Just kill him!" Mercer shouted over the soldier, backing up toward the far wall, away from the door.

Bershad ripped the two spears out of his body. The wounds closed in seconds. There were three soldiers left. Two rushed him with their spears while the third moved in front of the emperor. When the closest soldier jabbed his spear forward, Bershad caught it by the point and rammed it backward into his gut, doubling him over. He parried the second guard's thrust and stabbed him in the chest—pushing his sword through the steel breastplate as if it was made of cheese. Bershad moved toward the emperor, slicing the top of the doubled-over guard's head off as he passed.

The final sentry was standing in a middle guard but his hands were shaking so much it barely counted as a defense.

"Im-impossible," he whispered.

Bershad grabbed the sentry's blade and shoved it into his forehead. The sentry crumpled into a dead heap at the feet of the emperor. Bershad held up his palm so that Mercer could see his skin knit itself back together.

"Are the consequences of your death feeling a little more pressing now, Emperor?"

Mercer's gray eyes flicked around the room, looking for a way to escape. "I don't suppose you're willing to renegotiate our terms?" he asked when he didn't find one. "An emperor is a powerful person to have in your debt."

"No."

Mercer swallowed. "Ashlyn Malgrave sent you here to kill me, didn't she?"

"That's right."

"I see. That's the difference between an emperor and the queen of some muddy forest. She sent one man to slit my throat. I stole her entire country from underneath her feet. The Malgraves are finished."

"You're pretty confident for a dead man."

"Killing me won't change anything. You can stop this cull, but you can't stop the tide that's coming. Nobody can. Ashlyn won't outlive me by very long." His voice caught in his throat and he took a moment to collect himself. "She's no better than I am. She's digging for power inside the bodies of dragons just like me, except what she's found won't keep a cold person warm at night. It won't help the hungry or sick or starving. It will crack this world in half. No, she's not better than me. She just sent a fucking demon to do her dirty work, that's all."

Bershad didn't know what Mercer was talking about. Didn't care, either. This was only going to end one way.

"You can die with a weapon in your hand if you want."

Mercer nodded. Then he bent down and pulled the sword out of the sentry's forehead. Shifted the blade to his left hand and moved to a low guard. His grip and form were well-practiced. Confident. He attacked with an elegant series of strikes. He was a capable swordsman, but it didn't matter. Bershad parried and dodged until Mercer came at him with a sideways attack toward his chest. He let Mercer's sword dig deep between two of his ribs where it got stuck, then Bershad stabbed down through Mercer's collarbone and into his heart. Mercer sighed lightly as if he'd just been told an unhappy truth by a lover. He died on his feet, propped up by the length of steel rammed through his body.

Bershad dropped him. Stood there taking long, deep breaths while the damage to his own body disappeared. He'd put hundreds of leagues under his heels to reach this moment. Now that it had arrived, Bershad didn't feel any different. No sudden and warm feeling of relief flooding his conscience. That's what made life such a bastard—guilt rode on your back heavy and hard and relentless. Redemption was light as a feather. Easy to forget entirely.

35

BERSHAD

Balaria, Burz-al-dun, Imperial Palace

Bershad stood in the room of corpses trying to think about his next move. He glanced at the door. There were no sounds or signs of more soldiers coming. Might be he could slip out of the room and find another one of those servant passages. Somehow get out of the palace, sneak aboard a ship, and smuggle himself out of Balaria. But it was a long shot. And even if he had a clear path out of the city, he wouldn't have taken it. Bershad turned back to the bookshelf.

Osyrus Ward knew what was happening to his body, which meant Bershad needed to talk to him. It was that simple.

The hidden latch was behind a thick tome called *The Conquests of Emperor Junock III*. Bershad opened the passage and waited for it to close behind him. Then he found a pulley mechanism on the opposite side, stuck his sword into it, and bent the contraption so it wouldn't open again. He headed down the narrow, spiral stairs. As he descended, the rosemary perfume of the castle faded until there was nothing but the faint scent of dragon oil and mold.

The stairwell ended in a large subterranean room. A few lanterns burned at the far end, but otherwise it was too dark to see much right away. Still, he got the sense the room expanded for a long distance in all directions. There was also a low vibration reverberating from the floor.

As Bershad moved toward the lanterns, his eyes adjusted to the gloom. He caught the dim outline of large objects to his left and right that looked vaguely like massive crossbows, although each one had a heavy, mechanical case the size of a horse's chest attached to it. Bershad figured those had to be the ballistas that Mercer had told him about. He really did have hundreds of them.

Past the lanterns, there was a low-ceilinged hallway that opened into a much smaller and better-lit chamber. There was a fire in one corner, and a thick oak door reinforced with steel studs in another. Lanterns covered the walls. A large, wooden table was bolted to a stone pallet in the center of the room. The surface was littered with scraps of bloody organs, dragon scales, metal tools, and glass beakers set over low-burning flames. Next to the fire, there was a simple wooden desk against a wall. Osyrus Ward sat on a stool in front of the desk, smiling at Bershad. His wild beard and oiled hair made the shadow behind him look like an Almiran totem.

"Welcome to my workshop," he said in a sandpapery voice.

Bershad looked around for weapons or sentries but saw neither.

"We're alone, I assure you," Osyrus said. "Which means I can drop the silly custom with your name. Lord Bershad, I have wanted to meet you for a very long time."

"Don't you want to know how I got down here?" Bershad asked, motioning to the blood on his clothes.

"I know how you got down here. You killed everyone upstairs."

Bershad stepped into the room. "Would have thought you'd have a stronger reaction to the murder of your emperor."

Osyrus shrugged. "Emperor Mercer was a vital ally, but his role in my work had mostly run its course. I shall carry on without him, as I always do."

"Carry on," Bershad repeated. "You mean the cull of Tanglemire?" Bershad asked, tightening his grip on the sword.

"Don't be ridiculous. That was Mercer's project. I aim far higher with my work." He smiled to himself, revealing a set of oddly perfect teeth behind his feral beard. "I'm afraid the lizard cull will not happen this year. And who knows where the world will be in five years, when the next Great Migration occurs? Perhaps it will not be necessary at all. That's what you wanted, wasn't it?"

"That's not the only thing I want." Bershad hesitated. He'd come down here for answers. It was time to get some. "I want to know what I am."

"You are a paradox. Both the creator and destroyer of dragons."

Bershad frowned. That didn't make sense. "Why does the moss heal my body?"

"It's quite remarkable, isn't it? I'm very excited to learn more from you—you'll be a very interesting specimen to study."

"You're not going to study anything, old man. You're going to answer my questions and then maybe I won't kill you."

"I assure you, Lord Bershad, you are not the one controlling this situation."

Bershad raised the sword in his hand. "You sure about that?"

"Oh, yes. Because I know something that you don't."

"What's that?" Bershad asked, taking a step forward. If he had to beat the answers out of the crazy old man, he would.

"That if you combine canistine root with the embryonic fluid of a dragon's egg and simmer at low heat for forty-three hours, you'll create a tranquilizer that is so strong, no living creature can resist its potency, regardless of whatever . . . irregular strength they might be carrying within their blood."

"What are you talking about?"

Bershad was halfway across the room.

"Allow me to demonstrate," Osyrus said, digging one knobby hand inside of his jacket. He produced a small crossbow and shot Bershad in the chest. The impact pushed Bershad onto his heels, but didn't do much more—it was a small bolt. Bershad was about to grab Osyrus, but his balance rolled over and his vision blurred. His face hit the ground. Everything started going dark.

"You see?" came Osyrus's voice, although it sounded far away now. "Don't worry, Lord Bershad, we will continue our conversation later, under more favorable conditions. But since you're about to lose consciousness anyway, I'd like to perform an initial test."

Osyrus rummaged around out of sight for a few moments, then appeared over Bershad with a thick-bladed machete in his hand.

"Tell me, Lord Bershad, have you ever lost and then regrown a limb?"

Bershad tried to respond, but the words wouldn't form on his lips. It felt like he'd drunk an entire barrel of wine.

"I didn't think so." Osyrus pulled Bershad's left foot away from his body a little bit—the one that had been savaged by a Red Skull years ago, and was covered in scar tissue. "Brace yourself, Lord Bershad. This is going to be quite painful."

Osyrus hammered the blade into Bershad's ankle with a sickening crunch. Bershad felt nothing at first, but he heard blood splattering against the stone floor. The pain came a second later—hot and blinding, like someone was holding a white-hot poker against Bershad's flesh and bone.

He blacked out.

———

Bershad woke up, blinking a few times as the ceiling of the dungeon came into focus. His wrists and ankles were bound to the table by thick steel manacles. He was naked except for his deerskin breechcloth. His head was foggy and pounding. He pulled against the manacles, but was met with uncompromising resistance.

"Don't bother, you can't yank those out of the floor," Osyrus Ward said from somewhere behind him. "The steel is fused to a rock that goes fifty strides into the ground. A full-grown Red Skull wouldn't be able to break free."

Bershad turned his head to find Osyrus Ward sitting at his desk, writing notes on a brown length of parchment.

"You've been asleep for some time. Things are rather chaotic up above," Osyrus said, not looking up from the parchment but pointing at the ceiling with his quill. "The poor emperor, slaughtered just one day before his brother was scheduled to marry an Almiran princess. And the assassin is nowhere to be found." Osyrus smiled to himself. "Balarians are nothing if not adaptable, though. You've missed the first combined marriage and coronation ceremony in the history of the empire. It was quite an affair—the citizens of Burz-al-dun are quite taken with your Kira. Funny how easily a pretty face and a few charming words will win over a large crowd of people, even if they are supposed to be mourning the death of their previous leader. Emperor Ganon and Empress Kira Domitian rule Balaria now. I think their reign is full of interesting possibilities."

Bershad was too disoriented to follow most of what Osyrus was saying. He managed to lift his head just enough to see down his body. But instead of the ankle stump he was expecting, Bershad saw a perfectly normal foot. All of the scar tissue from his previous injury was gone.

"Remarkable, isn't it?" Osyrus said, looking up from his parchment. "With the proper treatment, the strength of the growth matches the nature of the wound. There are limits, of course. But not many."

"What did you do to me?" Bershad asked.

"Nothing you haven't done to yourself dozens of times before, judging from the ruination of scars across your body. I just did it better. Cleaner."

There were dozens of empty glass flasks sitting on a small tray next to him, and there was an oak cask halfway filled with dark green moss. Bershad could see the blue flowers and smell the rich loam.

"Do you know what that is?" Osyrus asked.

"I know what it does."

"Yes, of course. Almirans call it Gods Moss, but it has had many names throughout the ages. It's extremely rare."

"You've got a shitload of it."

"Yes, well. I have unique resources when it comes to collecting Gods Moss. All of this came from a warren located in the heart of the Soul Sea. Very remote. Very dangerous to visit. But worth it. You see, any kind of common moss will accelerate your healing to some degree. You could scrape some dusty bits from an old brick wall and heal a minor scrape. Or pack a bunch of slimy river muck into broken flesh and bone, and repair yourself in a week or so. But warren moss works on an entirely different level. And of the three types of warren moss, only a healthy supply of extremely fresh Gods Moss, like this, has the potency to regrow lost limbs. This information alone is a landmark discovery, Lord Bershad! You have no idea how much I've learned from you in the short time we've spent together."

"Is it magic?" Bershad asked. It was all he could think to ask.

"There is no such thing as magic, Lord Bershad. Just unanswered questions." Osyrus got up from his chair and crossed the room so that he was hovering over Bershad's face. "If you showed a barbarian from the jungle nations a suit of steel armor and told him that you forged it from a bunch of rocks, he would call that magic, no? My craft is the same. But with this kind of work, everyone is a barbarian except for me. No, what happens to you is a gift from your fore-fathers. Passed down unseen through the blood and the ages, just like your green eyes."

Osyrus produced a tool that looked like a sharpened spoon and, without any warning, scooped out a chunk of flesh from Bershad's new foot.

"Fuck!"

Bershad tried very hard to punch Osyrus in the face, but the man-acles held strong. He tried again, but the thick steel wouldn't budge. The old man leaned in to scoop another chunk of flesh out of Ber-shad's thigh. More slamming. More failed attempts to break Osyrus's face.

When Bershad calmed down, he looked down at his foot and saw the wound was already healing—open flesh knitting back together and starting to scab. But the hole in his thigh was leaking blood onto the table like any normal wound.

"Fascinating," murmured Osyrus. "Do you know what that means?"

"I am going to rip your lungs out, old man."

"The Gods Moss left your system hours ago, but the accelerated capacity for rejuvenation remains in the new limb. Extraordinary. Of course, there's no way to know how long it will last without care-ful observation. Could be days or weeks. It could be forever."

He moved back to the fire and started writing excitedly in his notebook again. Bershad just lay there breathing, trying not to lose his composure. He was going to die in this dungeon.

Osyrus finished his note. "You came down here for answers," he said. "You have already resolved many questions of mine; it's only fair that I answer some of yours. There is no reason we can't be civi-lized about this."

"Civilized? You just cut off my fucking foot."

"And then helped you grow a new one. A better one, even! But if you'd prefer to continue as we have, that is fine with me. I was only trying to be polite."

Bershad swallowed. Took a few breaths. If he was going to die down here, he wanted to die knowing what he really was.

"Have you found others like me?"

"Yes." Osyrus said. "The other seeds taught me many things in their own way, but you'll teach me more."

"Seeds?"

"That's what I call people like you. Everything needs a name, after all." He cleared his throat. "You spent time in dragon warrens as a child, yes?"

"How did you know that?"

"An attraction to warrens is a common indicator of your condition."

"What's going to happen to me? Am I . . . going to turn into a dragon?"

Osyrus smiled. "Maybe. There is a potency in your blood that's tied to the earth. And to dragons. It is the reason that you heal so rapidly. I suppose that sounds a bit mystical, but that is only because I don't fully understand it. Yet. But I do know that you are an extremely dangerous creature. The condition that has saved your life so many times will eventually kill you in an involuntary and destructive process. You may take another form afterward, but the man will be gone."

"You're sure?"

"You cannot stop the inevitable, Lord Bershad."

Bershad took a few breaths. His mouth had gone bone dry. "How long do I have before that happens?"

"To be honest, I'm amazed that you've managed to last this long, given the way you've occupied yourself for the last fourteen years. Each time you use the moss to heal a wound, you inch closer to the bloom. I expect you've begun to feel changes in your body beyond the healing that comes with exposure to moss. I already know you've discovered the strength Gods Moss can bring—that's how you got out of those irons upstairs and killed eight soldiers by yourself. But there is more, yes? You feel a deeper connection to the natural world. An intimacy with wild creatures."

Bershad thought about the bone tremors that the presence of dragons caused. The burst of sound and smells when he was inside the warren in the Razorback mountains. The sizzle of fish heartbeats when he was healing in the boat on the Lorong River.

"Yes."

"That means you're very close, Lord Bershad. But your capacity to delay transformation is unique among your kind—perhaps you could carry on for another fourteen years like this. Or perhaps I will cause too much trauma and you'll bloom in this dungeon, which would not be desirable at all. You would kill me. And half of Burz-al-dun, probably."

"You keep saying bloom. What does that mean?"

Osyrus smiled. "I believe it is once again my turn to ask the questions." He returned to his desk and took more notes. Bershad tried to process what he'd learned. "You haven't begged for your life yet," Osyrus said. "I find that strange."

"Would you let me go if I did?"

"An interesting question." Osyrus stopped writing. "Tell me, Lord Bershad, if I did release you right now, what would you do?"

"Murder you."

"After that."

Bershad hesitated. He'd been so focused on getting his job done, he hadn't thought about what he'd do if he was still alive when it was finished.

"I'd go back to Ashlyn." He thought of her face. Her hands. And then the armies of soldiers outside her walls. His throat clenched. "I never should have left her."

"Back to your lover, and back to Almira. That could be very interesting."

"Well, seeing as I'm bolted to a table in a fucking Balarian dungeon, it doesn't really matter if it's interesting, does it?"

Osyrus seemed to consider that. "Perhaps not. And I'm afraid we must proceed a little further." Osyrus moved to the shelf and picked up the machete. "Let's remove an entire leg this time, shall we? Try not to bite your tongue off. They're a tricky organ—it will be very uncomfortable to grow another one."

It took dozens of chops for Osyrus to cut off Bershad's leg. Each messy hack sent a shot of pain through Bershad's leg that spread throughout his body. He screamed until his throat turned raw, then he pissed himself. When it was done, Osyrus picked up the amputated limb and put it in a rough-spun sack. Blood was everywhere. Osyrus crammed four fistfuls of the Gods Moss into the gory wound before it stopped bleeding. The awful pain in Bershad's leg changed to soft comfort, like it had been dipped into a warm pond.

Bershad thrashed and moaned curses, unable to form a full sentence. Osyrus wrote more notes in his book. Then he felt Bershad's wrists and neck, counting his heartbeats.

"This is very exciting, Lord Bershad! You're quite stable. Yes. Yes, let's take things a little further. A little further and I'll have the answers that I need."

Bershad tried to protest, but before he got the words out Osyrus picked up a scalpel and slit Bershad's throat. He passed out while his mouth was filling with blood, and Osyrus was filling his neck wound with more moss.

———————

Bershad woke up to an empty room. The fire had burned down to embers. His leg was regrown. The new limb felt strange, like a living thing that was attached to him, but not a part of him.

He stared at the ceiling, which was wreathed in copper pipes, wondering what stupidity had caused him to be so curious about the truth of his body. He hadn't even learned much about his healing, except for the fact that it would kill him one day and was tied, somehow, to dragons.

Bershad was so occupied with berating himself that didn't notice the scraping sound at first. It was soft but steady—metal rubbing against stone. Back and forth. Back and forth. It was coming from the corner to his right, where a small, rusty-orange grate was set into the wall.

Bershad looked over, frowning, just as the grate started to shake up and down. After a few moments, the entire thing pushed forward and then to the side, revealing a square black hole.

And Felgor's face, smiling at him.

"You're in a bad fix, dragonslayer."

"Osyrus," Bershad whispered. "Where is he?"

"Relax," Felgor said, pulling himself out of the hole and into the chamber. He'd cut his hair short and was dressed as a Balarian palace servant. "The crazy man left the palace half an hour ago. I shadowed him over to the docks. He told an assistant he'd be gone for the rest of the day and muttered something about a broken ship. That being said, lingering around here isn't a good idea."

Felgor inspected each of the manacles, then he produced a lockpick from his belt.

"I can get you out of here," Felgor said. "If that's what you want."

"What else would I want?"

Felgor drew a long, curved dagger from his hip.

"The trick with the moss was one thing." Felgor grimaced. "Growing feet and legs is something else. Might be you just want to end things. Only fair I give you the choice."

Bershad looked at the knife's edge. Even a skinny man like Felgor could get his head off with one good chop of that blade. A clean death was tempting now that he knew a terrible one waited for him down the line. But something Vera had said to him up in the mountains stopped him from accepting Felgor's offer. She'd told him that he should use his strength to protect the people he cared about. Rowan and Alfonso were dead, but Ashlyn was still alive. Bershad might be cursed. Might be a demon, even. But he wasn't done yet.

"Get me off this fucking table," he said.

"Aye," Felgor said. "Good choice."

Felgor started fiddling with the manacles. Two minutes later, Bershad was free.

"Can you walk?" Felgor asked.

Bershad put his feet on the ground and took a few tentative steps. There were no calluses on his new feet, so moving felt strange after so many years of walking on hardened skin, but otherwise he was fine.

"Good enough," Felgor said. The thief dug around in a trunk near the shelves, and managed to produce a set of black linen pants, a leather shirt, and good boots. Felgor threw them to Bershad, then rummaged around the room while he got dressed, pocketing anything that looked valuable.

"You ready?"

"Not yet," Bershad said, looking around the room until he spotted a large barrel of dragon oil that Osyrus must have used to refuel his torches. Bershad picked it up and headed back toward the large chamber with the ballistas.

"What're you gonna do with that thing?" Felgor asked, following him.

"Finish what I started."

Emperor Mercer wasn't alive to order the dragon cull anymore, but there was only one way to be positive it didn't happen.

Bershad cracked the barrel open and poured oil up one row and down the other. Then he took a lantern off the wall and dropped it.

The flame snaked across the floor, illuminating the room so Bershad could see how many machines were in there. Hundreds. Rows upon rows. Bershad watched the fire spread.

"Uh, not sure that was a great idea," Felgor muttered, pointing up. With all the fire, it was now easy to see that the ceiling was covered with thousands of copper pipes—some were no wider than a man's arm, others were the width of a city street. All of them thrummed and vibrated. Bershad realized the massive gear running through the middle of the palace must be right above them.

"Huh."

"We need to get out of here," Felgor said. "Quick."

"Agreed."

"It's just a question of whether you'll squeeze through that hole in the wall."

It was close, but Bershad managed to shove through the opening by going in headfirst, blowing all the air out of his lungs, and pushing himself through with his legs propped up against the stone torture slab. Felgor replaced the grate after he slipped through behind Bershad.

"Good news is that if we don't get blown up, our tracks should be pretty much covered," Felgor said. "Should give that crazy fucker something to wonder about. Maybe he can write the mystery down in that notebook of his."

"How long were you watching?"

"Long enough to see some shit I'll never forget." Felgor shifted the grate until it fell into place. "We best keep moving."

The cramped tunnel connected to a larger drainage pipe that was almost tall enough for Bershad to stand up inside. There was a shallow trickle of water flowing down the middle of the pipe. They followed the water for a long time, and eventually they reached a locked grate that emptied into a small river. The lock was the size of a man's head and unreachable from the outside.

"We lucked out," Felgor said as he started picking the lock. "This is one of the older locks, which can be opened without a seal. If they'd slapped a new one on here, we'd be fucked."

Felgor still had to fiddle with the lock for almost fifteen minutes before he got it open and they tumbled into the cool evening air. They were almost a league away from the palace.

"Good. We're near the harbor," Felgor said, squinting and looking around. "The whole city was looking for you at first—hundreds of soldiers roaming the streets with torches and blades, hunting for anyone with blue bars on their face. But things cooled down after the wedding. Funny how quickly commoners forget royalty after they're gone, isn't it?"

Bershad rinsed his face and hair. Fought the temptation to poke and prod his regrown limbs.

"Do you know what happened to Vera?" Felgor asked. "I tried to get back to her, but that part of the castle is locked up tight now. Impossible to get in."

"Wouldn't have done any good if you did," Bershad said. "Kira wanted to stay in Balaria, and Vera stayed with her."

"Well, the little spider always could take care of herself."

Bershad nodded agreement. "Why'd you come back for me?"

Felgor blew a large lump of black snot from his nose.

"I don't always have a good reason for doing dangerous things. When I broke into that palace as a kid, I didn't want to steal anything in particular. I just wanted to stir shit up for the nobles. Relieving Balaria of their emperor's assassin will most definitely stir shit up, too."

"That can't be the only reason," Bershad said. "You could have died."

Felgor hesitated.

"That man was cutting off pieces of your body, Silas." Felgor looked at his feet. "I couldn't just let you die down there. Not after everything we've been through."

Bershad didn't know what to say. Felgor saw his face and smiled.

"Don't get all emotional on me, dragonslayer. Doesn't suit you. Now, we can't stay in this city very much longer. So where do you want to go?"

"Almira," Bershad said. "I need to get back to Almira."

Felgor scratched at his chin. "Um, last I checked, you don't have an army. Isn't that what it usually takes to break a siege?"

"Other than you and Vera, Ashlyn Malgrave is the only person in Terra that I care about. And she's in danger. If there's even the smallest chance I can help her, I have to take it. Otherwise, I might as well just have you slit my throat right here."

"Almira." Felgor nodded. "Fuck it, why not?"

"You don't have to come. You've paid your debt, Felgor."

"I got a death sentence in Balaria, remember? But Almira owes me a big juicy pardon." His face got serious. "And with Rowan gone, you could use a second pair of eyes looking over your shoulder. Trouble seems to follow your footsteps pretty close."

"Thank you, Felgor. For everything."

Felgor waved the gratitude away and glanced out over the harbor. "Stealing a ship from the Bay of Broken Clocks can be difficult, but—"

Felgor was interrupted by a low boom echoing out from the direction of the palace. They both turned to see the Kor Cog come to a grinding stop. A pillar of black smoke started drifting up from the palace dome.

"Huh," Felgor said. "That'll make things quite a bit easier."

"Why?"

"The gear stopped a few times when I was a kid. It powers the whole of Burz-al-dun. All the checkpoints. All the pulleys and faucets. Whole city'll be on lockdown till they fix it." He pointed away from the palace. "But the harbor's just over there—no checkpoints to cross. Compared to sneaking into the Imperial Palace through a shit-pipe, I figure stealing a boat amid the confusion and riding out of the harbor will be fairly straightforward."

36

ASHLYN

Almira, Castle Malgrave

Ashlyn watched from a porch on the King's Tower as Wallace's catapult team hauled a diseased cow onto the machine. Using a Papyrian lens, she could see that the crew were all wearing wolf masks. When the cow was in place, all of them moved away but one, who then released the trigger. The cow sailed high over the city wall and landed in an abandoned square. Blood and gore splattered across the cobblestones, leaving a dirty red streak on the ground. Wallace had just recently switched from massive stones to dead animals during the day. An attempt to spread pestilence and disease, along with destruction.

The roof of a nearby building was burned to cinders from one of Cedar Wallace's explosive charges, which he liked to use at night when they could be seen from everywhere in Floodhaven.

The barrage had been continuous and consistent since Cedar Wallace's army arrived. The catapults had pushed soldiers and citizens away from the outer walls, which had allowed Cedar Wallace to move his engines closer and begin hurtling missiles into the civilian districts. Yesterday, twenty-three wardens and eighty-seven commoners had been killed. Fourteen buildings were destroyed. The Malgrave high-wardens rotted in the trees—their eyes pecked by crows, their bellies bloated and full of gas.

In addition to the siege, the summer solstice was rapidly approaching. If the fleet didn't launch soon, it would be too late.

Ashlyn had known being queen would be difficult, but she'd always expected the larger problems of Terra to be her main concern. The global economy and food supply. Politics with foreign nations. Preserving the populations of dragons and the health of humans. But on her way toward solving those issues, she'd become stuck in the mire of Cedar Wallace's small-minded thirst for power. It made her furious. And yet, she couldn't think of a way to convince Wallace to give up the siege without giving up her throne, and with it her last chance to stop the cull. She could not force his eyes to see the wider circles of the world. Instead, Ashlyn had to deal with Wallace's hobgoblin greed on his terms before moving forward to what really mattered. Perhaps that's what frustrated her the most—even as queen she was servant to the patterns of history. The avarice of men.

Still, she had to try something. Allowing herself to sit besieged in Floodhaven while every dragon in Terra was murdered was not acceptable.

Ashlyn went back inside, where the remaining members of the High Council waited for her around a circular table. Hayden, Shoshone, and High-Warden Carlyle Llayawin were also in the room, standing behind the table.

A map of the city and the locations of Cedar Wallace's siege engines was laid out in the middle of the table. Ashlyn had calculated the catapults' ranges in the margins of the map and circled the most vulnerable areas of the city so that Carlyle could position his men accordingly. There was a part of Ashlyn that had found the mathematics of siege work fascinating, but the process of reducing dead men and destroyed buildings to a set of numbers on paper had made her skin crawl.

It hadn't been easy to keep the city under control during the siege. Food was scarce. Wardens were just as likely to join a riot as they were to stop one. And most of the lords who'd been in the city during her coronation had bunkered themselves into their villas. Shoshone and her widows had the castle and docks under control for now, but that wouldn't last forever.

Something needed to change, and soon.

Linkon Pommol wore a white tunic and pants. Doro Korbon was sweaty with nervousness. One of Yulnar Brock's servants had brought him a ceramic bowl of ribs drizzled with some kind of brown sauce. The commoners were eating rats and cakes made from sawdust, but Yulnar still didn't go an hour without a snack.

"I need an update on our forces inside the city," she said to the group. "Number of fighting men, casualties, and morale. High-Warden Llayawin?"

He stepped forward, arms folded in front of him. His eagle's mask, which had a bright orange slash down the middle, was hanging from his hip. "I had four hundred and fifty men under my command at the start of the siege. We're down to four hundred and seven, but most of our losses came in the first two nights, before you worked out the range of Wallace's catapults." Carlyle motioned to the map in the center of the room. "As long as we monitor any repositioning of their siege engines, I believe that I can hold the walls with the men I have."

"Morale?"

"Unwavering, my queen. My men and I will die on those walls before we come down from them."

Ashlyn nodded. It had been a rare stroke of luck that Carlyle's men had taken such small losses, given their position on the front lines.

"What of the wardens under the command of the Atlas Coast small lords?" Ashlyn asked him. She'd been forced to put them on the front lines as well.

Carlyle winced. "I'm afraid they've taken heavy losses, my queen. I don't have exact figures, but . . . it's bad. I'm not sure how much longer we can rely on their support."

Damn.

"Lord Linkon," she prompted.

Linkon cleared his throat. "I've lost two hundred men. Another three hundred have been injured and aren't fit for battle. That leaves fifteen hundred able-bodied men. Morale is strong."

"Define strong."

Linkon cleared his throat before continuing. "There are no deserters in my ranks, my queen."

"Korbon."

"I have three thousand able-bodied wardens in the city," Doro Korbon said. "But a large chunk of those are country wardens who came into the city for your coronation, my queen. They've only recently sworn allegiance to me, and I barely have control over them. If they had a chance to flee the city, I believe many would take it. In another week, they'll kill me just to get into my food stores."

"What about you, Lord Brock?" Ashlyn asked. "What of your eleven sons and their promise to be the first on Balarian shores?"

Yulnar Brock hesitated. Looked down at his bowl. Ashlyn noticed that he hadn't actually taken a bite of his food yet.

"My men saw the worst of the bombardments when Wallace began to move his catapults forward. Almost a thousand were killed. Less than half of my remaining wardens are in fighting shape." He lowered his voice. "And just last night, three of my sons were killed when an explosive missile destroyed a stable where they were preparing their mounts. I'm sorry, my queen, but my men have lost heart. They have homes outside these walls. Families. There's nobody to protect them from Cedar Wallace's men. He could be raiding the countryside at will right now." He hung his head. "I wonder if trying to strike a deal with Wallace isn't the best way out of this."

"I see."

Ashlyn didn't need to hear anything more to know that the wardens inside Floodhaven wouldn't fight in a pitched battle against Cedar Wallace, let alone sail across Terra to fight a war with Balaria. Not unless something changed very soon, and very dramatically.

"Perhaps Lord Brock is right," Linkon said. "A diplomatic solution may be the only option we have available."

Ashlyn thought about that. She had been at the mercy of fate and circumstance for her entire life. Her brothers died and she became the heir. Her father died and she became queen. And then, one by one, Malgrave allies had disappeared, forcing her to compromise over and over again. She was sick of it.

"There is another option," she said. "Send a messenger to Cedar Wallace. I challenge him to a duel for Floodhaven. Tell him that I will meet him inside a chalk circle tomorrow at midday."

———

That night, Ashlyn spent an hour using the latest dragon-sighting reports to update her map of the Great Migration. The impatient adolescent males had already crossed the Sea of Terra. They would spend a few weeks alone in Tanglemire, fighting each other and crying out mating calls to nobody. Meanwhile, the older dragons and females were gathering all over the coast of Almira. Any day now, they would leave in a huge swarm so large that it would blot out the sun. All of them heading to Balaria.

When she was finished, Ashlyn looked through some of her older drawings, made when she was still betrothed to Silas. He used to climb up the Queen's Tower and sneak through her window so they could sleep together. Afterward, she would bring her sketches into the bed and tell him about each dragon. Where it lived. What it ate. How it touched their world.

That time in her life seemed so far away that it belonged to another person.

If Ashlyn failed to protect the dragons of Terra, all the compromises she'd made so far would be for nothing. Sending Silas away. Getting thousands of Malgrave wardens killed. She couldn't give up now. Not after coming so far.

She opened her chest of alchemy ingredients and emptied it. Removed a false panel at the bottom and pulled out a small lockbox. There was only one key. She took it from her neck and opened the box. Picked up the vial of Gods Moss that was inside.

One way or another, Cedar Wallace's siege ended tomorrow.

37

GARRET

Almira, Floodhaven

Garret watched the coffeehouse. It was on the northwest side of the city, which the locals referred to as Foggy Side, and sat so close to Castle Malgrave that the building spent the whole morning in the shadow of the King's Tower. The constant barrage from the catapults was far enough away that it didn't seem to deter patrons, either. Highborn women passed by him in their expensive silk gowns— their hair stuck with dozens of pins and fixed into intricate designs. Wardens patrolled the streets, hands resting on heavy swords.

The coffeehouse took up half a city block—two stories and built from massive oak columns and granite stones. It had ten massive windows. Garret's employer was inside. He circled the building once, pretending to haggle with a sausage vendor while looking for other entrances to the building. There was a serving door on the east side that opened onto an alley, and what looked like a walled-in, private well out back. One good escape route and one dead end.

Garret opened and closed his hand a few times, checking for any remaining signs of the dragon rot infection. There were none. Jolan's tonic had worked perfectly.

He adjusted the position of his hunting knife, then went inside.

The place was crowded. Patrons were sipping their drinks happily. Garret found it interesting that while this area was full of well-dressed nobles enjoying their everyday comforts amidst a siege, he'd passed two women fighting over a dead rat on his way to Foggy Side. He'd also seen dozens of corpses in the streets—the only care they were given was the occasional mud statue molded near their final resting place.

Compared to Burz-al-dun, this city was a backwater gutter. But some things were the same no matter where you traveled in the realm of Terra. The poor always suffered first, and hardest.

"May I assist you, my lord?" A raven-haired woman with a form-fitting black gown asked him. She radiated a calculated mix of sexuality and shrewdness.

"I'm a guest of Lord Paltrix," Garret said, rounding off his accent so he sounded like the son of an Almiran small lord. It matched the expensive silk clothes he'd stolen earlier that morning.

"I see." The woman nodded once—as if acknowledging the sensitivity of the situation—and motioned for Garret to follow her. She headed to the back of the coffeehouse, gown shimmering as her hips moved. The woman produced a key from between her breasts and opened an oak door for Garret. She did not enter. Didn't even look inside.

"Appreciated," Garret said.

"Of course, my lord." The woman nodded again, then swished away.

Garret closed the door behind him. The room was a small, circular shape but it extended all the way to the roof. The space was illuminated by a large, eye-shaped skylight, and a half-dozen candles placed on small ledges against the walls. In the middle of the room, there was a squat, circular wooden table with four cushions set up around it. A stylish lord was sitting on one of the cushions and looking at Garret. He wore a blue jacket and had long blond hair that was tied in place by a few strips of black silk.

"Lord Paltrix, I assume?" Garret asked, switching to a Ghalamarian accent. He sat down across from the man who'd hired him to splatter noble blood across the Almiran backcountry.

"We can dispense with the deception at this point," the lord said. "My name is High Lord Linkon Pommol. You are the hangman?"

"That's right."

"How did you sneak past Cedar Wallace's siege lines?"

Garret shrugged. "Sneaking past things is my job."

"Sneaking quickly doesn't seem to be," Linkon said. "You're twenty-two days late."

"I'm twenty-two days behind schedule, but I made it very clear when we began that delays are a part of this business. If your country had just one properly paved road, it would have made things easier."

Garret's journey back north had been crippled by delays because the main highway had been washed out by a mudslide. The back roads had been so choked with oxen carts and farmers that some days, Garret had barely moved at all.

Linkon tapped his lips twice with two fingers. "Well, I shall not niggle. You've done an excellent job so far. Ashlyn was forced to send nearly all of her soldiers out of Floodhaven to clean up the messes that you made."

"And then Cedar Wallace killed them."

Garret had seen the wardens swaying from the trees as he came into the city.

"Indeed." Linkon smiled. "Ashlyn is still the queen, but my wardens practically control Floodhaven now. Beautiful, isn't it?"

Garret tried to bite back his irritation with Linkon, but failed. He could not stand the amateur mistakes that so many highborns made when they involved themselves in his work. Linkon should have kept his lordly fingernails clean and let a professional handle this.

"*Beautiful* is not the word I would use. Your work is sloppy, and it has made my job considerably more difficult. I was supposed to arrive in Floodhaven and assassinate a queen with no friends, allies, or army. Instead, I had to sneak into a city under siege by some war-crazed Gorgon lord, where I find Ashlyn Malgrave has surrounded herself with hundreds of Papyrian widows whose sole purpose is to protect her. I would not say that you are in control of anything."

Linkon's smile faded. "Yes, well, Ashlyn has proved more resourceful than expected. I could hardly prevent her from taking advantage of a Papyrian alliance she somehow formed in secrecy."

"Do you have any idea how difficult it is to kill just one Papyrian widow? The entire point of my work in the backcountry was to erode her protection. You have stood by and let her bolster it beyond recognition. And what is this I hear about an assassination attempt at her coronation?"

Linkon cleared his throat. "Cedar Wallace saw an opening and wanted to take it."

"That was a mistake."

"I don't think you realize how much worse things could have become," Linkon said. "If I hadn't had the foresight to send a hundred of my best archers outside of Floodhaven to shoot down Ashlyn's bloody pigeons, she would have summoned every warden in Deepdale back here to help her. Probably would have called down a thousand more Papyrians. I am the only man in Almira who realized how dangerous those damn birds of hers are."

"When we started this, you said that you could control Cedar

Wallace. You stood for his actions, which means you are responsible for his mistakes."

"I'll admit things are a bit more chaotic than intended. I am more than willing to pay you extra. Say, double your initial fee?"

Just like a highborn to try and buy his way out of a mistake.

"This isn't about money, Linkon. You have underestimated Ashlyn Malgrave and tainted my work. That cannot be undone." Garret leaned forward. "I have tightened men's throats for lesser mistakes."

"Is that a threat, Garret?" Linkon put his cup of coffee back onto the table without taking a sip. "Remember who you're talking to. I am a high lord of Almira."

"I was hired to kill a queen. Why would killing some special lord be a problem?"

Linkon raised an eyebrow at that, but didn't spook. "Speaking of your job, our resourceful little queen is going to do it for you tomorrow."

Garret had to give Linkon credit, his hands were only trembling a little as he picked up his cup again, took a sip, and waited for a response to his gambit. In the distance, a stone missile crashed into a building. Screams and alarms followed.

"Explain."

"Emperor Mercer was wise to want her dead. Ashlyn is so bent on invading Balaria that she's willing to do anything to end this siege. She has challenged Cedar Wallace to a duel tomorrow."

"A duel? Is she going to use a champion?"

Linkon shook his head. "We don't have that custom in Almira."

"Does she know how to fight?"

"She's a woman."

"That's a foolish assumption. I've known plenty of women who were just as dangerous as men. Some, far more so." Garret paused. "It doesn't make sense for Ashlyn to start a fight she can't win. She must have a plan."

Linkon dismissed the thought with a wave of his hand. "Ashlyn thinks she can consult her ledgers and messages and outwit everyone else, but she can't. The woman doesn't have the stomach for this kind of work. She'd have made an exceptional steward, but she is a terrible queen. She probably thinks she can bargain with Wallace before the duel starts. She'd have more luck negotiating with an actual wolf. Trust me, she's as good as dead."

"I don't trust you at all, Lord Linkon. But if you're so confident, why did you even bother calling me to this meeting?"

"Ah, yes. Why indeed?" Linkon paused in a pantomime of thought. "You see, while I'm confident that Ashlyn will see her last sunrise tomorrow, Cedar Wallace is a separate issue. You said yourself, I don't have him under control. I am worried about what he will do to me once he's defeated Ashlyn."

Garret didn't say anything. Just stared at Linkon.

"If you kill Cedar Wallace for me tomorrow, I'll match your fee for killing Ashlyn, who will be dead anyway. You'll make twice the money for the same amount of work."

"This isn't about money."

"Everything is about money, Garret. Anyone who says differently has never watched a fortune be squandered. They've never been forced to rebuild a dynasty using debt and ridicule as support beams."

Garret dug underneath a fingernail with his thumb, thinking for a moment.

"Tell me, Lord Linkon, when Ashlyn Malgrave and Cedar Wallace are dead, what sort of king do you plan to become?"

Linkon smiled at the question. Leaned back in his chair and began a well-practiced response.

"Ashlyn Malgrave is a relic of the past. She clings to her studies and theories while our poor and backward country goes to rot atop a massive fortune of dragon oil. Once she's gone, I will finish the trade agreement with Balaria, which she turned to shit, and begin harvesting and exporting our oil like a normal country. After my treasuries are full, I will build roads. Infrastructure. An organized government with a national army instead of this patchwork quilt of warlords. I will pull Almira out of the darkness, and into the light."

"Hmm." This skinny lord's words reminded him of Emperor Mercer Domitian. Garret wondered if he might actually last more than a month or two as king. He certainly had the ambition and cunning required to rule a country. But that was not Garret's problem. Making sure Ashlyn Malgrave actually died tomorrow was. That meant he needed to go along with Linkon's plan.

"To get this done, you will need to bring your wardens outside the gate tomorrow."

"Not a problem," Linkon said. "The queen trusts me."

"I also need a detailed map of the city and surrounding country-side and one set of your warden's armor—mask and all."

Linkon relaxed. "So we have a deal, then?"

"I always finish my work, Lord Linkon. Surely the emperor told you that."

"He did. Anything else?"

"Yes." Garret glanced out the window. It was already dusk and he had much to prepare. There would be no time for sleep. "A coffee would be nice."

38

BERSHAD

Almira, Floodhaven Harbor

Bershad and Felgor spotted the coast of Almira an hour before dawn. The silhouette of Floodhaven was drawn in fire against the horizon. Every few minutes, a new fireball was lobbed into the sky and exploded somewhere in the city.

"Well, that's a sight," Felgor said, scratching his head.

"Yeah," Bershad said.

They'd fled Balaria on a stolen theater troupe's schooner. Felgor said it was just like the one he'd grown up on. Getting out of Balaria wasn't nearly as difficult as getting in, seeing as the palace was on fire and the city in chaos. They sailed straight out of the harbor. Felgor was able to cross the Soul Sea in half the time it had taken them on the *Luminata*—and bragged the entire time about secret currents—but they'd hit a bad storm the night before. Both sails were nearly ruined, more than half their rigging had been lost to the sea, and the rudder wiggled back and forth like a tooth that needed to be pulled. Still, they had made it.

Bershad studied the port. There was a wall of warships protecting the entrance to the harbor.

"Ashlyn summoned the Papyrian fleet," Bershad said.

"Why're they just sitting in the harbor?" Felgor asked, squinting. "Couldn't they use 'em to sail away?"

"They could," Bershad said. "But she doesn't know that I killed the emperor, which means she still plans on going to war with Balaria. Can't do that if she runs away."

"Who's doing all the siege work, do you think?"

"No idea."

Felgor let go of the ship's wheel to adjust one of their sails. "Well, we're here. What's the plan?"

Bershad studied the shoreline.

"Just head for the harbor," he said.

"What about all the warships?"

"The sun'll be up in an hour. There's no room for subtlety on this one."

"I like subtlety."

Bershad gave Felgor a look. "If I'm right, someone on those ships will have orders to let us through."

"And if you're wrong?"

Bershad shrugged. "At least our souls won't have trouble finding the sea."

———————

Once they came within a league of the harbor, a Papyrian frigate diverted from the blockade and chased them down. The ship was nine times the size of their schooner. When they came up along their portside rail, the bald heads of two Papyrian sailors appeared just long enough for them to throw two roped harpoons into the deck of their ship.

"The fuck?" Felgor shouted up. "Not like we're gonna run off."

"Not with that torn-to-shit boat, you're not," someone called in a Papyrian accent.

"That's my point! You're wasting harpoons."

"Not really. We'll just pull 'em out of the deck after we kill you two idiots. Who else is on the ship?"

"It's just us," Bershad replied. "Who's in charge up there?"

Things were quiet for a moment.

"I'm the captain," came a deeper voice. "Who are you?"

"Come get a look at my face," Bershad said. "Trust me, you'll know it."

A moment later, the sunbaked face of a Papyrian popped over the deck. His eyes were stuck in a permanent squint and his jaw was covered with scraggly gray hair.

"Step a bit closer, yeah? Eyes aren't what they used to be."

Bershad moved forward. Brushed the black hair away from his cheeks. He could hear some of the crew whispering to each other, but couldn't quite make out what they were saying. The captain spat into the sea, but otherwise his face remained unreadable.

"Caught yourself a pair o' blue bars, I see. Not a unique problem."

Bershad rolled up his sleeve to show the long line of dragons running up his arm.

The captain sucked on his teeth for a moment. "That, on the other hand, is a fucking sight to see. Silas Bershad, welcome home." He paused. Scratched his jawline. "It's just you two? Queen Ashlyn said her sister would be with you."

"Afraid not. But I need to see Ashlyn right away."

The captain winced. "That might be a bit difficult, given her plans for today."

"What do you mean?"

"Best I explain on the way to the harbor. Come on, I'll take you in." He gave the ship a once-over. "We might as well just let this shit-heap sink."

———

Bershad jumped over the ship's gunwale when it was still five strides from shore. The shock of landing splintered the bones in his left foot, but they shifted back into place three steps later. The healing power of the regrown limb hadn't gone away yet.

"Hey!" Felgor shouted, working his way down the gangplank. "Hold on, will you? We can't all grow new fucking legs."

"No time!"

Bershad couldn't believe what the captain had told him. Ashlyn was going to get herself killed over an army that didn't need raising anymore. A war that didn't need fighting. He had to reach her.

"I'm not passing up the chance to meet the queen I did all this shit for—that's how you get cheated out of a reward," Felgor said, hopping onto the dock. "Where we headed?"

The captain had told him that Ashlyn was meeting Cedar Wallace outside the main gate of Floodhaven. The road from the harbor would lead them straight there.

"This way. Keep up or I leave you behind."

39

ASHLYN

Almira, Floodhaven

Ashlyn walked out of Floodhaven with all her widows by her side. Behind her, Carlyle Llayawin and his wardens followed, along with Linkon Pommol's much larger force. Linkon had volunteered his archers to guard the castle walls so that Ashlyn could keep the last of her wardens nearby.

She wore leather riding pants and a silk shirt with loose-fitting sleeves to hide her wrists. Over her chest, she wore the sharkskin breastplate of a Papyrian widow. The castle blacksmith had taken it from one of the widows who died during her coronation and refit the armor. She carried no steel. Had no metal of any kind on her body.

Linkon stood to her left, gazing out over the field. He was wearing an expensive set of green armor—the metal was acid-stained to look reptilian. His neck looked almost comically skinny with so much thick metal around it.

"Ashlyn, I must ask you one more time," Hayden said. "Do not do this."

"I agree with Hayden," Shoshone said. "We could have you on a ship to Papyria in an hour. Dying on that field doesn't help anyone or anything."

"Neither does fleeing to Papyria."

Both widows had spent the morning trying to convince Ashlyn to change her mind, but she was resolute. This was the only way. Ashlyn thumbed the vial of Gods Moss that she'd tucked inside of her right sleeve. The dragon thread was tied to her left wrist.

"I will go to the circle alone," Ashlyn said. "Everyone else will stay close to the walls, where our archers can provide cover. Protect yourselves and protect the city, no matter what occurs. I will not have any more people dying for me."

Linkon nodded. "By your orders, my queen."

Ashlyn looked at Linkon for a moment, but didn't say anything. There was no turning back now. She motioned for Hayden and Shoshone to come closer.

"If this doesn't work, go south to Umbrik's Glade, then east along the river until you reach a watermill."

Hayden frowned. "My queen?"

"That mill has a bird trained to return to Himeja castle. The miller will know where to find the others that are still scattered around the Dainwood, too. If I die, you have to get word to Empress Okinu. Do you understand?"

Hayden frowned for a long time. But eventually nodded. "Yes, my queen."

───────────

Ashlyn walked across the field alone. The sound of her feet crunching on dry summer grass filled her head. She wasn't scared. Things couldn't get much worse than they were, and there was a strange comfort in that kind of resignation. She wondered if Silas had felt the same way when he went to kill his first dragon.

There were a hundred wardens marching toward her from across the field. Ashlyn could make out a white-haired man in the lead. He wore red armor. A green twinkle flashed over his right shoulder. An emerald in the pommel of a sword.

Cedar Wallace.

The chalk circle was ringed with dozens of mud statues, all of them holding scraps of steel. Ashlyn stepped between two of them, entering the dueling grounds. As Wallace's men approached the line from the other side, they spread out along the border in a semicircle, letting Wallace cross alone. Only two people were allowed inside the circle.

Ashlyn and Wallace approached each other. Stopped when they were a dozen strides apart. Cedar's silver hair was combed and tied into a neat bun, his beard trimmed. He'd painted three mud streaks through his hair in the western style. His armor was made from hundreds of red enameled scales that shifted with his movements like a snake's hide.

"Didn't think you'd show," Wallace said.

"You were wrong."

Wallace grunted. "Let's get on with it, then."

"I have a question for you, first."

"Don't try and talk your way out of this, half-breed." Wallace took a step forward. "The circle's for fighting and nothing else."

"Linkon Pommol helped you get extra soldiers into my coronation, didn't he?"

That stopped Wallace, but he didn't respond.

"Someone tipped you off that I was moving a group of my wardens from the walls to the castle. The high lords were the only ones who could have known about it."

She'd suspected Korbon or Brock for a long time. But something in Linkon's face as he was calling for a horse and joining his men outside the castle walls had bothered Ashlyn.

Wallace smiled. "You're dead anyway. Guess there's no harm in you knowing. That's right—your skinny, indebted confidant betrayed you. He's been against you longer than I have."

Ashlyn clenched her teeth. Felt the thread on her wrist start to sizzle.

"He'll die next, then."

"Probably," Wallace said, drawing the blade from his back and swinging it into a relaxed low guard. "But it'll be me that does him."

Wallace stalked toward Ashlyn. She moved to Wallace's left so he'd have to strike from across his body. She touched her wrist with a fingertip. Felt the energy waiting there.

"You were never fit to be queen," Wallace said as he moved toward her, slow and confident. Ashlyn kept bobbing left, watching his hands and feet for the right moment. "For all your drawings and studies and conviction, you never saw what the world truly is—a brutal and cruel storm." Wallace crossed his feet to follow her circuitous path. "All anyone can do is carve out a small corner and protect it. Your father understood that, but you—"

Ashlyn slammed the vial of Gods Moss into her palm hard enough to break it. She unwound the dragon thread and ripped her bleeding, moss-covered hand down its length. The familiar spark of energy filled her fist, and then something far more powerful spread into her body. It cascaded up her arm and snaked inside her veins. Every nerve ending in her body spun into a raging turmoil. She pulled the storm deep into her chest, the way she'd practiced all those long nights alone. Felt skeins of lightning skimming across her lungs and heart, then she opened her palm and watched the energy run back down her arms and pool at her fingertips.

Wallace froze. Sword hanging limp at his hip.

"What the fuck is that?" he muttered.

"My carving knife," Ashlyn said.

She fired a single bolt of lightning at Cedar Wallace. It struck his right arm—red scales from his armor spilled across the grass, starting little fires on the ground. The second blast struck him in the breastplate, knocking him on his ass.

Cedar's eyes widened.

"Sorceress!" he screamed. "Demon-fucking bitch!"

His panicked eyes looked for help from his men outside the circle. They had drawn their swords, but hadn't crossed the chalk.

"Help!" Wallace shouted to his men, his voice cracking. "Help me!"

The wardens hesitated for a moment—the chalk circle was a sacred boundary in Almira. But so was the line between demon's magic and men. They rushed across the white chalk a moment later, screaming for her death.

It was Ashlyn's turn to stalk forward. She grabbed Wallace by the throat and lifted him off the ground as if he were a child. The energy in her body gave her unnatural strength.

"Wait!" Wallace shouted. "Just wait!"

Ashlyn squeezed.

Smoke poured from Wallace's mouth. She pushed the full power of the moss-fueled dragon thread into his body. The grass at her feet turned brown, then black with heat, rippling and expanding in time with her hammering pulse. The mole on Cedar Wallace's face cooked under the blistering glow.

There was a pop. Everything turned white.

40

GARRET

Almira, Floodhaven

Garret closed his eyes and shielded them from the explosion with his hand, but his vision flashed orange anyway. The veins inside his eyelids were momentarily ignited. When he opened his eyes again, Cedar Wallace and the wardens around the circle were gone.

Ashlyn Malgrave stood in the center of a scorched ring. Shoulders rising and falling with each long breath. Curls of lightning were still rolling up her shoulders and snapping around her eyes. A whirling cloud of dark ash swept through the empty field, then into the sky where it dissipated to nothing. Garret had seen a lot of strange things in his life, but he had never seen anything like that.

"What happened?" asked a warden near Garret.

"Where'd all of 'em go?" came another.

A steaming corpse landed at Garret's feet with a wet smack. The scales of Cedar Wallace's armor were glowing pure white, as if they'd spent an hour at the bottom of a blacksmith's furnace. Some of the chinks were fused to skin and white hair. His face was a melted ruin.

Linkon had been right, one part of Garret's job was done for him, but it looked like the other half of his work was going to be more difficult than expected.

The widows broke formation and rushed across the field to their queen. None of Linkon's wardens stopped them, but none of the Malgrave eagles rushed to help, either.

The men around Garret broke into nervous, muttering chatter.

"Gods . . . is that Cedar Wallace?"

"How did she do that to him?"

"She's a witch. She's a fucking Papyrian witch."

"What do we do?"

"Fuck knows."

"If Ashlyn won the duel, the siege is over, isn't it?"

"Who gives a shit about the siege now?" The warden pointed

across the field. "She just turned Cedar Wallace to steaming mush and killed a hundred of his men in the blink of an eye!"

Garret glanced down the line and spotted Linkon Pommol, who was shifting his focus between Wallace's wolves and the widows rushing to create a perimeter around Ashlyn. The high lord wasn't a warrior, but he was smart enough to know what needed to happen if he was going to end this day as the king of Almira.

41

ASHLYN

Almira, Floodhaven

Ashlyn's vision sparked and crackled. Her body burned—every vessel and nerve alive with heat. She knew the thread should have brought agony beyond comprehension. But pain wasn't the right word for this feeling.

She ached in a way that she would miss once it was gone.

Time slowed. An invisible current spread down Ashlyn's body and through the earth, connecting to the heartbeats of every human on the field. It was the way Ashlyn imagined a Ghost Moth felt while hunting from the skies—a world of prey connected to the tangled pulse of her body. She felt the wild rush of her widows crossing the field to protect her. The fixed uncertainty of Linkon and his men holding fast by the wall. And the panicked rage of Cedar Wallace's now leaderless army—all wolf masks and white eyes, hungry to avenge their fallen lord. They were the closest to her, and the largest threat. The front line locked shields and started moving toward Ashlyn at a run. They'd reach her before the widows, and with twenty times the numbers.

Ashlyn rooted her feet onto the burned grass. She started counting wolf pulses the way she once counted mortar seams on her bedroom wall. The only difference was numbers.

She opened her palms and unleashed the dragon thread's current—white lightning slicing over grass and mud before exploding into the mass of wardens. The electricity surged across their shield wall, expanding like a spider's web that sparked and popped against armor and flesh before slamming thousands of men onto their backs as if they'd been struck by an invisible wave.

A fraction of the warriors in the vanguard had deflected the lightning with their shields. Maybe three hundred men. They kept charging her. With a grunt of pain, Ashlyn squeezed down on the thread, pushing more blood and moss into the reaction. The lightning cracked and grew until it was flowing from her right arm like an enormous whip. She lashed out at the incoming wardens, tossing them into the air like scattered coins. They landed near the tree line from which they'd charged, bodies bouncing once and then going still.

When it was done, Ashlyn fell to one knee—all the power and energy drained from her body. Her fingers were numb. Vision blurry. Just as she was about to fall, a strong pair of hands caught her.

Pulled her up.

42

GARRET

Almira, Floodhaven

Garret kept his eyes on Ashlyn until the widows obscured his view. Hard to tell if she was truly hurt. She had definitely fallen.

Ashlyn hadn't killed all of Wallace's wolves, but she'd come close. Most of his army was nothing but a pile of smoking meat. The trees behind the destruction were roasted and split. Leaves burning. It didn't take long for the smell of cooked flesh to reach Garret's nostrils.

The wolves on the periphery of the line were still standing, but the decimation of their numbers had swallowed whatever fight they had left. The line wavered as men dropped their weapons and ran into the forest.

Linkon's men seemed ready to do the same—they glanced nervously at the closed gate behind them. Many were edging backward, angling to be the first underneath once it opened again. Ashlyn was on the cusp of defeating two armies all by herself. That was impressive, but also unacceptable. Garret worked his way over to Linkon, who was staring at the destruction.

"She's hurt," Garret hissed. "Vulnerable."

"You're sure?" Linkon asked, not in any rush to lose his army, too.

Garret looked back across the field. It was hard to spot Ashlyn between the wall of black leather, but he was pretty sure she was still on her knees. It was a risk, but Garret always finished the job. And even sorceresses died when you wrapped a noose around their neck and pulled.

"Order your men to charge those widows," Garret said, motioning to his rope. "I'll take care of her."

Linkon squinted toward the circle of widows. Prodded his horse forward a few paces. "Wardens!" he shouted in a powerful voice. "Hear me!"

The men looked to their lord.

"You are men of Almira. True warriors. Not some pack of frightened wolves who scamper from a fight!"

That earned a low rumble of approval. Funny how far a confident voice will carry men.

"We are sworn to protect Almira and her people against all enemies." Linkon drew his sword and pointed it at Ashlyn. "We do not tolerate demon-fucking witches. She's been weakened by her devilry, I can see it! We need only finish off her foreign protectors and destroy the dark magic she's brought to our land."

The men howled agreement. Linkon waited a moment before speaking again—allowing the wardens to rile themselves up. Garret wondered how he'd gotten so good at war speeches. This had to be his first one.

"Kill the widows!" Linkon shouted. "Then bring me the witch's head!"

The wardens bellowed a cacophony of war cries. Banged their swords and spears against shields. A chant rippled through the lines.

"Kill the witch! Kill the witch! Kill the witch!"

43

BERSHAD

Almira, Floodhaven

Bershad and Felgor were about to reach the ramparts when the second blast of white light filled the sky. The archers on the wall crunched their eyes closed. Twisted their faces away. One of them loosed his half-drawn arrow, plunking it an inch from his own foot. Bershad sprinted to the top of the wall and looked out.

Ashlyn was crouched alone in the middle of the field with lightning arcing around her. She looked hurt. A large circle of blackened grass stretched around her, and several hundred Papyrian widows were rushing to protect their queen. Past Ashlyn, an entire army had been massacred near the tree line. The few wardens who remained alive were busy running away—swords dropped in the grass, men's backs disappearing into the woods.

"That her?" Felgor asked.

"That's her."

"You didn't mention the, uh, lightning thing."

"It's new."

Bershad tried to absorb the situation. There were several thousand wardens in turtle masks standing in tight formation beneath the shadow of the wall. Each man carried a spear, sword, and shield. There were also a few columns of Malgrave eagles, about four hundred men. Everyone looked ready to run as far away from Ashlyn Malgrave as possible. The sound and smell of burning grass and flesh was everywhere.

A man in a turtle mask who was riding a white destrier called out above the din. At first, his words got lost in the shouts and cheers from his men, but the last part reached the ramparts loud and clear.

"Kill the widows! Then bring me the witch's head!"

The man's wardens charged across the field. As soon as the wardens left the shadow of the wall, the rider signaled for the gate to be opened, and disappeared underneath. The Malgrave eagles stayed where they were. A high-warden with an orange slash down the middle of his eagle's mask moved to the front of the column. It took Bershad a moment to realize it was Carlyle Llayawin—the man who'd led him into Floodhaven. He drew his sword.

"Dunno about the rest of you!" Carlyle called. "But I swore an oath to protect Ashlyn Malgrave. Didn't swear shit to Linkon fucking Pommol. Agreed?"

The men behind the officer slammed the butts of their swords into their shields, creating a single, unified boom.

"Aye," Carlyle said. "Best get to work then."

The eagles charged, lagging behind the turtles by a few hundred strides. They were outnumbered three to one, but if the widows could hold off the attack long enough for the Malgrave wardens to hit them from behind, they had a chance.

"I'm going down there," Bershad said. "You need to get as far from here as possible."

"Not happening," Felgor said.

"What?"

"I'm not repeating the whole 'you've done your part, save yourself' thing. We covered that already. You and I are in the shit together now. I'll go steal another boat for us. Just tell me where I should wait for you."

"Felgor, there's no time."

"Totally agree. So answer me."

Bershad looked at Felgor's face and saw he wasn't going to budge. "Fine. Just north of the city there's a harbor with a white domed rock at the mouth. Wait for me there."

Bershad didn't think there was much chance of him making it to that harbor alive, but at least it got Felgor out of the city.

"Archers, Carlyle and his wardens betray Lord Pommol!" a sergeant shouted from farther down the rampart, pointing at the eagles. "Fire on those bastards at my command!"

"Fuck," Bershad muttered, twisting around to see the archers lining up on the wall. "I'll meet you in that harbor, Felgor. Now go!"

Bershad started sprinting down the line, rushing to the sergeant. Ten paces away.

"Nock your arrows!" the sergeant shouted.

Five paces.

"Draw!"

Bershad grabbed the sergeant's head and slammed it into the rampart, then threw him over the wall. Watched his body bounce on the field below. It was a fifty-stride drop, at least. The archer next to him turned, face twisted into a snarl. Bow rotating around to Bershad's chest.

"Shoot the dragonslayer!" he shouted.

Bershad punched the archer in the throat, sending him reeling backward into the man next to him. Then he jumped off the wall.

44

GARRET

Almira, Floodhaven

Garret charged with Linkon's men. The first volley from the widows' slings came when they were two hundred strides away from the queen. A whooshing sound followed by an eerie silence. Garret slowed down and ducked behind a wide-shouldered warden, whose head promptly exploded. Garret picked up the dead man's shield and rushed to get inside the range of the horrific weapons. They'd cleared another fifty strides before the second volley was released.

"Shields up!" Garret called. "Shields up!"

Garret felt the shock of four shots thumping into his shield, then lowered it and kept moving. There wouldn't be time for a third volley.

As they closed in, the widows broke their circle and formed a defensive formation shaped like a large horseshoe that was just wide enough to make flanking them difficult. For bodyguards, the widows operated well in a pitched battle.

The grass beneath Garret's feet changed to charred black. He reached the widows' line at a dead run and locked blades with a tall Papyrian. She tried to knee him between the thighs and when that didn't work, she spat in his eye. Garret crossed blades with her a few more times, realized he was outmatched, then ducked beneath a slash of her steel and rolled backward, abandoning the duel and retreating behind the wardens' line.

Garret had only been hired to kill one woman today. No sense risking his life against a hopelessly outnumbered force of widows. That's what Linkon's men were there for.

He still couldn't see Ashlyn, but he didn't see any more lightning snapping across the field, either. Good. Garret just needed to wait for Linkon's men to break through the widows' line and this would be over.

But when Garret reached the back of the column, instead of finding an empty, safe field like he'd expected, he slammed into a charging warden wearing an eagle mask with an orange slash down the middle. Garret was so surprised that he barely managed to dodge the warden's first strike, and when the Almiran rammed the pommel of his sword forward, Garret took the hit on the temple.

Everything went black.

45

BERSHAD

Almira, Floodhaven

Bershad didn't wait for his shattered foot and ruined knee to heal before he started charging across the field. His muscles and tendons shrieked with pain for the first ten strides, but both legs were repaired before he'd left the shadow of Floodhaven's wall.

Two arrows snapped into the ground to his left. Then three more thumped into his thigh, back, and neck. Bershad stumbled, regained his footing, and tore the arrows out of his neck and thigh. Felt the wounds close. Nothing he could do about the one in his back besides leave it there and hope it wasn't deep enough to kill him.

Up ahead, Carlyle and his wardens had attacked Pommol's men at a full charge, turning the tide of the battle. Instead of a one-sided slaughter, everything was confusion and chaos. Bershad got behind one of Pommol's spearmen, drew the man's sword from his hip, and stabbed him through the spine, lifting his boots off the ground. The man next to him jolted in surprise. Bershad hacked his forehead open and snatched his spear.

Bershad shoved and stabbed and speared at the turtle wardens.

Without armor on, he caught a dozen different wounds in the few seconds he spent pushing through the battle. Most of them were outside the places that Osyrus had changed, so they didn't heal right away. He was nearly past the fray when someone slammed a shield into the side of his head and put him on his back. The warden raised his spear, snarling and preparing to push it through Bershad's heart.

There was a blur of black leather behind the warden, and his throat opened. The man tried to breathe. Tried to speak. Then he fell onto his back and died.

The widows were everywhere. Wardens were being pelted and stabbed and strangled. Others stumbled around, disoriented and gushing blood from puncture wounds at the seams of their armor— groins, armpits, throats.

Bershad had lost his sword when he fell, but half of the spear was still in his hand. He got up and continued pushing toward Ashlyn, his wounds shrieking at him. Almost there.

46

GARRET

Almira, Floodhaven

Garret regained consciousness after someone stomped on his stomach with a steel boot. The turtle mask he'd been wearing was gone. His nose was broken and one of his teeth had been knocked out. Garret ignored the pain. Looked around.

Pommol's wardens had lost the upper hand. The eagles had taken them by surprise and were carving through the back of their line. If they met the widows in the middle, this battle would be over. Garret moved through the fray, staying low. Past the heavy fighting, thirty widows had encircled Ashlyn in a tight barrier. A score of Pommol's men had cleared the main battle and were harrying the circle with swords and spears, but failing to penetrate the wall. Garret didn't need to break through—he just needed one moment with a clear view of Ashlyn's throat.

He roamed the circle of widows like a jackal searching for a weakness in the pack. Every few seconds their formation would shift and a widow would fire her sling from a gap in the wall of black leather, pegging a warden in the face or throat. Pommol's spearmen rushed forward one at a time or in small groups to attack, but they all stumbled away, bleeding from three or four puncture wounds.

Garret kept moving. Bided his time. Eyes focused.

He caught sight of Ashlyn's pale neck. Planted his feet. Threw. Felt the noose catch. Tugged once to tighten. Then heaved with all the strength he had left. Ashlyn Malgrave flew out of the circle of widows and landed at his feet. The pull hadn't broken her neck for some reason, but that didn't matter. He had her now.

Garret drew the hunting knife from his belt. Just before he was going to plunge it into Ashlyn's heart, he was stopped by the sound of an animal growl.

47

BERSHAD

Almira, Floodhaven

Bershad collided at a full run with the man who was holding a noose around Ashlyn's throat. His spear popped through the man's stomach and sent him tumbling onto a pile of smoking bodies. No time to finish the bastard off—Ashlyn was choking. He turned around and knelt at her side, slipping his fingers beneath the hemp rope and tugging it loose. She sucked in a long, sharp breath. Steam poured out of her mouth and nose when she released it.

She was still alive. Bershad touched Ashlyn's cheek. Her skin was burning. One of her hands was covered with blood and moss, the other was clutching that translucent strand.

"Silas?" Ashlyn squinted at him. Confused. "How did you get here?"

"Doesn't matter right now." Bershad looked around. The man he'd stabbed with the spear was gone. "We need to get you out of here."

Bershad moved to stand up, but was stopped by a searing pain in his side. There was a hunting dagger hilt-deep in the side of his chest.

"Shit."

Two widows were rushing toward them. One of them had a forked scar running across her mouth, and the other one was Hayden, who was swinging her sling over her head, eyes focused on Bershad.

"Hayden, wait!"

Too late. She released the shot. Bershad heard a wet impact behind him. When he turned around a warden wearing a turtle's mask was on the ground twitching. There was a gaping hole in his chest.

Bershad picked up the dead warden's sword and shield, wincing at the awful pain in his side. He searched for another turtle to kill but couldn't find one. There were only widows and eagle wardens left standing. Nobody celebrated. Just looked around, breathing hard. Waiting. The blackened grass was littered with corpses.

The gates of Floodhaven opened and more wardens poured out—a myriad of different animal masks on their faces, swords drawn.

"Are those your wardens?" Bershad asked Ashlyn.

"The only loyal wardens I have left are standing on this field with me," Ashlyn said, struggling to stand up. She was still dazed.

"Then we have a problem."

It was too many to fight. Far too many. But if Bershad was going to die somewhere, this was where he wanted to do it. He got in front of Ashlyn and raised his shield. Without orders, the remaining eagle wardens lined up next to him. Carlyle Llayawin was among them— the orange slash on his eagle mask was hard to see through all the splashed blood.

He gave Bershad a firm nod. "Don't know how you got here, but it's good to see you again, Lord Bershad."

"Likewise."

The widows got behind them and started swinging slings over their heads.

"Make every shot count!" Hayden called.

The other wardens charged, weapons high. Bershad could see the different-colored scales and snouts of their masks. Hear their chain mail rattling. He tightened his grip on the sword. Focused on the warden at the head of the attack—a tall bastard with a double-headed axe and round shield. Bershad could get him, at least. Maybe two or three more.

Something crackled over Bershad's shoulder, then a bolt of lightning jolted into the man with the two-headed axe. He froze, then exploded. Blood and bones burst outward. His shield hit the man next to him and sent him cartwheeling sideways from the force.

Hundreds of weaker lightning tendrils radiated from Ashlyn's arm, turning the charging army rigid. Blood came from Ashlyn's nose and ears. Her face twisted into a strange mixture of agony and pleasure.

Her eyes rolled back in her head. The lightning stopped, and Ashlyn fell unconscious onto the grass. Most of the charging men had fallen to the ground, but they weren't dead. Ashlyn didn't have the strength to destroy another army, just to slow this one down.

Bershad picked Ashlyn up, wincing again at the dagger in his chest. It had gotten into his lung for sure. Maybe worse.

"I can get her out of here," Bershad said.

"How?" Hayden asked.

Bershad motioned north, to a heavy copse of oaks. "Up the coast. Might be I have a boat waiting."

As long as Felgor didn't get himself killed stealing it.

"We'll hold them off here," Carlyle said. "Cover your escape."

"No," Bershad said. "Order your men to scatter. Everyone in different directions." He looked at Hayden. "Widows, too. The only way Ashlyn survives is if they can't tell which direction we took her, and guess wrong."

"I go with you," Hayden said. "And three other widows."

"Agreed," Bershad said, eyes on the wardens Ashlyn had stunned. Some were still on the ground, others vomiting on their knees.

Hayden turned to the widow with a forked scar on her face. An unspoken question passed between them.

"Empress Okinu will want to keep open eyes in Almira. And drawn blades. My sisters and I will stay."

Hayden nodded. "Umbrik's Glade is not close, but you can lose any pursuers once you reach the Dainwood. So push hard to get across the Gorgon."

"Understood," the widow replied.

Most of the wardens were standing now. Getting their bearings.

"Everyone ready?" Bershad asked.

The wardens and widows grunted affirmation.

"Now!"

Bershad carried Ashlyn through the woods. He didn't look back to see if they were being followed, just ran full tilt, hoping they got lucky. After a few hundred paces, the snarls and calls of wardens on their trail caught up with them.

"Faster!" Bershad called. "Keep moving."

They cleared the trees and Bershad's feet hit the white sand of the hidden harbor. He twisted his ankle and fell over. Turned around to see a score of fox- and badger-masked wardens swarming out of the trees. When they were within five strides of Bershad, all of them were killed by a volley of crossbow bolts.

"What the . . ." Bershad muttered, turning back to the water.

Instead of a stolen fishing boat, there was a Papyrian warship waiting in the harbor just off the shore. The gunwale was lined with sailors holding crossbows.

"Onto the ship!" called a voice with a Papyrian accent.

Bershad picked Ashlyn up and tried to keep going, but collapsed on the bone-white sand a moment later, heaving air but feeling like he was underwater. The blade in his ribs had done some real damage.

"Take the queen," Hayden ordered one of the widows. "I will carry him."

Hayden slipped an arm underneath Bershad's shoulder and picked him up. Bershad stumbled in the shallows and went face-first into the water. Hayden picked him up again.

"Get me a seashell," he muttered. This felt like the end somehow.

"Don't be an idiot," Hayden said. "We're almost there."

The three widows hauled Ashlyn onto the deck. Then everyone struggled to get Bershad up and over the gunwale. By then, he couldn't breathe at all.

"The dagger's in his lung," someone said. "Pull it out."

"It's also in his heart. If you pull it out he'll bleed to death."

"Leave it in and he'll suffocate."

Bershad's vision started going dark. Funny, to have survived so much only to be done in by such a small piece of steel. At least they were close to the sea.

"Moss," came a familiar voice. "Get him some fucking moss!"

Felgor.

Bershad struggled to get an eye open. Saw the blurry outline of Felgor scurrying around the dock.

"What's that shit in the queen's hand? Is that moss?"

"I'm not sure, it's all blackened and—"

"Yes, that's Gods Moss," Hayden said from somewhere.

"Perfect. Looks like there's still some green bits." Felgor hunched over the queen, scooping her palm clean with his hand. "Hope this is enough."

Felgor appeared over Bershad, his face serious.

"Hold on a little longer, I've got you."

Bershad felt the dagger being removed from his chest. Heard the sound of his blood splashing onto the deck. Then the hard pressure of Felgor's hand over the wound. Warmth flooded into his body—his organs and bones and flesh started knitting back together.

Bershad inhaled a long, full breath.

Felgor's face broke into a smile.

"Saved your life again, Silas." He looked up the coast. The sailors were pulling anchor and dropping oars. "I'm feeling like the real hero in this whole mess."

48

ASHLYN

Almira, Atlas Coast

Ashlyn woke up in the dim hold of a ship. She could feel the motion of the waves rocking back and forth. Her head was pounding. There was a terrible, metallic taste in her mouth. On instinct, she touched her wrist. The thread was still there. Her memory of the battle was foggy, but clearing with each passing second. She'd killed Cedar Wallace, and then how many others? Hundreds? Thousands?

"You're awake."

Ashlyn sat up on the cot. Silas was sitting next to it. There was a bandage wrapped around his bare chest, but no blood on it. He held out a ceramic jug.

"Drink this," he said. "It helps."

She took a long swallow from the jug. It was full of cold rice wine that washed the foul taste out of her mouth. When she let the jug fall, a tendril of steam rose from her lips. She wondered how long that would last.

"How did you get back to Almira?" she asked, her throat sore.

"That's a question with a very long answer," he said. "But you're safe. Hayden is safe. We're on a Papyrian warship. Still not sure how Felgor managed that trick, but we're both in his debt."

"What about Floodhaven? The other widows? Carlyle and his wardens?"

"We all scattered. Not sure if they made it." Bershad took the jug from her and drank a long sip of his own.

Ashlyn looked at Bershad's body. "You were hurt so badly earlier. I saw arrows in your back. A knife in your chest."

She pointed at the bandage.

"This? It's just to humor the sailors—they're already having a hard time with their witch-queen cargo. Figured they could do without a demon dragonslayer, too." Bershad unwrapped the linen cloth. The flesh beneath was unmarred except for a thin white scar below his heart. He folded the bandage up and put it on the ground next to him. Looked at her.

"When I left you in the spring, we were both carrying secrets. After today, I don't think either of us can keep them from the world anymore, let alone each other."

"I think you're right."

They stayed in the hold for a long time, telling each other what had happened. So many lives had been lost. Her father. The Grealors. Rowan. Alfonso. Bershad told her about Kira, and what he'd done to the emperor of Balaria. What was done to him in the dungeons below. She told him about the dragon thread and Cedar Wallace and the mess that Almira had become.

"You kept your promise," Ashlyn said. "You came back. But I can't keep mine. The Dainwood is no longer mine to give. I'm sorry, Silas."

Bershad hesitated before responding. "I've spent fourteen years punishing myself for the past. Aimless and angry and lost. But you gave me a way out of that. I know my place now. It's not in the Dainwood. It's next to you. No matter where you go. No matter what happens."

Ashlyn didn't know what to say. She paused. Thought of Linkon Pommol sitting in the King's Tower. She clenched her fist so hard that her nails dug into her palm. "I don't deserve your loyalty anymore."

Bershad looked like he was about to say something, but stopped. He looked up at the ceiling, suddenly alarmed.

"Silas? Are you all right?"

Before Bershad could respond, the hatch to the deck opened and a smiling face appeared. It was the Balarian thief Ashlyn had sent across the sea with Bershad. She remembered him because he had the smallest teeth she'd ever seen.

"Something's happening up top that you two'll want to see," he said.

Bershad helped Ashlyn get above deck. It took her a moment to get her bearings—the Papyrian warship was moving north along the coast of Almira. Hayden and three other widows were on the deck. Their armor and hair were still covered in blood, but their faces had been washed clean. Ashlyn looked behind her and could just barely make out the silhouette of Castle Malgrave. There was a heavy plume of black smoke rising from the west where the battle had taken place.

"You're looking the wrong way, Queen," Felgor said, turning her around and pointing east, over the sea.

The sky was filled with thousands of dragons. Ghost Moths. Blackjacks. Needle-Throated Verduns. So many of them that they cast a long shadow across the waves of the Soul Sea. Their bodies flickered and swooped across the sky. Their screeching calls filled Ashlyn's ears.

"There won't be any Balarians waiting for them in Tanglemire," Bershad said, staring at the sky. "We saved them, Ashlyn. You and me. Forget about deserving loyalty, Ashe. I love you. Always have."

Ashlyn watched the dragons, feeling tears well up behind her eyes. When Ashlyn spoke again, she did it very slowly. "There is at least half of my promise that I can keep. Lord Silas Bershad, I hereby lift your banishment and absolve you of your crimes. You are a dragon-slayer no longer."

Bershad took her hand and squeezed.

"If you want revenge for what happened today, I'll help you kill everyone who was involved. If you want to sail away from this realm, we can turn this ship toward the mouth of the Soul Sea and never look back. You can go anywhere you want, Ashlyn, but I am coming with you."

Ashlyn kissed him. Pressed her body against his. She knew the

dragon thread wasn't just a weapon that could turn armies to cinders—it was part of a larger world that had been hidden from her
until now. She had to learn more about the power she'd unlocked in
herself and unleashed on the world. There was only one place she'd
be safe to do that.

"Papyria," she whispered. "Let's go to Papyria."

49

VERA

Balaria, Bay of Broken Clocks

Vera waited for Osyrus Ward to arrive. Thumbed the hilt of Bershad's sword and looked at Kira. Osyrus had given her the blade after
she'd agreed to stay as Kira's protector. A show of good faith, he'd
called it.

"You're doing it again," Kira said.

"Doing what, Princess?"

"Empress now, remember?"

"Sorry. Doing what, Empress?"

"Scowling at me."

Vera looked out at the Bay of Broken Clocks—full of choppy
waves and jagged rocks. For some reason, Kira had insisted they venture beyond the city and visit this remote cove today. There was
something she wanted Vera to see, but she refused to say what it was.

"I am sorry, Empress."

Kira gave a small nod. She was wearing a crown made from dragon
bones that Ganon had placed on her head during the coronation and
wedding ceremony. It was a Balarian custom for the bride to wear it
constantly for a full moon's turn to better the chances of a quick preg-
nancy. Besides Bershad's dagger, it was the only preserved dragon
bone that Vera had ever seen.

"I don't see why you're so upset. I'm alive, I'm empress of Balaria,
and you can protect me again. Aren't those the things you wanted?"

She had wanted to return Kira to Almira where she'd be safe, but
she'd failed. Now Vera didn't know what to do.

"Are you still bitter about me ringing that bell?" Kira pressed.

Vera didn't say anything.

"I already explained that. Those soldiers were going to arrest Bershad whether I rang the stupid thing or not. This way, I've built favor and trust with the Balarians, which we'll need. And anyway, Bershad escaped. Everything turned out fine."

Before Vera could object to Kira's logic, Osyrus arrived with his greasy hair and long green leather jacket.

"Empress Domitian." Osyrus approached and bowed. Vera repositioned herself so it would be easier to slit his throat if necessary. "Will our new emperor be joining us today?"

"No," Kira said. "He is preparing for tonight's gala."

"Wasn't the gala yesterday?"

"There is another one tonight. But don't worry, your work is far more interesting to me than parties."

"I am glad to hear that, Empress."

"As we left the city to come here, I noticed that the Kor Cog began turning once again," Kira said. "Are the checkpoints working again as well?"

"Yes, Empress. The disruption was unfortunate, but it is resolved."

"Good. And thank you for doing this, Osyrus," Kira said to him. "I know you're busy, but I am having trouble wiping that scowl off Vera's face."

"An empress never needs to thank a lowly engineer such as myself, but I appreciate the sentiment." Osyrus looked at Vera. His eyes made her skin crawl. "I'd have thought you would be more satisfied, Vera the widow. Things have not turned out so badly."

"That's what I said!" Kira piped.

"For example," Osyrus said, keeping his eyes fixed on Vera, "I can tell you were fond of Silas Bershad. Are you not happy that he escaped after committing his heinous crime?"

Osyrus smiled as he said those last two words. Of all the people in the royal palace, Osyrus Ward seemed the least upset about the death of the emperor and the escape of Silas Bershad. He'd been the one to call the manhunt off after just three days. Even the massive fire in the palace and ensuing lockdown of the city hadn't seemed to cause the royal engineer much concern. Vera did not trust Osyrus Ward. She planned to watch him very carefully.

"Forgive me," Vera said. "This is all very new."

"Enough talk, can we show her now? I know she won't believe me until she sees it."

"As you command, Empress." Osyrus motioned to the water. "Vera, if you'll turn your attention to that frigate, they will begin shortly."

There was only one ship in the hidden cove, so it was easy to spot. The frigate was an uncommon design for Balaria's navy, sitting far lower in the water with a wider deck.

"What am I looking for?" she asked.

"Just wait," Kira said. "You'll see."

It took a few moments, but the water around the frigate began to swell as if some great beast below was trying to devour the ship. But instead of a yawning mouth and a sprout of tentacles from some children's story, two massive and bloated skins rose from the water. They were suspended by long support beams that stretched out from both sides of the frigate like wings.

The carrack began to rise from the water. Misty sea spray dripped from the black hull. Once it was above the surf, Vera saw that the bottom of the flying ship was dominated by a complicated apparatus built from the remains of dead dragons, but also wreathed with metal piping and copper wires. If the dragon-bone crown was noteworthy, preserving so many tons of great lizard carcass was downright unfathomable.

Wide sails were drawn across the newly arisen wings. They billowed to life as they filled with wind. The smell of burning dragon oil wafted over the water and filled Vera's nose. The carrack tipped one way, then the other, like an eagle finding its balance after jumping from a pine tree.

"Black skies," Vera hissed. As the ship continued to rise in the sky, Vera imagined how easily it could soar over even the highest castle walls. Seaside fortresses that would have once required months of blockades and land sieges to conquer would fall in a matter of hours. This ship would change warfare forever.

"The world is made of interesting ingredients," Osyrus said from behind her. "Rock and wood and living creatures, kept upright by meat and flesh and bone. We make up rules. Make up a vision of the world and the limits of what it can become. It is amazing what you can accomplish if you're willing to ignore those rules. And strong enough to break them."

"How many of these do you have?" Vera asked. She had her hand clamped down on Bershad's sword. Knuckles white.

"Let's just say that the harvesting of dragon oil is not the only reason the great lizards have become so rare in Balaria. But don't let my flying armada scare you. I serve at the pleasure of the empress."

Vera looked at Osyrus for a long time. "Do I look afraid to you?" she asked.

"No, Vera the widow. You do not."

They all watched the ship for a moment. Eventually, Kira broke the silence.

"Almira was my prison," she said in a cold tone that Vera didn't recognize. "Always at my father's beck and call. Or Ashlyn's. Go to this feast. Make the small lords laugh. Sit in front of that crowd. Wave. Smile. Wave some more. I hated it." Kira took a breath. She was practically snarling. "But that is over now, Vera. I'm finally free. With these ships, nobody will ever put me in a cage again. Imagine the places we can go. And how small everyone will look when we look down on them from above."

Kira turned to Vera. Her seething expression melted into a perfect smile.

"This will be fun."

APPENDIX

—

THE DRAGONS OF TERRA

(As compiled from the field notes of Silas Bershad and Ashlyn Malgrave)

Needle-Throated Verdun/*Draconis grimensis*

> *Green hide, queer orange eyes, medium size. Vicious, quick, but not very smart. They fall for the horn call every time, but be careful not to rile them up too much before making a pass or they'll make you regret it.*
>
> *They stick to the foothills of mountain ranges and will generally burrow a lair in an area with good sunning rocks and a consistent source of food. Sheep and goat, especially. Verdun blood heats up faster than average. Attacking after it's sunned itself for more than an hour is suicide.*

Common dragon of eastern Almira.

    Coloring: Green-hued scales ranging from deep olive to the light carapace of a praying mantis. Carrot-orange eyes suggest poor vision during the day but excellent night vision for navigating lairs and burrows. The needles on their throat are a defense against rival males.

    Average length: 11 strides from nose to tail tip

    Average weight of heart: 1½ stone

    General notes: Female raises the brood alone and becomes highly territorial during this time. They are opportunistic hunters, but prefer cloven-hooved creatures, which makes them unpopular with shepherds but vital to meadows of the Atlas Coast.

Mountain-Dwelling Red Skull/*Draconis rex cranis*

> *Huge and hostile. Will rampage if not killed quickly. Best time to make a pass is an hour before dawn, but start blowing your horn a half hour before that because they're heavy sleepers. Even when you get them early, they will not make it easy on you. If you have a choice between two writs, take the one that isn't a Red Skull.*

Rare dragon that nests in the Razorback Mountains of the east and the Gorgon Mountains of the west.

Coloring: Scale hues on the body are obsidian black but shift to red hues along the neck that range from crimson to coral. Top of skull is always a deep blood red and devoid of scales.

Average length: 27 strides from nose to tail

Average weight of heart: 6½ stone

General notes: Thickened skull is a product of violent head bashing during mating rituals. Despite their reputation for aggression, Red Skull males are extremely doting fathers who watch over their broods with a dedication that is unrivaled by any other breed. They nest in the mountains, but typically hunt along the foothills and flatlands. Diet includes moose, elk, and cattle.

Common Thundertail/*Draconis tonitrui cauda*

> *Early risers. Very difficult to surprise. You won't even need the horn—get within half a league of their lair and they'll come out to greet you. Scales are thin enough to jam a spear through, but it's hard to get close because of those damn tails. You can tell when they're going to strike because they'll twitch the ear on the same side the tail's coming from. Bring a thick shield, take the blow as a glance shot, then play dead. When it comes to sniff out the kill, you'll have a clear opening to the brain or the heart. Don't miss, you only get one chance before that tail comes around again.*

A common dragon known for its unique tail.

Coloring: Blue scales ranging from robin's egg blue to pigeon-wing gray.

Average length: 17 strides from nose to tail

Average weight of heart: 1 stone

General notes: Males typically grow five to seven barbs on their tails during puberty, which can reach up to one stride in length and are razor sharp. Breed occurs in Almira, Ghalamar, and Balaria. Diet varies dramatically depending on their location, but all of them tend to favor medium-sized omnivores that come to drink along riverbanks. I have detailed the damaging effects of the Balarian variety's extinction in my folio: *The Murderous Monkeys of Southern Balaria*.

Horned Black/*Draconis corniger habitus*

> *Black scales, medium size. Don't worry about the horn—it looks intimidating but they don't use it to defend themselves. Very predictable attack pattern. They circle twice and then pounce like cats. As long as you catch it before noon, it'll be sluggish enough to peg through the eye without much trouble.*

Forest-dwelling breed of medium size.

Coloring: Scales are uniformly obsidian black, hence the common name.

Average length: 14 strides from nose to tail

Average weight of heart: 2 stone

General notes: Males have a horn that grows halfway down their snout and can reach two strides in length. However, it is not a defensive anatomical feature, as many believe, but a part of their mating ritual where two males will interlock the horns and tug until one of them submits.

Dunfar Sand Strider/*Draconis arenus natans*

> *Very sneaky. They like to build false lairs in the shade of tall cactus trees, then burrow a foot or two underneath the sand near the mouth of the lair, waiting for something to walk past. Look carefully for queer impressions in the sand and you can generally spot them. Throw a rock at the beast, let it strike the stone, then rush in to cut its head off.*

Small, golden desert dragons with a very limited dispersion. No samples studied.

Western Ghost Moth/*Draconis wisp somnium*

> *Since Ghost Moths don't eat livestock or attack people, writs aren't generally put out for them. It's a good thing. The Moths are gentle and graceful. Driving a spear through one's brain seems wrong somehow.*

An extremely rare, medium-sized dragon occurring in Almira and Papyria.

Coloring: Scales are pale white, with hues ranging from ivory to gray-smoke.

Average length: 18 strides from nose to tail
Average weight of heart: 5½ stone
General notes: The common name, Ghost Moth, comes from the pale coloring and twin tendrils that run down the breed's snout and resemble the antennae of a moth. There is a white powder on the tendrils that may assist the dragon in locating the dens of subterranean prey, such as foxes and badgers, which are common in both Almira and Papyria.

Known for their lack of aggressiveness toward human settlements as well as their rolling, almost ethereal wing beats, as if they are swimming through the air instead of flying.

A lesser known but equally important characteristic is the breed's longevity. The natural lifespan is anywhere from eighty to one hundred and fifty years. This unique attribute has led to certain anatomical irregularities that require further investigation.

Ghalamarian Stone Scale/*Draconis lapis numquam*

> *These are tricky bastards. Their scales are the same color and thickness as rock slabs. They'll generally tuck in between a few boulders and ambush unsuspecting mountain goats or unlucky travelers. They're basically fortresses while they're lying in wait, but vulnerable while they're eating. If you think you've found one, find a vantage point from above and throw a goat at it. When it starts to eat, a gap in the scales between their spine and skull opens while they're chewing. That's where your spear goes.*

Large and reclusive breed occurring primarily in the foothills of the Razorback Mountains.
Coloring: Scale hues range from sandy gold to bark-brown skin.
Average length: 47 strides from nose to tail
Average weight of heart: 10½ stone
General notes: The stonelike scales are durable beyond comprehension—acids that normally dissolve dragon scales within a few hours appear to have no effect. A blacksmith could spend an hour pounding on a scale without causing damage to anything except the hammer.

The material would make for wonderful armor if a scale the size of a woman's hand did not weigh as much as a full-grown warden.

Naga Soul Strider/*Draconis mare spinatea*

> *Massive and terrifying, but luckily they stick to the open water. Not sure how you'd kill one. Tow yourself behind a boat as bait with a seashell in your mouth?*

Large dragon that roosts on the rocky, uninhabited islands of the Sea of Terra.

Coloring: Scale hues range from azure to indigo.

Average length: 33 strides from nose to tail

Average weight of heart: 7½ stone

General notes: Tail is twice as long as the body, which makes it slow moving and cumbersome on land, but an unrivaled fisherman when flying across the sea. Breed will typically hook the tail beneath its body and trawl the ocean. Diet includes marlin, sea lion, dolphin, and on rare occasions, orca. Adolescents and males will typically eat their catches fresh, while mothers with a brood will return to the interior islands to feed their hatchlings.

The breed's role in the underwater system of Terra is both mysterious and enticing. What must the marlin think of this airborne creature that appears from nowhere and snatches it upward to the waterless hell above?

Almiran River Lurker/*Draconis flumine daeas*

> *Massive, muddy-brown river demons. Best to try and kill them in the winter, when the rivers are cooler and they're sluggish until early afternoon.*
>
> *You can spot their underwater lairs because the mud along the banks will be a lighter shade of brown and the water lilies will be tall, healthy, and topped with blue flowers. Get a longboat—at least thirty strides from bow to stern—and paddle out until you're right above the lair. Drop a big rock down there and it'll surface for you, but it'll have to distend its jaw to account for your boat, which leaves it vulnerable. Stab it through the roof of its mouth as it breaches the surface. If you hit the brain, it'll be dead before it can close its jaw and devour you.*

A large, aquatic breed native to Almiran riverways.

Coloring: Scales appear muddy, but can actually range in hue from emerald green to azure blue.

Average length: 42 strides from nose to tail
Average weight of heart: 11½ stone
General notes: Diet consists mostly of bottom-feeding river shrimp and catfish, or the occasional unlucky otter, but their intimidating size has made them needlessly feared by the people of Almira.

The River Lurker, as they're called colloquially, is vital to the natural balance of Almira. Their feces enrich the riverbanks, leading to healthy water lily and creek-side plants whose roots prevent erosion during the rainy seasons while also providing food for herbivorous wildlife.

Snub-Nosed Blackjack/*Draconis var coruptan*

> *Size varies—some are no bigger than a horse, others can tear down city walls. They have thick scales and a ridged back. They generally bed down like deer in meadows—ask around for groves with a lot of Dainwood trees if you're on the hunt. They like to burrow beneath them for some reason.*
>
> *The upturned snout makes it difficult to stab it in the eye. Use a longer spear and go for a nostril—the shorter snout means you can reach the brain from there.*

A common dragon in the Dainwood jungle.
Coloring: Unique marble scaling of jet-black and bone-white hues.
Average length: 12 strides from nose to tail (note: average not representative due to many outliers)
Average weight of heart: 1¼ stone
General notes: Breed is prone to respiratory infections, likely due to their unique snouts. It's possible they are able to alleviate these breathing problems by ingesting a white fungus that thrives on the roots of Dain trees. This has created an interesting and mutually beneficial relationship. If one species were to disappear, the other would also perish.

Almiran Lake Screecher/*Draconis luc vocifera*

> *Not very large or dangerous, so you don't see many writs for Screechers. If one of them spends too long at a lake near town, most small lords will just send out a few of their wardens to deal with it. That way, they don't have to pay taxes on the oil they harvest.*

> *If you pulled a light duty and are hunting one, they are easy to find. Just bend down by the side of an Almiran lake and start splashing the water. They'll find you.*

A common dragon of the Atlas Coast and Gorgon Valley of Almira.
>   **Coloring:** Deep green scales that typically present as black, especially when wet.
>   **Average length:** 7 strides from nose to tail
>   **Average weight of heart:** 1 stone
>   **General notes:** The presence of a resident Lake Screecher is a clear sign of a healthy body of water. Just as herons keep frog and fish populations in check, the Lake Screecher typically hunts medium-sized mammals, such as otters, coyotes, and raccoons. If a lake no longer receives frequent visits from a Screecher, these mammals tend to overhunt the nests of local birds and snakes, which disrupts the balance of these delicate systems.

Yellow-Spined Greezel/*Draconis hallucina favar*

> *Most are only the size of large dogs, but don't let that fool you. Small means their blood heats up quick, and they move faster than a diving falcon. You've got to get them on the ground, but be careful when you start grappling. Those yellow spines are poisonous, and you will not like the visions they bring.*

A small dragon common to the deepest parts of the Gorgon River Valley. They have also been known to skirt the Papyrian islands during the summer months.
>   **Coloring:** Black scales on the body, bright yellow spines on the back.
>   **Average length:** 2 strides from nose to tail
>   **Average weight of heart:** ½ stone
>   **General notes:** Their compact bodies are extremely efficient when it comes to generating heat. The most remarkable aspect of this breed is the venom carried in their spines, which causes hallucinations, tremors, and, in some cases, a paralysis that leads to death. Juveniles do not begin producing the toxin until their second summer, suggesting that their diet plays a role in the poison's creation. More research needed to draw further conclusions.

Gray-Winged Nomad/*Draconis ravus vargus*

> *Medium-sized, color of smoke. Very difficult to hunt because they spend almost the entire day in flight, covering hundreds of leagues between dawn and dusk, then making their lairs on isolated peaks. But they have a soft spot for Almiran giant river turtles. Tie a turtle down as bait on an uninhabited river island so the Nomad thinks it's safe, then hide in a blind nearby. The Nomad is vulnerable while it's trying to crack open the turtle's shell. Go in through the mouth.*

A rare dragon with the largest range of any known breed in the realm of Terra.

Coloring: Hues range from white-smoke gray to deep charcoal.

Average length: 17 strides from nose to tail

Average weight of heart: 3½ stone

General notes: Due to their massive hunting range, this breed affects almost every environment in the realm of Terra. They typically feed off animals watering themselves along the riverways, which keeps the bankside plants and algae from being overgrazed.

There is a rumor that Silas Bershad forged a functional dagger from a Gray-Winged Nomad tooth, but efforts to replicate the process in the eastern tower have been unsuccessful.

Papyrian Milk Wing/*Draconis pallida vela*

> *Only killed one. The beast was sick—both eyes rheumy and generally it was disoriented and unwilling to fly. Not sure how or why it came so far south. Walked up and jammed a spear through its eye. Felt like shit afterward.*

Common dragon native to the Papyrian Islands.

Coloring: Consistent hue pattern of pale-white wings and jet-black body.

Average length: 14 strides from nose to tail

Average weight of heart: 3½ stone

General notes: Native to Papyria and rarely observed anywhere else. Diet primarily consists of smaller fish and woodland game. Despite their common name, the breed's oil is a thick and viscous black, which Papyrians dilute and then use to dye the hulls of their ships.

Apparently, a single dragon can provide coloring for nearly one hundred ships. Curious what other properties this oil may have that are, as of yet, unknown.

Ghalamarian Green Horn/*Draconis cortex circumsta*

Big, green, and aggressive. They heat up fast, too. Had one take flight twenty minutes before the sun rose once. Look for them in aspen and cedar groves. You can track them by following the trail of chipped and scarred bark—they rub their horns against them all day.

The horn makes it hard to spear them in the eye, but their underbellies are soft. Squat down with your spear over your head when it charges. If you're lucky, the mean bastard will disembowel itself.

Common dragon in the forests of Ghalamar.

Coloring: Hues range from turtle-skin to light mint green.

Average length: 23 strides from nose to tail

Average weight of heart: 4½ stone

General notes: Curious habit of rubbing their horns against tree bark. Upon dissection, discovered hollow ducts that run from the horn all through the body. Remarkable—the horn rubbing is used as a method for heating the body, which explains the breed's alacrity and energy in the morning.

Overhunting in Ghalamar has led to the breed congregating in confined and remote areas. Reports of widespread aspen deforestation have become more and more common.

ACKNOWLEDGMENTS

Writing is a solitary process, but making a book is not. Many people helped me along the way, and without their aid the Flawless Bershad and his crew would never have traveled beyond the recesses of my brain.

First, I would like to thank my agent, Caitlin Blasdell, and my editor, Christopher Morgan. They believed in me and my story from the beginning, and provided me with invaluable advice, insight, and wisdom every step of the way. I would also like to thank the talented team at Tor, as well as Bella Pagan and everyone at Tor UK.

Thank you to Melora Wolff, Greg Hrbek, and Gary Blauvelt for the dedicated instruction and confidence you bestowed upon me as a young writer. Thank you, Justin Anthony, for reading one of the earliest drafts and encouraging me to keep going.

Thank you to my mother and father. Without your love and support, none of this would have happened. Also, my brother and sister, who never let me get away with anything.

Lola, my brave and stalwart German shepherd, slept at my feet while a large portion of this book was written and came up with all the good ideas.

Most of all, thank you, Jess Townsend. You have brought immeasurable joy to this story, and to my life.